D0616323

Berkley Sensation Titles by Carolyn Jewel

SCANDAL
INDISCREET

INDISCREET

CAROLYN JEWEL

B

BERKLEY SENSATION, NEW YORK

THE BERKLEY PUBLISHING GROUP
Published by the Penguin Group
Penguin Group (USA) Inc.
375 Hudson Street, New York, New York 10014, USA
Penguin Group (Canada), 90 Eglinton Avenue East, Suite 700, Toronto, Ontario M4P 2Y3, Canada
(a division of Pearson Penguin Canada Inc.)
Penguin Books Ltd., 80 Strand, London WC2R 0RL, England
Penguin Group Ireland, 25 St. Stephen's Green, Dublin 2, Ireland
(a division of Penguin Books Ltd.)
Penguin Group (Australia), 250 Camberwell Road, Camberwell, Victoria 3124, Australia
(a division of Pearson Australia Group Pty. Ltd.)
Penguin Books India Pvt. Ltd., 11 Community Centre, Panchsheel Park, New Delhi—110 017, India
Penguin Group (NZ), 67 Apollo Drive, Rosedale, North Shore 0632, New Zealand
(a division of Pearson New Zealand Ltd.)
Penguin Books (South Africa) (Pty.) Ltd., 24 Sturdee Avenue, Rosebank, Johannesburg 2196,
South Africa

Penguin Books Ltd., Registered Offices: 80 Strand, London WC2R 0RL, England

INDISCREET

A Berkley Sensation Book / published by arrangement with the author

PRINTING HISTORY
Berkley Sensation mass-market edition / October 2009

ISBN: 978-0-425-23099-2

BERKLEY® SENSATION
Berkley Sensation Books are published by The Berkley Publishing Group,
a division of Penguin Group (USA) Inc.,
375 Hudson Street, New York, New York 10014.
BERKLEY® SENSATION and the "B" design are trademarks of Penguin Group (USA) Inc.

PRINTED IN THE UNITED STATES OF AMERICA

10 9 8 7 6 5 4 3 2 1

ACKNOWLEDGMENTS

As usual, I have a number of people who deserve a big thank-you from me. A heartfelt thank-you to my agent, Kristin Nelson, for her straight talk and keen eye for story and detail. Thanks are also due to Megan Frampton and to my editor, Kate Seaver, for believing in me. The Berkley Sensation art department totally rocks. Thank you for the beautiful covers! My family puts up with a lot from me when I'm on deadline so thanks to you all, especially my sister, Marguerite, for being my biggest fan, and my son, Nathaniel, for being so good about the really quick dinners and in general for being the greatest joy of my life. To Jasper, Jake, and Speed Brick for all the lap time while I'm writing, thanks fuzzy guys!

One

How everything started.

This incident took place at about two o'clock the morning of September 3, 1809. The location was the back parlor of a town house owned by the Duke of Buckingham but lived in by the Earl of Crosshaven on a ninety-nine-year lease, presently in its twenty-third year. It should be remarked that Lord Edward Marrack, the younger brother of the Marquess of Foye, was in attendance that night. Lord Edward had been something of a rake until his engagement to the daughter of a long-time family friend. The Earl of Crosshaven currently was a rake.

LORD EDWARD MARRACK REFUSED MORE WINE WHEN the bottle came around in his direction. Instead, he leaned against his chair while his friend the Earl of Crosshaven raised a hand—Cross was inevitably the center of attention—and said, with significant stress, the two words, "Sabine Godard."

The other men in the room looked impressed. No one, including Lord Edward, doubted for a moment that Cross had indeed secured the person of Miss Sabine Godard.

Up to now, the young lady's reputation had been unassailable. She was an orphan who had been raised by her uncle since she was quite young. They made their home in Oxford, the city of spires, Henry Godard having been a don there and a noted philosopher until his recent retirement from those hallowed walls. She and her uncle had come to London so that Godard could receive a knighthood in recognition of his intellectual contributions to king and empire.

They had not been long in London, the Godards, but Lord Edward recalled hearing Miss Godard was reckoned a pretty girl. Very pretty and quite unavailable. She was, if he had his facts in order, her uncle's permanent caretaker, as was often the fate of children not raised by their parents. Her uncle was now Sir Henry Godard. By several large steps, quite a come up in the world for them both.

The unavailable Miss Godard had been pursued by Crosshaven. That, too, Lord Edward had heard. The Earl of Crosshaven was angelically, devilishly, beautiful. His manners were exquisite and his intellect absolutely first-rate. Lord Edward would not bother with a friendship if that were not the case. But Crosshaven, in Lord Edward's opinion, was not as familiar with discretion as he might be. Something he was proving tonight.

Though Lord Edward liked Cross exceedingly, this boast of his was infamous. Ungentlemanly, in fact. That Cross had refilled his glass far too often in the course of the evening was no excuse for his revealing to anyone that he had seduced a young woman of decent family.

And, one presumed, abandoned her to whatever fate her uncle might decide was fit for a girl who strayed from what was proper.

"How was she?" asked one of the other young bucks.

Cross kissed the tips of his fingers and arced his thus blessed hand toward the ceiling. That engendered several ribald comments, some having to do with Cross's prowess in the bedroom and others having to do with Sabine Godard and what Crosshaven may or may not have taught her about sexual congress and how to fornicate with elan.

In Lord Edward's opinion, Cross, though just short of thirty, and for all his lofty titles, had now proved he had a great deal to learn about honor and decency. This evening, which had begun as a pleasant interlude with men he liked, no longer seemed very pleasant.

"A seduction," Lord Edward said to no one in particular, "when properly carried out, pleases both parties for the duration, while a break humiliates no one."

"Who says I've broken with her?" Crosshaven asked.

"I do," he replied. "And any fool with half a brain."

Crosshaven shook his head sadly. "Is this what happens to a man when he falls in love? If I didn't know better, I'd accuse you of not wanting to go to bed with a pretty young woman." He winked. "Without benefit of marriage, I mean." He gave Lord Edward a sloppy smile, then looked around the room with his glass held high in a mock toast. "To Sabine Godard."

"Hear, hear," said a few of the others. Most just took the opportunity to sample their wine.

Crosshaven took another drink of his hock, but he kept his eyes on Lord Edward as he did. He'd noticed Lord Edward hadn't joined in the toast. "Don't be such a bloody bore, Ned," he said with a roll of his eyes. "You're not married yet, old man."

"True." But in three months time he would be. God, he was weary of this, of nights like this spent drinking or whoring and living as if there weren't something more to be had from life. He wasn't married yet, but wished Rosaline was already his wife.

Lord Edward put down his glass and stood. He felt a giant. With reason. He towered over everyone in the room, standing or not. "Good evening, gentlemen, my lords."

"What?" said Cross. He was a bit unsteady on his feet. "Are you leaving already, Ned? It's early yet."

Lord Edward could not bring himself to smile to soften his disapproval of his friend's behavior. Nor could he remain silent. "I do not care to hear any lady's character shredded for the sake of a man's reputation."

Cross focused on Lord Edward, registered the slight to his honor, and said, "She's no better than she ought to be."

"True," Lord Edward said. "But the consequences of indiscretion always fall hardest on the woman. Tonight, you are lauded for your seduction of the girl, deemed ever more manly. Your reputation as a cocksman is firmly established."

Crosshaven bowed amid a few catcalls. He straightened, grinning. Lord Edward was probably the only one in the room who wasn't grinning back.

"What reason had you to prove that fact at the cost of her reputation? No one disputes your appeal to the fairer sex." Lord Edward sighed. There was no point in lecturing Cross. No point at all. "Tomorrow," he said with regret soft in his voice, "Miss Godard will not find the world so pleasant a place. That is a fate you ought to have avoided for the girl."

"She's still no better than she ought to be, Ned." He pretended to sober up, but as a drunk would do. Sloppily. "I mean no disrespect, Lord Edward. But it's true about the girl. No better than she ought to be."

He acknowledged Cross with a nod, without smiling because he was disappointed in his friend. "Nor are you."

As he walked out, Lord Edward thought it was a very great pity that Miss Godard was so thoroughly ruined. Beyond repair. Crosshaven's boast of her would be everywhere by noon tomorrow. He did not know the girl personally but did not like to think of the disgrace that was soon to fall on her and her uncle. They would both be touched by Crosshaven's indiscretion.

He thought it likely the newly knighted Sir Henry Godard would put her onto the street.

Two

*One year and eight months later,
give or take a few days,*
May 5, 1811

The former Lord Edward Marrack was now the Marquess of Foye and a guest at the palace of an English merchant in Büyükdere, Turkey, about twelve miles outside Constantinople. Europeans were not permitted to live in the city, and Büyükdere was a favorite summer residence for expatriates from any number of countries. Including England. A good deal of the diplomatic corps resided in Büyükdere, which overlooked the blue, blue waters of the Bosporus.

The finest woman here tonight was Miss Sabine Godard.

How strange that he should cross paths with Miss Godard so many thousands of miles from home. Foye wasn't surprised to find she was a lovely woman.

If Crosshaven had noticed her, and, quite infamously, he had, it stood to reason she would have something. She did.

Foye sat on a chair not so far from the center of the assembly that he would be thought aloof, though he'd been accused of that and worse since he'd begun his tour of countries that had the single advantage of being far from England. He was not by nature a gregarious man and was even less so now, or so he'd been told by people who had known him before. True enough. For the second time in his life, he was a changed man. What a pity he didn't like the change.

Now that he saw her before him, he understood why so many men had spoken of her looks and why Crosshaven had chosen her; it wasn't so much that she was beautiful. She wasn't quite that. A man didn't catch his breath at the sight of her. She was not a very tall woman, though from what he could see of her, her figure was a nice one. He stared at her, trying to pin down for himself the reason that she was a more attractive woman than she ought to be.

Her features were too strong for beauty in the classic sense, though anyone meeting her for the first time would think her pretty. She smiled often, and he'd watched several men stare, besotted, when her mouth curved a certain way. Her hair was an astonishing shade of gold. Curls at her temples and brow gave her an air of sweetness without being cloying, and there weren't many pretty young women who could manage that. A lace cap was on her head, a jade green ribbon threaded through the material. She wasn't beautiful, no, not that, but she was pretty. Exceptionally so.

She had something else as well, and he was determined to put a name to whatever elusive quality that was. What a shame Crosshaven had ruined everything for her. She might have done well for herself, had she stayed in London. There were any number of pretty young girls who'd married up. Some decent young man would likely have thought himself lucky to marry a woman like her. Foye couldn't help feeling at least partially responsible for the fact that she hadn't.

At the moment, Miss Godard was sitting at a table surrounded by men in uniform; sailors, soldiers of the Royal Artillery, Royal Engineers, or otherwise attached to the military here in Büyükdere. She was reading tea leaves for them and having a grand time, too. Despite her smiles, and despite the men gathered around her, she appeared unaware of the flirtatious looks and remarks sent her way, but not, he thought, unaware of her looks.

Miss Godard knew very well that men found her attractive, Foye decided. But she was not a flirt.

Her uncle, Sir Henry Godard, sat close enough to her that she could easily lean over and touch his arm should she care to. Sir Henry was deep in conversation with one of the merchants who worked for the Levant Company. The topic at hand, from what Foye could overhear, was the merits and demerits of St. Augustine. A heady subject for afternoon tea.

So far, Sir Henry had the advantage in the argument. He was a wily debater. Leading his prey to make admissions that seemed reasonable enough while in reality he was laying a trap such that when it sprang his victim would have no choice but to cede Sir Henry's entire point.

Experience had etched deep lines in Sir Henry's face and yet had taken a disproportionate physical toll on the rest of his body. His upper back was hunched, throwing his leonine head forward. His hair was that off shade of white, a yellowish silver, common to men who'd been blond throughout their adult lives. Notwithstanding the depredations of age and illness, Sir Henry was a man of considerable presence. His profession remained in his manner of speech, his temperament, and even his gestures. It was easy to imagine him addressing a lecture hall of young men and terrifying them into listening at peril of their very survival.

The salon was filled with guests holding teacups and guarding plates of cakes, biscuits, and sugar wafers. There were tables piled with watermelon and bowls of sherbet in silver cups with delicate silver spoons. The merchant whose palace this was, Mr. Anthony Lucey, had invited only Englishmen and women this afternoon, though naturally men outnumbered the women, who were, for the most part, wives or other relatives of the soldiers. Some of the men were longtime employees of the Levant Company who had raised families here. A pretty English girl wasn't unheard of in Büyükdere. Not by any means.

Lucey himself, a longtime friend of Foye's late father,

stood in the center of the room telling a story Foye had
heard before about the time he'd gotten lost in Mayfair and
had mistakenly knocked on the Duke of Portland's private
door. Lucey was such an excellent raconteur the tale still
amused more than forty years after it had happened.

He was beginning to think, though, that he ought to go
get himself introduced to Miss Godard. Just to see what
she was like. Naturally, he was curious. And since he was
here, if the circumstances offered, he might explain what
had happened.

Foye resisted the urge to smooth down his hair. There
really was no dealing with his curls. They were contrary
by innate disposition, it seemed. A good match for his face,
which was one of the reasons he'd let his hair grow and
never cut it short again. With a face that defined "ill made"
and a body that tended to intimidate by sheer size—he had
always been prone to muscle—Foye was used to women
looking past him or away from him. Though since he'd
become Foye, that happened marginally less often.

He plucked a crisp sugar wafer from his plate and took
a bite. A touch of almond, he thought, and he had a taste
of bliss melting over his tongue. Lucey's cook was superb,
a Neapolitan man he'd succeeded in hiring away from the
Italian ambassador's residence. The story of Lucey's raid
on the Italian kitchen was amusing, too. Foye took another
bite of his wafer and savored it while he watched yet
another lovesick young officer beg to have his fortune told
by Miss Godard.

Perhaps, he thought, it was something about the way she
looked at a man. Yes. Something about her eyes. And her
complete disinterest. What bold young man didn't want the
very woman who wouldn't have him? Given all that he and
Miss Godard had in common, he ought to at least meet her.
It was, however, quite plain to him that to get anywhere
with the niece one must start with the uncle.

When Foye was done eating, he asked Lucey for an
introduction to Sir Henry.

The old man was formidable, that had been apparent even

from a distance. Closer up, he seemed no less so for all that his frailness was the more evident. He had, Foye recalled, read one of Sir Henry's treatises, the 1805 *On Hubris*.

When Lucey walked him over to the philosopher, Foye was speared by a pair of iron gray eyes that would have been at home in a man forty years his junior, they were that bright and perceptive. He did not believe it was an accident that he should think back on his university days with some sense of dread. This man would have had no compunction whatever about sending a prince packing for want of preparation. No more a mere second son—all that Foye had been in those days.

Foye bowed when Lucey completed the introduction. Already the object of much curiosity on account of his appearance, more stares came his way when his titles were pronounced. Lucey, unfortunately, knew the entire list. Marquess of Foye. Earls of Eidenderry and DeMortmercy. He was used to them now, at last accustomed to the change in his identity from Lord Edward to Foye. There were days now when he could hardly recall a time when he hadn't been Foye. His first titled ancestor had been ennobled before the reign of Charlemagne. The Marracks of Cornwall had never been viscounts. Their nobility had begun with an earldom.

It was with him that the Marrack line would end. With the death of his brother without any living children, he was the last of the Marrack men. When he died, his properties and titles would revert to the crown. What a failure to take to his grave, to leave no one to carry on the name.

"Well, well, young man," Sir Henry said, laboriously craning his neck sideways to look at him. "That is a mouthful of names."

Foye smiled despite himself. He had not been called a young man for a good many years. It wasn't as though he was old, but at thirty-eight, he wasn't a boy anymore. Godard held out a gnarled hand for Foye to take, which he did, gently. The philosopher was crippled with the gout, and his skin was hot to the touch.

"Yes, Sir Henry, it is, indeed, a mouthful." He smiled, aware of Miss Godard's attention to their exchange. Would he tell her, if the opportunity arose? He ought to but didn't know if he would. She seemed to have made a life for herself here, far from England. Why bring up what could only be painful memories for her? Because, Foye thought, if he were her, he'd want to know the truth. "I hope you were not bored listening to all that."

"Not at all." Sir Henry bobbed his head. "I am pleased to make your acquaintance, my Lord Foye."

"The pleasure is mine, Sir Henry." Foye was aware that Miss Godard had stopped her inspection of someone's teacup—what nonsense that business was—to listen to the introduction.

Did she recognize his name from his connection with Crosshaven? Perhaps she did not know he and Cross had been friends and that Foye knew what had been done to her. Or perhaps she did, and now wondered if her reputation was to be ruined again by someone else who knew only the lies.

"Foye. Foye," Sir Henry said, tapping his chin with a finger permanently hooked into a claw. He narrowed his eyes and gave him a sideways look. "A King's College man, weren't you?"

Foye bowed. For a split second, he racked his brain for the essay he must have failed to write. "Yes, sir."

"Your elder brother, too, if I'm not mistaken."

"You are not."

"I thought so." Sir Henry grinned and nodded. "You were Lord Edward then, not Foye. That's why I didn't know who you were until you were close enough for me to see you." He pulled at a blanket spread over his lap. "Took a first in maths, didn't you?"

"I'm astonished you should know such a thing." It was at university that Foye had learned there were women who cared more for what he offered when they were intimate than what he looked like in broad daylight. He'd also discovered he had a talent for pleasing his partners. He'd made himself an assiduous student of the delights to be had between a man and woman. Well. No more of that for him. Those days were long gone. He was done with that life.

Godard waved a misshapen hand. "I made it a point to acquaint myself with the names of all the young men of promise. If we were at home, I would send Sabine to find my entry on you." He smiled, and the effect was disconcertingly sly. His niece looked in their direction at the mention of her name. "I kept a ledger, my lord. I followed you in Parliament, you know. Heard your maiden speech. I am rarely wrong in my predictions."

"Am I to be flattered by that?" Foye asked. He did not look at Miss Godard, though he burned to do so.

"I should think so. I saw you once or twice at university." He chuckled. "No mistaking you for anyone else."

He smiled again. "No, sir."

"I should think you learned early on it's better to have something here"—he tapped his temple—"than to have a handsome face. Too many young men these days spend hours primping at the mirror when they would profit more from improving their minds."

"Godard," his niece murmured. She put an arm on her uncle's sleeve in a gesture familiar enough to be habitual. Foye could easily imagine her needing to restrain her uncle's bluntness. For all Sir Henry's rudeness, he rather liked the man for it. He wasn't a pretty man, after all.

"What?" Sir Henry said, turning his torso toward his niece. "With a face like his, do you think he bothers much with enriching his tailor over his bookseller?"

"I think Lord Foye is very smartly dressed," she said.

"Thank you," Foye said. In point of fact, he was vain of his appearance. Even as Lord Edward, he had never walked out of his house without clothes that made other men beg him for the name of his tailor.

"Look at him." One thin arm shot into the air. "Do you think he spent his time at King's with his mistresses instead of in the library?"

Good God. Foye held back his shock at Sir Henry's speech. Miss Godard, too, felt the indiscretion, for her

cheeks pinked up. Sir Henry didn't seem to think anything
of his declaration.

"Godard." She slid a glance at Foye, and their eyes met.
Hers were brown. There was nothing extraordinary about
her eyes, but for the intelligence there. She was no ordinary
girl, he thought. "Forgive him," she murmured.

"For what?" Foye said. "It's true. I am no model of masculine beauty. I am not offended by Sir Henry pointing that
out." Age had its privileges, after all, and Sir Henry had to
be nearer seventy than sixty. He had decided to be amused.
There was brilliance yet in the old man.

"Sensible of you, my boy."

Foye nodded to Sir Henry, but he was absorbed by Miss
Godard. She was a far more interesting woman than he'd
expected. All this time, whenever he thought of Crosshaven
and what he'd done that night, he'd been imagining a sweet
young woman, weeping for her lost reputation. Naïve and
mourning the infamous wrong done her. Miss Godard was
hardly naïve.

"Have you been in Anatolia long, my lord?" Sir Henry
asked.

"No," Foye replied.

Miss Godard was now indisputably a part of their conversation. He could not help but look at her. Her eyes were
not a common brown after all, but something a more poetic
man might call dark honey. From the shape of her mouth,
the tilt of her eyes with their thick, dark lashes, to the
sweeping line of her throat to her shoulders, she was the
sort of woman who made a man think of darkened rooms
and whispered endearments. He understood very well why
Crosshaven had chosen her.

"I arrived in Constantinople yesterday," Foye said to Sir
Henry. "And you?"

Sir Henry folded his crippled hands on his lap. "We
have been in Büyükdere coming onto a month. Is that correct, Sabine?"

She answered without hesitation. "In Anatolia,
forty-three days. In Büyükdere, twenty-one, Uncle."

Again, Foye felt his understanding of Miss Godard to be maddeningly incomplete. Not a woman wronged and mourning her fate. Not a pretty girl who knew and used the power her looks gave her over a man. And to speak so crisply, with such unhesitating precision. He preferred it when the people he met fell into neat categories. Irascible old man. A young woman wronged. Foye did not yet know where to fit Miss Godard.

"Twenty-one days, my lord," Sir Henry told him with a smile that conveyed his pride in the precision of his niece's recollection.

The naval officer whose tea leaves she'd been reading bid Miss Godard adieu. She nodded, said good-bye, and though the officer waited for her to say something more, she didn't. For the moment, her table was empty of a companion, yet all the other men who had been waiting for their chance found themselves dismissed without a word.

"You have an able assistant, sir." There was an awkward silence during which Foye expected to be introduced and was not. He cleared his throat and returned a bit of the older man's directness. "May I meet your niece, Sir Henry?"

"What for?" Sir Henry's eyes scalded. Foye could only thank the Lord he'd never been in one of Sir Henry's lectures when he was at Oxford. He would have quailed under that gimlet eye. Because, in truth, he had spent more time with his various mistresses than with his studies.

"Godard," Miss Godard said, firmly this time.

Sir Henry tipped his head toward her. "Very well. I suppose there's no hope for it. Sabine, will you meet the Marquess of Foye?"

She stood to curtsey but did not extend a hand to him over the very small table at which she sat. He bowed in return. "Delighted to make your acquaintance, my lord."

"My niece, sir. Miss Sabine Godard."

"Miss Godard." He was aware he was staring too hard. She was still so very young. He doubted she was much beyond twenty. Crosshaven ought to rot in hell for what he'd done to the girl.

She cocked her head at him, and at that moment he would have given anything to know what she was thinking.

"Would you read my future?" he asked.

Sir Henry snorted. "It's nonsense, my lord," he said. "She knows that, too."

Miss Godard's gaze flicked to her uncle; she remained unruffled. "If he is on your list of men who will make something of themselves, Godard, I daresay he is well aware my tea reading is a nothing more than an amusing way to pass the time." She turned to him. "My lord, have you a cup you've been drinking? If not, you'll need fresh."

He pointed in the direction of the table on which he'd set his tea. "There."

"That should do." She smiled at him, but with no particular interest in him beyond what was polite and no indication that she cared anything for his title or his consequence. Or his lack of beauty, for that matter. How egalitarian of her. "I'll wait, my lord."

He returned with his nearly empty cup and sat on the chair opposite her. His legs were too long to fit underneath the table, leaving him no choice but to sit sideways or remain as he was with his thighs wide open. He turned on the chair. Miss Godard took his cup and looked into it. "Can you bear to drink another mouthful or two?"

He nodded. He would tell her, he decided. He would tell her about Crosshaven and then apologize for his role in her ruin, limited as it had been. He took back his cup, drank it nearly empty, and extended it to her.

"No," she said, refusing his cup. "Hold it just so and swirl the contents thus." She demonstrated the desired motion with her arm.

"Nonsense, all of it," Sir Henry said.

"Yes, Godard," she said without looking at her uncle. But he saw a smile lurking on her mouth. "Excellent. Now upend your cup on the saucer."

"Shall I first cross your palms with silver?" Foye asked.

"Certainly not." Her eyes, her very fine eyes, flashed

with humor. There was more to Miss Godard than she meant to let on, he realized. "If I allowed you to pay me in order to learn your future, my ability to accurately assess what tomorrow and beyond may hold for you would be compromised."

"Consider the offer rescinded, miss."

Her mouth quirked. "Anyone who takes filthy lucre is no better than a rank charlatan."

Obediently, he swirled his cup and did as directed, upending the cup over the saucer. Though he did not like to admit it, she interested him. What was she? What had she become since Crosshaven? "And you, being above remuneration, are no charlatan, I presume?"

Her smile became a direct and knowing connection with his gaze. "I am the worst charlatan in Christendom if you believe a word I say, my lord." She righted his tea and stared into it. "This is utter nonsense, as you well know."

"My future?" He sighed. "I feared as much."

Miss Godard laughed softly. "Divination, my lord. As much as I admire the great civilizations of the past, I have concluded there is a reason men of modern learning do not maintain a belief in the ancient ways. Just as there were no gods on Mount Olympus, there is no magic by which one can infer the future from random patterns made in tea leaves." She quirked her eyebrows at him. "Or the entrails of a goat, for that matter."

He very nearly laughed. Nearly. My God, she was quick-witted and not afraid to show him. "Nevertheless, this"—he indicated the teacup—"is, as you say, quite a charming pastime for a lady to have."

"Thank you." She raised her voice. "You see, Godard, that I am vindicated by Lord Foye."

"What's that?" Sir Henry said.

"The marquess finds the reading of tea leaves to be an amusing occupation." She spoke so drolly and with such affection for her uncle that Foye was hard-pressed not to grin. Miss Godard handled her irascible uncle quite well.

"More the fool he," Sir Henry said.

Miss Godard lifted a hand and pressed the other to her upper bosom. "A moment of silence while I read the portents, my lord."

She could have been an actress, the gesture and tone of voice were so perfectly done. No wonder the officers vied for her attention. For one thing, she was miserly with it, and when she did look at you directly, there was so much there to see in her eyes, a man could not be faulted for wanting more. He leaned his side against his chair, his elbow over the back, and stretched out one leg while he watched her. "I believe," he said in a low voice, "that we have a mutual acquaintance."

Without taking her eyes from his cup, she replied in a soft voice, "Not a mutual friend, I am afraid. Unless you mean someone besides the Earl of Crosshaven."

"I do not."

Her expression closed off. "You have a bouquet of flowers, here." She pointed to a mass of leaves. "That signifies you are to be happy in love."

"I was," he said. "Once. But no longer."

She looked at him. "I am not reading your past, my lord, but your future."

"Happy in love?" he said, looking into her eyes. "I fear that is quite impossible."

"The tea leaves never lie," she replied.

He wriggled his fingers over his cup. "Pray continue."

Three

HOW LOUD HER HEART BEAT IN HER EARS. HER FINGERS would be shaking if she hadn't curled them around the tea-cup in front of her.

Sabine kept her attention fixed on the leaves clinging to the interior of the marquess's teacup and wondered how much Lord Foye knew about her. Safest for her to assume that the man sitting across from her had heard every boast Lord Crosshaven had ever made concerning her; all of them lies, whether said in relative private to his cronies or pronounced at some assembly to which she and her uncle would never have been invited. Lies to which a rebuttal proved impossible.

How many thousands of miles from England did she have to go before she could live without fear of being thought a whore? Or would Lord Foye, whom she had not met when she and Godard were in London, be like the others who had assumed she was now fair game for seduction? She flicked a glance at him, resentful and apprehensive at the same time. He might do her a great deal of damage if he desired. Better she find out now than later.

He was a physically formidable man, which she did not care for. Not only tall but muscular, with broad shoulders and chest, and thighs shaped by vigorous activity. And unlike Godard, she was well aware that his clothes were exquisitely made. He probably did spend hours before his mirror.

Lord Foye was head and shoulders taller than she. His hair was dark, not quite black, and quite willful in its curls. His eyes were the same blue as the Mediterranean. His nose was hooked, and the remainder of his features were set irregularly in his face, as if someone had put the parts together and then given him a hard shake before everything had quite settled into place.

She had, in her life, never met a peer until she and her uncle went to London where he was knighted. The aristocracy she'd found terrible in the extreme. They were a proud lot, too aware of their consequence and too overbearing in their expectation that she would be transported by the honor of an introduction.

Her mistake in believing the same of Foye became clear the moment he sat down to have her read his tea leaves. Not so much a proud man, she decided, as reserved. His consequence fit him like his clothes: exquisitely and without ostentation, but underneath there ran a river too deep to sound.

No one could spend five minutes in a room with the Marquess of Foye and not understand that here was a man to be reckoned with. Despite his title, despite his connection to Crosshaven, and even despite that he quite obviously knew every word that had been said about her, Sabine wanted very much to like him.

She was no longer so willing to believe the best of anyone.

Lord Foye sat sideways on his chair, one leg crossed over the other. When she looked up, he caught her glance. She'd been silent in her thoughts for too long.

"You have a complicated future," she said.

"Take your time," Foye replied. He had a deep voice. He spoke quietly, sure of himself, with a fullness of tone in his words that suggested nothing but that he hoped to be amused. There was no mistaking his voice for anything but that of a mature man, which, to be honest, was a pleasant change from the eager young soldiers and sailors she found so tiresome. "I should like my fortune read properly, Miss Godard."

She returned her gaze to his teacup. "I endeavor, my lord."

Lord Foye was not a handsome man. She had, in fact, been watching him since the moment he came in, even before she knew who he was. How could one not? He was tremendously tall, and, as Godard had so baldly pointed out, not very handsome. If one felt inclined to generosity, and she had not yet made up her mind on that account, one might call him an arresting man.

"You will take a journey soon," she said.

He leaned forward to peer into the cup with her, a motion that put their heads close together. He smelled slightly of sandalwood. "What tells you that?"

"This arrangement here." She pointed to the place she meant. "Three horseshoes in near proximity to each other. Nearer the handle than farther, so the time of your journey is closer to the present than it is distant. Your more immediate future."

"Those are horseshoes?"

"Yes." By now, she didn't care what shapes the tea leaves made, which in the event was nothing much at all. This was, indeed, complete nonsense. She could no more tell someone's fortune with tea leaves than she could detect a scoundrel before it was too late to avoid making his acquaintance. The clumps near the handle of the cup were vaguely U-shaped; therefore, she styled them horseshoes.

Her idea of reading tea leaves seemed an unlucky decision now. She'd thought to amuse herself and perhaps a few others, that was all, not find herself cornered by some crony of Crosshaven's. "Horseshoes arranged just so signify you will soon go on a journey."

And may it be soon, she thought. She wanted to be nowhere near Lord Foye. She wanted nothing to do with anyone who knew Lord Crosshaven.

"I am on one now," he pointed out.

She glanced up. "The tea leaves do not tell your past." His eyes were guileless, completely clear of any salacious motive concerning her. Some of the tension in her shoulders fell away. But not all. He had been careful to make sure she knew of his acquaintance with Lord Crosshaven, and now she must work out why he would have done so, if not to suggest his willingness for an affair. He would not be the first man to make her such a proposition. "The leaves show only the future as it might be at the time you overturned your cup, my lord."

He waved a hand. His fingers were long and slender. He did not wear any jewelry. "Do carry on."

"You will journey through rugged terrain, as you may see from the lines surrounding the horseshoes." She improvised, as she had during all her readings so far. "Mountains, I suspect. The second horseshoe implies your journey will be a pleasant one, but I think—" She tapped the tabletop with a fingertip. While she did not believe in fortune-telling, she saw no reason not to attempt to follow the geometrical logic. She found it a rather stimulating exercise. "With the mountains surrounding, one should interpret this as an arduous journey successfully made. Yes, I think that is the correct divination." Travel in Turkey and the Levant was never easy, so she took no great risk there. "Now, this third horseshoe portends a woman."

Lord Foye looked uninterested in that possibility.

"Lady Foye, perhaps?" she said in a sweet voice.

"No," he said after too long a silence. "There is no Lady Foye."

She looked up, interested more by his flat tone of voice than by his declaration of bachelorhood. He wasn't looking at her. His attention was interior, on some deep and private pain. She hadn't expected to see anguish, yet that was what she saw in his eyes, and her heart pinched a little on his behalf.

"Another woman, then," she said. Looking at Lord Foye, with his irregularly put together face, was suddenly too intimate an experience. His eyes were too raw with loss. Had she inadvertently reminded him of a lost love? "Someone who will love you, my lord. Exactly as you deserve."

Without thinking, she leaned forward, peering into his face. Foye's gaze came back to the present. Their eyes locked, and with no warning, her breath caught in her throat. Her skin prickled up and down her body, all in pointed awareness of the man sitting across from her. He wasn't handsome. He wasn't at all. But Sabine's heart beat hard against her ribs as if he were.

She leaned away, still struggling to get enough air into her lungs. She felt she had not moved soon enough, that she had unwittingly allowed an intimacy she would never permit in actual fact. A spark of fear settled in her chest because even with the distance between them, she remained lost in his eyes. Lost.

It was Foye who broke their gaze. "What else do the tea leaves predict?" he softly asked.

Sabine thought that in all her life she'd never heard a more seductive voice. But her lesson had been a harsh one well learned. Her own future did not include love or marriage. She returned to his tea leaves. "Here," she said, pointing. "A dragon."

His expression was remote. Distant but pleasant. She was reminded that he was a great deal older than she. This was not a man to be bothered with young ladies. If he happened to be looking for a lover, she suspected he would prefer a woman older than her twenty-three years. And a woman with some independence as well. She knew how things were done, if he was discreet. A married woman. Or perhaps a widow. Someone closer to his own age.

He leaned forward again and frowned. "A dragon, you say." He squinted and tilted his head. "Are you certain it's not a snake? Or a stick. Or even nothing more than an accidentally formed clump of leaves clinging to the inside of a cup?"

"Oh," she said, laughing. His mouth twitched, too, and she felt another breath hitch in her chest. "Accidental? Impossible, my lord."

"Why ever so?"

She flicked a look in his direction. "Why, because then we would be wasting our time over this when we could be speaking of politics or mathematics or Newton's first law of thermodynamics."

Lord Foye sat back and crossed his hands over his very flat stomach. His eyelashes, she noted, were very thick and dark. "What a great many words just came out of your mouth. My head swims with all those syllables." That wasn't a smile, not precisely, lurking around the edges of his mouth, and Sabine waited breathlessly for one to appear. "I prefer that you tell me of this dragon in my tea, Miss Godard. What is it doing there, and what does it portend?"

"That's easy enough to divine. A snake signifies misfortune, and I see no misfortune in this cup. As for a stick, I assure you, there is never anything so mundane as a stick in one's tea leaves. No, I am quite confident this is no snake but a dragon, and it portends change. Typically with the dragon, the change is sudden and unexpected."

"And how is that different from the unfortunate snake?"

"Change isn't always a misfortune," she said. The more she looked at him, the more she itched to pull out her sketch pad and take a likeness of him. He was possessed of a fearsome intellect, and sooner or later, intellect always affected one's impression of a man's appearance. Lord Foye probably did quite well with the ladies, if he was a man inclined to dally. She peeked at him. Yes. He was a dangerous man.

And what a fascinating face he possessed. If she were to force herself to select Foye's best feature she would have to choose his eyes. They were lovely. Deep set, wide, and blue, with his lovely, thick, dark lashes. As for the rest of him? Quite unlovely. And unconscionably large. Not just in height but in sheer mass, and he was not in the least fat.

"Are you thinking of dragons?" he asked with a wry twist of his mouth.

"Oh dear." She felt her cheeks flush. "I have been caught out."

"In what transgression, Miss Godard?" His voice went low and inviting, and the sound made her shiver inside. My heavens, yes, he was dangerous. "Something amusing, I hope," he said in that tone of warm silk.

"Not very, I fear." She licked her lower lip. "I was thinking that Edward IV, the Black Prince, was said to have been six feet and three inches."

"I am taller than that by three inches." He held himself quite still, but his focus—and she was not mistaken in this—was on her mouth, and that made her anxious and something else as well that was not entirely unpleasant.

"Is it inconvenient to be so tall?" The words were out before she could stop them. How trite, she said to herself. He must think her a fool.

"There are advantages," he said. The edges of his mouth tensed, and some of the warmth vanished from his eyes. She was sorry for that. Somehow, she had lost control of the conversation.

Sabine glanced away to hide the flush she knew was coloring her cheeks. "Forgive me, my lord," she said. "I have been rude. You must hear such questions far too often." With regret for the loss of even a hint of a smile from him, she clasped her hands on the table in front of her. "I am five feet and three inches tall. Provided I stand very straight when I am measured. A full twelve inches shorter than the Black Prince. And, my lord, because I know you are far too polite to ask, yes, it is often inconvenient not to be taller."

He didn't smile, but he did incline his head, and she was actually relieved to have succeeded even a little at smoothing over her blunder with him.

She pushed aside the teacup. "There. We are even, my lord. Now, tell me, after Constantinople, where will you travel? Have you an itinerary?"

"I've plans to visit Maraat Al-Numan, Palmyra. Damascus, of course." His near smile returned and without thinking, Sabine smiled back at him. He cocked his head to the side, a thoughtful look on his face. "But I am ever in pursuit of recommendations. You and your uncle have been in the country for a while. What should I see, Miss Godard?"

She pushed his teacup another inch closer to him. "We were in Egypt until recently. Before that, Greece and Crete. Macedonia because I was intent on seeing the home country of Alexander the Great."

"And in Minos did you find the labyrinth or the Minotaur?"

"No sign of either, I'm afraid," she said. "And Egypt was—not comfortable for us. We arrived shortly before Ibrahim Pasha's massacre of the Mameluks. After that event, the army was everywhere and the soldiers quite tense." Lord Foye was easy to talk to, and even though she knew it was unwise to speak so unguardedly, she did. He was not trying to flirt with her for one thing, his reference to Crosshaven notwithstanding, nor did he speak as if her gender required platitudes or meant she lacked a subtle mind.

"I'd heard something of that," Foye said. "You and your uncle were in Cairo at the time?"

She nodded. "Godard and I were glad to leave. Even here they whisper of another march through the desert. There was some talk of Turkish reinforcements. I convinced Godard we would be more comfortable farther from the troubles in Egypt, so we came here to Constantinople."

His eyes stayed on her, and she could not for her life be sure of what she saw there. Curiosity? Admiration? She knew men often admired her looks. But his regard of her was not what she'd come to expect from men. There was so much more to see in Lord Foye's visage that she felt out of her depth where he was concerned, and that was a rare thing for her. Men did not often disconcert her.

"What have you seen that you would recommend?" he asked.

She considered whether to answer honestly or offer some polite and not very useful response. Before Crosshaven, she would not have hesitated to give her opinion. Until London, she hadn't known just how peculiar a woman she was, or what the consequences of that would be.

"Your honest opinion would be appreciated," he said.

Sabine was not entirely blind to her faults, and yet she did not want him to think her odd when he must already believe the worst of her morals. "Godard toured the mosque at Topkapi Palace, which I would heartily recommend to you."

Lord Foye remained leaning back on his chair. His face was remarkably fluid. There were fine lines around his eyes, but they added character rather than detracted. "What of the sultan's Seraglio?" He grinned at her, and her heart skipped a beat. "I think I should like to visit the sultan's personal harem exceedingly well." He touched his teacup and gave her an innocent smile. "Perhaps my pleasant and successful journey will be to the Seraglio."

Sabine pulled his teacup back to her. "I see no portents of death or dismemberment in here. You will not visit the Seraglio, my lord."

"A very great disappointment, to be sure." He shook his head. "Or perhaps not." He shifted his long legs. "How long will you and your uncle stay in Constantinople?"

"I can't say," Sabine said. She glanced at her uncle. "Before much longer we'll head north to Kilis. Nazim Pasha has invited us to his palace there. Godard is quite keen to go."

"Kilis?" Lord Foye said. He turned to Godard and waited until he had her uncle's attention. "Are you certain that's wise, Sir Henry? To travel through the north of Syria? So many unpleasant stories of the Wahabi rebellion emanate from there."

Godard lifted a hand from his lap and let it fall back. "If we go, when we go, we shall be perfectly fine, my dear fellow. We will be the honored guests of Nazim Pasha. We could hardly be safer."

"Nazim Pasha." Foye grimaced. "An infamous man by all accounts."

"We shall be perfectly safe," Godard said.

That, as it turned out, was not the case.

Four

🐌

About four in the afternoon. Near the village square of Büyükdere on a day somewhat warmer than usual. Meaning it was more than eighty degrees Fahrenheit. Baking hot for the English who were not raised in such constant heat. At the shops nearby, a good many people sat under canopies or umbrellas eating sherbet sold at two paras the cup.

"I WAS VERY SORRY TO HEAR ABOUT YOUR BROTHER," Anthony Lucey said. "Mrs. Lucey and I were devastated by the news."

Foye nodded. He and Lucey were walking from Lucey's palace toward the village square at a leisurely pace. He'd rather take a brisker walk, but Lucey, though a trim and hale man, was years older than he. He let Lucey set the pace.

Their plan was to stay in the shade of the fruit trees that abounded here and to buy a cup of sherbet from a favorite vendor of Lucey's. "Your letter arrived the day before I left England. Your memories of him as a boy were a comfort to me."

"I am glad to know that."

"It was unexpected," Foye said. His father and Lucey had been friends since their Eton days and had maintained a correspondence throughout the years Lucey had been living in Turkey, up to the day his father died. After that sad occurrence, he and Foye had continued a warm and cordial exchange of letters. He'd corresponded with Foye's brother, too, though not quite as often. He'd found Lucey's letters among his brother's effects.

"High time you got married, don't you think? You're not going to let your disappointment put you off the idea, are you?" Lucey asked. The man was quite serious. Well. There wasn't anyone left to push him on the matter, was there?

"I do not expect to marry, sir." He suppressed a smile as they stood to one side to let a pair of Grecian ladies pass them by. Both women looked at Foye. One grabbed her companion's arm to hurry them past while the other gave him a glance that lingered at his groin.

"Not marry?" Lucey came to a full stop but hurried to catch up when Foye continued walking. "Not marry?"

"That is my decision, sir." He spoke firmly. Decisively. The problem was he knew it for a lie. He would marry. Eventually. To the woman of his choice. An older woman with some experience of life.

"Your father should have insisted you get married before he passed. I know he wanted to see you settled down with a wife and children. He told me so." Lucey kept his hands clasped behind his back. "More than once. What father doesn't wish to see his children happily married?"

They passed beneath an almond tree, and Foye reached up to snag a twig from a branch. "Oh, he tried, sir. But I didn't see the point in tying myself down then." He shrugged. He'd been too busy then with a string of mistresses, opera girls and ballet dancers. Besides, his brother had been married and at that time had a son. Who, alas, had not lived. At the time, he saw no reason to be married and a great many why he should not be.

But then he'd met Rosaline, and marriage had suddenly seemed the most desirable state in the world. For a time.

He had written to Lucey of his broken engagement, but

perhaps in too few words; there was to be no wedding after all, he had said, and he was in the process of returning any gifts that had been sent in advance of the wedding. Nothing more.

"I would have been a wretched husband had I married."

"Nonsense," Lucey said.

He laughed to himself. "I appreciate your support of me." He dropped his twig, stripped bare of leaves now. "I suppose Miss Prescott thought so, too, though." He was pleased to discover that he could speak of Rosaline without feeling as if his heart were being crushed all over again. "I would have been a poor husband for her. Doubtless she is happier now than she would have been married to me."

"Tosh," Lucey said, releasing one hand and waving it in the air as if that proved Rosaline's error. "The girl was a fool to marry anyone but you, and that's a fact." He clapped Foye between his shoulder blades. "Didn't mean to stir up old wounds, my lord. I only meant to say that if you'd married when you were merely Lord Edward, as you ought to have done, you'd have been in a position to marry after your heart."

"I was very much in love with Miss Prescott," Foye said. He wondered, though, if that were true. Rosaline had not loved him. What would have happened if he'd married Rosaline and then discovered she did not love him? Well. She had saved him that humiliation, hadn't she? The prospect of unending years spent bound to any woman without love or even the smallest affection deadened him inside.

"You'll love again," Lucey said.

"No. I shan't." Foye held up a hand when Lucey started to speak. "Spare me the protestations. It's not a matter of meeting the right woman. Nor waiting for my broken heart to heal." Very true. When he married, his wife would be suitable and experienced enough to understand love would have no place in their marriage. "There's nothing more to be said on the matter."

Lucey sighed. "The shop's just there." He pointed.

"I must warn you, my lord, that Mrs. Lucey has designs upon your single state."

Foye laughed despite himself. He had been dodging matchmakers for quite some time now. "What is her name?"

"Miss Anna Justice." Lucey looked at him, abashed. "A lovely girl, if that matters."

"No." They changed course for the direction Lucey indicated. A girl. Therein lay the problem.

"Who knows," Lucey said. "You might change your mind."

"Isn't that Sir Henry and Miss Godard sitting just outside?" Foye asked. He recognized them right off and was grateful for any excuse to speak of something else.

He shaded his eyes against the strong sun. "So it is."

"Interesting man, Sir Henry," Foye said, just to keep things on track.

"Ill-tempered, but brilliant. Quite brilliant. Mrs. Lucey finds him endearing. I don't know why. Fortunately, his niece hasn't inherited his disposition." Lucey gave him a sideways look. "Shall we join them, or would you rather not?"

"Join them, by all means."

Lucey chuckled. "A lovely young woman, Miss Godard."

"Yes." Foye saw no reason to deny the obvious. "But from that it does not follow that I will wish to marry her."

"Pity, really. You and Miss Godard would suit rather well."

Foye stopped walking. "She is too young, sir. I've no wish to marry a girl. Lovely or otherwise."

He threw up his hands. "I'll say no more!" He lifted his hat and wiped his forehead with his handkerchief. "Twenty-five years I've lived in this country and I still long for fog." He stuffed his handkerchief into a pocket. They started walking again. "Whatever you think of her, she's a dear thing. She'll make someone a fine wife, I'll warrant you that."

Thank goodness word of her disgrace had not made it to this side of the world. He looked toward them again. He and Miss Godard had a great deal in common. "I did not have the impression she was looking to marry."

Lucey came to a stop. "Furthest thing from her mind, I'd say." They stood in the direct sun rather than in the shade along the side. It was devilishly hot. Lucey rocked up to his toes and back as he stood there, sweating.

Foye walked toward the Godards and shade.

"Sir Henry!" Lucey called out when he and Foye were nearer the table where Godard and his niece sat. An empty cup of sherbet on the table was overshadowed by the mass of papers spread over the surface. Sir Henry pushed his hat farther back on his head while Miss Godard bent over a sheet of paper, writing something. She had her tongue stuck into the corner of her mouth.

"Good afternoon, Mr. Lucey," Sir Henry said. He rapped a misshapen finger on the table near his niece. "Did you get that down, Sabine?"

She kept writing. "Yes, Godard."

How strange that she addressed her uncle with such a lack of intimacy. Or, rather, that she addressed him as if she were a male companion of his.

She glanced up, taking in Lucey and him, then returned her attention to her page, writing the entire time. Her penmanship was excruciatingly neat. Which he found an astonishing accomplishment considering the speed with which her pen moved over the page.

"May we buy you and Miss Godard another sherbet?" Lucey asked.

Foye watched Miss Godard. She'd done writing and was now scanning her page for errors, he presumed. She wore a white cloth over her head, hiding much of her golden blond hair. Her frock wasn't a very interesting one but for the way she fit into it. She had a lush figure for so small a woman.

"You've brought Foye along." Sir Henry nodded in approval. He gestured for them to sit. "I am afraid, however, that you cannot buy us both another sherbet."

"Are you quite sure?" Lucey said. Foye fetched two chairs from another table, and Lucey sat, gratefully, in the shade. Foye stayed on his feet since he expected he would be the one to procure the sherbets. Miss Godard appended another sentence to her document. At minimum, he was fifteen years her elder. The difference in their ages and experiences was simply too vast.

"He means, Mr. Lucey," Foye said with a nod at the empty cup, "that since only one of them has indulged it is impossible to procure another for them both."

Sir Henry let out a bleat of laughter and thumped his cane on the ground. "Very clever, my lord. What did I tell you about him, Sabine? Did I not tell you he was a man to watch?"

"Yes, Godard, you did." She capped her bottle of ink.

Foye wondered what it must be like to be constantly in the company of a man like Sir Henry. One had to admire her for her fortitude. If she was perhaps a bit odd, he understood why.

"Lord Foye is precisely correct," Sir Henry said. "Sabine hasn't had a sherbet, Mr. Lucey, so it's impossible to buy her another." He thrust his head forward, eyes sharp as the edge of a sword. "You may, however, buy me another if you like."

Miss Godard laid a hand on her uncle's arm. "Godard," she murmured.

"Orange for me," Lucey told Foye.

Foye took a look at the remains of Godard's sherbet. "Will you have orange again, Sir Henry?"

"Clever fellow, you are." He bobbed his head. "Very clever, wouldn't you say, Sabine?"

"I cannot say, Godard." With movements economical and precise, she closed up the box that held her writing supplies. "He is, however, observant."

"Hah!" Sir Henry craned his head sideways to look at him. "Thank you, my lord, yes, I should like another orange."

"And you, Miss Godard?" Foye asked. Would she look at him or not? "Will you have a sherbet, too?"

She stopped straightening the papers on the table in an attempt to make room for Lucey and him. Sheaf of papers in hand, she smiled at him, and Foye had several competing reactions as a direct result. Why, he wondered, did she look surprised by his question? Another thought was that Miss Godard was even prettier when she smiled. Stunning, actually. Her smile was not in the least flirtatious or suggestive. She gave no sign that she found his title any reason to behave differently. She was merely . . . sweet. In fact, she looked pleased to have been asked, and that made him pleased to have done the asking.

"Can there be any question?" Lucey said. "Of course a sherbet for Miss Godard. Will you have orange?"

"Thank you." Her smile at Lucey made her entire face light up. She was still smiling when she looked at him, and Foye's body reacted even though the remains of her smile weren't meant for him. "Pomegranate, please," she said with a curt nod.

Foye bowed to her. "I am delighted to indulge your every whim, Miss Godard."

She did not smile, and why should she, given his connection with Crosshaven? Why indeed?

He went inside the shop and found, to his relief, that the shopkeeper spoke enough English for him to return with a white-turbaned native servant behind him carrying a salver with the requisite sherbets: three orange and one pomegranate.

The table was clear of papers now, with but a slim stack remaining at Miss Godard's elbow. She accepted the sherbet from the servant with a nod and a phrase he took for the local language.

Foye sat down, sweeping his coattails behind him once he'd angled his chair so his legs did not hit anyone else's. "You speak Turkish, Miss Godard? I'm impressed."

"That was Arabic, my lord." Spoon in one hand, she rested her arm on the table. "Enough to say please and thank you and not much more. My Turkish is somewhat better."

Good Lord. She was a solemn thing, wasn't she?

"Don't believe her for a moment," Lucey said. He accepted his sherbet from the servant. "I've heard her chattering away like a little magpie. Perfect accent, every word."

Miss Godard gazed at Lucey, alert and focused. "I am not fluent, Mr. Lucey. As you well know."

"Every time I hear her speak, I think I'm listening to a native with an imperfect command of the grammar."

"You are a frighteningly accomplished woman, Miss Godard," Foye said. She was waiting, he realized, for her uncle to start eating.

"I excel at languages," she said. This she stated as fact, not a boast. She leaned toward her uncle and resettled the napkin over his lap. Only when Sir Henry had begun, laboriously, eating with the spoon clenched in his crippled hand, did she relax and start on her own sherbet.

His was delicious. Cool and sweet. The perfect refreshment for a hot afternoon. "I considered choosing the pomegranate, Miss Godard, but found I hadn't the courage."

She pushed her bowl toward him. "You may taste mine, of course. Please."

He dipped his spoon into her sherbet.

"Well?" Lucey asked.

"Hmm." He closed his eyes and pretended to savor the taste for a while. "I'm not sure. May I try more?"

"Of course."

He took another spoonful. "It's very slightly tart," he said. Damned if he wasn't determined to get a smile out of her. "And, yet, I'm not certain, Miss Godard. One more?" He waited for her to nod before her took yet another spoonful. "Do you know," he said when he'd eaten that, too, "I'm still unsure." He looked into her cup. "I may need to eat the rest before I'm able to decide. In the spirit of a proper inquiry, do you mind?"

Lucey and Sir Henry laughed, and even though all he got from Miss Godard was a tiny smile, hardly even a smile at all, Foye felt his body clench. Breathtaking. Absolutely breathtaking. Foye signaled to the shopkeeper, and when he came out, he ordered another pomegranate sherbet.

"That's not necessary."

"Yes, it is." He held her dish in one hand while he scooped up a heaping amount of what remained and ate it. "Yours is practically gone, and I don't think you've had more than a spoonful."

"It's quite all right," she said.

But the second sherbet was bought, and Foye handed over the necessary coins. He leaned against his chair and relaxed. Sir Henry, for all that he was sometimes so gruff, was an engaging conversationalist, deeply knowledgeable on a great many subjects. Their conversation ranged from philosophy and natural history to the sights they'd each seen during their travels. As for Miss Godard, she was never at a loss. She was much like her uncle in respect of her knowledge and insight. No one questioned her participation, least of all her uncle. Presently, though, the sherbets were consumed and the point reached when they must leave or admit a closer acquaintance.

Foye surprised himself by saying, "May we escort you and Sir Henry home, Miss Godard?" If they did, perhaps he'd manage to get a proper smile from her.

She glanced at her uncle. "We ought to finish your chapter," she said.

"And how is the book coming?" Lucey asked.

"Book?" Foye said.

Sir Henry pushed away his empty cup with a look of regret. "I am engaged in the writing of an account of our travels, my lord. Sabine is my official secretary for the endeavor." He grinned. "And a hard taskmaster she is."

Foye stood, knowing very well that Miss Godard had used her uncle's project as an excuse to see him on his way. Lucey did the same. He was sorry they were parting and perhaps sorrier that Miss Godard had wanted to stay behind. "Good afternoon, Sir Henry." He turned. "Miss Godard."

She reached for her uncle's papers just when he expected

her to offer her hand. There followed an awkward moment
when his hand was extended in the expectation of bowing
over hers. She did not proffer hers in return, and Foye lowered his arm while she said, holding a stack of papers, "It
was a pleasure seeing you again, my lord." Foye was coming to hate that crisp, impersonal tone of hers. "Mr. Lucey,
do give Mrs. Lucey my regards."

On their way back to Lucey's house, Lucey said,
"Extraordinary woman, Miss Godard."

"I found her rather cold," he said.

"The girl needs a husband, no matter what her uncle
says." They kept walking. Though Foye said nothing in
response, he could not help thinking that had it not been
for Crosshaven, she might already be married. His opinion
wasn't so different from Lucey's. "Well," Lucey continued,
"My dear wife often warns me not to meddle, but I tell you,
Foye, I am determined to find her a suitable husband. Especially now that you tell me there's no hope for you."

"None whatever," he said.

"There's a dozen soldiers who would do quite well
for her. Sir Henry's not going to live forever, you know.
None of us are. What's to become of her if she hasn't got a
husband?"

Foye said nothing to that, either. He was struggling with
the unpleasant realization that for some reason, he thought
of Miss Godard as his. She wasn't. What's more, he did not
want her to be.

His.

Five

❧

Constantinople, Turkey. The suq (bazaar),
MAY 13, 1811

A hot day outside. Inside the covered portions of the suq
the temperature was considerably cooler. There were
two groups of Europeans present. The first consisted of
Lord Foye, Lieutenant Russell of the Royal Artillery, and
two other soldiers from the same company. The second
included Miss Godard, Sir Henry, and Sir Henry's native
servant Asif. The former were aware the latter were here,
somewhere. The latter were unaware of the former.

SOMEONE CURSED ANGRILY IN TURKISH, AND SABINE
turned to be sure the argument was not going to spread. Asif,
the Syrian servant who attended to Godard, also turned. He,
of course, being large and armed with a pair of pistols tucked
into the sash around his waist, was the only one of them in a
position to do anything if the altercation got out of hand.

After some shaking of mutual fists, the disagreement
abated, and Asif returned to assisting Godard with trying on hats. Sabine did not return to the shopping effort
because among the crowds in the suq, she saw the Marquess of Foye heading in their general direction. He was
certainly easy enough to pick out.

Her pulse sped up as she watched him, wondering if he
had seen them and whether it would be possible to avoid
him. She wanted nothing to do with him. He continued
toward them. He had seen them, though, because their eyes

met across the crowd. Well, then. There was nothing for it
now. She would have to endure another meeting with him,
wondering when he would slyly, or perhaps even boldly,
get around to her immoral past. What a shame Godard
liked the man.

"Godard," she said, placing a hand on her uncle's arm.
Her stomach clenched.

"What do you think of this one?" Godard said, holding
up a hat that resembled a beret.

"It's too large, isn't it?" She leaned to her uncle and
spoke in a low voice. "Lord Foye is here." It occurred to
her then that the marquess was alone. How odd that was.
Perhaps he was lost, separated from whatever servants he'd
brought with him.

"Lord Foye?" Godard swung around and the hat slipped
off his head, fortunately caught by Asif at the last minute.
The servant returned the hat to the vendor.

The marquess was almost upon them, quite plainly
working his way to them. With a sense of dread, Sabine
watched him move through the crowd. Most people simply got out of his way, but when that was not possible, he
slipped with fluid grace between bodies or around knots of
shoppers or merchants delivering goods, ignoring all the
calls for his attention. A half-dozen children, many of them
barefoot and in rags, ran after him, begging for coins.

She picked up an embroidered silk hat decorated with
pearls and glass beads. The sort of hat that would be
worn to a wedding. Godard would never buy such a bit of
frippery, but that did not mean it wasn't lovely. The spot
directly between her shoulders tingled as she examined the
needlework. She looked over her shoulder.

A few feet from where they stood, Foye had paused to
take some coins from his pocket. He was passing them out
to the children, who babbled happily at him in a combination of Turkish and Arabic. She pretended to be absorbed in
her examination of the hat. And then, he was here. Standing not two feet from her. The children followed, begging
more coins from him.

Done for the moment with the children pressing him for more money, he bowed and she guessed would have offered his hand to her, but she held the hat in both hands. He deftly turned to her uncle. "Sir Henry," he said. "How do you do, sir?"

"Fine, thank you. And yourself?" Godard extended a hand, and Foye hardly shook it, a gentle touch, for which she was very grateful. She already knew this trip into Constantinople would cost Godard dearly later in the day and into tomorrow. Godard knew, too, of course. His fortitude in dealing with his constant pain was only one of the many reasons she admired her uncle. They managed, the two of them. Even when they disagreed, even though Lord Crosshaven had destroyed Godard's trust in her, they got on.

A fact for which she was eternally grateful. The outcome of their London trip could have been much worse than it had been.

Foye turned to her again. "Miss Godard," he said. His blue coat made his eyes stand out even more than usual. They were the color of an early morning. Pale but not washed out.

She lifted her head but deliberately did not smile. He wore riding clothes, buckskin breeches that snugly covered his legs, a plain cravat, and a bronze and gold embroidered waistcoat with gold buttons. His knee-high polished boots looked soft as butter. He held a beaver hat in one hand. She wondered why he left his hair so long. He'd have some luck controlling his curls if he kept it short.

Sabine bent a knee. "My lord."

Beside them Godard continued trying on hats. "No, Godard," she said when he put on one of a violent red. She tried to ignore Lord Foye, but it wasn't easy. Her back tingled with awareness of him.

"Asif?" Godard said, with a look at the servant. Asif shook his head and squinted as if the color hurt his eyes. "Hmm," he said with a puff of air from between his pursed lips. "What do *you* think, my lord?"

Foye looked Godard up and down, then put a hand to his chin while he studied the hat. Slowly, he shook his head. "I don't believe, sir, that red is quite your color." He continued his perusal. "Might I suggest a richer color? Forest green or perhaps bronze or midnight blue?"

"A man milliner, are you?" Godard returned the hat to the merchant.

The marquess waited in silence, as if he knew Sabine would not be able to resist looking at him much longer, and, drat the man, he was right.

"I've found you without even trying," he said when she broke down and looked. While she wondered what that meant, he scrubbed a hand through his hair. A curl flopped over his forehead, then several more.

"You were looking for us?" she asked.

There. That was very blandly said. She did not at all sound as if she thought that remarkable. Godard continued his examination of hats, and she affected fascination with the process.

"Well, no." With an oddly guilty glance behind him, he said, "I came here with others who are."

That got Godard's attention. He stopped with a hat halfway to his head. "Looking for us?" Godard said. "Pray tell, who? Mr. Lucey, perhaps? I should be pleased to see him."

Sabine kept her expression as neutral as possible, but she knew her uncle's too careful tone of voice. She knew precisely what he wondered.

Foye's attention moved from Godard to Sabine. The moment his blue eyes met hers, her stomach filled with butterflies, and there was no reason for it. There was no reason at all that she should have any reaction to the marquess.

"Lieutenant Russell, for one." He said the name as if it ought to be significant to her. It was not, but the damage had been done. At her blank expression, Foye added, "of the Royal Artillery?"

She barely remembered the name. She made a point of not remembering any of the gentlemen and officers she met and so could summon no face to go with the name. Not that it mattered. She was acutely aware of Godard scowling at her. In London, he had sworn he believed her innocent, but he hadn't. Not really. Not truly. She put down the silk hat. The air smelled of spices, saffron, cinnamon, pepper, sandalwood, and a dozen other aromas. If they were to walk to the spice merchants, the smell would overpower even the omnipresent thick and bitter scent of the coffee the merchants brewed for themselves.

"Red," Foye replied. "He has red hair. A very nice red, to be sure," he hurried to add.

Sabine bit back the urge to tell the marquess she didn't care what color Lieutenant Russell's hair was. She wanted nothing to do with him or any officer.

Godard waved aside the merchant's offering of another hat. He wheeled about, his cane gripped hard with both hands, leaning a shoulder against Asif's upper arm when he faced Lord Foye and craned his neck to see him. "What the devil does that young puppy want with Sabine?"

"I am unable to answer on his behalf," Foye replied. He inspected the lay of his waistcoat. "Though I should think that obvious, given that he is a handsome young man and your niece a pretty young girl."

The merchant, fearful of losing his customer, selected another hat from among his wares, speaking in rapid Turkish that, thankfully, required Sabine's concentration. His hats were the most excellent hats in all the world. The workmanship was exquisite, each hat so lovingly made that even an infidel should wear one.

She happily turned her back to the marquess while she told the merchant in no uncertain terms that she did not want her uncle wearing an inferior hat. Her stomach was sour, a very pleasant day ruined. She wished the marquess had never seen them.

At the end of her discussion with the merchant, Godard ended up with another hat on his head, this time a dark blue felt embroidered with gold and silver thread. She rolled her eyes and made a gesture that was neither approving or disapproving. She did enjoy bargaining.

In English, she said, "You look very handsome in that hat, Godard." For the merchant's benefit she gave the hat a scathing glance and shook her head.

Sir Henry removed one hand from his walking stick. "Asif," he said, "what do you think?"

The servant kept his hand on the hilt of one of his pistols and bowed. In Turkish, he said, "It seems ill fitting to me," a sentiment he punctuated with a dismissive gesture and an expression of distaste. Sabine agreed in the same language.

The merchant launched into a rebuttal.

"It is the finest one yet, Godard," she said in English.

"Very well, then," Godard said. "This one."

And now, they must find a way to purchase that very fine hat for less than the money she had budgeted for the expense. She gestured to Asif, who bowed and bent to pick up a parcel that had been sitting at his feet.

The vendor began extolling the virtues of this hat in particular and why it was worth ten times what Sabine intended to pay. The marquess stayed at her side, listening intently. She wished him to perdition. At the end of the negotiations, she handed over two coins, and the shopkeeper wrapped the hat in paper and handed it to Asif.

Sir Henry craned his neck to look up at Foye, pushing up on his walking stick to gain another inch or two of height. Godard would be in bed the moment they returned to Büyükdere. Tomorrow, he would stay in, barely able to walk. His condition meant they traveled slowly with more days spent recovering than traveling. Perhaps they were slow, but so far they had seen a great deal more of the world than many able-bodied men. "We did not expect to see you in Constantinople, my lord. If we'd known, you might have traveled with us."

"My visit was wholly unplanned, Sir Henry. I rode in with some officers who were coming to the bazaar this morning." One side of his mouth pulled down. "As I said already, I suppose. At any rate, I'd not been to the suq yet and thought I should not miss the opportunity."

Godard scowled terribly, and Sabine knew that if Foye had been a different sort of man, he would have quailed under that disapproving eye. He wasn't and so did not. Whatever the marquess thought of her, he was beyond being intimidated by her uncle. But then he was a grown man. Mature in his years and experience of life. And of a social position few men matched and even fewer exceeded.

"Have you been here long? At the suq, I mean," Foye said, as if he'd not noticed Godard's displeasure at the mention of Lieutenant Russell.

Sabine said nothing. It would do no good to deny an interest in the lieutenant now. Godard, she was certain, was convinced otherwise. Why else would a soldier come haring all the way to Constantinople, if not because of some nefarious plot against her virtue? No matter how often he denied it, Crosshaven and the disastrous aftermath had instilled a bone-deep distrust of her in her uncle. And of every handsome man to show an interest in her. She was blameless, yet every day since the gossip had begun, she lived with the consequences.

She took her watch from a pocket of her frock. "It's nearly two, Godard," she said, fiercely glad to have a reason to put an end to this agonizing encounter. She pressed her fingers over the watch and felt the satisfying click as the metal cover closed over the face. "We have just time to find the rug makers, if you feel up to it."

"That way." Foye pointed behind him. "I passed them on my way here."

"Thank you," she said. She took care to keep any hint of thankfulness from her expression or the words.

Foye fell into step next to her. Godard was on her other side, clinging to Asif's arm. His cane thudded on the ground. Unfortunately, Godard did not think the marquess posed a danger to her, or he would even now be attempting to chase him away.

Godard said, "My niece and I have been discussing our Roman history, my lord." The curve of her uncle's spine meant he had to turn his entire upper body in order to look at Foye.

"Have you?" the marquess said.

"Sabine is partial to the writings of Marcus Aurelius." He lifted a hand from his cane, and Asif stepped forward, in position to assist if it were needed. It wasn't. "But then," he said in his gruff way, "she is a sentimental female."

"You find the Stoics sentimental?" Foye asked her.

She leaned toward Godard because she did not like her awareness of the marquess. Perhaps the subject would distract Godard from the thought of Lieutenant Russell searching the suq for her. "Yes, my lord, I do."

Godard cackled. "She is not a lover of Latin. If Aurelius had written in Latin instead of Greek, I'd have had a devil of a time convincing her to read him."

"Really, Godard," she said. "I enjoy the Romans as much as anyone." She glanced at Foye. He was watching Godard, and Sabine took the opportunity to study his face. She did not have to like or trust him to find his face interesting. Perhaps when they were home, she would attempt to draw him from memory. All the lines and angles that did not meet in harmony, the mouth that, when he smiled, transformed him utterly. "Plato's dialogues was my first great triumph, my lord." In London, she had learned that gentlemen found her education both peculiar and off-putting. She smiled and wondered at her not thinking of this sooner. "When Godard agreed that I had mastered that—"

"She was sixteen, my lord," Godard said with a look at Foye that made her wonder at the slyness of it. "Sixteen!"

"—I never said I was an excellent pupil, Godard," Sabine replied evenly but with a vicious and satisfying sense of irony. "Merely a proud one. I thought I needed no further improvement once I had Plato dissected." She looked at Lord Foye. "I ask you, my lord, what could the Romans be after that but anticlimactic?"

They proceeded slowly along a passageway lined with merchants sitting cross-legged amid their wares. The noise was louder here, the scent of spices fainter, the smell of coffee and dirt stronger. More children ran after them, calling out, "Pretty lady! Beautiful lady!" Sabine passed out a few coins—she hadn't many to spare—and in Turkish shooed the rest away. Above them, in a canopy spread over a vendor and his merchandise, a monkey on a leash chittered loudly.

"I suppose," Foye said, leaning in so that she could hear him, "that I would say to you, what of Livy or Pompey or Cicero, or any of the Caesars?"

"I may grant you Cicero," she said. She didn't care what he thought of her. She only wished him gone. Without the children running after them, the noise was considerably lessened.

"Thank you," Foye said.

"Which Caesar is your favorite?" Godard asked. "Is there one who captured your imagination as a young boy?"

"Don't say Julius," Sabine said, since she suspected that Julius Caesar would be exactly who he would name. "It's too simple." If Plato did not drive him away, perhaps the Romans would.

"Not Julius, eh?" Lord Foye said. He scratched a cheek.

She smiled and didn't care at all that he would take it for triumph. "Your reply may tell us something of your character, don't you agree, Godard? Your favorite Caesar besides him. Or Marc Anthony. Let us exclude him as well."

"Am I allowed Caligula?" Foye's smile transformed him from plain to arresting. Her stomach dropped a mile. He wasn't handsome. Not in the least, so why, then, did she find him so compelling? How aggravating that it should be so.

"That is acceptable," she said.

"Caligula," Godard said. "An excellent choice, my lord."

"Thank you, Sir Henry." Foye's attention returned to her, and she felt that same soaring sensation in her stomach. "And your favorite, Miss Godard?"

Before she could answer, someone called out, "My lord! Is that you, Lord Foye?"

They stopped and all four of them, Asif included, turned to see a soldier running toward them. Foye remained beside her.

"Lieutenant Russell," she said with a sinking heart. The soldier was, indeed, a handsome man. "I recognize him now."

"Do you?" Foye said.

How appalling, she thought. With Lieutenant Russell bulling his way toward them, she was actually glad that Foye was here.

"His hair is red," she said with a glance in the marquess's direction. "I thought you were making that up."

He looked down at her, eyebrows arched. "You really don't recall him, do you?"

She shook her head and wondered what it was about Foye that made her stomach take flight.

Six

&

LIEUTENANT RUSSELL CONTINUED MOVING THROUGH the bazaar to where Foye stood with Sabine and her uncle. From somewhere deeper in the suq, an ass brayed, the sound carrying above the noise of commerce. Russell's two companions were nowhere to be seen. Godard's servant, Asif, dressed in the Ottoman style of a white turban, baggy pants that tightened at the ankle, and a flowing, long kaftan over a jacket and shirt, put a hand on one of the pistols at his waist.

The lieutenant was a strapping young man of perhaps twenty-five or -six. Quite possibly younger, Miss Godard's age even, with a head of dark red curls. He was tall and well made and brimmed with the confidence that comes of knowing one is young and beautiful.

As he watched Lieutenant Russell hurrying toward Sabine with a smile of joy on his earnest, handsome face, Foye's heart clenched. He envied the lieutenant and wondered, not so idly, if Miss Godard thought him hand-some. Ah, but did that matter? She did not look pleased to see the man working his way toward them.

"You found her," the lieutenant said to Foye when he reached them. "Splendid of you, milord. Just splendid." A little out of breath from his dash through the crowded suq, the lieutenant clapped a hand on Foye's shoulder, completely unaware that Foye might be a rival. "I'd nearly given up, and then I saw you, and well"—Lieutenant Russell looked at Sabine with cow's eyes—"here you are."

"It is more accurate to say that I chanced to find them," Foye said. He was careful, too, to include Godard. He'd not been blind to the tension earlier when Godard had realized Lieutenant Russell was looking for his niece. Nor did he appreciate being greeted as if he and Lieutenant Russell were intimate friends. He hardly knew the man. Neither did he care for the implication that he had found Miss Godard on the lieutenant's behalf. Bloody hell to that.

"However it happened, I've found her now, and that's a delight to be sure."

Good Lord. Must he be so enthusiastic?

Russell bowed to the Godards, but his attention was for Sabine. "Sir Henry. How do you do?" He grinned even when Sir Henry glared at him with narrowed eyes.

"And you are?"

"Lieutenant Russell, sir," the young man said. "We were introduced at Mr. Lucey's, as I'm sure you recall."

"Humph." Sir Henry kept his hands on his cane. "I don't believe I do recall."

"You were introduced to all the officers there that night," Russell said. His grin never faded. "I certainly recall meeting you."

"I don't recall you."

Foye was quite certain Sir Henry did remember the fel-low. Which amused him more than it ought. Miss Godard was consulting her watch, oblivious to the well-favored young officer at her side. He did not mind at all seeing someone else the recipient of her indifference.

The lieutenant, however, was impervious to the tension. "And how are you, Miss Godard?" He held out a gloved hand. "Are you well? I must say you are looking especially lovely today."

That remark got the lieutenant nowhere. Foye didn't doubt Miss Godard knew she was a lovely woman, but she didn't seem to care much.

She curled her fingers around her watch. "I am very well, thank you, Lieutenant."

"Sabine," Sir Henry said. This he accompanied with a bang of his cane on the ground that made Miss Godard jump. "Pray do not address a man to whom you have not been introduced."

This, Foye realized, was one of the consequences of her time in London. Her uncle, however proud of her intellect, did not trust his niece. He suspected she'd been made to pay for that in large and small ways every day since the scandal.

Lieutenant Russell, to his credit, did not lose his composure or his damned enthusiasm. "Sir Henry, I assure you she's done nothing improper."

"Humph."

"Miss Godard and I have been introduced."

"Since I don't recall you, I should very much like to know how that could be," Sir Henry said.

"Mr. Lucey introduced us."

"I have no such recollection."

"Godard," Sabine said with a patient, pleasant expression belied by the tension in her shoulders. She was crushing her watch. "Mr. Lucey did introduce you to him. And to me."

He narrowed his eyes, pretending, Foye was quite certain, to think. "Is that so?"

"Yes, Godard, that's so. We were introduced to all the officers that evening."

"Not a very memorable fellow, then, is he?"

"Godard." Sabine laid a hand on her uncle's arm. "Please."

Lieutenant Russell completely misinterpreted the exchange. He beamed at Miss Godard. To Foye, it was patently obvious that she was genuinely appalled by Russell's adoration of her and was doing all she could to distance herself from the man without overt rudeness. The lieutenant thought she was defending him out of fondness. The poor, deluded fool.

They stood there, all of them, with Lieutenant Russell hoping he would be asked to join them and Godard having no intention of doing so. Miss Godard fell silent. The longer the invitation went without being made, the more awkward the moment became.

"Lord Foye," Sir Henry said.

"Sir?" He awaited this development with interest.

"Walk ahead with Sabine, won't you? I want a word in private with this young fellow." Sir Henry smiled rather like a hawk would smile right before it dove for a hapless rabbit. "I should like to discover everything he knows about the history of his regiment."

"I should be delighted," Foye said, turning to Miss Godard with his arm extended.

Her gaze slid over his proffered arm. Instead, she started walking, and Foye, after bowing to Sir Henry and the lieutenant, followed.

"Poor Lieutenant Russell," he said in a low voice. He was curious to know what she might say now that they were alone. "Sir Henry will question him until his brain turns to pudding."

She stopped walking and looked back to where her uncle stood with their servant and the lieutenant. "I don't know whether we ought to stay well ahead of them or if it would be best to remain close. I think we should remain nearby, don't you?"

"He won't go far," Foye said. "Your servant is there if he needs assistance." He clasped his hands behind his back. "If Lieutenant Russell is to be told he is not welcome as an aspirant to your heart—"

"I've done nothing," she said. She looked into his face,

and he was struck again by how pretty she was, and by how miserable she looked. "Nothing that would allow anyone to think he could have any legitimate hopes where I am concerned."

"I agree," he said. "In any case, it's best if you are not near while your uncle deals with him. If we stay where we are, he will see us. Do not humiliate him."

"No," she said, and started walking again. "That would not be well done of us."

"Better if you and I continue in our discussion of Roman emperors," Foye said. He offered his arm, but she busied herself with shaking out her skirts, an occupation she kept up until Foye lowered his arm. "I don't believe you told me which was your favorite."

"I did not."

"I insist on knowing." He felt awkward walking beside her here in the crowded suq without taking her arm.

"Does it make a difference?"

He gazed down at her. Had he really hoped for better treatment from her when her uncle was not watching her every utterance? "No," he said. "No difference at all." She flushed at his curt reply, and it was a measure of his irritation with her dislike of him that he hardly cared. "It is at least a subject of conversation to occupy us. Better than stone-cold silence between us."

She looked over her shoulder, then quickly back. "Very well." She took a breath. "As a girl, my lord, I divided the Roman rulers into two groups, those who died unnaturally and those who did not."

My God, she sounded as though she were giving a lecture.

"The former may be further grouped according to whether they were assassinated, murdered by the Praetorian guards, executed, a suicide, or killed in battle. I was astonished to learn that for quite a long while it was unusual for an emperor, and I use that term loosely here as many emperors never so styled themselves, to die anything but unnaturally."

"Had you a favorite among the various groups?" He was interested despite himself, despite a strong suspicion that she intended to put him off with this display of erudition.

"Comodus. Assassinated, it's said, by a wrestler, and Hadrian because I was born near Hadrian's Wall."

"I am ashamed of my single choice of Caligula."

"He was a fine emperor." Her face was intent, and Foye wondered if she knew she'd gotten carried away with the subject. "I approve of your favorite, my lord." She nodded to herself. "Godard would say it shows you have a discerning mind. But then, you are on his assiduously maintained list. I expected no less."

"I am flattered you think so," he said. He meant it. She distrusted him, and if she admired his mind despite that, he was well pleased. He could see himself in twenty, forty, or even fifty years, still being fascinated by her mind.

Now that was quite a thought for him to be having.

"I admire the Romans no matter what I say about the Greeks," she went on. "Don't let Godard convince you otherwise about me. The Roman influence went geographically farther, and they did take knowledge of the Greeks with them." She gave him a sideways look. "Have you been to Serjillo?"

"Not yet." Serjillo was an abandoned Roman city in northern Syria, one of many in the region, and yes, he did intend to see at least some of the Roman ruins. "But I shall certainly place it on my itinerary now."

They came to a section of the suq where the merchants were selling jewelry, and Foye slowed. The rug merchants were still a ways distant. "The Roman ruins are to be a chapter in his book," she said.

"The one you're helping him write?"

She nodded.

A glance behind them gave Foye a glimpse of Lieutenant Russell walking quickly away from Sir Henry. And he had said nothing of Crosshaven yet. He stopped walking and decided it was time to take his honor in hand and let her know what had happened. "Perhaps," he said, "we ought to bring a few matters into the open."

Her mouth tightened. There was something forlorn about the way she went so still, as if she were bracing herself for tragic news. She nodded to him, a very small movement of her head. "Good God," he said, both offended and appalled. "You think I'm going to proposition you, don't you?"

"You would not be the first acquaintance of Lord Crosshaven's to do so."

"Crosshaven and I have parted ways." Foye heard the touch of anger in his voice but seemed powerless to suppress it. "He is no friend of mine. Please be assured of that, Miss Godard."

She started walking again. Foye took a long step to catch up and was shocked to see her near tears. He drew her arm through his, but she moved sharply away.

"This is nonsense," he said. "It is polite for a gentleman to take a young lady's arm when they are walking out."

"We are *not* walking out."

"That isn't what I meant, and well you know it." He bent closer. "Even if I thought you had been to bed with Crosshaven, I would offer you my arm. Without designs on your person, I might add. Because I assure you I do not wish an entanglement of that sort with you or any other woman."

She gazed at him, eyes wide, and he had absolutely no idea what she was thinking.

He let out a long breath. "Miss Godard, I attach no blame to you for what happened in London. I know that Crosshaven lied."

"And how do you know any such thing?"

He kept still as he came face-to-face with his reluctance to speak. "I was engaged to be married not long ago." There. He'd done it. The first time he'd directly referred to Rosaline with someone who was not an intimate of his, and he felt hardly a pinch.

Her eyebrows went up. She had, he realized, misunderstood him. "Is she waiting for you in England?"

"No." He felt his disappointment again. But to his

surprise, the hurt had faded. His regret was bittersweet
rather than a wound yet to heal. "She married someone
else."

"I'm sorry," she said gently. In her pale brown eyes he
saw understanding, not pity. He was going about this all
wrong. He still had not made her understand.

"It was Lord Crosshaven," he said. "She eloped with
Crosshaven two months before our wedding."

"I'm very sorry to know that," she said.

He lowered his voice. "You are wondering what my broken engagement has to do with you." He shook his head. "It
has everything to do with you, I'm afraid. When you were
in London, you and your uncle, Crosshaven was at that
time actively courting Rosaline. My fiancée. In secret, as
you may well imagine. And she," he said stiffly, "returned
his feelings, despite that we were to be married. I was not
at that time Foye, but merely Lord Edward." He reached
for her shoulder but at the last minute let his hand fall to
his side. "Cross, who was one of my dearest friends, pub-
lically lied about you to divert my attention from what
he was doing. He wished for me, for everyone, to believe
he had seduced you. To draw attention from Miss Prescott
and him."

She tipped her head to one side and returned his gaze.
There was no pity in her eyes, just a steady assessment of
him that made his heart thud against his ribs. "Do you hate
him?" she asked.

Foye had the unsettling idea that what she really meant
by her question was that she hated Crosshaven, too. "Hate?"
He thought about that. He had been deeply hurt. Betrayed.
Disappointed beyond words. He gazed down at her and
felt like a damn beast next to her. Rosaline had been far
taller. It was one of the reasons he'd offered for her. "No.
I don't hate him." He hesitated, but once again unwise
words came out. "Do you?" To hell with doing what was
wise, anyway.

She tilted her chin so she could stare into his face. Her
expression was ferocious. "Yes," she said in a gentle voice.

A gentle voice and such a contrast to the raw emotion in her eyes, the set of her mouth, the way her hands clenched at her sides. "I hate Lord Crosshaven enough for us both."

Foye held her gaze, feeling the pull of an expected and sharp desire for her. "That is a subject to be further explored between us, don't you think?"

Seven

૨&

Evening. At a ball held at the marble-covered palace of
Mr. Anthony Lucey. The ballroom faced the Bosporus on
one side and an almond orchard on the other. In addition
to several officers of the British army and navy, guests
included the Italian ambassador and French and Russian
diplomats. Sir Henry Godard and his niece Sabine were
also in attendance. Lord Foye had just arrived.

BUT FOR THE COLORFULLY PATTERNED AND TILED CEILING,
the room might have been anywhere in England. If Foye
were to close his eyes, he could easily imagine himself
back in London. He didn't, though, because he was not a
sentimental man. The music was achingly familiar, at the
moment, a contredanse that had the couples on the floor
laughing and flirting as they moved through the steps.
The orchestra, consisting of violin, cello, flute, and French
horn, was first-rate.

Though he was thousands of miles from London, the
scene reminded Foye of Rosaline. She had loved to dance.
For all he knew, she still did. No doubt Crosshaven was
kept busy dancing. For love of Rosaline, Foye had attended
and danced at nearly every ball for the entire season of
their engagement. He had been pleased to do so because
it made her happy, even though he did not enjoy dancing.
Since then, he'd slowly come to believe he'd made as lucky

an escape as Rosaline. Their marriage would have been a disaster for them both.

Foye stayed where he was, just inside the doorway wondering if he could bear to stay long enough to avoid being thought a boor. He would at least have to greet Lucey, but after that was done, he could leave without anyone noticing much. There was no compelling reason for him to stay.

He was not going to dance tonight.

Candlelight flashed off the gold braid, pins, and tassels worn by the officers. Thankfully, there were enough men not in uniform—either employees of the Levant Company or noncombatants attached to the military—that the ballroom did not have an overwhelmingly martial feel. He was no more conspicuous than usual. As for the ladies, Foye did not see a single able-bodied woman who was not dancing.

God. What a pathetic creature he'd become to so begrudge the young their romance. So be it. He would pattern himself after Sir Henry and decline into his old age without caring a whit what anyone thought about him. He scanned the room in search of something that would distract him from his puerile mood. His attention eventually landed on one young woman who was not dancing.

Miss Godard sat with her uncle at the side of the ballroom. She wore a frock too plain for a ball, with her hair arranged in curls at the back of her head. The color of her hair was unbelievably gold. A few brave soldiers lingered near, but with Sir Henry scowling as he was, Foye was not surprised no one dared approach her.

While he stood there like some love-struck dolt, which he most certainly was not nor would he ever be, Miss Godard looked directly at him. Across the room their eyes met, and damned if he didn't feel a shock of sexual anticipation. He'd been abstinent too long, but regardless of his state of sexual self-denial, she was a very, very pretty woman. Not a girl. A woman. And he wanted her. Quite badly.

She broke the contact, leaned over to say something to her uncle, and afterward left her seat. Foye watched her circle the room, heading toward him. He was not the only man to react to her. As she moved along the perimeter of the ballroom, other men watched her, some openly, others with sly, quick glances, depending on whether they were with a young lady who ought to be the focus of their attention.

Miss Godard drew the male eye despite her plain gown, which did not bare enough of her shoulders or bosom to be interesting. And yet Foye doubted he was the only man whose thoughts were painted over with lust. She had about her an air of self-possession that made a man think, *Here is a woman worth having at the end of the pursuit.*

Of course, there would be no pursuit. He could control his urges as well as the next man. Besides, she had no romantic interest in him. Or any man.

She stopped just shy of where he stood. Notwithstanding her self-possession, she was all of twenty-three, he reminded himself. And he was fifteen years her elder. She surely saw him as too mature and too unfortunate in his looks to be considered anything but an acquaintance.

She curtseyed and slid her gloved hands behind her back so that all he saw of her arms was the bare flesh between her elbows and the ends of her short sleeves. There was an entire civilization of thought behind her eyes. Her youth deceived; her looks misled. Sabine Godard was mature beyond her chronological age. The aching sweetness of her face and the curve of her bosom did not mean she was without complexity of thought or mind, something he was sure most other men failed to comprehend.

Conflating her appearance with her character was, he realized, the mistake other men made with her. Indeed, she was young and lovely enough to arouse any man's interest. With her, though, the usual courtship always failed; witness Lieutenant Russell. Sabine Godard was not a woman to be won with flattery and gallantry. One must woo her mind, not her heart, which, like his, was set someplace very far away.

"Lord Foye," she said. He took a breath and smelled

attar of roses. "When I told Godard you were here, he sent me to fetch you to him."

He looked down at her and smiled faintly. "Miss Godard."

"Come, my lord, and say good evening to Godard." She smiled, and for the first time since he'd met her, he was the recipient of a genuine smile of hers. That his desire, his inappropriate ardor for her, only increased did not improve his mood. "He will be so pleased if you do."

"Very well." He held out his arm and waited. "Oh, come now," he said in a low voice. "We've had this conversation. Did we not come to a satisfactory conclusion, then?"

She looked at his arm and smiled, a private sort of smile. Then, she placed her hand on his arm. "Yes, my lord. We did."

"Excellent." He decided that Mr. Lucey was right. Miss Godard ought to be married. Just not to someone like Lieutenant Russell. A military marriage had its rewards, of course, but she needed not a man of uniform but one of intellect. A man who would appreciate the uniqueness of her mind. "Now, are you enjoying yourself tonight?"

"Mr. Lucey gives a ball at least once a fortnight." She looked up at him, as of course she must given their relative heights. The crowd was thick and they could not walk quickly. They were at ease with each other, or, more accurately, she was at ease with him. It seemed confession was indeed good for the soul. "Godard enjoys the spectacle, I think."

"There is at least good conversation to be had," he replied. His sentiment had the advantage of being honest. Dancing interested her as little as it did him, and he did enjoy conversation with men of intellect such as Sir Henry. And his niece, for that matter.

"Mrs. Lucey expects skulduggery tonight," she said.

"Indeed?"

"Don't look just yet, but there to your right is the Italian ambassador. In the dark gray coat. He's very charming. Mrs. Lucey and I suspect he means to attempt to lure his cook back tonight. I advised her to post footmen at the entrances to the kitchen. And to offer the cook another salary increase."

He laughed. Not only because it was polite of him but also because she had so unexpectedly amused him.

"Do you think you will dance tonight?" she asked.

Foye looked down at her, eyebrows raised. Now here was an interesting development. A door opened wide for any other man. "I am too old for dancing, Miss Godard."

She tipped her head sideways with her chin tilted toward him. There was amusement in her eyes. For a moment his breath really did stop in his chest. What the devil was she thinking? That he was foolish? Prematurely old? Or was she smiling because he hadn't followed with the question every other man would have asked after being led to the well, so to speak?

"I'm quite sure several of the young ladies will be swooning at the thought of dancing with a marquess. Miss Anna Justice among them, I am quite sure."

"Anna Justice." He stopped walking, and so did she. He felt perfectly foolish for thinking for even a moment she had been hinting at anything with respect to her. She stayed with her head cocked, assessing him. "The notion of young ladies swooning to dance with me is absurd."

She gave him another of those penetrating looks of hers, the kind that sent a jolt of heat through him. Her eyes were the reason, he decided. The way the outer edges tipped up just enough to make the shape exotic. Her eyes made him think of sleepy kisses at the conclusion of an exhausting night.

"I expect," she eventually said, "that you underestimate your appeal to the fair sex."

"I think not."

They stood looking at one another, and for Foye, the ballroom ceased to exist. Noise died away for him as he lost himself in her eyes. What was she thinking? He would give a great deal to know. He wanted to reach inside and touch the spark that flickered there and make it his.

"But why?" she asked. And quite genuinely. Without any recognition of him as a man and her as a woman. He had never, ever met a woman so completely immune to the possibilities inherent in their differing gender.

Ridiculous. What he was thinking was ridiculous beyond words. Beyond comprehension.

Foye looked over his shoulder as the world rushed back. He was just in time to see an overly enthusiastic dancer veer too far from his pattern. The gentleman lost his balance and, one arm flung wide, sent several spectators reeling toward the wall. Someone shouted, "Look out!"

The warning was inadequate and too late. Three soldiers tumbled backward into the spectators. One fell and caused two more guests to trip. A collision was unavoidable. Foye turned his back just in time. More shrieks and shouts went up. Bodies careened into him, hitting him hard and carrying him and Miss Godard toward the wall. He grabbed her around the waist with one arm and held her tight against him because if he hadn't, she would have been knocked to the floor or crushed against the wall.

He fought to keep his feet and managed to stop their tumble by jamming his other hand against the marble wall. Pain shot up his arm from his wrist to his shoulder. Miss Godard ended up trapped between his body and the wall.

"Are you hurt?" he asked. Oh damn, but his wrist ached.

A hum of sexual tension shot through him when he looked down. Her eyes were open wide and fixed on him. One of her hands was trapped between their torsos, the other gripped his upper arm. Initially, he continued holding her because the crowd around them remained unsteady. Not everyone was up yet. At least one of the parties involved in the collision was drunk, and Foye wanted to be sure there would not be a further disturbance before he released her.

She continued to look up at him. Into him, and he was aroused almost beyond endurance. Around them, people groaned or laughed or asked if someone was hurt. A woman who'd fallen to the floor was crying.

"No," she said. She was breathing hard, trying to catch her breath and failing, and my God, but he had a view of her breasts that put wicked thoughts in his head. "I can't breathe," she said.

Eight

༈

FOYE'S ARM REMAINED TIGHT AROUND HER WAIST because, well. Because. She pushed against his chest, but he didn't release her. Good God, but her mouth was lovely. He had an absolutely mad desire to kiss her.

She blinked, and Foye fell into her eyes all over again. Deep. She swallowed hard, and all he could do was watch her mouth.

He let her go. "Better?" he said.

She stepped away, not far since there was quite the crush of people about them. She shook out her skirt, trembling. She pressed a hand to her chest, and he was still lost in her eyes.

"Miss Godard?"

"I'm all right now," she said. But her voice quavered. Not that he would not have known otherwise that she was lying to him. She wasn't all right. Patently not. What woman wanted to be crushed by a monstrously large man like him? He looked around for someone he could trust to take her someplace where she could get a breath of fresh air. Someplace far from all these infernal people.

Lucey was nowhere in sight, and the people he saw were sailors and soldiers, none of whom he knew—hardly men to whom he could entrust her. Lieutenant Russell was a few feet away, assisting a fellow soldier to his feet. For the space of half a second he considered calling the officer over. And did not.

Instead, he put a hand to the back of her shoulder and ushered her through an arched doorway. The corridor, at the moment, was entirely unoccupied while being in full view of the ballroom. Another archway flanked by two columns led to a semicircular room with an upholstered bench all along the curved interior wall. A carved marble table stood in the center of the domed room. Lamps hung from hooks set in the wall, casting enough light to see.

"You're not well," he said. "You're trembling. Sit down, Miss Godard, before you fall down."

She went still. She looked at the room in which they stood. Quite alone. And he watched while suspicion filled her eyes.

"You're pale as a ghost and shaking." He took several steps away from her. "At least stay here until you've recovered. Shall I fetch Lieutenant Russell?"

"Lieutenant Russell?" Her eyes snapped to his, questioning.

"Sit down," he said. "Catch your breath."

She sat on the padded bench and opened the fan hanging off her wrist. She waved it under her chin and took several deep breaths in a row. "I was certain we were going to be crushed."

"You mean you feared I would crush you," he said wryly.

She stopped fanning herself. "No. I don't mean that at all. I said quite plainly that I feared *we* would be crushed."

"At fourteen," he said in a low voice, "I was six feet tall. Taller than my father and brother. By seventeen I'd grown another three inches taller than that." He gave a bitter smile that rose up from a dark place inside him he hadn't realized was so easily accessed. "As tall as the Black Prince and yet I added another three before I was twenty-one. You never saw a more awkward boy than I. Believe me, I am more than aware of my size and its effect on people."

"I never thought you were going to turn me into a crepe," she said. "In fact, I knew you would not." She stared at his hand. "You hurt yourself so that I would not be. Don't bother denying it. I saw your face when it happened."

Foye gazed back at her and felt the ground beneath him shift in precisely the wrong direction. Good Lord, what foolishness. He wanted to amuse her, to make her smile and think him a clever man. He'd wanted the same for Rosaline, with disaster the result. "Most women find me beastly."

She gave him a sharp glance, eyebrows drawn together, but he didn't give her a chance to interrupt.

"I have few illusions about myself, Miss Godard. I am uncommonly tall and uncommonly large. God forbid I should ever get fat. They could not build a bed to hold me in that case or find a horse capable of carrying me." He kept his hands behind him. "Combine that with my rough-hewn face, and there you have it. I am ever destined, I fear, to play the beast to feminine beauty." Some of his anger bled though despite his intentions. There was nothing worse than an attempt at self-deprecation gone flat.

After a silence, she said, "I don't find you beastly, my lord." Her hands fell to her lap, her fan still open. "You are a striking man, as I am sure you are well aware."

The noise of the gathering faded away for him. There was nothing now but her staring at him as if she thought he'd lost his mind. He took a step toward her and ended up wondering how that had happened.

She glanced down and refolded her fan. "I don't say that to flatter you," she said. "Not at all. Why would I?"

"Indeed," he said. Why had Rosaline said she loved him up to the very day she eloped with Crosshaven? "Why would you?"

Well. He seemed to have offended her.

"I will not marry, my lord. That was the case before Crosshaven, by the way, and remains the case now. My place is with Godard." She stood up, lifting a hand to prevent him speaking. "Spare me, my lord. Do not deny you thought I had set my cap for you."

He waited a bit before he answered. He ought to let that go, but he didn't. "Haven't you?" he drawled.

She inhaled deeply. "Oh, you are an infuriating man. I understand you. If I say no, you will say it's because you are a monstrous man and no pretty woman could want a beast like you." She walked to him. "If I say yes, you will say that a woman looking to marry so far above her will tell any lie at all."

He shrugged. "Think what you like. But be warned. I don't intend to marry, either."

"Then we are well matched, wouldn't you say?"

"Two peas in a pod," he said.

She astonished him by laughing. "Oh, Lord Foye, when we have so much in common, can't we be friends?"

"I have little interest in being friends, Miss Godard." They were so close he could smell the attar of roses in her hair. His remark flew right over her head and made him feel a heel. But, really, need she be quite so innocent?

She wasn't looking at him just then, which gave him a view of her profile that showed the line of her neck and shoulders. He was beastly after all, because all he could think was that he would like very much to see her naked. He had been a long time without a lover, and he was beguiled by everything about her. He shouldn't be having such thoughts. Not about her. But he was. The inappropriate, ungentlemanly thought remained when she looked at him again.

The stillness deepened and threatened, absurdly, madly, to become too intimate.

"Miss Godard," he said, trying to put some formality in the utterance of her name. Oh hell. She understood now at least something of what was in his head. She seemed so impossibly young and innocent that his heart broke. He forced himself to stay where he was. He wanted to take her into his arms and slay whatever dragons needed slaying.

"My lord," she said. Her eyes were wide. Cautious. Curious?

He breached the space between them, tracing a fingertip beneath her mouth. "You know nothing of men and their desires."

"Untrue."

Where was all the air in the room? Her mouth parted, and he traced her lower lip a second time. "You don't know mine, then. Shall I tell you?" She nodded. "Very well, then. You beguile me, Miss Godard. But you're too young for me. Too pretty. Too sweet. Too innocent for a man like me."

She cocked her head, studying him. "Are you going to kiss me?"

"No." Somehow the space between them disappeared, and he was very much afraid that it was his fault, that it was his feet that had closed the gap.

Her eyebrows drew together. "Do you want to?"

"My God, you try me to my soul." For his life he could not step away from her. His body was tense with desire, he was half-erect, and he kept touching her, sweeping his finger beneath her so delectable mouth. And she continued gazing up at him. "If I do," he said gruffly, "you understand nothing can come of it."

"Of course."

"I won't," he said. She was innocent and inexperienced, and he shouldn't. He really shouldn't. "It's madness to kiss you."

She bit her lower lip, and his noble intentions flew off to some other hemisphere of the world. "I understand that, too."

Foye decided he didn't mind if he went to hell. He bent his head and she stretched to meet him. Just a brush of his lips over hers, he told himself. Just the sort of kiss any young lady might experience without threatening her virtue. Or his.

Foye's body clenched when Sabine's mouth touched his. He didn't react at first because he wasn't sure that what was happening between them was real. But it was. He wasn't imagining this. This was her kissing him, not him losing control. Her choice. Her lips on his.

Had he ever wanted anything as much as he did this? He didn't care that she was too young for him or that he didn't want an entanglement. Or that there were a hundred reasons why he shouldn't be letting this happen, the very least of which was that this was hardly the time and place for kissing any woman.

Except her mouth was so soft, and she was trembling and a little hesitant—that was sweet, so very sweet. He knew what it had cost her to do this because right before she'd closed her eyes, he'd seen she expected him to stop her, and the thought of hurting her like that was a dagger through his heart. He wanted her about as badly as he'd wanted any woman in his life. More.

Her mouth was every bit as soft as he'd thought, softer even. His arms snaked around her waist, pulling her closer to him. She was a slight woman, but indisputably a woman. She was awkward at first.

Miss Sabine Godard didn't know the first thing about kissing. He reached for her arms and put them on his shoulders and just kept kissing her. And then she was not awkward. They were not awkward. She figured out what to do with her hands and when and how to tilt her head, and he bent just enough and she went up on her toes just enough. Matters between them became a good deal more dangerous.

He ought to have known she'd be a quick study. He opened his mouth over hers even as he told himself, *Enough*. It wasn't, though. He pulled her hard against him, and she brought his head down to hers. Her fingers brushed his hair, and just bloody, bloody hell, he was in a world of trouble.

While he was wrestling with all the reasons he shouldn't

be kissing Sabine Godard, his body continued to mutiny. He held the back of her head with one hand and set the other between her shoulder blades. She was still tentative, as if she had no idea that he'd capitulated to her. He pulled her close. Her indrawn breath rocketed through him, from the sound of that soft gasp to the change in the pressure of her body against his.

God help him, he wanted more than she could give him. More than he could decently ask of her or any woman of her age and standing in society. Just when he thought he could extract himself from this headlong plunge to disaster, she was kissing him the way he wanted her to, lips parted, tongue playing, touching, meeting his. This time the gasp came from him. Lost. He was lost.

What a bastard he was to let this happen.

He didn't give a damn.

He took control of the kiss, and still holding her head, he swept his tongue into her so soft and pliant mouth, and she, quick study that she was, returned his boldness. Kissing was harmless enough, he told himself. This didn't have to go beyond kissing.

The problem, it seemed, was that kissing Miss Godard was not harmless.

Foye lifted his mouth from hers and watched her eyes slowly open. He had his arms around her, one hand cupping the back of her head, the other, well, his other hand seemed to have wandered perilously near her backside while his erection was trapped between them.

"You kiss wonderfully well," she said in a low, velvet voice. Christ, she sounded as drugged with pleasure as her eyes suggested. He suspected he didn't look or sound much different. "It's lovely, kissing you, Lord Foye. It really is."

"Confess, Miss Godard. You've never done that before."

"You mean kiss a man? No. I confess I haven't."

"Mm," he said. "You were very good at it."

She smiled. "Why, thank you, my lord."

He forced himself to bring both hands up to her face

while he held her head, using his thumbs to trace a line
beneath her eyes. What more might she allow him? Would
she, would she, would she?

"Perhaps you ought to kiss me again," he said. "To be
sure you've got the hang of it."

Sabine laughed, and he had his usual reaction to that.
"Yes," she said. His gut clenched at the sight of her smile.
"I think I should."

She slid her arms around his shoulders, and while he
was thinking about how wonderful that felt, she buried
her fingers in his hair and pulled his head to hers, and hell.
Just hell. The difference between this kiss and their first
was the difference between hot and searing. He recipro-
cated wholeheartedly, willingly, greedily. Where she led,
he followed.

Somehow, somehow, she was tight against his body, and
he couldn't get enough. Not enough. She arched against
him. He wanted a good deal more than kissing from her,
and he was fast heading toward the point where his sexual
urges would overrun his good sense and decency.

By the time they parted he was panting, and so was
she. And she looked liked a woman thoroughly kissed. He
stared at the carved wooden ceiling while he fought for
control.

She touched his face, following the line of his cheek.
"I'm sorry if I've upset you."

Foye stared at her. "Upset? Upset that I've been indiscreet and ungentlemanly?"

"You haven't been." She drew in a long trembling breath
while he scrubbed his hands through his hair. "Well, perhaps a bit indiscreet."

"Indiscreet. It was a good deal more than that, Miss
Godard."

After a bit, she said, "I suppose we should find my
uncle."

He agreed and would have told her so, but he looked at
her mouth and instead said, "In a moment."

"Very well." They locked gazes, and the heat started up

again to the point where he wondered which was worse, staying in here or letting her leave looking the way she did, with her so very kissed mouth.

He sighed. "Shall we find your uncle?"

She nodded. At the exit to the ballroom, he sent Sabine on ahead and lingered for several minutes in the dim corridor, listening to a gavotte. How in God's name had he allowed that encounter to spin so horribly out of control? And part of him wondered how soon he could do it again. He wouldn't. They couldn't.

When he returned to the ballroom, there she was, not far away, with several officers gathered around her, Lieutenant Russell among them. She looked too solemn for a pretty woman at a ball, surrounded by admirers whom she did not admire.

In a way, she was as isolated as he was.

She looked relieved when he appeared. "Lord Foye," she called out. "There you are."

He joined her. "Miss Godard," he said. He nodded to the lieutenant and got a sullen, suspicious nod in return.

"Godard still wishes to see you, my lord." She smiled at the officers. "Good evening, gentlemen."

"But Miss Godard," the lieutenant called out.

She tilted her head. "Yes?"

The lieutenant's heated gaze flicked to Foye for a moment before returning to Miss Godard. "You've not promised me a dance."

"I do not dance," she said with a curt nod. "Good evening."

Well. Thank God for that, Foye thought.

They reached her uncle at last. "Godard," she said. "I have brought you Lord Foye."

"Come sit by me and say something intelligent," Sir Henry said to him. The music stopped, but not because a set of dances had come to an end. The violin halted mid-crescendo. Conversation ceased in a wave from the front of the room to the back. "What is it?" Sir Henry asked. He grabbed his cane and struggled to his feet. Sir Henry's servant Asif came around from behind the chair to stand at Godard's side. The fellow was almost as tall as Foye. "Somebody tell me what the devil is going on."

There was an advantage to Foye's height, namely, that he could see over everyone's head. A Turkish gentleman, very splendidly dressed, had walked into the room, accompanied by at least a dozen servants. The Turk wore a traditional robe but a singularly gorgeous one: silk embroidered with gold thread and decorated with pearls and gems. His skin was swarthy, his nose regally hooked, his mustache and beard full and luxurious. "I believe," Foye said to Sir Henry, "that Nazim Pasha is paying a call."

Miss Godard said something to the servant that Foye did not understand. The reply was brief and, it appeared, in the affirmative.

"What are you and that devil Asif talking about?" Sir Henry asked.

"Lord Foye is correct," she said, turning to her uncle. "It is Nazim Pasha."

Foye watched Anthony Lucey cross the now cleared ballroom floor to greet the pasha. The pasha wore a diamond-encrusted sword at his side and a pair of enameled, gem-encrusted pistols tucked into the sash around his waist. His retinue was armed with a less decorative and far more utilitarian assortment of pistols and muskets. The crowd melted away around him and before long, even the two Godards had a view of Nazim Pasha and his men, with Anthony Lucey walking at his side. Foye glanced at Miss Godard. "Is this usual?" he asked in a low voice. "For a pasha to appear among so many infidels?"

She shook her head. "No. But he and Godard got on quite well when they met before, and Mr. Lucey has had several years' acquaintance with him. Perhaps he's curious about us."

Nazim Pasha came to a stop in front of Sir Henry, bowed, and greeted him in perfect French. Sir Henry returned the greeting in kind.

In the exchange that followed, one thing became

perfectly clear to Foye: Nazim Pasha was quite taken with Miss Godard.

He had been jealous of Lieutenant Russell. The soldier was young and handsome and sickeningly in love but, ultimately, no real threat. Miss Godard had no interest in him. The pasha was another matter altogether. He was no puppy, for one thing. Here was a man for whom, by reputation at least, robbery, fraud, murder, and even rape were merely the means by which he obtained whatever it was he desired. Without compunction or remorse.

If Nazim Pasha acted on his attraction to Miss Godard, Foye was quite certain she would vanish, never to be seen again.

He was surprised to discover he had a very personal intention to see that did not happen.

Nine

❧

About four o'clock in the morning. Lord Foye's accommodations in Büyükdere. Specifically, Foye's bedchamber. Foye was wide awake.

His bedroom was pitch dark and silent. Yet he could not sleep. Foye lay in bed twitchy with the urge to physically exhaust himself. Ever since he'd kissed Sabine Godard, he'd been on edge and uneasy in himself. He'd had no business allowing that to happen. None. But it had, and he wasn't precisely sorry.

He knew he'd never get back to sleep. He called for his servant Barton, who acted as his valet, butler, footman, and general factotum, and after dressing ate a quick breakfast and gulped down coffee.

He headed for the center of Büyükdere. In addition to his unsettled state as regarded Miss Godard, his sleep had been disturbed these past nights by dreams of her that were by turn too explicit for his comfort or else involved him saving her from some deadly peril, after which she would melt in his arms and confess her undying love and gratitude. Spiritually and physically.

Last night, he'd had both sorts of dreams. There was as well the fact that he was not the only man to have noticed Nazim Pasha's attentions to her and interpreted them as sexual in nature. When the subject had been broached—he didn't even recall who had first brought it up—the consensus had been one of concern for her safety. Miss Godard was universally liked. Nevertheless, the pasha's admiration had been duly noted. There had been talk. Nothing to her detriment so far. She was too far from being a flirt for anyone to entertain the notion of her having, somehow, encouraged the pasha's interest.

Foye continued walking, his hands clenched behind his back and his head down as he increased his stride. A long, hard walk, he hoped, would clear his mind. His vague intention was to see the sun rise and then, whenever it happened that he discharged the nervous energy that filled him, to return home and plan the remainder of his day. He wondered if he ought to leave Constantinople and avoid entirely his increasing infatuation with Sabine Godard. It would not do to entangle himself and possibly embroil her in scandal.

When he arrived in the village square with the sky still more dark than light, he knew if he returned home, he'd only need to walk out again. He headed for the strand. Not only would a walk along the Bosporus be pleasant, it would also allow him to extend his exercise in whatever direction he so decided: south in the general direction of Constantinople or in the opposite direction toward the Black Sea.

But for Lieutenant Russell's silent suspicion, the incident between him and Miss Godard at Lucey's ball had gone unnoticed. Aside from some hilarity over the toppling soldiers, and even one or two amusing reenactions, no one so much as mentioned that Foye and Miss Godard had been caught up in the mayhem.

But he could not forget the pure terror in her eyes when he'd caught her and held her to prevent her falling. She might have been injured, for God's sake, if he'd done nothing. Ten steps slower or faster and they'd have avoided the entire debacle. He'd never have taken her anywhere alone nor lost his head. Nor discovered that Sabine Godard kissed like an angel. Nor would he have seen her expression when she claimed to find his face arresting. As if she found that a fine thing for his face to be. And he believed her.

It was also the case, he'd learned, that more than a few residents of Büyükdere had thought Sir Henry had boasted of his friendship with the pasha. The man's arrival at the gathering, no more the personal conversational exchange between the two, put that lie to rest. There was yet more talk about Sir Henry when, the day after the ball, Nazim Pasha had called on them privately and made it known he had renewed his invitation for them to visit him in Kilis. He had also presented both of them with outrageously lavish gifts.

To Sir Henry, the pasha had given a kaftan embroidered with gold and silver thread, seed pearls, and diamonds, too. To Miss Godard he had given ivory hair combs topped with gold and inlaid with matching rubies, three of them the size of Foye's fingernail, which detail he knew because Sir Henry had proudly displayed both their gifts to anyone who called. Yes, he had called. At one of the rare times when he knew she would not be at home. His express purpose had been to tell Sir Henry of Crosshaven's infamy, to make him understand that she was innocent in the matter. It was the least he could do for her, and he had done so. That obligation was now discharged in full. He learned a great deal more, too, about the Godards and the pasha.

Her gift was not just the hair combs, extravagant all by themselves, but also a matching bracelet and brooch. From anyone else, such a gift was worse than inappropriate. From the pasha? Most excused the extravagance. The pasha was rich. He'd made other such gifts to various members of the various diplomats in Büyükdere and Pera. The rubies were of magnificent quality. Too personal, Foye felt. He'd taken one look at those gemstones, so exquisitely set, and known them for the sort of gift a man makes of a woman with whom he hoped to be intimate.

He reached the strand and set out in a southerly direction,

toward Constantinople, though he did not think he would walk quite as far as that since he would have to walk the twelve miles back, too. Büyükdere Castle was a possible destination. Some six miles distant, it was built at the edge of the Bosporus with a sister fortress on the other side of the waterway. The two castles had been constructed for the sole purpose of choking off access to the Black Sea. There began and ended everything he knew about the castle.

He considered returning home, but he was too full of nervous energy, with too much on his mind. He would walk to the castle, he decided. Why not? No one expected him anywhere, and his valet, Barton, was used to his long and solitary excursions. He had a few paras in his pocket, a small denomination coin of the local currency; enough for a decent luncheon. He set out with the sun just barely over the horizon.

The trek took him less than two hours, heading south in the direction of Constantinople and staying more or less along the Bosporus. Another advantage to his size. With his longer stride, he covered more distance than a man of average height. This morning his body, as it did in general, relished being pushed. The walk itself was not difficult at all, but he moved as quickly as he could to put himself past a comfortable walk. He succeeded in putting Miss Godard out of his mind precisely twice.

The entrance to the castle was on the water's edge. The structure was built on a hill overlooking the Bosporus and was in geometry a misshapen rectangle with three massive crenellated towers. In construction, the castle was very much like any number of English castles. The decorative stamp of the Byzantines clung to parts of the interior in the portions of carved marble edifice that must have at one time entirely covered the stones. A solitary column stood near a wall covered with the remnants of a typically Byzantine pattern carved in the marble facing.

There still remained some cannons, though many were rusted and in poor repair. No one would be firing across the Bosporus from here. He spent some time examining them and peering across the strait to what remained of the sister castle. A canny location, at once defensive and yet capable of preventing access to the sea or Constantinople. Since the barbican wall was in good repair, he decided to walk along the perimeter and enjoy the view of the water. He headed first toward the tower that overlooked the water.

Seabirds circled overhead, calling out for someone to provide them a ration of fish. Alas, he had none to give them. A native ship sailed slowly toward Constantinople. As he walked the ledge, he caught a glimpse of someone sitting near the first tower that was his destination. Some Turk, perhaps, mulling over his country's history and contemplating what had been a glorious past. Foye was not one of those men who thought the Porte could protect its territorial reach much longer. Büyükdere Castle would not be in such a state of disrepair otherwise.

He continued walking, and before long it was plain that his Turkish contemplator was, in fact, a woman. And since no Turkish woman would be permitted here by herself, she must be European. Another few steps and he recognized the golden hair visible from beneath her hat.

Sabine Godard.

Ten

🕊

About half past six in the morning. The site of a very
great coincidence. Or perhaps just fate.

"MISS GODARD?"

Sabine started when she heard her name. She turned
away from her sketch, shading her eyes to see who it was.

Lord Foye was instantly recognizable. She didn't know
anyone else that tall. Her pulse sped up as he continued
toward her. Sabine kept her place at one of the crenellated
portions of the castle wall. Until Lord Foye had called out,
she'd been bent over a sketch pad set atop the stone, pencil in
hand. As she straightened, the toe of her shoe hit the leather
case at her feet. It was open to show more paper and her col-
lection of pencils, charcoals, chalks, and gum rubbers.

Lord Foye stopped about a yard distant from her and
snatched off his hat. He shook his head to resettle his curls.
Her heart sped up even though she knew they would not
kiss again. He'd told her nothing would come of it, and so
far he'd been true to his word. He smiled. "It is you, Miss
Godard. I wasn't certain at first."

She knew she ought to reply, *Yes, my lord. It is I.* Or perhaps, *Good morning, my lord.* But she didn't because this was the third time her awareness of him had surged out of proportion to what was proper. The truth was she found him attractive, from the jumbled line of his cheeks to the hook of his nose. Even though nothing could ever come of her feelings for him, as he had so appropriately warned her.

She put a hand on her paper to keep the breeze from blowing away her work while she was distracted. This morning Lord Foye wore a burgundy waistcoat striped with a gray satin that matched his dove breeches. His charcoal coat fit his narrow waist and fell straight over a flat belly. Sabine wasn't used to noticing a man with such detail, or rather, she wasn't used to having the details affect her this way. Still, they could be friends. That would be enough.

Foye bowed to her and then said, "Good morning."

She had to lift her chin in order to look into his face, and as she did, she remembered in torturous detail the sensation of his arms around her, holding her. His mouth on her, so soft and gentle. Her first and only kiss. The moment their eyes met, her stomach took flight, and she had to press her hand down hard on her sketchbook to maintain a sense that she remained connected to the ground. One heard and read of such feelings, of women who claimed to be transported at the sight of one certain man, but she'd thought the reaction was exaggeration, a mere fancy of an overactive imagination, and that even if it were true, such a thing would never happen to her. And here she stood, staring at Lord Foye, wondering if her legs would hold her.

For her life she could not decide if he seemed glad to have come across her or if he was annoyed. She tucked her pencil behind her ear and summoned her self-control. Nothing would come of this, they were both determined, and she was dashed if she made a fool of herself.

"Good morning, my lord," she said. This meeting was no different than any other she might have with a gentleman of her acquaintance. She made an awkward curtsey in his direction since she was keeping her hand on her sketch. After all, he was Lord Foye. The Marquess of Foye. A man so far above her in society, she shouldn't be feeling anything about him at all. She put away her memory of their kiss in a faraway place to be brought out and remembered at some other time. "What brings you here so early in the day?"

He kept the distance between them, and Sabine was certain that any moment he would nod and take his leave. "Mr. Lucey recommended that I tour Büyükdere Castle. So here I am. Sightseeing." He pointed to the water with a grin she felt from head to toe. "Calculating what it would take to fire a cannon across the water into Asiatic Turkey."

They were alone here. Completely alone, and she wasn't afraid or worried he might make an improper advance. Her nerves were for an entirely different reason. *"Rumeli Hisari,"* she said.

He frowned. "I beg your pardon?"

"The natives call this *Rumeli Hisari*, the Roman Fortress." She spoke too quickly. But, my God, she was actually trembling. Such a foolish woman she was. Her voice didn't sound like her own. She'd never been nervous around any of the other gentlemen she'd met in her life. "I don't know why they call it that." She scraped a strand of hair away from her face. She was babbling, but couldn't seem to stop. And Foye was too polite to interrupt her. "It was built by Fatih Mehmet the Conqueror, beginning in 1451. Not very Roman I should say. By then even Caesar Augustus was long buried. Have you seen the cannons?" She pointed to the far side of the castle to a tower away from the water. "Over there is the gunpowder tower."

He didn't look in the direction she pointed. He just cleared his throat and pressed the rim of his hat between his long fingers. "You are a veritable font of information, Miss Godard. As ever."

She gazed at him, speechless with the horror of realizing she wasn't just feeling a fool but was indeed making a fool of herself. Another strand of hair came free of her

confining hat and blew across her cheek. She ignored it.
"I can't help it, you know."

"Can't help what?"

"I was raised by Godard." She shrugged and kept her
ground when he came nearer. As near as any two people
might stand when they are acquainted. He meant nothing by this, and yet she stared at his mouth and wondered
what it would be like if he were to kiss her again. "Facts
stay with me. I did not know when I was growing up that
it was unusual for a girl to be educated as I was. But so
I was, and now I am unable to forget a fact I have heard."
Silly, ridiculous words tripped from her mouth. "I was
eighteen before I learned we women are expected to hide
what knowledge we have." She raised her hand and waved
it just above her head. "All these facts I have here. They
are trapped now. Languages and chronologies of history,
calculus, and geometry. Sometimes I forget I ought to dis-
semble, and something unfortunate spills out." She smiled
at him. "Have you not noticed that about me?"

He blinked. "Calculus?"

Well, then. She'd done enough damage already that
more could hardly make a difference. Her intellectual odd-
ities were hardly a secret from him. "Godard and I made a
thorough study of Newton's *Principia*."

"And?"

He was never going to kiss her again. They were safe.
She was safe. The knowledge calmed her. While her feelings were real enough, her hopes were not, and in that
she could take a measure of relief. Lord Foye was far too
polite to let on he thought her silly. He would preserve her
dignity.

"We muddled along, Godard and I," she said. Her nerves
settled, and that made it easier to marshal her thoughts.
"I am afraid I disappointed him. He had hopes for me as
I excelled at arithmetic."

"Did you?"

She nodded. "It happens I am not very good at
mathematics."

Foye smiled, and her heart gave a twist. Madness! This was madness to find him so attractive. "Your uncle has given you a better education than most boys of your station in life."

"Oh, yes, my lord."

He gave her a look. "You may call me Foye, if you like." He gestured. "I was going to walk the perimeter of the castle." For a moment, he stared down at his hat. "Would you care to put your mountain of facts to use and be my guide?"

She set a hand to the back of her head and looked into his face as if there she would see the motive for the request. She saw nothing there but his blue, blue eyes, the uneven features of his face, and the curls around his forehead. At last, at a loss to think why he'd asked, other than that he really did want the benefit of her knowledge, she said, "If you like."

"I would," he said.

She bent to her art case and put away her gum rubber, keeping one hand on her sketch pad against the breeze coming off the water. Her pencil must have rolled off the surface because she didn't see it on her sketch pad.

"Allow me," Foye said. She didn't know he'd come close until he placed his much larger hand on her sketch. She knew him well enough now that his being so near didn't bother her in the least, aside from the butterflies in her stomach, that is.

"Thank you," she said from her half-crouch over her case. The location of her pencil continued to elude her.

"Is something amiss?" he asked.

"Yes," she said, without looking up. "I've lost my pencil."

"Miss Godard."

She looked up in time to see him smiling as he reached for her. Her breath caught in her throat. She forced herself not to react, but her expression must have given her away, because his smile vanished.

"No," he said. "Not that."

She shook her head, meaning to deny that she'd been thinking he intended to embrace her. No words came. And perhaps that was for the best.

Foye plucked her pencil from the side of her ear. "Your pencil," he said softly. He held it out to her, and she took it from him. Her bare fingers brushed his.

"Thank you," she said. She dropped the pencil in the case and closed it. Without rising from her crouch, she stretched out a hand for her sketch pad. Foye handed it to her without remark. "Thank you, again."

"You are a talented artist."

She was engaged with closing up her case and didn't look at him. "That's kind of you to say so, my lord. I'm told my father had the same knack."

"How old were you when he died?"

"Both my parents died when I was two."

He touched her shoulder. He meant nothing by it, she told herself. "I'm sorry."

"I don't remember them. But I miss them all the same. Isn't that queer?"

"Not at all, Miss Godard." He pointed to her art case. "Are you self-taught? Or did your uncle see that you were instructed in art as well?"

"Art was never a subject Godard set me to. He does not encourage that particular talent of mine. I suppose because he never got along with my father. At any rate, I soon discovered that if I am to practice I must do so in secret." She rose, tucking her case under one arm, all very efficient. She had to tilt her chin up to look at him, and when she had, she felt as if all the air between them had disappeared.

"I cannot fathom why," Foye said. One side of his mouth quirked, and Sabine could not stop a smile in return. "A proper young lady is not accomplished unless she can sketch and paint a watercolor."

Sabine laughed. "I don't think Godard ever thought about that."

"No," he said slowly. "I doubt that he did." He rubbed the side of his face. "I've often wondered since we met whether you were born like Athena, fully grown from the head of Zeus. Fully educated."

"Perhaps I was." She tipped her head to one side, and he stayed quite still. Sabine studied him.

"I shudder to think what thoughts are running through your head just now, Miss Godard."

"You have such an interesting face. I would love to sketch you one day." Foye's eyebrows rose. "Ah," she said. "That was out of order. Forgive me." She adjusted her cap with one hand. "Shall we walk?"

He continued to look at her. "That would be delightful."

The skin along her arms prickled as she switched her art case to her other hand so that Foye could take her arm. They set out. For the most part the wall was in good shape, and they walked comfortably side by side.

"How is it you were able to leave your uncle behind in Büyükdere?" he asked after a few moments of silence.

"Asif is taking him to the baths today. Godard finds the heat soothes his joints provided they are gentle with him." She glanced at him, and her stomach dipped again. He did not think of her that way. He had once, for five minutes, but that was in the past. Irrevocably in the past. "Since ladies are not permitted when the gentlemen bathe, I find myself with a free morning when he goes to the *hamam*."

"How fortunate for you."

"Yes." She was dreadfully aware of him walking at her side, of the warmth of his body, the scent of sandalwood. She was even more aware that she liked the sound of his voice. He had a marvelous voice.

"You should not have walked out alone."

She didn't answer right away, and when she did, her reply was more evasion than anything else. The fact was, she had not expected to meet anyone. "This is not England, my lord."

Foye laughed. The soft sound rolled over her. "Indeed it is not."

"Do you miss England?" she asked.

"Sometimes." He worked very hard not to crowd her on the wall, which she did appreciate, but here and there the stone wall was crumbling away and they were forced closer together. She did not entirely mind. "You?"

"I miss Oxford and Godard's friends and the students who used to call. But there's a great deal I do not miss." She shrugged. "As you might imagine, I was very glad to leave England."

"I suppose you were, Miss Godard."

"It was an unpleasant time." She shrugged again. They had reached a part of the barbican wall that trended upward into the hill on which the castle was built. The going was more difficult, and in places vegetation and time had done their worst. Foye put a hand to the back of her arm when she stumbled, only for a step, at a rocky section. Her heart jumped at the unexpected contact. She kept walking, willing herself to calm down even as her pulse raced. It was nothing. Lord Foye had done nothing but make sure she didn't fall. He meant nothing, one way or the other, by the contact.

But she could not stop herself from thinking that they were alone and wondering if she would want to cling to him again, if he decided to kiss her after all. He wouldn't, though. Such thoughts were nothing more than silly fancy.

When they came to a section where the wall had almost entirely crumbled away, they stood at the edge of the break for an awkward moment until he said, "Will you allow me to assist you across?"

Sabine nodded. "Yes, of course, my lord."

"Foye."

"Foye," she said.

"Ready?" She nodded and he picked her up, one arm behind her knees, the other around her middle back. His arms were rock hard. "Are you all right?" he asked.

She nodded even though she wasn't sure she was. Being held so tightly made her breath come hard. Foye's arms tightened around her, and he stepped across the gap in the wall.

"You see?" he said when they were over. His voice was low and soft in her ear. "There is an advantage to keeping company with a beast of a man. You may be easily lifted over obstacles that would otherwise stop you from your goal. We are across and the victors in the battle."

He did not release her, not until he'd taken a third step. He ought to have put her down already. Why hadn't he? She looked at his face, and their eyes met with a shock that ran from her chest to her low, low belly. She wanted this, she'd thought of this—his arms around her, this closeness. With him. Perversely, now that the moment she'd been longing for was here, she was terrified of what might happen.

He set her down close to him. Too close, and yet, Sabine thought, not close enough. She didn't ease away from him, though she could have. Though he expected her to. He left his hand on the side of her hip. She suppressed the urge to whisk away the curls dangling over his forehead.

"Safe and sound," he said.

She couldn't help herself; she reached up and swept away the wayward curls. She stopped, on her tiptoes, with her fingers on his forehead. "Your hair is so very soft, Foye." She brushed away a few more curls. "It doesn't look it, but it is."

He reached up and took her hand in his. She'd never put on her gloves, so her fingers were bare. Slowly, he brought her fingers to his mouth and kissed the back of her hand. His lips touched her bare skin. "Sabine," he whispered, "what am I to do with you?"

"What is it you want to do?"

He did not step away, and, God help her, she trembled with anticipation. He tipped his head to one side. "To make up my mind about you." The skin around his eyes crinkled when he smiled. "Am I too beastly for you, Sabine? Or is that something you can overlook?"

She was aware that the future of her relationship with him, whatever that was to be, hung in the balance now. Her whole life was about to change, and this time the choice was hers. Her chest felt tight. She could hardly breathe. "You and I will continue to disagree on that, I think."

Foye slid his hand from her hip upward to her ribs, coming to a rest just beneath her breast. She swallowed once. His eyes, such a lovely blue, stayed on her face. He grimaced. "I have no angel's face for you to adore."

"Yes, you have." A breeze caught at her hair again, but she ignored it.

His fingers tightened on her. "Then, again, I must ask, what am I to do with you?"

"Kiss me again?"

"A deplorable idea." But he brought her close and kissed her anyway. Briefly, but his mouth opened over hers, his lips caught at hers, and she could not help feeling this was nothing like the kiss they'd shared before. This was gentler, sweeter. He drew back. "What else?"

She tried to take a deep breath and couldn't. The air caught in her lungs. She licked her lips. There were no words, just a nameless emotion building up in her and leaving her without any words to express what she felt. "What are you asking, Foye?"

He drew in a long breath and put a hand on her shoulder. "Damned if I know." They both stood very still. Waiting. He placed his hands on either side of her face and kissed her again. Longer this time. Far more assertively. Enough that she swayed toward him and threw one arm around his neck. Her art case banged against his leg, and after a bit, he set her back and took the case from her. He set it down. "Sabine, please, if I might be so bold with you as to call you that. Allow me to speak my mind. Please."

She nodded. Foye took a step closer until there were only inches between them. His finger brushed the top of her neck and slowly down until it rested on her collarbone. "Very well, then."

His smile melted her. "Perhaps," he said, "I don't wish to speak."

"Then what are we to do?"

"This." He used his finger to brush away the strand of hair that had escaped her hairpins and traced a line from behind her ear to the nape of her neck. He stood close enough to her that her cloak and skirts were trapped against his legs. He bent his head over her so that his breath warmed her skin. He pressed his mouth to the side of her throat, just beneath her ear. "Tell me what you want from me," he whispered.

She wanted this. She wanted him to kiss her again and again. "Foye. I want you, Foye."

"Even though I'm an old man compared to you?"

"Stop that."

"You have me, then, Sabine." Slowly, he drew back. She was crying, tears slipping silently, wetly, down her cheeks. "Sabine." He peered into her face, searching for something there. "My God, what are these tears?"

"I can't leave Godard," she said. Her heart broke for want of him. She whispered, as her heart shattered, "I won't."

"Hush," he said. His hands tightened on her. "I've not asked that of you."

"Then what?" she said, still crying. "Nothing? All this between us and you want nothing at all?"

He bent down and kissed her again, and Sabine clung to him in case this was the last time he ever wanted to hold her again. He wasn't so gentle this time when he kissed her. Heat pooled in her belly and between her legs and still he kissed her. When he stopped, she held him tight and he said, "I'll wait for you, Sabine. Don't you know that? For as long as I need to."

Eleven

₰

Büyükdere,
MAY 26, 1811

Three fifteen in the afternoon. A private courtyard at
the home of Mr. and Mrs. Charles Faber. A fountain in
the middle of the courtyard cooled the afternoon heat.
There was a pond with tiny golden fish and finches in the
almond trees. Inside the house, any number of people
were having tea and listening to Miss Anna Justice play
the pianoforte.

SABINE SAT ON A STONE BENCH KNOWING FULL WELL
she was nothing but the worst kind of coward. She ought
to be inside helping Mrs. Lucey in her scheme to bring
together Lord Foye and Miss Justice, only she couldn't face
either of them. She felt she was deceiving Mrs. Lucey. She
was. Foye wanted nothing to do with Miss Justice, but he
was in there now pretending.

Dozen of finches flitted about in the almond trees
planted in the courtyard. She listened to them calling to
each other and to the fountain burbling, but neither sound
blocked out the noise from within the house. Miss Justice
was still playing the pianoforte. She was very good. Not
just competent. Ah. And now she was singing.

A high stone wall enclosed the courtyard to which she'd
escaped—she could likely cross the entire length in twenty
steps. Probably fewer. Behind her was the corridor that led

here from the house. There was a bend in the passageway so that if she were to look, she would not see the house. She could easily imagine she was entirely alone here with no need to rejoin the others and pretend all was well with her when it wasn't.

She did not wish to feel as if her heart was no longer her own, yet that was her predicament. She was not, however, required to give in to those feelings. She didn't dare. Strength of character belonged to her, and with that asset, she could move through her life outwardly unchanged until Lord Foye returned to England or she and Godard left Büyükdere. Perhaps in ten or twenty years she and Foye would be together. Or he would have forgotten.

She crossed her forearms atop her thighs and stared into the pool, watching for a flash of piscine fin in the water. If she'd known she would find fish here, she would have brought bread crumbs. The sense that time was passing too quickly set her nerves on end. She would have to return soon. Godard would be asking after her. She'd have to go back inside and watch Foye with Miss Justice.

"Sabine?"

She stood, turning, knowing already who it was before she saw him standing in the doorway. His voice reverberated in her ears. She curtseyed to him and held out her hands. Her heart broke all over again. "Foye."

He walked into the courtyard. As ever, she could not guess his thoughts when he was somber, as he was now. His expression was pleasant. "You seem very deep in concentration. Am I intruding?" he asked.

"Never," she said. She could not stop the rush of heat through her body nor the leap of her heart.

"You looked so thoughtful." He pulled her into his arms, and she raised up for a kiss. "We haven't much time. They'll miss us both before long, and I have a question to ask of you." He kissed her. But he sensed something had changed, and he set her back. "Is everything all right?"

"No." Her heart pounded. How wretched this was, to be

so affected by anyone. No matter how often she told herself to be happy for whatever moments she had with him, her thoughts kept rushing to the future that must separate them.

He didn't say anything, and neither did she. The silence was . . . not precisely uncomfortable. Then they both spoke at the same time, overrunning each other.

"What is your question?"

"What is it, Sabine? What's—"

"Hold me, Foye. As if you'll never let me go."

"—happened?"

He obliged her, and she threw her arms around his neck and kissed him until he was kissing her back. Again, though, he set her back. "What's wrong, Sabine? Tell me and I'll try to make everything better."

They ended up staring at each other, and Sabine's head filled with the memory of them on the barbican wall at Büyükdere Castle. "Not yet," she said. "You first. What is your question?"

"The other day, you said you wished to sketch me."

Sabine studied him, trying to work out why he cared to bring up a comment she'd made almost as an aside. "Yes, I did say that. I suppose I ought to be flattered you even recall."

He gazed at her. "I recall every word you said that day."

"Do you?"

"I want you to take my likeness, Sabine. As soon as you can manage the time away from your uncle." He hooked a thumb in the pocket of his waistcoat.

She nodded and blinked back tears. There was no more time.

"Excellent." He grinned. "When is the next time he goes to the baths?"

She opened her mouth to speak, then realized she had no idea what she ought to say, only that she did not want to tell him yet.

"Now what," he said in a low voice, "is going on in that clever mind of yours?"

"I want to draw you. I do. I would in a heartbeat if it were possible. But I cannot."

"Why not?"

She clasped his hands in hers and brought them up to her mouth to kiss them one at a time. "Godard and I are leaving Büyükdere tomorrow."

Twelve

MAY 26, 1811

About five o'clock in the evening. The Godards' rented house in Büyükdere. While a modest home, the house did boast a partial view of the Bosporus. Much of the interior was in disarray since the Godards were preparing to leave for Nazim Pasha's *pashalik* in Kilis.

"SIR HENRY," LORD FOYE SAID IN A VOICE THAT SENT A shiver down Sabine's spine. She did her best to suppress the reaction. She did not want to start crying and have to concoct some explanation as to why she'd grown so unnaturally fond of Büyükdere that she couldn't bear to leave. She bent her head over her writing; she was working on the Egyptian section of Godard's book. Supposedly. If she'd written half a line, she was fortunate.

Foye stood in the center of the room, having just been shown into what she and her uncle called the Divan Salon because they had left it furnished, with one exception, in the Turkish style. Asif came forward to take his greatcoat. Foye handed over his hat and gloves first, both of which he had been holding in one hand.

"Thank you," Foye said as he slipped out of his lightweight coat. Asif bowed and withdrew.

Sabine tried very hard not to be so aware of him. But she

was. Terribly aware of what had happened between them at *Rumeli Hisari*. She sat at her desk, pretending to write about Ibrahim Pasha's massacre of the Mameluks while her thoughts strayed to the idea of kissing Foye. Even in the abstract, the possibility of such an intimacy with Foye set off butterflies in her stomach. If only they could, just one more time before she and Foye were separated.

Her hand on the desk fisted. Her breath cut off, and she closed her eyes and tried to suppress the tears welling up in her throat and burning behind her eyes. She despised this pretense. Despised it. But Godard had given up too much for her. She refused to leave him. How could she leave him when they were so far from home? Eventually, they would return to England and perhaps there she and Foye could find a way to make a life together.

"My lord," her uncle said from the divan upon which he sat. Along the windowed wall that overlooked the court-yard and the adjoining wall was a divan on a raised plat-form. Embroidered and tasseled pillows covered the silk upholstery. The divan was for sitting or resting or even napping. A narghile, or water pipe, sat on the floor, unused at the moment. Her uncle enjoyed Turkish tobacco almost as much as he enjoyed their coffee. He'd become a devotee of both.

Sabine stayed where she was, silent and ill at ease. She unfisted her hand. Her fingers hurt as she straightened them. She spent too much time thinking about Foye—Lord Foye—and the sweetness she felt when he kissed her, the shivery, giddy darkness that ran through her whenever his lips touched her. Stolen moments, every one of them.

Foye had not yet realized she was present, or else had a far better command of himself than she did. His attention was on her uncle, and with her desk tucked away in the corner opposite the divan, he wouldn't have seen her when he entered. He might appear calm, but her nerves were far from settled. What would Godard think of his calling on them? Would he guess what had changed between them?

"What a pleasure to have you call on us before we are on our way," Godard said from his place on the superior, rightmost corner of the divan.

Sabine relaxed. Of course, Foye would take his leave of them. That was only natural and polite of him.

"I could not let you leave without making my good-byes," he said. His gaze flicked to her and then away. So serious, he looked. "Besides, I am to depart myself in a day or two."

Sabine's heart lurched. They had so little time left, and yet the hours between now and their parting seemed infinite. A curious paradox. Every moment was to be savored, though. She watched Foye without, she hoped, seeming to stare, drinking him in, memorizing his face, the set of his shoulders, the way he held his body. God only knew when they would see each other again. It might be years.

At last, Foye turned to her, and she forced herself to sit calmly, her expression pleasant and bland. His clothes fit him amazingly well. As always. His taste was impeccable. She felt such a sense of restrained energy from him that she expected he might burst into motion at any moment.

"Miss Godard." He bowed, rather stiffly. You'd never think he'd ever passionately kissed her or held her close in his embrace. His eyes on her burned with heat. "Good afternoon. Please." He held up a hand. "Do not stand on my account."

She stood and curtseyed anyway; as brief a curtsey as his bow had been economical. "Good afternoon, my lord." *Rumeli Hisari* might never have happened, she told herself. He had never held her or kissed her or looked at her as though she were the only woman in the world. "I hope you are well."

"I am, thank you." He studied her a moment, but she could read nothing in his face. "You should not have arisen, Miss Godard."

Sabine curtseyed again. Her heart raced on his account and no other. Ruthlessly, she tamped down the reaction. She wanted so badly to slip her arms around his neck and tangle her fingers in his curls and whisper to him that she loved him.

"Do please sit down, my lord." She sat so that he would be able to do the same.

Foye nodded curtly, and remained standing with one hand behind his back and the other gripping the lapel of his coat so hard his knuckles were white.

Sabine wasn't any less held by strong emotion than Foye. What a wretched state in which to exist, to feel—to know that she had met a man she could admire beyond all others and yet, they could not be together. She had imagined once or twice what it would be like if she left Godard. She could. She could confess to her uncle that she was desperately in love. There was nothing, objectively, to stop her from doing so. Except for obligation. Godard had raised her. He had been the best parent to her that he knew how to be. He had loved her and raised her and sacrificed for her. No one knew better than she did the sacrifices he'd made on her behalf. No matter how bitter his disappointment over what had happened in London, Godard had never blamed her for the damage to his career and reputation.

Now that his gout was debilitating, her uncle relied on her. He needed her to write his letters and organize his papers. She was his voice in the written world. Without her assistance, he would never be able to write his book. For all the peculiarities of his character, he needed her, and she loved him for every moment of the life she'd had. How could she abandon him now?

Foye returned his attention to her uncle, and Sabine was left to her desk and papers. She continued observing Foye without her uncle being aware she did so, with her right hand on her cheek and her head turned to one side while she held a pen in the other, making desultory lines on the reverse side of a sheet containing her description of the Ibrahim Pasha's slaughter of his political rivals in Cairo. Ibrahim Pasha had invited his enemies to a celebration of the birth of his son and then slaughtered them all. Every Mameluk in Egypt.

Her desire to sketch Foye remained as strong as ever. There were so many angles from which she might decide to draw his face. She could, she should, before she left. Then she'd have something to remember him by.

The table at which she sat was cluttered with papers, pamphlets, correspondence, and several pages of Godard's manuscript besides the chapter on Egypt. There was a mountain of books, too, some of them brought with them from England, others acquired during their travels. Not all were in English. Sabine was making a study of written Arabic. There was such beauty in the characters. There was also blank paper, pen and ink, pencils, even a nub of charcoal. In short, all that she needed to draw Lord Foye.

In the meanwhile, Godard slid off the divan and laboriously pushed himself to his feet, leaning heavily on his cane. She knew what it cost him to stand, but he was stubborn, and if she didn't wait for him to ask for help he would refuse any assistance at all. She wished Asif had stayed, for he was one person who Godard reliably permitted to assist him.

"I hope," her uncle said to Foye with a grimace as he stood, "that you do not mind we preferred to keep this room as would the sultan himself."

"Not at all," Foye said. Quite sincerely, Sabine thought. There were many reasons to admire Foye. More than admire. She loved him. Not the least of those reasons was his decency to her uncle. Godard was not always a pleasant man to be around, particularly when his joints were hurting him as they were today. He had done too much this morning and now paid for it in pain.

Godard gestured at the divan. "Won't you sit, my lord? I assure you, you will never be more comfortable in your life as you are on a Turkish divan."

He smiled at Godard. "And I assure you, Sir Henry, that I find the Turkish style as comfortable as you." Foye's voice was amiable, and so lovely to hear. One day, she thought, she would ask him to read her poetry. The sonnets of Shakespeare, Donne, and Plutarch. Perhaps verses of Milton or Dante.

With both hands pressing down on his cane, Godard arched his back. Every degree of movement was painfully achieved. As his illness progressed, their lives narrowed with the incremental restriction of his mobility. There was so little time left for him to travel. One day, he would not be able to walk or even stand. Her heart broke for him as she watched for signs she must intervene in his moment of independence. Though he swayed a little, his hands, both gripping the top of his walking stick, were steady enough. She was ready, though, to insist he sit down again, his pride be dashed.

At last, Foye sat, just as another of the native servants brought in tea, coffee, and a selection of delicacies. Foye took the left corner of the divan. There was as much precedence involved in where one sat in a Turkish room as in any salon in London. Or Oxford, for that matter.

The two men settled in, declining tea in favor of smoking. Another servant prepared the narghile, filling the bowl at the top with the honey-soaked tobacco her uncle preferred to use. Since she was unnoticed for the moment, she slid her sketchbook from beneath the post that had arrived just this afternoon, found a pencil she had not worn down to a stub, and sketched Foye because she wanted to remember his face and their time together.

She made light strokes to capture the power in the line of his cheeks. There was a great deal of character in his uneven features. For so large a man who had expressed some dissatisfaction with his size, he was quite at home in his body. She would love to sketch him in the nude, to capture the leonine majesty of him. A brazen notion, but true. How marvelous it would be to draw him from life.

Foye and Godard talked a great deal between pulls on the narghile, which gave her time to work. She stared at her sheet of paper, unhappy with the result. She had not captured his essence, the beauty that shone from his eyes and took up residence in the way he arranged his body on the divan. She began again and quite lost track of the time.

"I had another purpose in this call, sir," Foye was saying

to her uncle when she surfaced from her period of concentration. She blinked and looked down at her page. So inadequate, her efforts at drawing him.

"Sabine," her uncle said, "would you send for more coffee, please?"

"Of course." She slipped her so inadequate efforts beneath a book and went to the door to speak to the servant waiting outside. When she returned, she could not shake the notion that Foye had watched her all the way there and back. She wished he would not. Or perhaps she wished he had. She retook her seat until the servant came with fresh coffee.

She poured their coffee into one of the small ceramic cups made expressly for the drink. Unlike the tobacco, which she found unpleasant, she loved the smell of coffee. She brought a cup to Foye.

"Thank you," he said as he took it from her. Their eyes locked, just for a moment, and he didn't do anything to soften the impact of what she saw there. Oh, unfair. How unfair to break her heart again.

"You're welcome." She served her uncle next, taking care that he had a firm grip on the cup before she let go. She moved a tray, with its pistachios and oranges and other sweets, within reaching distance for the marquess. For her uncle, she prepared a plate of his favorites, taking care to shell the pistachios for him. He could have nothing that required dexterous motion. His fingers lacked agility and strength. That done, she retreated to the other side of the inlaid table and sat on a pillow on the floor, her legs curled to one side.

Foye glanced at her. "The weather is quite mild today, don't you agree, Miss Godard?"

Her uncle laughed. "More days than not, the Levantine climate agrees with me," he said, still laughing. "But, my dear Lord Foye, you needn't make polite conversation on account of Sabine. Think of her as a man, and we will all get on better. You may speak frankly before her."

"But she is not a man." Foye looked at Godard with

raised eyebrows. "And one always speaks politely in the presence of a lady, sir."

"An hour in her company and you will soon forget her gender," Godard said. He waved a gnarled hand. "We shall have a very dull time of this visit if you insist on considering her a woman, my lord. The kind of insipid conversation one must endure on account of female sensibilities? Bah. No talk of the weather here, my lord. We may indulge in any subject."

"Very well, Sir Henry." Foye drank some of his coffee. "I will speak frankly to you both." Godard gestured for him to continue. "You must not go to Kilis."

"Why the devil not?" Godard's eyebrows drew together. "We have been invited by Nazim Pasha himself."

"I have had a most interesting and revealing conversation with Anthony Lucey. There are reports, Sir Henry, of violence in the north. Three Germans robbed and killed. And I have heard, on the very best authority, that not far from Aleppo, Bedouins attacked a native family on their way to a wedding. I urge you to cancel your plans. It is not safe for you to travel north, no matter who you intend to visit while you are there. If you find Büyükdere and Constantinople dull, you are welcome to join me on my way to Palmyra. There are Roman ruins there as fine as any at Serjillo." He glanced between Godard and her. "There is just as much that is fascinating and new in the south as the north."

"We will be traveling with Nazim Pasha himself," Godard said. "Who, pray tell, do you think will have the nerve to attack him?"

"And later—when you leave Kilis?"

"What interest will anyone have in a crippled old man and a woman of no consequence?"

Foye clenched and unclenched his fist. "You are English, Sir Henry. Infidels. For some, that is more than enough."

"Bah."

"Is there really no dissuading you? No swaying you with reminders of the dangers to which you expose your niece?"

"Have some pistachios, my lord." Godard pushed a bowl of the nuts toward Foye. "They were a gift from Nazim Pasha himself."

Foye stilled. "No, sir." He leaned over and put down his empty cup before he stood. "I have another engagement. I hope we will meet again before one of us leaves. I beg of you, for your niece's sake if for none other, to reconsider."

"We were in Egypt during the recent unrest there, my lord," Godard said. "The violence is between the natives."

"Folly, sir." He bowed again. Sabine tried and failed to catch his eye.

Godard waved a hand. "What sort of travelogue can I write if I do not travel? I cannot write of the East without including the north. Shall I leave out descriptions of the Syrian province?" He rested his hands on his lap. "I thank you for your concern, my boy. Now, good day."

Foye went to Sabine but did not offer to take her hand. She was at once nervous about him being so near and distraught at the thought of not seeing him again. He bowed and looked her straight in the eye. In a low voice pitched so that her uncle would not overhear, he said, "May we have five minutes alone? I'll wait for you by the fountain."

Thirteen

❧

WITH AN UNSETTLED MIND AND A HEART THE WRONG size for the space in his chest, Foye walked downstairs to the interior courtyard of the Godards' house. Would Sabine come down? What if her uncle interfered or refused to let her leave him? They might not see each other before she and Godard left.

He jiggled some loose change in his coat pocket as he waited. Not English coins. Turkish paras. He hadn't felt this anxious over a woman since he was twenty, for God's sake. He was resigned to the path his heart had led him to. He had not come to Turkey to fall in love, and yet he had. He wanted Sabine as badly as ever. More, even.

The sound of footsteps on stone made him look up. Sabine was crossing the courtyard at a brisk pace, and his heart dove toward his toes. There had been any number of nights when he had been perfectly happy to send himself to perdition by self-satisfying an urge for sexual release. None of those longings had ever involved wishing for a partner to assist. Until now. He was in a bad way over her.

She walked toward the fountain where he'd stopped to wait. The sway of her skirts more than suggested the curves beneath the muslin. For a small woman, she had extremely feminine curves. He knew that. He'd held her in his arms often enough to know. He was a patient man, or thought so until now. He did not want to wait to make Sabine his. He wanted her to be his so there would be no chance of her changing her mind or falling out of love with him. So much might happen between now and whenever it was that they were back in England and able to deal with her situation. Hell, Sir Henry could live with them, if he wanted to. Or he'd move to Oxford himself and live with the Godards. So help him, he would.

Foye stopped jingling the coins in his pocket. She was smiling at him, a little sadly, he fancied. At that moment he would have given his life for the right to take her in his arms in front of anyone who might be looking. It wasn't as if he intended to make off with Sabine and ravish her, though true enough, he had a growing set of fantasies about her in which he did just that.

"Thank you for coming," he said when she was near enough to hear him clearly. Her mouth was tense, and one of her hands was fisted at her side. He didn't move toward her or change his position in any way. No sense letting the servants guess.

She stopped a few feet away so that, should anyone happen to see them, they would see nothing improper. "Foye," she whispered.

When he looked into her eyes, he knew she was seeing more than he wanted anyone to see about the man he was. A turbaned servant crossed the courtyard, and they fell silent until the man disappeared into another part of the house. Foye had on his overcoat, but he was still holding his hat, and he studied the brim while he chose his words because he didn't want to say the wrong thing.

"I wish we weren't going," she said while he was still

trying to marshal his thoughts into words. "I wish we were staying here. Or that we were going with you."

"We knew you would be going to Kilis," he said. The last thing he wanted to do was make her unhappier than she already was. They would be separated for a while. So what? Lovers and couples parted company all the time without the distance spelling disaster for the relationship. "You'll return, or I'll join you in some other city. In any event, we'll be back in England one day."

"And you? Are you really leaving Büyükdere? Where will you go?" She took a step closer. "How will I write to you, Foye?"

"Write care of Mr. Lucey. He'll see my correspondence is forwarded." He took a deep breath. "I'll write to you at the British consulate in Aleppo." So long as the Godards left word of their next destination, his letters would eventually find her.

Her eyes glittered with unshed tears. She nodded. "Yes, all right."

"I'll be returning to England before long," he said. "After Damascus, I expect. By the new year, I should be home. Write to me at Maralee House in St. Ives, Cornwall, after that. If I'm not in London, I'll be there."

"Maralee House, St. Ives, Cornwall." She nodded.

"If you're not sure where to direct your letters, direct them there."

"I shall, then. Thank you."

"You'll see the house one day and love it as I do."

She swiped a hand over her eye. "Yes, I'm sure I shall, Foye."

Foye took a folded slip of paper from his coat pocket. "In the meantime, if anything should happen, if you should find yourself in need of any assistance, whether you are in England or here, and the Luceys cannot help you, write to my solicitor, Mr. George Brook." He gave her the paper on which he had written his lawyer's address. "I've already sent him instructions on your behalf. If you do write him, my letter is likely to have arrived beforehand."

"That's very generous of you." She took the paper and scanned the address before she put the sheet in her pocket. "Thank you." The corner of her mouth pulled down.

Foye stepped forward. But, damn, he didn't dare touch her. "My love, don't cry."

"I shan't." She gave a tight shake of her head.

"Will you draw me a likeness of you, Sabine?"

She didn't answer him.

"Will you?" He took a step toward her. "Or do you intend to send me away with nothing by which to remember you?"

She raised her face to his and smiled. He thought his heart would break at the sight. "No lock of hair, my lord?"

He locked gazes with her. "A self-portrait, Sabine, so I may remember you and know with each stroke of your pencil that you thought of me."

She didn't answer, and in the silence, Foye could guess nothing of her thoughts. She nodded. "Very well."

He squeezed the brim of his hat and brought himself to the mark. "I love you, Sabine. You've become my heart and soul since we met. I will wait for you."

She reached for his hand and curled her fingers around his. "And I you, Foye."

"When you are able, we'll be married, if you'll do me the honor."

She gently squeezed his hand. "If you say you love me still, I shall, Foye."

They stood like that, hand in hand, each silent and knowing they must part. "Convince your uncle not to visit Kilis," he said. "Have nothing to do with Nazim Pasha."

"Do you think I haven't tried?" she asked.

He stared at her, keeping the contact between them even when it went beyond polite. "His hands are nearly useless," he said. "He can barely walk. Try as he might, he cannot hide his frailty from anyone. Tell him he mustn't make the journey. Nor should you trust Nazim Pasha." He tightened his hand around hers. "This is madness. He admires you too much. His reputation is not a pleasant one, Sabine."

Her forehead wrinkled in puzzlement. "The pasha, you mean?"

"Yes, the pasha. He admires you too much. Everyone saw it. I am not the only man to have noticed his attentions to you."

She opened her mouth to say something, then didn't. The edge of her mouth twitched. "But I love you," she said. "Not the pasha."

He took a step toward her and then stopped. "Sabine, you will not be safe." He tipped his chin in the direction of the upper portion of the house. "Ask your uncle's servant. Ask him if Nazim Pasha isn't making a fortune buying and selling women. Ask him."

She nodded. "I will try. But I can't promise you I'll succeed."

Foye dug his fingers into the brim of his hat. He wanted to tear the damn thing apart. "With all due respect to your uncle, you should not have to convince him of anything. He should be concerned for your safety. He should know it is his duty to protect you at all costs. I fail to understand why he puts you at risk." He threw a hand in the air. "He treats you as if you are a man. No matter how clever you are, no matter that you can run rings around anyone ever to graduate Oxford, you are not a man."

"He wants to finish his book. The north is one of the last places we have to visit. I think if we go there, I can persuade him it's time to go home. To England."

"And if his doing so puts you in danger, what then?"

She shrugged. "Finishing his book is his dream. The only one left to him. And you know I am the reason this is all he has left. Oh, Foye. Please. I won't take that from him, too."

His anger, always slow to boil over, flashed hot. Enough. This was enough. He closed the distance between them, dropping his hat to grab her by the shoulders. "If it were me I'd give my life before I put you in danger. Your uncle doesn't feel about you the way I do, Sabine. He doesn't love you."

"But he does love me." She smiled, a sad, heartbreaking curve of her mouth, and Foye caught his breath because that so sad smile tipped him the rest of the way. The very last of his resistance to her ripped away.

He mastered himself, and it was not easy. "I know," he said. "I know he loves you, as a father would. We love you differently. And God help me, I hope you love me differently!"

She laughed softly. "Yes, Foye."

"If you cannot persuade him, Sabine, then at least promise you will let me send some of my men with you. I will be in Büyükdere long enough for that. If you cannot convince him, I'll arrange to send additional armed men with you on your journey." He met her gaze. "They will be loyal to you, not Nazim Pasha."

Her mind was more than quick enough to grasp the importance of that. "Thank you," she said. "That is an excellent precaution."

Foye nodded. Inside he was wound up tight. He was a man of varied experience. He'd had lovers and mistresses in his life, and when he fell in love, he had been faithful. And yet, he stood before Sabine Godard feeling like an absolute tyro.

"Perhaps it would be wise for you to gather your extra men now. There might not be time later. Nazim Pasha promised we were to leave first thing tomorrow morning."

"Consider it done." He glanced behind him, saw a shadowed corner beneath the interior courtyard stairs to the upper floor, and pulled her into the niche formed there. He wrapped his arms around her waist and brought her close up against him. "Promise me you'll be careful," he said.

"Foye," she said, "someone will see us."

"I don't care." He cupped her chin and tilted her face to his. "Promise me, Sabine."

"I promise."

He kissed her, and he didn't hold much back at all. She stretched up to him, opening her mouth under his, and he swept his tongue inside. He felt her momentary hesitation, and then she relaxed against him and, well. Yes. She *was* a quick study.

Eventually, he had to let her go. The servants were busy packing for the Godards' removal tomorrow. The house would be closed up but remain a base of operations while the Godards were in the north. If he kept Sabine here much longer, someone really would see them, and the last thing he wanted was for her to be the subject of gossip again or find that Godard was allied against him before he'd even had a chance.

"Write to me every day," he said. "And send me your portrait."

"I shall."

This was it, then. The last time they would see each other for who knew how long. Sabine brushed her hand through his hair, tangling her fingers in his curls. "Foye," she said, "promise me you'll be careful?"

"I will," he said.

"Good-bye," she said.

"Not good-bye." He pulled her into his arms and kissed the top of her head. "We'll see each other again."

From upstairs, a male voice called for her in heavily accented English.

She stepped away, brushing at her skirts and wiping at her cheeks with the sides of her fingers. "Good-bye, Foye."

"Adieu, Sabine," he whispered.

Fourteen

❧

Northern Syria, Aleppo, Kilis, and
the pashalik of Nazim Pasha,
JUNE 29, 1811

Kilis lay roughly eighty miles northeast of Maraat
Al-Numan, where Foye had briefly gone, through
Syria with its factions and tribes all looking to establish
independence from the sultan or from Ibrahim Pasha in
Egypt now that he'd massacred the Egyptian Mameluks
out of existence. Nazim Pasha, it was believed, aspired
to control the entire province without the nuisance of
allegiance to any higher authority. With or without the
assistance of France or Russia. Or Britain.

FOYE WAS FIVE DAYS REACHING KILIS BECAUSE HE STOPPED
in Aleppo for supplies and to check whether any of his letters to Sabine had arrived at the consulate, and if any had,
whether she and Sir Henry had been by to collect them.
Three of his letters were there, uncollected. He did learn,
however, that the pasha had been through the city on this
way to Kilis, and that the Godards had been with him. Both
in good health.

As for why he was on his way to Aleppo? The hell with
Damascus, and the hell with being separated from Sabine
when it wasn't yet necessary. When it was madness to allow
Sabine and her uncle to travel alone with the pasha, into an
area known to be politically unstable, then he ought to put

a stop to it. Let Godard think what he would of Foye's join-ing them. He could at least have Lieutenant Russell's cour-age in facing the man on behalf of the woman he loved. He intended to do whatever it took to convince Sir Henry that he loved Sabine and deserved his blessing for a courtship.

In addition to replenishing the supplies necessary to get his men and himself to Kilis and back, he had with him a set of English dueling pistols to present to the pasha when he arrived at his palace, as it seemed that was where he must go to join the Godards. The pistols were a common gift made to princes, pashas, and various warlords who were in de facto control of the remote provinces of the sultanate.

He also hired more men while he was there—mercenaries and former Janissaries—to accompany him to Kilis. If there was trouble, he wanted to be prepared, and that meant men and weapons, neither of which were in short supply here. There were a good many retired fighting men in Aleppo, as well as ferocious-looking men from any number of the tribes indigenous to the area.

He chose men who looked like they'd be bastards in a fight and paid them enough to secure their loyalty with a promise of half as much money again when he discharged them. In the end, Foye outfitted and armed twenty men in addition to his personal guard. His valet, Barton, knew his way around a pistol, and his young dragoman, Nabil, though still a boy, kept a pistol tucked into his sash and a sword over his back. Including those two, his retinue num-bered nearly thirty. More than enough, he hoped, to deter any bandits or Bedouins they might meet on the road.

Well provisioned and armed, Foye left for Kilis two days after arriving in Aleppo and a month since leaving Büyükdere. The journey between Kilis and Aleppo was just long enough to require an overnight stop. A man on a fine horse might make the trip in a day, but with a small army and the pack animals carrying their supplies? If there was trouble on the way, he wanted his men fresh, not hun-gry and exhausted from hard riding.

Their stop came at just past the halfway point, at a

village where the people stared at him with wide eyes,
likely having never seen a European man as tall as he
was. They were followed by children begging for food and
money. Emaciated dogs nipped at the heels of their horses.
Nabil secured them lodgings in an inn that served surpris-
ingly good food.

After they ate, Foye took Barton and Nabil with him for
a walk. With Nabil interpreting, he was able to discover that
the pasha had stopped here, too, when he came through on
his way to Kilis. Not surprising, given that Sir Henry was
unable to travel quickly.

With full dark at least an hour or two away, they continued their tour of the village. There was a public fountain
erected at the side of the road that continued on to Kilis,
and several more in the village proper. As they walked,
a dozen children followed after him, begging for coins,
which he handed out amid laughter and shrieks of joy. He
spent some time at the village bazaar, where he found some
exceptionally fine embroidered silk and another merchant
who had a superb selection of emeralds. Foye sat with the
vendor, and again with Nabil interpreting, they smoked and
drank coffee and haggled over a price for the emeralds.

His lack of Arabic or Turkish was no barrier to commerce. Where money was involved, all one really required
was an expressive face and the will to walk away. Nabil
translated when necessary, but for the most part, Foye con-
ducted the matter on his own and came away with the gems
he wanted at a more than agreeable price. Barton tucked
his purchases into a satchel, and they continued their walk.

The farther north they went, the fewer Turks there were,
and this was as true of Aleppo as it was of this village.
The population was more and more tribal: Arabs, Bedouin, Druze, Turkmen, Syrians, and even Christians. At
the end of one street they reached a spot where an Arab
had erected a small rug-covered dais. Ten youths sat on
the rug with one blackamoor woman, hugely pregnant,
and two paler-skinned women, both of whom were quite
young and very pretty. The Arab was, Foye realized with a

start, a slaver, and he was even now displaying his female merchandise to a man who looked disinterested in what he saw. Foye saw no blondes, no other women of any color but the two Caucasian girls. His heart misgave him at this evidence that, indeed, the trading of women was a practice that survived in the north.

Thank God he already knew the pasha and the Godards had passed safely through here.

They reached Kilis about eleven the following morning. Nazim Pasha's palace was on a rise on the northern outskirts of the city, well situated to withstand an assault should anyone be foolish enough to attack the pasha. Foye ordered the bulk of his men to make camp out of sight of the palace. He saw no reason to alarm the pasha by approaching with what was, in effect, a small fighting force.

With just Barton and Nabil, Foye rode to the pasha's palace. Planted in the dirt inside the entrance were two wooden spears, each with a cow's tail affixed to it. They were the literal symbol of the pasha's standing; Nazim Pasha was a two-tail pasha, a man of significant rank in the eyes of the Ottoman Porte. Three tails, and he would be sitting in the High Porte, Sultan Mahmud II's private court, with the title of vizier or something equally lofty.

A white-bearded man greeted them at the courtyard entrance, which was wide with a gate high enough to admit an entire caravan of camels and donkeys. Foye relayed via Nabil that he was most anxious to meet the pasha and present him with a gift as a token of his esteem. They were admitted, and Foye let out a breath of relief. He would see Sabine again, within the hour he hoped.

The Godards had been staying in opulent quarters indeed. The interior of the palace was a grand affair, with marble floors and columns, mosaicked walls, and windows and doorways with inverted teardrop-shaped tops. From what he saw, the general layout adhered to the traditional courtyard-based constructions he'd seen in Büyükdere and elsewhere in the provinces of Turkey. There were two minarets and, so Foye assumed, at least one mosque.

With frequent bows and salaams, the white-bearded servant escorted him to an interior courtyard with a marble floor laid out in a pattern of dark and light tiles. Barton and Nabil followed him. Covered walkways lined the perimeter of the rectangular courtyard, with marble columns supporting the arched openings. Fruit trees and flowering bushes offered shade, and two fountains, one at each end of the enclosure, cooled the air.

The *irwan* to which the servant escorted him was as magnificent as the rest of the palace. This high-ceilinged, domed room was entirely open to the courtyard. The marble-lined floor-to-ceiling walls were decorated with tiles inlaid in the pattern of black and white so common in the north. Bright rugs covered the floor, and a divan glittered with pillows in jeweled tones of silk. The massive fountain at the near side of the courtyard was surrounded by palm, orange, and lemon trees. Finches flitted from branch to branch. It was here, the servant told him, that he would meet Nazim Pasha. First, of course, he must freshen himself after his journey.

Half an hour later Foye returned to the *irwan* with Nabil at his side. Foye looked for the Godards but did not see them yet. Servants had brought food and drink to the *irwan*, arranging the selection on what looked like upside-down chairs with platters laid over the legs. Soft music of flutes and stringed instruments came from an enclosed structure on one side of the *irwan*. He adjusted his grip on the dueling pistols, wrapped in a velvet bag, that he intended to present to the pasha and crossed the remainder of the courtyard.

The infamous Nazim Pasha reclined on the divan, a narghile at his feet, his robes as extravagantly embroidered as before. Gold and silver thread embellished his heavy silk kaftan, and a teardrop pearl adorned the front of his turban. As was the custom, Foye and Nabil removed their outer shoes before they entered the *irwan*; Foye retained the thin slippers he'd worn inside his shoes, a convenient custom he was happy to have adopted. Without a word,

Nabil installed himself on the floor, legs crossed and hands resting on his thighs.

As expected, the pasha was established in the rightmost corner of the divan. He wore a large ruby on his left hand. A long-limbed Moor in a striped kaftan served fresh coffee, hot and strong and almost unbearably sweet, and then retreated to the lower portion of the floor to sit with Nabil until he was needed again.

Foye presented the dueling pistols, which were graciously received and exclaimed over.

"Excellency," Foye said in French once the pasha had set the pistols aside. He sat on the left corner of the divan, cradling his coffee in his hand. After a clap from the pasha, the Moorish servant moved a tray of nuts and sherbet within his reach. "I hope my arrival here is not inconvenient."

Nazim Pasha waved a desultory hand. "It is delightful to see you, my lord. I do enjoy my European visitors."

"I confess, Pasha, I had hoped the Godards would be here. Have they left Kilis already?"

"No, Marquis."

"I hope they are well, sir," he said. "I am anxious to see them, as you must be aware."

"Alas," the pasha said in his near flawless French. He peeled a fig as he spoke. His fingers were expert. "I regret to tell you that only a few days ago Sir Henry fell very ill."

Foye leaned against the divan, his chest tight. He'd done the right thing, then, coming after Sabine. "Distressing news indeed." If what the pasha had just said was true, it did explain why the Godards had not joined them in the *irwan*. He only wished he knew whether he ought to believe the pasha. "How is Sir Henry now? Has he recovered?"

The pasha bowed his head. When he looked at Foye, the mournful cast to his eyes sent a bolt of dread lancing straight through to his soul. *"Je suis désolé, Marquis. Il est mort."*

Foye didn't understand the words at first, even though the pasha spoke quite clearly and simply. His confusion must have been quite evident. The pasha swallowed his bite of fig before he spoke in heavily accented English. "It is my very sad duty to tell you, *Monsieur le Marquis*, that Sir Henry died three days ago."

Foye started to say something, then stopped. His heart gave a gigantic thump against his ribs, so hard and loud he was sure the pasha could have heard it from where he sat. He gathered his thoughts. "And Miss Godard?" he asked. He tightened his fingers around his coffee cup. For three days, Sabine had been here on her own, grief stricken and alone with no one to look after her and see that she was safe. "How is she? Is she all right?"

"Such sad news to tell you, Marquis." He lifted a bejeweled finger. "She is doing as well as one can expect after the loss of a beloved uncle."

Sir Henry Godard was dead. God ought to strike him deaf and dumb, for his first thought was that Sabine was free. What kind of beast was he that he felt even a moment of pure, clear relief in the knowledge?

"I can see that you are quite undone at my news," the pasha said. "Please accept my condolences, Marquis. I was not aware you were such close friends."

"Yes," he said. "The news is most shocking. Forgive me, I did not expect this. It is fortunate I came when I did," he said. Good Lord. What if he hadn't? What if he'd continued his self-pity and gone on to Palmyra? Or Damascus? "I'll see to everything, of course. Have you notified the British Consulate? They knew nothing of this when I left Aleppo."

A flash of impatience showed in the pasha's dark eyes. "She is grieving, naturally. I have done everything possible to console her."

Foye set down his coffee. His fingers trembled. The pasha's impatience made him sit up straight. Without her uncle, Sabine was without any influence. She was an unmarried woman alone in a country with far more restrictive notions of a woman's place in society than Sabine was used to. "You will be relieved, I am sure, to know I am prepared to oversee Miss Godard's immediate and safe return to England."

The pasha raised his eyebrows. "Miss Godard's every need has been satisfied during this difficult time. She is disconsolate, you may imagine, Marquis." If not for their surroundings, Foye could have believed himself in a Paris drawing room. "My own personal physician attended Sir Henry in his final days, and even knowing that his faith was not the true one, I nevertheless summoned a Christian priest to preside over his burial."

But he hadn't informed the British consul of Sir Henry's illness or of its fatal result. The pasha had—deliberately?—left Sabine isolated from her countrymen all this time. Foye drank some of his coffee, even though he didn't want any, in order to think through what he ought to do.

"You have my sincerest thanks for all your troubles on their behalf, Excellency. I am sure that everything you did for her and her uncle was a comfort to Miss Godard." He forced himself to loosen his grip on his cup.

"It was nothing," Nazim Pasha said. "I was more than happy to be of assistance to her."

Foye rose from the divan and stood looking down at the pasha. "Would it be possible for me to speak with her now? We have much to discuss, and I would like to be on our way first thing tomorrow."

"But of course, Marquis."

The pasha's answer disarmed him. He had, he realized, expected to be denied. From the moment he'd heard that Godard was dead, he'd believed his worst fears about what might happen to Sabine were to come true.

Nazim Pasha clapped his hands, the usual method of summoning a servant, and gave instructions in a language that, to his admittedly untutored ear, did not sound like Turkish or Arabic. He saw Nabil cock his head. Curious. Foye's uneasiness returned. The servant bowed and left the *irwan*.

"While we wait for Miss Godard to join us," the pasha

said, "perhaps you will tell me about your country. I am
curious to know more about England." He reclined on the
divan, a pillow behind him. "Have you a large estate?"

Foye replied with some nonsense about English weather
and that when he was not in London, he lived in Cornwall,
the loveliest spot in the whole of the British Isles. How the
hell long did it take to fetch one young lady? When the servant returned, it was without Sabine. Foye listened, maddeningly, to an exchange in language he did not understand.
He had become adept, though, at reading expressions. It
was Foye's distinct impression that there was nothing out
of place with the servant. He was reporting to his master on
a subject that was, for him, entirely mundane. The pasha,
however, was another matter. Foye did not like anything
about the way he listened to his servant. Every instinct in
his body reminded him that the man before him was an
opportunist.

But surely there was no reason for him to feel so apprehensive. Sabine was here, by the pasha's own admission.
When she was able, he would see her. There was no reason
for Nazim Pasha to keep him from seeing her. None at all.

When he had dismissed the servant once again, Nazim
Pasha pressed his hands together and addressed Foye.
"Alas, Marquis, such ill luck!" His dark eyes glinted.
"I have been informed that Miss Godard is not here."

Fifteen

❧

"Not here?" Foye had no reason to think the pasha was lying, yet he so believed. Every rumor he'd heard about the pasha came back to him: that he'd held people for ransom; that he engaged in the selling of women into harems; his admiration of Sabine. The extravagant gifts to her were no rumor. The pasha's interest in Sabine was another fact. "Forgive me, I'm not certain I understand what you mean when you say Miss Godard is not here."

With a smile, the pasha bowed his head. "Allow me to restate, Marquis. Of course Miss Godard is here"— he gestured with a hand that took in the entirety of their surroundings—"but she has gone for a walk in one of my orchards. Oh, not alone, I assure you. She is accompanied by the servants I have put at her disposal during her stay here. You see, I have been looking after her comfort. My servants have been instructed to inform her of your arrival the very moment she returns."

"Can you not send someone to fetch her?" He spoke casually, but his interior state was far from casual.

"But of course!" The pasha smiled. "I have done so already. She will return any moment, I am certain." A servant came forward to refill and light the coal that would heat the tobacco in the bowl at the top of the narghile. The pasha gestured to the food set out. "While we wait, please, my lord, eat."

"I'm sure you won't object if in the meantime I arrange to have the Godards' things prepared for removal. I don't wish to put you to any trouble, so naturally, my servants will take care of everything." Asif, Foye thought. He needed to find Asif. Godard's servant would surely know what had happened here. "I should like us to leave at first light tomorrow."

"So soon? But you have just arrived." The pasha stroked his beard. "You English are always in such haste. Allow me to properly entertain you before you hurry off."

"Nazim Pasha, as I am sure you can foresee, with the death of Miss Godard's uncle there are formalities to be seen to. The consulate must be notified. The sooner Miss Godard and I are in Aleppo, the better."

"All will be seen to in due time." The pasha clapped again, and another servant came forward to receive instructions. He, too, hurried away as had the other. Foye itched to follow him. About now he'd lay odds that the servant was stopping out of sight and doing nothing but waiting where he would not be seen. Jesus, he was seeing treachery everywhere. It was quite possible that Sabine was indeed engaged at the moment and not available.

Foye's stomach roiled with tension. No matter how reasonable he told himself it was for Sabine not to be immediately available simply because he wished her to be, he was convinced that every passing moment increased the likelihood that Sabine would be lost to him. The bloody orchard, if it even existed, couldn't be so far away that she would be hours from the palace.

Just as he did not believe Sabine was walking in any orchard, he did not believe the pasha had directed his staff to cooperate in readying the Godards' belongings for transport. Again the servant returned, and again there was a rapid exchange between the pasha and his servant.

Foye, in his turn, signaled for Nabil to join him. When the man was at his side, Foye spoke in a low voice. "Can you translate any of what they are saying?"

"They are talking about Miss Godard," he replied. There was concern in his eyes.

"And?" Foye did not need to tell Nabil to keep his voice low. The boy's eyes were wide and frightened. Their lives might well depend on maintaining the fiction of the pasha's excuses, and both he and Nabil knew it.

"Nazim Pasha has told his servant to post a guard at her door."

Foye schooled himself. "I want you to find a man, a native, who worked for Sir Henry Godard. His name is Asif. Find him, tell him I am here. Find out whatever you can about what happened. Then find Barton and tell him we're to leave at first light tomorrow with the Godards' possessions."

Nabil bowed and hurried away.

"Has Miss Godard returned from her walk?" Foye asked when the pasha's servant had bowed his way back to a place on the floor of the *irwan*.

"Indeed, Marquis, she has. But I am informed now that she is sleeping." He gestured. "Of course I am deeply concerned for her. My physician has been monitoring her for signs of the illness that took her uncle. She must not be disturbed. Be patient." He drew deeply from the narghile. "There is time for all that and more. When we are certain her health is not at risk."

"Has she been told I am here?"

The pasha lifted his hands. "That I do not know. You English wish the world to move so quickly." He shook his head. "This evening, Marquis. You will certainly see her later this evening. In the meantime, please, enjoy yourself. There is much to see here in Kilis."

"Respectfully, Pasha, Miss Godard is a British citizen

and in need of assistance from her countrymen in her time of need. She is alone, without her uncle. There are a hundred details to be attended to in this matter. Surely she can be awakened and told I am here, willing and ready to assist her."

"One wonders," the pasha said, reclining against his silk-covered divan while a servant—a slave?—slowly fanned him, "why you are here instead of the consul in Aleppo. I have met Mr. John Barker. We have dined together from time to time. He is a most amiable and competent man."

"No doubt he is," Foye replied.

"How can all be taken care of as it should be without his authority?" He crossed an arm over his middle, one hand holding the water pipe. "You are surely aware that you are not in Britannia. There are legalities among the Turks, Marquis, that should be seen to as well." He fingered the luxurious fabric of his kaftan. "Customs that should be observed."

Foye tilted his head. "I am sure," he said slowly, "there are ways to repay you for the trouble you've been to on behalf of your British guests."

"I think," the pasha said with thoughtfulness that was not the least genuine, "that it would not be right or proper for me to deal with anyone but the consul himself where Miss Godard is concerned. I understand that now her uncle is dead there is no other male relative here to represent her interests."

"You are correct, Pasha."

"How can I release her to you when you are not her uncle or brother or a male relative who will protect her as a woman must be protected in these dangerous and uncertain times?" He shook his head mournfully. "Such things are not done here. It is not our way to entrust a woman to a man who is not her relative. Has she really no family who can come here and retrieve her?"

"I'm sure the consul can assist in clarifying her status, Pasha."

"You are doubtless correct in that." The pasha exhaled a stream of smoke. "These things take time. A very long time."

Foye knew what the pasha intended. He knew it in his soul. First, Foye would be required to pay a bribe that would be more than he could possibly have on hand. He would have to return to Aleppo to raise the money and convince the consul to deal with the pasha. Nazim Pasha would either refuse the ransom, demand an even greater sum, or, more likely yet, arrange to have Foye robbed of it on his return to Kilis. And what would happen to Sabine in the meantime or afterward?

His chest turned cold with fear. A thousand unpleasant outcomes occurred to him, each worse than the one before. The pasha would establish her in his harem or sell her to someone else. One heard that the Turks prized European women in their harems. Was it not whispered that the sultan's own mother had been a Frenchwoman? No mere rumor, alas. This was the nineteenth century, not the fifteenth, and yet so many old customs remained alive and vital.

"Certainly," Foye said easily, as if it were the most natural thing in the world, "I insist on seeing you are compensated for you troubles on her behalf, Nazim Pasha."

While Foye waited for a response, the pasha took up the narghile again. A cloud of bergamot-laced smoke floated in the air. He smiled broadly. "Compensation would be most generous of you. My good friend Mr. Julius Ghyoot was my guest here for half a year." Unfortunately, Foye knew this to be fact. Ghyoot's trials at the hands of Nazim Pasha were the stuff of legend among the diplomats in Büyükdere. "He will tell you himself he was entertained every day of his stay."

"At no small expense to you."

"Precisely." He grinned. "How quick you are to understand. That is what I so like about you British. But I wonder. Surely, in six months, perhaps a little longer, some relative from England might bestir himself to come for her. That would resolve both difficulties: the expense of her stay here and the difficulty in putting her into the hands of a man who is not her relation."

"I have five very fine horses with me," he said. "You may have your pick of them. For your trouble."

"Only five?" Nazim Pasha laughed, one hand on his belly. "I have a dozen in my stable now. Do you value Miss Godard so little, Marquis? Five thousand Arabians would be a small price to pay for a woman such as she is." He touched the ring on his index finger, twisting it around and around. "She is . . . a pearl without price, do you not agree?"

"Not without price," Foye said.

"Agreed," the pasha replied with a laugh. He lifted his hands. "You see I am a reasonable man. There is, indeed, always a price."

"The question to be settled between us," Foye said, "is what I will agree to pay you to put Miss Godard into my custody."

The pasha's smile sent a thread of ice straight to his heart. "There is the matter of the sultan as well."

"The sultan?"

Nazim Pasha leaned back, stretching an arm along the top of the divan. "He would be pleased, I think, if I sent her to him. A gift to demonstrate my great esteem for him."

Foye stared into his coffee until he was certain his face would not give away his emotions. Everything depended upon him remaining calm. "I assure you, the British government would not look kindly upon such an action."

"And yet, I am moved to do so." He held out one hand, palm up. "I spoke of customs. This is a custom among us. Not at all an uncommon transaction, Marquis. I am free to make a gift of any woman in my harem. Or to sell any concubine I wish."

"Of course, but Miss Godard is not in your harem. She is a British citizen."

"A small detail, Marquis." Nazim Pasha slowly stroked his beard. "It means nothing to me and is, in any case, easily remedied."

But Foye had learned at least something of the art of bargaining from watching Sabine. "If not five horses, then perhaps a hundred pounds?"

"A hundred pounds?" The pasha laughed, hands on his belly. "You insult me. A hundred pounds. Five thousand pounds sterling would be a pittance for what you ask me to give up. A woman such as her?"

"It's wartime, Pasha. I doubt very much I could get my hands on any significant amount of specie. I might be able to manage two hundred pounds."

"I have many expenses, Marquis, and you are a nobleman in your own country. Can five thousand be beyond your ability to gather?"

Their negotiations carried on for the next hour, punctuated by coffee and the nearly constant use of the narghile. Eventually, they settled on the sum of nine hundred fifty pounds. A ruinous sum Foye agreed to deliver in specie and any other combination of coin or gems that Foye could amass in Aleppo or Constantinople.

He returned to his room before eleven that night, having politely declined the company of one of the pasha's dancing girls. He spent an hour with Barton and Nabil relating a less than complete version of his bargain and what he intended to do about it. At this point, Foye did not trust anyone. He barely trusted Barton, and he was an Englishman. When he'd sent them away, each with his own set of instructions to follow, all he could do was wait for them to be carried out and count the minutes ticking away.

When Nabil returned, Foye gathered what he needed and left his room.

In the courtyard that shared a wall with the wing in which he'd learned the Godards had been housed, Foye stood motionless, a light but bulging satchel slung across his body as he listened for sounds that indicated he should continue to wait. He listened to the noises of the palace. Distant conversation. The sound of night birds. The faint scent of smoke in the air. Nothing out of place or unsettling. Well, then. It was time to act.

He adjusted the satchel so that the bag hung from his back. With his height and strength, he had no difficulty pulling himself up and through an open window. He'd

been prepared to break one open if need be, but that proved
unnecessary. His heart nearly hammered out of his chest
at the noise from him opening the window wide enough to
admit him. He pushed through and landed hard.

Foye crouched until he was certain the guards Nabil
had warned him of had heard nothing. From his satchel, he
removed a small lamp and the implements required to light
it. In the ensuing faint light, he could see the Godards'
trunks stacked in the center of the room awaiting removal
to Aleppo in a few short hours. That, at least, was not something the pasha had seen fit to prevent.

At the interior door that connected Sir Henry's room to
Sabine's, he paused and steeled himself against the thud
of his pulse. Beyond a preference that he not die, he didn't
care so much for his fate. If this was the night when the
Marrack line came to an end, it would at least end in an
honorable cause. But it wouldn't be only his life that ended.
Any mistake or misfortune now would consign Sabine to
whatever fate the pasha had in mind for her. Nothing very
pleasant, he was sure, whether it was confinement to Nazim
Pasha's harem or the Seraglio in Constantinople.

If he was overheard, and provided he wasn't shot dead
soon after, he wasn't sure if he could subdue both the guards
on her door. On a purely physical level, yes, he didn't doubt
he could eliminate the men if it came to that. Whether he
could do so without rousing more of the pasha's men was a
question he preferred he not be forced to answer. The fact
was, he was prepared to die or commit murder on Sabine's
behalf. In either case, he would stand at the gates of heaven
sure that he had done what honor required.

He kept the lamp shielded behind his hand and opened
the door to Sabine's room. The native custom was to sleep
on mattresses laid on the floor at night and put away during
the day. Thus, he could make out Sabine's sleeping form
at the far side of the room. Her mattress had been laid out
next to the carved cabinets that held the bedding during the
day. He moved as silently as he could through the darkened
room. Thick rugs covered the marble floor and muffled

the sound of his shoes. A few feet from the mattress, he stopped. She slept soundly, unaware of his presence in her private chamber.

The quilt that covered her was a thin, striped gold silk. One bare foot poked out, as did one of her slender, pale arms. He felt like some vile seducer who, having obtained the key to an innocent's bedchamber, had now crept in to have his wicked way with her person. He was aware that awakening her was likely to frighten her, and he could not afford to have her make any noise that would inadvertently alert the guards.

In her sleep, she turned over so that she ended up facing him, a slender, feminine shape under the covering quilt. One hand disappeared under her covers. In the flickering light of his lamp, her golden hair gleamed softly.

She looked so very young and innocent.

And here he was, in a way, as intent on her seduction as the pasha himself.

Sixteen

❧

Three fifteen in the morning. The palace of Nazim Pasha in Kilis, Turkey. A chamber in which Sabine Godard had so far contrived to stay since her uncle's death. She had in fact not left the room since her uncle died. She was aware there were now armed guards at her door. She was also aware that strangulation was the preferred method of disposing of inconvenient women, and was therefore relatively confident the men were not there to murder her at some agreeable moment in time.

SABINE LAY ON HER MATTRESS UNABLE TO SLEEP. HER body and heart were heavy with grief and disbelief. She hadn't slept much since before Godard had died, and when she had managed to close her eyes, she kept waking up in tears or in the grip of fear. Twice now, she'd tried to leave the palace, but each time her instructions were countermanded or simply never carried out. Nazim Pasha had a charming, infuriating habit of agreeing that she must return home, and yet nothing ever happened. His promises were always for a tomorrow that never came.

She'd known for days that Foye had been right. Nazim Pasha's interest in her was indeed personal. Sexual in nature. From the very beginning of their arrival in Kilis, overtures had been made and carefully misunderstood. The pasha wished to be—intended to be?—intimate with her. The thought of him touching her like that turned her cold and hollow.

She could not help but consider the fate of Aimée du Buc de Rivéry, Empress Josephine's cousin who was rumored to have ended up in the Seraglio sometime after 1788 when the ship she was sailing on was attacked by pirates. That Sabine might share such a destination could not be discounted. The pasha himself had a harem. She'd passed by the cloistered quarters several times, and once, just once, in the first days of her stay at the palace in Kilis, she had been given a tour of the women's quarters.

They lived quite well, if one did not mind that these women's lives were confined to this single area of the palace. The pasha's wives had a freer existence, but his concubines were not so lucky. She was sorely afraid she would end up in the harem.

In the middle of these myriad thoughts, typically unpleasant for her of late, she heard the door between her room and Godard's creak. But that room was empty of life now. The door had been firmly closed for days. Sabine lay motionless, convinced, hoping, praying that her thoughts about the Empress Josephine's cousin had led her to hear things, to mistake the sound of a servant outside her door for the sound of an intruder in her room.

Someone was here. The soft pad of footsteps on the carpet wasn't her imagination. Nor was the flicker of light from a lamp. Terror slid like ice down Sabine's spine. This could not be happening. Surely not. Not to her. And yet, someone was in her room. Creeping from the interior door toward her bed. She had a fascinating and paradoxical desire to cover her head with her blanket in the hope that whoever it was would realize he'd made a mistake and leave her alone, a bit shaken, but none the worse for her fright.

Sabine willed herself not to move or change her breathing while she processed what she was hearing. The choice of doing nothing, which still exerted considerable pull over her, was unthinkable and illogical.

Whoever was in the room was being very quiet. Stealthy. She forced her limbs to relax as she turned to face the door and slide a hand beneath her covers. She palmed the pistol she kept with her at all times since shortly after Godard had died. She clenched her hand around the butt of the weapon and prayed she would not shake when the time came to pull the trigger. No one, not even the pasha himself, would take her anywhere without first learning that she was going to fight for herself.

The intruder stopped walking. She peeked from beneath her lashes. If she was going to shoot a man, she intended to get a look at him first. He was large. Far too tall and too slender to be Nazim Pasha.

Had he sent someone to strangle her after all?

Underneath the covers, her fingers searched for and found the safety on her little pistol. My God, the man was a giant; at least as tall as Foye. With her heart pounding and with her trying to maintain an even breathing that simulated sleep, she registered the impossible fact that, from what she could see, her interloper was wearing English clothes.

Foye was not here. There was no reason on earth to think he would be. They had parted quite finally in Büyükdere. By now, he must be hundreds of miles away in Palmyra or Damascus or even further south, if not, in fact, entirely gone from the continent. He might already be on his way to England, to the lovely city of St. Ives.

She steeled herself against the fear ripping through her. There was no ignoring the terror, but she would not meekly accept whatever the pasha intended for her. She turned onto her back, heart racing, and brought up her pistol. She pointed the weapon at the man's heart when he knelt at her bed. "Get away," she said in Arabic. "Or I will shoot you like a dog."

In the darkness, she could see her attacker was an Englishman.

Before she could react, she was pinned to the mattress by a large and heavy male body. English clothes or not, he squeezed her wrist in a painful grip that prevented her from firing the gun. In the same motion, he covered her mouth with his bare palm.

He held her completely immobile. There was nothing she could do to combat the truth that she did not have the physical strength to free herself. His lower body lay on top of her, heavy and immovable. Panic tore through her again, and she exploded against the restraint. She squeezed her fingers around her pistol. If she got the chance, so help her, she would shoot him dead before she let him touch her.

He put his mouth by her ear and whispered in a low, desperate voice, "Sabine. It's Foye." English. He was speaking English to her. He tightened his grip on her. "Be still or all is lost."

She went quiet even though it occurred to her she might be dreaming. Maybe none of this was happening. Foye, or whoever he was, did not remove his hand from her mouth nor ease the weight of his body pinning her to the bedding. Each lungful of air she sucked in brought her in closer contact with his torso. He raised up enough that she could see his face in the light of his tiny lamp.

Without releasing his hold on her, he leaned over her enough for her to confirm that it was, indeed, Foye. Her breath caught in her lungs. She recognized the uneven features, the hooked nose and his light eyes. She didn't understand how or why he was here, but he was. Emotion choked her. She wanted to cry with relief, but she couldn't even do that much.

In the same low, low voice as before, Foye said, "Nod your head if you understand I am Foye and not here to do you harm." She nodded, and slowly, he removed his hand from her mouth, ready to stop a cry if he'd misjudged her or the situation. "I presume," he said in the same whisper, "that you no longer intend to shoot me."

When she shook her head, her lips brushed his palm. He lifted his hand from her mouth.

"Nor that you are averse to leaving this place."

"I am not," she murmured back. Foye's eyes were fixed on her, looking into her. He seemed unaware that he remained lying across her, his body trapping her against the mattress. Despite everything, from the moment she'd recognized Foye, her panic eased.

"Excellent."

"Is it really you?" she whispered. "Foye?"

"Yes." He lay a finger cross his lips. He torqued his upper body to reach for something that he dropped beside them. A battered satchel. He did not release her wrist from his viselike grip until he'd reached in and taken her pistol. He set the trigger lock and slipped the gun into his coat pocket. From the satchel, he brought out a bundle of something, clothing, she thought. He continued in a voice so low she had to strain to hear him. "Put these on."

She took a breath and pulled aside the covers. Her body felt too light, and her heart fluttered in her chest, a sparrow trying to find a way out. Her thick cotton shift, quite English in its hideousness, hid her from the top of her throat to all but an inch or two above her ankles. She was quite safe from him seeing much that was indiscreet. Foye watched her as she unrolled what proved to be clothes and a pair of shoes. She separated the various pieces.

"Men's clothes?" She, too, spoke in a low voice.

"You must pass for a native boy." He stayed close, his mouth near her ear. "For the illusion to succeed, wear nothing but these clothes. Nothing occidental. Nothing womanly. These clothes and nothing else, clear?" He pressed her elbow. His fingers were warm through the fabric of her nightdress. "Make haste, Sabine. There is little time to spare."

She looked at the unfamiliar clothing. She'd seen any number of men dressed in such a costume, but that did not mean she knew how to don one herself. She could only guess the order in which they went on.

If she was to leave the palace as a boy, her costume must be precisely right. For that, she would need Foye's assistance. Her body hollowed out, but she nodded curtly and like him, stood.

"The *shirwal* first." He picked up the baggy trousers, demonstrated how she must step into them, then handed them to her. Foye's tiny lamp did not cast enough light for her to put on clothes with which she was so unfamiliar. What's more, she knew from his miserable expression he had already anticipated the difficulty. "I'm sorry," he said with such abject wretchedness that she felt, if not better, then at least less awkward.

So be it. She hiked up her nightdress high enough to step into the *shirwal*.

Foye turned his head while she pulled up the trousers, but he had to fasten them for her while she held her night-dress above her waist. His fingers brushed her bare skin in incidental touches she suspected were more awkward for him than for her. When the trousers were managed, he fumbled around on the bed a bit before he selected a long, narrow length of fabric. He hesitated, staring at the cloth in his hands.

She grabbed his wrist until he looked into her face. "We do what we must," she told him, squeezing her fingers around him for emphasis. "There can be no modesty now."

Foye nodded. She did not think she was mistaken about his relief.

With some fumbling, they got the fabric in place enough that she could hold it over her chest while Foye removed her nightdress in a swift, efficient motion. Despite that she was not tall, she did not have a boy's figure. She understood, as Foye had anticipated, that her bosom, if left free beneath clothes intended for a man, would give the lie to her supposed gender. Foye grabbed the ends of the strip and tightly wrapped the length of silk twice around her in an improvised corset of sorts. She could hardly breathe after he tied a knot in the back and stepped away.

Relieved, she supposed, that the need to touch her was over with. As was she.

He reached into the satchel and took out a clay jar about the size of his hand. She frowned and forgot that she was indecently covered when he opened the jar. A pungent smell filled the room.

"Closer," he said, gesturing. She did so, and he slathered some of the contents of the jar on her bare shoulder. "A walnut extract," he explained, "to darken your skin." Indeed. If she was to pass as a native boy, best she not be English pale. Between the two of them, they covered her upper body and arms with the lotion. The intimacy of him touching her naked skin hardly felt intimate at all. Instead, she worried that in the dimness of her room they would miss some crucial spot. They covered her face and throat last. Sabine applied the ointment using both her hands, and when she thought she was done, she lifted her face to his so he could examine her for spots she'd missed.

Foye picked up the lamp, taking care to keep his body between the light and the door, and slowly examined her. His perusal was thorough. He used the side of his thumb to even out the application on her cheek and underside of her jaw.

"Thank God you've got brown eyes," he said. "Otherwise this would be doomed to failure."

She rubbed a place on her cheek that still felt damp, then waved her arms to make sure the lotion was sufficiently dry on her skin.

Foye snatched a shirt from what was left of the bundle on her mattress. She glanced up while he positioned the garment over her head and confirmed her arms were correctly placed for the sleeves. He brought the shirt down, she thrust her arms through the sleeves, and he continued the downward motion. She was covered now.

The worst was over.

"When we get outside," he said, "do not touch anything. Most especially, don't rub your face."

She nodded. When she had her arms free to finish adjusting the shirt, he picked up an outer shirt of a light-weight fabric with narrow vertical stripes. They were in the process of getting it settled on her when a loud bang from outside her door startled them both.

Seventeen

❧

THEY FROZE, FOYE WITH HIS HANDS ON THE TOP PORTION of the striped overgarment where her breasts would have been obvious were she not tightly bound, her with her hands pulling the garment down from hip level. From outside her door came the sound of a violent argument in Arabic, muffled so Sabine could not immediately decipher what they were saying.

"Bugger," Foye whispered. His hands gripped the fabric as they waited, not even breathing, either of them, while the shouting continued.

Cheating.

Sabine leaned her head against Foye's chest. They were arguing about cheating. Foye, of course, did not know that.

"It's nothing to do with me," she whispered. She touched Foye's arm even though what she wanted to do was throw her arms around him and hug him to her. She did not, of course. Her pulse slowed from a gallop to a trot. "One of the guards has accused the other of cheating at dice."

Foye let out a breath, the only sign that he had been affected by the fright that had paralyzed her. Presently, the argument died away and the palace fell back into silence. He retrieved another item from her mattress, a cloth sash to be wound several times around her waist.

"Here," he said when the ends of the sash were secured. He took her pistol from his pocket and slipped it between the folds of the sash. "Next time, don't hesitate to pull the trigger."

"I won't," she said.

"Shoot anyone who gets even half that close to you," Foye said.

She nodded. Over the outer garment and sash came a waist-length embroidered coat with sleeves that ended at the elbow. This, she knew, was left open. For her feet were a pair of red slippers to be worn inside a pair of sturdy boots. The boots were a very close fit, but she could walk in them and that was all that mattered. Last was a brown traveling cloak.

Foye produced a knife from his satchel. "Can you pin your hair or must we cut it?"

There was no time for her to fumble in the dark for pins let alone fasten it securely enough. Nor could they risk her hair coming loose during whatever period of time she must spend dressed as a boy.

She turned her back to him. To her shame, her throat closed off at the thought of losing her hair. Her hair was one of her few vanities. It hung nearly to her waist in thick golden curls, and every night, she counted out one hundred strokes of her brush. By the time she retired, every strand was soft as silk. "Cut it," she said.

Foye gripped her braid, and she winced even though he wasn't hurting her. He cut in several passes, all very close to her neck. She felt the pull of his hand on her braid, the blade sawing through, and then, nothing. Weightlessness.

He dropped the severed plait, but she stooped and handed it back to him. Better no one knew for certain that she now had short hair.

"Burn it later or some such thing," she said.

"Good man," Foye said. He smiled when he said it, but even though Sabine knew he meant to ease the insult of what he had done to her, the loss of her hair nearly undid her. The direness of her situation came home in force. All she really wanted to do was climb back into bed and go to sleep in the hope that this entire episode turned out to be a misunderstanding. Nazim Pasha did not intend to establish her in his harem; the delays in arranging for her return to the consulate in Aleppo were due to his concern for her health.

No matter how badly she wanted that to be the truth, it wasn't. She knew that in her heart. Sabine clamped down on her emotions. Better to be bald than trapped here. Her hair would grow back.

Foye held out the jar again, and she rubbed ointment through her hair until he was satisfied with the result. The guards outside cursed at each other again, in shouts that increased in heat until a sudden silence. Her heart pounded again. This was taking too long. They would be discovered, surely they would.

When she was done with her hair, she rubbed her hands together to even out the ointment left on them then scrubbed her hands through what was left of her hair to get it as dry as possible. There wasn't time to wait. Foye laid a thick, dark scarf across her damp hair that fell down to her shoulders and secured that with a knotted head rope. He stuffed her shift into his satchel. They both knelt to attempt to shape the bedding so anyone who did not look closely might believe she was there.

Foye coiled her braid into his satchel, too, then sheathed his knife and shoved that into one of the outer folds of her sash.

"Tolerable," he said, looking her up and down. "Keep your head down. You are to go by the name Pathros. You

are a Christian of Syrian descent and my dragoman. I
brought you with me from Aleppo. We are infidels, you
and I. You are my servant, so for God's sake, defer to me in
everything. Do not question anything I tell you."

"I understand."

"You have consequence among the other servants on
account of your working directly for me," he said, "but
never forget you are in my employ. Do as I say when I say
and ask no questions. Defer to me in all things. Our lives
depend upon you remembering that. Is that clear?"

"Very."

He stooped for his lamp. They walked through the
adjoining room to her uncle's apartment. Nothing remained
to prove Godard had ever been here but his trunks stacked
by the door. Sabine Godard no longer existed, she told herself. She was Pathros, the English lord's interpreter. Her
unfamiliar clothes, she found, assisted in her attempt to
leave Sabine Godard behind and become young Pathros.

Foye did not head for the door but for the opposite side
of the room, along the wall where the high, narrow windows looked onto the courtyard. She followed to within a
few feet of him. He reached up, so tall that he easily hooked
a finger in one of the window frames and opened it wide.
His point of ingress, and, she presumed, their egress. He
turned to her and said, "Is Anthony Lucey right about your
Arabic?" His gaze scoured her without any of the warmth
she was so used to seeing. The sight made her wonder if
she knew him at all. "Have you really no accent?"

"Very near," she replied. "I've improved since we came
north."

The way he looked at her so intently, the crisp tone of
voice, the tension in his body was new to her. He was not
giving orders as Godard had so often done, but neither
was there any doubt he was in command of this situation
and expected her to fall in. She had no intention of disap-
pointing that expectation just now. But she could not shake
the feeling that she was seeing a different Foye, a man she
didn't know and hadn't suspected existed.

"If we are stopped," he said, "say nothing." He took a step forward and grabbed her upper arms but immediately let her go. "If you do speak, do so in English. Not French. Do not let on you understand that language."

"That seems a wise precaution." She rubbed her arms. Her skin tingled from his touch. He had not held her tightly, but neither had his touch been gentle. "The pasha is not the only one here to speak French," she said. "There are others."

"If something important comes up in some language I do not speak, please, do translate," he said. In the dimness, she saw him smile, and that comforted her, to see something familiar about him when everything else was so unfamiliar. "I should hate to miss something crucial because you followed my directions too literally."

"I'm not a fool," she said. "You may trust my judgment in the matter of when I ought to translate."

"No doubt," he said. "But best if I make myself clear given a misunderstanding between us might be fatal."

"You are, of course, quite correct." She plucked at her overcoat with brown hands that startled her. A rather pretty brown, she thought. "You are right to be cautious." Her skin was not terribly dark, but she could—would, she hoped—pass for a youth who'd spent his life in the sun. Her clothes were a very good fit, but she felt awkward in them. Not herself. Unwomanly. Her bound bosom required that she breathe from the bottom of her lungs if she wanted to get enough air, and that was an adjustment to make. "If I do speak, I shall endeavor to limit myself to only a phrase or two."

"Good." Foye doused the lamp and stowed it in a cabinet. She waited for her eyes to adjust to the darkness. He'd planned this well and thoroughly. She was impressed. And relieved and grateful and any number of emotions she could not at present properly parse out. But then, she would never have expected less from Foye than this precise attention to detail.

He returned to her, his satchel slung across his body, and gestured. She approached. In the dark, he boosted her up, easily and without effort until she perched on the window ledge. Her stomach hollowed out when she looked out. How far away the ground seemed.

"Sabine?"

She twisted to look at him. "Pathros, my lord."

"Jump," he said. "It's not far. I'll be right behind you."

Not far. Perhaps not for someone his size. Sabine swung her legs over the ledge. Her stomach took flight.

"Sabine," Foye said, his voice low and urgent.

She held her breath and pushed off the window ledge into the air. The drop was far enough to make her legs feel like water. And mercifully short. She landed on her feet but not on balance. A lemon tree broke her sideways lurch. Fortunately, the branches did not scratch her badly, but her sleeve was caught in the broken twigs. By the time Foye landed on the ground next to her, she'd freed her clothes from the snags.

A perfectly balanced landing. He hauled himself up and pulled the window closed as best he could. When he faced her again, he handed her his satchel, and she slung it across her shoulders to rest on her left hip. Naturally, Lord Foye would not carry his own things, and she was no longer Sabine Godard, but Pathros, the Marquess of Foye's dragoman.

They crossed the courtyard to walk openly through darkened corridors until they reached the wing in the palace where servants hurried back and forth. They'd not taken but ten steps before Foye grabbed her elbow and hauled her back to him. She lifted her head as he bent down to whisper violently into her ear, "For pity's sake, Sabine, walk as if you have bollocks between your legs."

Her cheeks burned hot. How on earth did one do that?

"Let's not be discovered because someone notices that my dragoman walks like a woman."

"I shall do my best," she said.

He kept his grip on her elbow, and she saw a new fear in his eyes. What now? What new deficiency was there? "I presume you can ride?" he asked.

She took a breath, offended. How did he think she'd traveled through Egypt and Anatolia? She hadn't walked, and she certainly hadn't been carried. "Of course I can ride."

"Astride," he said. "You must ride astride, as a man would."

She bowed her head respectfully as a servant passed by. One of Nazim Pasha's men, she thought. The servant glanced at Foye as he passed, but that was all. If he noticed her, it was to recognize that she was of no importance. *"A'yan,"* she said. When the servant was past them, she said, "I can ride, my lord."

"Astride?"

"Astride," she said. Because she must. There was no alternative.

At last, Foye released her arm. She resisted the urge to rub the spot he'd gripped. Her skin tingled at the contact. They continued along the corridor with Sabine following. He walked quickly, with that sense of barely leashed physicality that had so struck her about him from the first. He kept walking, she following, taking two steps to every one of his, until they reached the main palace courtyard.

Pack animals, horses, and at least thirty armed men crowed one side of the flagstone courtyard. She recognized some of Nazim Pasha's staff among the men. A high, arched gateway led outside. To freedom. Would they ever ride through that gate, she wondered?

They hadn't been there long before she saw another Englishman supervising two native men carrying one of Godard's trunks between them. Asif was here, too, tall and somber, working with the others to prepare for Foye's departure.

The noise was considerable. No one bothered her, and yet with every minute that passed, she expected someone to point her out as an imposter. The servants were busy with their own affairs; packing trunks onto one of the braying mules; bringing out another of Godard's trunks; arguing; dealing with recalcitrant pack animals. She could see none of her trunks. Of course not. Everything she had brought with her to Kilis was going to be lost: her clothes, her slippers, stockings, books, her personal notes on their travels, and every sketch of Foye she'd attempted and abandoned since leaving Büyükdere. How odd that she would most regret those sketches of everything she was leaving behind.

Even when she and Foye walked into the thick of it, no one looked askance at her. In the hubbub around her, she was invisible. They saw what they expected to see: the English nobleman Foye with a native boy at his side.

The sky was still dark, but that would not last much longer. Already the stars were fading, and to the east, there was a faint graying glow at the horizon. She did not wish to be here when the sun was high enough for anyone to get a close look at her, and she believed herself correct in thinking Foye did not feel any differently.

He led her to a side of the courtyard where there were shadows aplenty. There, she saw the other Englishman again, holding the heads of two Arabians, a dark stallion and a lighter-colored mare. Foye's servant, obviously.

The mare was saddled in the native style, with a high-backed saddle and short stirrups. Saddlebags hung off the sides, and there was a rolled-up rug fastened behind the saddle. The sound of the hooves on the cobbles told Sabine the two animals were also shod in the native manner, with a plate that covered the whole underside of the hoof. The stallion's saddle was English. Foye's horse.

Ten Janissaries detached themselves from the main group and joined Foye as he headed in their direction. The Janissaries were already mounted, weapons stuck in the sashes around their waists, long-muzzled muskets slung across their backs. Several wore swords and knives, and three or four carried pikes.

With an unpleasant start, Sabine saw the pasha's

white-bearded servant keeping a close eye on Foye. He
stood at the edge of the courtyard, near the inner palace,
arms crossed over his chest. She put her back to the man
and ended up facing Foye's servant. Had Foye told him
what he planned? Did he know who she was? She saw no
sign of that. The stallion he held tossed its head, and the
servant leaned in to whisper to the animal, stroking the
animal's nose.

"Are we ready, Barton?" Foye said to his servant.

"Aye, milord."

Foye put a hand to the stallion whose head Barton held,
preparing to mount. His body moved with a grace that
made her breath hitch as he mounted effortlessly. Why had
she ever thought he was an ungainly man? He wasn't. Not
in any respect. The mare Barton also held sidestepped,
hooves ringing out on the stone courtyard.

While she waited for someone—Foye, anyone—to tell
her what was expected of her, a young man came forward
to address Foye in tolerable if heavily accented English.
"My lord, am I not to accompany you?" He saw Sabine,
in her guise as Pathros, of course, and his eyes widened in
what looked very much like injured pride.

Foye leaned down, one hand on the pommel of his
saddle. He looked at the young man and said, very pleas-
antly, "Nabil, you're to accompany Barton. He will be in
need of your services."

Nabil scowled. "My lord—"

Sabine understood his displeasure. Being shifted to
interpret for a servant was a demotion, a loss of status that
must sting. Asif stepped between Foye and Nabil, and facing Nabil with a hand to the other man's chest, said, in
Arabic, "Do as your master bids or you will be left behind."
He straightened his arm, pushing the boy away. "Go. Go!"

She knew she didn't imagine Foye relaxed when Nabil
did as he was told. Or that Asif had recognized her. She
held her breath, but Asif merely bowed to Foye and calmly
reached for the reins of her mare. Barton did not mind in
the least.

"Pathros," Foye said, declining to call her by the anglicized version of the name, "Peter." He raised his voice and looked back at the Janissaries. "Let us go now."

Asif reached back and brought around the mare. She could ride. Of course she could. But on her own English sidesaddle onto which she was always assisted. Never on an unfamiliar horse with a wholly unfamiliar style of saddle. She hesitated and her chest contracted. She understood the mechanics of how one mounted astride, but she'd never done so on her own. She was going to fail her first test.

"Pathros," Foye said, "Nazim Pasha's servant is headed this way. Mount up. Now." He sat his horse, face mostly in shadows that emphasized the sharp angles of his cheekbones. Everything depended upon her. Anything she did that led to their being discovered would result in Foye's death. Nazim Pasha would not willingly let her go, and Foye would not let her be retaken.

Heart in her throat, she walked to the mare, and, thank God, Asif was large enough to block her from view because she was not at all adept at mounting this way. He grabbed her arm as she emulated what Foye had done so effortlessly. She gave an ungainly hop, and her mare skittered sideways. Asif's hand tightened on her arm. Her pulled the mare back and kept her body in a forward tip as he boosted her upward.

She was on. Astride the mare and accepting the reins with heat flashing into her cheeks because the sensation was so utterly, horribly improper and unfamiliar. She discovered, too, that the manner of controlling her horse was a subtly different thing. She understood at once how it must be accomplished, with the use of her thighs and shifts in her weight, the pressure of hands on the reins at a different angle than she was accustomed to, but that insight did not transfer to muscles that had never been so tasked.

Her breath caught in her chest. This couldn't work. She would be recognized by her awkwardness if nothing else. Her eyes met Foye's, and he gave her a curt nod. Sabine's heart lurched. They were all of them, every soul in the courtyard, in danger because of her. If she were missed or recognized, they might all be killed.

Barton had already moved away to the portion of the courtyard where pack mules continued to be laden with her uncle's possessions. Asif rested a hand on her mare's neck and said, in Turkish, "Allah be with you," before he strode away.

The mass of activity and shouting increased. Someone dropped one of the trunks, and the uproar was deafening as everyone in the vicinity began shouting and cursing. In the middle of this chaos, Foye gave the ready sign and their party was off. Sabine froze momentarily and watched Foye's retreating back. The Janissaries started off, riding so quickly that Foye was soon hidden from sight. Barton, Asif, and Nabil would follow later. She inhaled as deeply as she could and urged her mare forward, toward the gate and freedom.

They headed out the arched gateway under the piercing eye of Nazim Pasha's majordomo. Sabine's heart hammered against her ribs as she adjusted to riding astride. She was so distracted by the experience she could think of nothing else until they'd passed through the high, arched gate and onto the road that led to Kilis. The commotion in the palace courtyard receded. Above her head stars shone in a still dark sky. The moon hung low in the horizon. That she could even see the sky seemed a miracle. And one she hoped would continue.

Foye set a brutal pace south, around Kilis to the road to Aleppo all while the sun was still rising. When Kilis was behind them, too, Foye signaled for her to join him.

"Pathros," Foye said, speaking just loudly enough to be heard over the noise of the other riders, "before much longer the pasha will discover you're gone, if he hasn't already."

"Understood."

"With luck, Barton will delay them coming after us,

but it's inevitable that we shall be pursued." She nodded. Nazim Pasha would not be pleased to learn she'd escaped. "If for some reason we must separate, I want you and as many of these men"—he gestured at the mercenaries riding with them—"as you can take with you to head for Iskenderun. Inform the captain of our Janissaries, if you will. Tell them you have a vital letter that must be delivered to Iskenderun. Clear?"

"Yes, Foye."

He frowned. "Even in English, to you I am my lord or Lord Foye, understood?"

She nodded. There were too many ways she could reveal herself. Too many.

"When you reach Iskenderun, ask for Mr. Hugh Eglender at the British Consulate. He's a personal friend of mine and will assist you in private, if need be. If he's not there, then find him at home, *Bayt Salem*, in the hills above Iskenderun. Tell him everything that's happened. Leave nothing out."

"My lord."

Foye leaned toward her, adjusting effortlessly in his saddle. "Take this." He folded the fingers of her extended hand over a small purse he drew from his pocket. "There's enough in there to purchase your passage to England if it comes to that. Not just money, but gemstones. Eglender will assist you in that as well."

"My lord." She took the purse and tucked it into her sash. With a bow of her head, she rode to the Druze captain of Foye's hired soldiers. Her first official task as Pathros. She relayed the relevant parts of what Foye had told her. The captain listened attentively, nodding when she'd finished, seeing not a woman disguised as a boy, but Pathros, the infidel dragoman employed by Lord Foye.

How strange it was to be Sabine Godard no longer. What sort of person would Pathros be during this journey? What behavior was most likely to keep the others from looking past the surface? Not craven, she decided. Pathros would

be as much like Foye as was possible. Outwardly calm.
Dependable. Aloof from her countrymen, an attitude easily
explained by their different religions. Brave. Decisive.

What other qualities did Foye possess that she had not
yet guessed?

She was quite certain she would learn the answers in the
hours and days to come.

Eighteen

FOR THE FIRST HOUR ON THE ROAD, SABINE WAS TOO nervous about the possibility of capture by Nazim Pasha to think about much but staying on her horse and keeping up. They all trusted their horses to find the way in the predawn dark, but it was Foye, riding at the point, upon whom everything depended. He rode at the head of their party, standing out on account of his size and his English clothing. No one protested that he set a pace that would have ruined English-bred animals.

When Sabine had made the Aleppo-to-Kilis trip, she had been with Godard and traveling with Nazim Pasha's entourage. They had taken two days to cover a distance Foye intended for them to complete in a day. At this pace, the thirty-five miles between Kilis and Aleppo meant a long, hard ride that would continue well into the afternoon.

As dark turned to morning with no sign of pursuit from Kilis, she relaxed enough to start analyzing her situation.

While she understood and wholeheartedly agreed with
Foye's decision to disguise her as a boy—a brilliant ruse,
she thought—she was profoundly unsettled by everything
to do with it. The experience made her a foreigner in her
own body; riding astride, the way her clothes fit, and perhaps most of all, the way others reacted to her.

As Sabine Godard, she had sometimes been dismissed
as inconsequential or uninteresting, but she had never
been invisible as she was now. Men, particularly young
men, always noticed her. They bowed to her and opened
doors and generally behaved as if she were fragile and in
need of protection. There were times at some gathering of
Godard's when her choice of action was to remain silent
or leave; she knew there were times when her opinions
were not welcome, whether she was expert in the subject at
hand or not. Those same men who expected silence or her
absence would hold a chair for her, and if she were to stand
whilst they were seated, they stood, too.

As it was now, she was being shaped inside and out by
the sort of person she was and by the expectations of those
around her. It made no difference that she was not used
to riding at the pace Foye set. Everyone, including Foye,
expected her to keep up and gave no thought at all the possibility that she could not. Indeed, there was no reason for
any of them to believe she could not.

The differences between being Sabine Godard and being
Pathros were fascinating. Being one who served rather than
one who was served was not so very different from her relationship with Godard. She must pay attention to Foye much
as she had to Godard, though without the benefit of years of
a lifetime's acquaintance. She could do this.

When did Foye need her near? What actions on her part
were to be expected as a matter of course? A dragoman
often provided more than translation, and in this case, she
was, so she surmised, something in the nature of a replace-
ment for Barton. Therefore, she must not only translate for
him but foresee his personal needs, carry his bags, see to
his clothes and hygiene as well.

She must do all this while, as Foye had so indelicately phrased it, she walked and rode as if she possessed bollocks. There was a whole series of hierarchies among the men of which she had not previously been so aware as she was now. Not only the hierarchy of class as one saw, for example, in the precedence of the English drawing room or the Turk's divan, but of servant and served, and most fascinating of all, a hierarchy of maleness that at times crossed the lines of class.

Full morning arrived with no one having asked how she was or having called a halt because she had wiped her brow or said that she was thirsty, which in any event she did not dare do. She stayed near Foye when she could, watching him when she was not fully engaged with the challenge of the road.

Conversation, when there was any, was either between men who spoke a dialect she did not, or in Arabic that often included the use of words and phrases she soon understood to be crude in nature. This was a very different use of the language than she was familiar with. Less formal. Less elegant. Very much to the raw point. The verbal equivalent, she thought, of walking as if one possessed bollocks. She tucked away her new words and phrases for future reference.

As the morning wore on, the sensation of trousers and robes instead of a riding habit and parasol began slowly to seem less absurd to her, and through a process of observation of the other riders and frank experience she learned the different carriage required of her when sitting astride. She became Pathros. A native youth who had been riding astride all his life. With bollocks between his legs and a vocabulary to match. Morning transformed to the full heat of summer. The silk wrapped around her bosom was tight and damp with perspiration, but thank God, Foye had thought of it, because riding without any restrictive garment beneath her clothes would have been disastrous. She could, bound as she was, almost forget the existence of her bosom.

As they left the foothills of the Taurus Mountains, the terrain flattened out. Vineyards and olive orchards, with their distinctive gray-green-leaved trees, predominated the vegetation. Everywhere she looked the colors were pale green interspersed with reddish soil and outcroppings of steel gray rock. The sun beat down, baking the land and sapping her of energy. Her throat was dry, and before long, she'd done as Foye and the others did, which was to wrap a length of cloth around the lower part of her face to avoid breathing and swallowing the dust kicked up by the horses.

Whenever she looked down at the reins, she was startled to see nut brown skin. Her hands were too feminine, she thought. Soft and useless. She ought to have gloves to hide their shape. In her costume, she was no different from the other natives here, aside from her apparent youth. The others were grown men. She had no beard or mustache, no eyes that looked with a distant gaze. And yet she was one of them.

No longer was she the only woman in the company and subject to the care of men. She rode astride as they did, with the same kit, the same sort of saddlebags. The very view from her native saddle was subtly altered. She could do as she liked, spit or curse or scratch herself, and no one would think twice. So long as they did not notice her soft hands. So long as she did not give away her gender.

Sometime around ten o'clock they ate their morning meal: a handful of olives, a sharp cheese, dry bread, and a mouthful of water, all consumed while riding. No one questioned Foye's decision to press on or looked in any way out of sorts, tired, or angry.

Conversation ceased as the heat beat down. The air around them smelled of dust, sweaty horses, and men. A constant drip of moisture ran down her back and along her temples. When she thought no one was looking, she wiped at her hands and face with the sleeve of her kaftan and examined the fabric for smears of brown. No telltale smudges that she could see.

Shortly after noon, Foye called their first full halt. Half an hour, Sabine translated for him, for them to feed and water their horses and prepare a larger meal than the one they'd eaten on the move. They moved off the road to a spot where olive trees offered shade and where, at the head of a spring, someone had erected a carved stone fountain. Water poured from the mouth of a roaring lion and splashed into a fluted basin. They dismounted, each of the men looking after their horses first. Sabine stayed mounted until Foye happened to turn around to look.

"Is it best," she asked in English and in a soft voice so as to avoid being overheard, "to have all my weight on this leg?" She tapped the leg in question.

"Keep your torso forward," Foye said in a similarly low voice. "Press down with that leg and swing the other around and down. Then slide free of the stirrup. If all goes well, you will end on your feet. If not, laugh, curse if you know how in their language, and dust yourself off." He looked tired and tense. "If you fall, I cannot help you up. Further, they will expect you to assist me, Pathros, so please don't delay."

"I understand." To her surprise she did not bumble her dismount. There was no humiliating fall and no need to curse her clumsiness. Another success in establishing herself as Pathros. She stood beside her horse and fumbled to unfasten her saddlebag and kit as the others had already done. Foye and the soldiers made use of the fountain to bathe their hands and faces, which Sabine did as well when her turn came. The coloring on her skin stayed fast.

The Mohammedans among them made their prayers and set to cooking. Foye untied his rug himself after she'd secured her mare near his chocolate brown stallion, but she made a point of spreading out his rug beneath one of the olive trees. Foye had already seen to watering his horse and was now feeding the animal. He made a point of working slowly so that she would see how it was done.

She did her best not to be hopelessly fumble fingered with the gear, but the truth was, she had never had to do such things by herself. There had always been servants to help her dismount from her horse, to look after her mount, lay down a rug for her, and see that she was settled in a shady spot. Nor had she ever handled a saddlebag full of gear on her own. Her own, far lighter bag, yes. But not one filled with the various supplies of the road. So many ways for her to betray herself, she thought. So many habits of dependence ingrained.

Her next difficulty was to avoid showing her shock and discomfort when the others, having secured their horses, walked a distressingly short distance from their stopping place to relieve themselves. Foye went further away to secure his privacy. What was she to do? Stand there with her eye closed? Pathros would hardly be shocked by the sight.

She had pressing needs of her own but lacked a penis to so casually expose. Unlike the others, she required privacy. She headed for a largish sort of olive tree about twenty yards away. Farther than anyone else, including Foye, had gone for the business. On the far side of the trunk, she kept her back to the others and finished as quickly as she could.

On her return, the men had a fire going and were preparing a communal luncheon of rice with lentils, bread, and cheese. Foye had unwrapped the cloth around his face. She joined him underneath the olive tree where he'd settled himself. He sat with his back against the trunk, forearms atop of his bent knees so that his hands dangled down.

"Are you all right?" he asked without looking at her.

"Yes, thank you." She tilted her face to look at him, safe in her staring. No one would think that odd of her. The back of his head rested against the trunk, his squared-off chin pointed slightly up. His eyes were closed, and his lashes made dark shadows on his cheeks. His cheek slanted too sharply down, then straightened out only to make an ungainly angle toward the centerline of his face. The hook of his nose formed the prominent feature of his silhouette. There was nothing remotely handsome about him, and yet she felt a pang just looking at him.

"You're doing well, Pathros," he said. He moved his

head, eyes open just wide enough to show the brilliant blue of his irises. Their gazes locked. He didn't say anything, just continued to regard her instead of averting his eyes. Her stomach bottomed out, and her chest felt fluttery, lighter than air. She was relieved to learn she could still react this way to Foye. She might have stared at him forever, but one of the Janissaries called out that the meal was ready.

When she returned with the two copper bowls she'd dug from their saddlebags, she handed one to Foye and sat down with the other in her hands. She had two new curses for her repertoire as well. Her stomach rumbled.

"Pathros." Foye leaned over and pulled on her arm before she could take a bite.

She swung her head around to see his warning glance at her legs. She was sitting, by habit, as she always sat. That is, with her legs folded to one side, her knees primly together. She adjusted her position before anyone noticed what she'd done. The others sat either cross-legged or with one or two legs up and an arm thrown over the knee if they'd finished eating. She elected the cross-legged position and dedicated herself to emptying her bowl.

When they were done, she washed out the bowls and packed them away. The Janissaries were done, too, and were now making coffee from personal supplies of beans they roasted over the fire. Sabine watched, concentrating on the steps in case she should find she was expected to make coffee for Foye one day. Not that she had the accoutrements. But one never knew.

Foye grabbed the heavier of his two saddlebags, lifting it as if it weighed nothing. From it, he took out a pistol, much larger than the one already hidden in her sash. "Keep this on your person, Pathros."

Sabine took the weapon and examined it. She had, of course, never in her life handled a weapon like this one. The principle, she expected, would not be much different. "My lord," she said.

Foye leaned to her again. "No different than with your

little weapon," he said. She nodded while he showed her, his fingers so deadly deft, how to unload it and then load the pistol. "Like so." Foye handed the gun back to her. "Now you do it."

With the scent of roasting coffee beans in the air, she loaded and unloaded the gun while he watched, again and again until he was satisfied. The gun felt heavy in her hand; she would never be as dexterous as Foye. She was used to her lighter, and less effective, weapon.

Their gazes met again, and though she had looked at Foye time and again since he'd come to Büyükdere, she was aware of him in a way she hadn't been before. Despite her men's clothes, her shorn hair, and new name, she was viscerally aware that he was a man and that she was not. There was a great deal more than just kissing that could happen between them, and for the first time she actually felt that truth. For the first time, she actually felt the pos-sibility of that *more*. She saw it in his eyes.

He dug in his saddlebag again to take out a box of ammunition and hand it to her. "By the way," he said, "I buried your braid out there among the olive trees."

"Oh." She was afraid of what might happen if she looked at him again and dared only a glance at him. His mouth was twisted in an ironic grin. "I'm glad that's done."

"I sang a mournful dirge as I did."

How like him to distract her from whatever it was that had just happened between them. She returned his smile. "That was kind of you."

They were safe enough speaking English, so long as she was appropriately deferential to Foye. That wasn't difficult. He was a nobleman after all, and just now he intimidated her. The gentleness of his manners from Büyükdere had disappeared somewhere between then and now. She won-dered if he was aware that he behaved differently. He must be; he was too intelligent not to be. A line between them had been erased, and she wasn't sure where, if anywhere, a new one might be drawn. She was a boy and not a boy. His servant and not his servant. Female and not female. And when she looked at him, her stomach leaped off the end of the world.

Everything changed.

She was safe with him and not at all safe.

"You're doing well." He held her gaze again, and Sabine didn't know how to look at him anymore. She wondered what he saw when he looked at her. A brown-faced boy? A woman who did not interest him? Or one who did? Or perhaps nothing at all. She kept her head down. Did he even love her still? Had that changed with everything else?

"We will come out of this," he said. He kept his voice low, though it was unlikely anyone would overhear, and even if they did, that they would understand. "I promise you, I'll see you through this."

The intensity of his voice made her look up. "I know that."

"I'll get us back to England and we'll be married." He laughed softly. "I swore I never would. I told Lucey I was prepared to be the very last Marrack. I knew that for a lie when I said it, but I planned to marry a much older woman. Not some pretty young thing like you."

"There's time for you to change your mind," she said.

"I shan't," he replied. "I find you suit me very well now." He was sitting very informally, with one knee up and an arm dangling off his knee. His boots were covered with dust, as were hers, for that matter, and he, too, had a line of sweat running down the side of his face. The cloth he used to wrap around his lower face was loose around his neck. "Before long, you and I will be sitting in front of the fire at Maralee House remembering what an adventure we had."

"Telling our children about it," she said without thinking.

Foye didn't reply. His gaze stayed on her.

"Forgive me," she said. Her cheeks burned hot. "I spoke out of turn."

"You didn't," he said softly. "It's just, I haven't even got us married yet, and you're on to the children. We will have them. But how many?"

She drew up her knees. "Half a dozen. Three girls and three boys."

"All as pretty as you," he said.

"All as handsome as you," Sabine replied.

"Heaven forbid," he said.

"We'll have beautiful children," she said, leaning toward him so she could keep her voice low. "Every one of them."

Foye threw back his head and laughed, not even caring that everyone looked at him. If Foye wanted to laugh at something his dragoman said, he was entitled. Sabine liked the way he looked when he laughed. His eyes sparkled, and his so unlovely face became, to her, preciously lovely.

Looking at him, she understood now the reason for her earlier failures in trying to draw him. In those attempts she had not known Foye nearly well enough and so had failed to capture what he was. She had missed the decency and honor of him in favor of replicating the ways in which his face did not please the eye, all the while knowing that something had not been right. "I do want to sketch you one day," she said.

He shrugged. "You will one day."

The little privacy they'd had ended with one of the mercenaries calling her over to fetch coffee for Foye and herself. She found cups in their kit and went to the fire for their share. She thanked the Janissary in his language, but too formally, she thought. Too much as if there were that barrier of gender that had colored her use of the language when she was a woman.

She took both cups back to Foye and sat down, this time remembering to sit cross-legged. She gave Foye his and sipped her own. She welcomed the sharp flavor, the aroma drifting up, invigorating even by scent alone. She'd been awake for too many hours to count, with several more facing her before any of them would have the opportunity to sleep.

After the coffee was consumed, the fires put out, and accoutrements stowed away, they watered their horses one last time. A few of the soldiers took another turn at the fountain. Her years of traveling with Godard had given her the ability to pack, thus she was no better or worse than the others at stowing away her utensils and Foye's, but her rug refused to be rolled as tightly as everyone else managed, and when she walked to her mare, she stood there stupid with the realization that she did not know the first thing about how to attach her gear. Her heart stuttered as she looked to see how the others were managing.

Foye walked over and under cover of engaging her in conversation, readjusted her rug, showing her as he did, the proper way to affix it. He did the same with her saddlebags. She had the same maddening awareness of him as she had before. Cognizant that Foye was watching her, she remounted on her own, and they were back on the road. Now that, she thought with no small pride, was well done of her.

They continued south to Aleppo. The sun beat down with no breeze but that generated by their motion. Dirt and sand constantly blew in the air around them. Sabine found herself glad for her headdress for it kept the wickedly hot sun from burning her head and neck. Like the others, she had a long cloth wrapped around her face to keep out the dust. Foye avoided her as he had previously, keeping his stallion at the front of the party, which had the chief advantage of being out of the dust. Before long she stopped hoping he would drop back and speak with her and simply concentrated on riding. Later in the afternoon, as they had in the morning, they ate hard bread, cheese, and bits of dried fruit, and sipped stale water in the saddle.

Their second stop came an hour or two before full dark. They ate the same meal for dinner as they'd had for luncheon, followed by more of the strong, hot coffee that Foye and Sabine drank sweet as she dared make it from the small supply of sugar in her kit. They barely rested after they ate, ten minutes at most. Everyone remounted without complaint. No one spoke to her. No one assisted her. But she'd learned her lesson well. She knew how to fasten her rug and saddlebags, and she could mount on her own. They continued to ride well past treacherous dark, their horses stepping unerringly around obstacles in the uneven ground heading toward the city. They reached Aleppo shortly after nine o'clock. Sabine was at the outside edge of their procession when their party passed the Citadel of Aleppo, the great gleaming white fortress that sat on a hill in the very oldest section of the town. The castle dominated the city's landscape.

They continued into this ancient section of the city to the khans, inns used by the caravans that stopped in Aleppo on their way east or west to the port city of Iskenderun. As at Nazim Pasha's palace in Kilis, all the khans had arched entrance gates wide and tall enough to accommodate a fully burdened camel. The interior courtyard of the one Foye led them to was large enough to hold all the animals from two or more caravans. She did not yet read Arabic well enough to do more than guess at the meaning of the words inscribed over the gateway as they entered.

After dismounting, Sabine looked after her mare first but left the animal wearing both blanket and saddle as was the custom. She followed Foye inside. The others remained in the courtyard. She remembered to walk as if she weren't a woman, which wasn't difficult given the hours she'd spent riding. If she'd had bollocks she was certain they'd be as sore as her posterior. The proprietor recalled Foye from his previous stop on the way to Kilis and spoke enough broken English that Sabine's services were not required. Foye secured their accommodations himself.

It did not occur to Sabine until it was happening that she would be sharing a room with Foye. Alone.

Her stomach felt as if she had stepped off a very high cliff.

Nineteen

❧

Aleppo, Haleb province of Syria,
JULY 1, 1811

A city continuously inhabited going back at least three
thousand years before the birth of Jesus Christ, and presently under the putative control of the Turks. The very
earth itself seemed to feel the regime could not last much
longer, but no one knew who would take over once the
Turks were gone. Nazim Pasha had his own opinion
about that. As did Ibrahim Pasha, who had so resound-
ingly slaughtered his Egyptian competition earlier in
the year. The French, the British, the Italians, and the
Russians had their separate ideas as well.

"THERE'S NO HELP FOR IT," FOYE SAID TO HER WHEN THEY
were alone in a second-floor room. He unslung the heavier
of his saddlebags and let it fall to the floor. The ceiling
was high and painted in creams, blue, and gold in intri-
cate patterns centered around flowing Arabic script. The
wood-paneled walls were just as intricately carved.

"I understand that, Foye," she said.

There was no furniture but for a low octagonal table
and a narghile at the edge of the divan. At each end of the
room, a lamp hung from a hook in the wall. Foye crossed
the room and dropped his other saddlebag on the floor,
near the divan.

"We aren't married yet," he said. He opened the

cupboards built into the walls until he found the rolled-up
mattresses. With both mattresses in hand he turned. "You
have nothing to fear from me," he said.

"I know." Sabine put down her things, too, and helped
him lay out the bedding. That done, she stood hands on her
hips, longing to take a deep breath but unable to because of
the cloth so tightly wrapped around her rib cage. Anxiety
curled in her belly. She was excessively aware of Foye.

He frowned as he removed his pistols from his coat
pockets and placed them beside his mattress. To them he
added two knives and a dagger. She took another uncomfortable breath. "Why are you breathing like that?" he
asked with a glance in her direction.

She gazed at him, knowing her cheeks were flaming red.
Could he tell under the artificial color of her skin? Here she
stood, alone with a man she'd kissed until her knees were
weak, and she still felt shy. Worse than shy. They were alone,
and he was not the polite and controlled marquess she'd
known in Büyükdere. As for why she was breathing as she
was, she wasn't sure she could bring herself to tell him the
problem, which was that her bosom was too tightly bound.

"Sabine."

For a man so temperamentally even, he had a talent for
skewering one with a single glance. "I am not comfortable,
Foye." He arched an eyebrow. She gestured at her upper
body. "Here."

"Nor am I—" He scowled at her, but understanding had
dawned. His gaze lowered to the vicinity of her bosom.
"Ah. Yes. Our solution to the problems of anatomy."

"As you said, there's nothing for it," she said. She
avoided looking at him by kneeling to unroll her rug and
spread it over her mattress. She brushed away as much dust
as she could. The room, beautiful as it was, was not very
large. They would be close here. Very close. But nothing
would happen. Would it? She kept her head down. Was that
what she wanted?

"Sabine," Foye said.

She did not want to hear anything from him about her

constricted bosom. She wished to God she'd never even alluded to the reason for her discomfort. All she'd done was destroy the illusion that she was Pathros and bring back all the discomfort from before. They were now both too aware of each other. Well, she was too aware of him.

"It would be best . . ." He coughed. "If we left our solution in place. Unless it's unbearable for you."

"No," she said. Lied. "It's not." She sat down, cross-legged, and was reminded that she too was armed when the weapons in her sash poked into her ribs. She took out both the pistols and the knife tucked into her sash. The purse he'd given her was there, too, but she left that for now. What had her life come to that she was pulling such deadly instruments from her clothing and thinking that perhaps she ought to have more?

"They make a rather impressive pile, don't you agree?" she said.

Foye looked over. "Formidable." He fetched his other saddlebag and moved both to one side. He, too, unrolled his rug and stretched out on the mattress. His feet hung off the end. "God willing, you will never use them," he said, tucking his hands under his head. "And, God willing, you will if necessary."

"Yes." She touched the larger pistol Foye had given her. Sabine would never have touched such a weapon. No one would ever think she could. But Pathros? He must be familiar and ruthless with such an instrument. "Do you think Nazim Pasha knows I'm gone?"

"Assuredly."

"He'll come after you."

"Yes. With luck, Barton has delayed him. We'll keep you out of sight if he catches up with me. I intend to play the innocent for as long as it lasts. With more luck we'll be on our way to Iskenderun before he finds us."

She removed her headband, scarf, and cap and ran her fingers through what was left of her hair. It felt sticky and damp with sweat and was uneven; longer in some places, primarily the front, and horribly short in the back. She did not care to imagine what she must look like. A fright. An absolute fright. She was glad there was no mirror to confirm her suspicions.

Foye gave her a regretful look. Lord, it must be even worse than she imagined. "I'm sure it's not much consolation at the moment, but your hair will grow out and the dye will fade."

"Better to look a disaster than to be identified because someone saw the color of my hair," she said.

He grunted.

"It's the first time I've ever wished I'd been born a brunette." She ran her fingers through her hair once more, trying to work out the tangles. "If someone were to see it now, they'd know something was wrong."

He didn't smile, but Sabine's heart beat a little harder anyway. They were alone, and even though he said nothing would happen and even though she was relieved by his assurance, she was still nervous. Her awareness of him as a man was too sharp. "You're right, of course," he said. "I've a pair of shears in my kit. I ought to cut it properly. Just in case." He pushed himself to his feet. "That's if you trust me not to butcher you even worse this time."

"Thank you." She made sure she sounded as if she didn't feel she would fall off that cliff any minute. Nothing would happen. "I think that would be wise."

"Anything for you, my love," he said in his familiar light tone.

"Anything?" She returned his teasing lilt. She had her head bowed away from him while she used her fingers to work out a snarl on one side and so could not see his face. "I shall begin a list. A bath, I think." She worked through the last tangle and looked up to see him watching her. Her stomach dropped again. "The moon and the stars? Can you give me those?" she asked softly.

Foye didn't answer her right away, and she was lost in the blue of his eyes. When he did reply, the humor was gone from his voice. "Anything," he said. He had the shears in his hand and now went onto his knees beside her.

"The universe?" he said. "Say the word and it's yours." His fingers brushed her shoulder. His gaze held hers. "You are magnificent," he said.

Sabine's breath hitched. The giddy, shivery feeling was back, centered in her stomach and lower, and she wasn't at all sure what to make of it, except that she was both frightened of her feelings and wishing that whatever restraint kept Foye from embracing her would vanish.

He reached into his satchel, dug around, and came out with a comb he held out to her. She took the comb and worked the teeth through her tangled hair while he held up the shears and scissored them with a madman's grin that made her laugh and broke the mood.

Everything would be all right, after all. Nothing would happen. She was safe from the emotions that rushed through her. She no longer felt like the naïve young woman who had kissed the Marquess of Foye and fancied herself in love with a man she didn't really know. Now, her feelings were far, far more complex and dangerous. He could hurt her, devastate her with a word or look.

He wrapped her blanket around her shoulders and went to work. "My God, I made a hash of this," he said. He took the comb from her. "I've no future as a valet or lady's maid. Don't move your head, Sabine." He shifted closer to her so that she could not help but feel the size of his body. He felt warm, and he made her feel safe. Beyond that just now, she refused to speculate.

She sat cross-legged with her back straight and her hands underneath the blanket around her, holding it closed. "I suppose you think me vain to regret the loss of my hair."

"No," he said. The sound of the scissors snipping her hair echoed in her ears. "Even I prefer to be presentable, insofar as that is possible."

Without thinking, she turned her head. "You really mustn't—"

He pulled away the scissors. "Have a care, or I'll lop off a piece of your ear."

"—talk about yourself as if you're hideous to behold."

Honestly, though, she remembered all too well that her first impression of his looks had not been charitable. She had once wanted to draw his face for the novelty of capturing the irregular line of his cheeks and jaw. Now she wanted to know if she could capture the way his eyes and smile transformed him utterly.

"You're not." She was insulted for him, since he would not be for himself. "Not at all."

Foye took her chin between thumb and forefinger and turned her head so that he had her profile. "Hold still, woman."

"Woman?" She snorted. "I am Pathros, effendi, and I spit on your calling me a woman. I spit on it!" He laughed, a low chuckle. "Don't change the subject, Foye. You're a far more attractive man than you give yourself credit for. Will you force me to speak to you sternly about this?"

He went back to cutting her hair. "As to your sex, Sabine, that you are female is rarely far from my mind, you may trust me on that." He moved behind her and resumed his work with the shears. "As to my appearance, thank you. I am flattered by your opinion. And I do not think you vain, by the way. You are so far from that, I think I ought to give you lessons in vanity. I will have you know I spend hours before the mirror achieving an absolutely precise fold of a cravat. It is an art to which every gentleman ought to aspire. So few succeed." He snipped more of her hair. "I'll turn you into a valet yet. Just wait until morning, Pathros, when I require you to tie my cravat to my exacting specifications."

"I endeavor to please, effendi."

Snip, snip, snip. He touched the back of her head, pushing slightly as he cut.

"When we're back in England, and your hair has grown out," he said, "I'll have your portrait painted." More hair fell onto her lap. "I said hold still. Do you want to keep your ear?"

"Yes, my lord, I do. Forgive me."

Presently, he reached around her to her forehead and

brought her head upright. "Almost done," he said. He studied her, squinting at her before he went to work again. "I've made you as masculine as I can." He tipped his head this way and that. "You'll have to tell me if you think I've ruined you."

She laughed. "If you have, I don't mind, Foye."

Too late, she realized how much could be read into what she'd said and how he must be taking it. Once again, the silence between them felt too large. "I didn't mean precisely that," she said. But was that true? What if she had? What if she wanted him that way? Now? "Not the way it came out."

"No," he said. He drew a finger along the line of her jaw. "You gave my heart a turn nonetheless." He put down the shears, but Sabine didn't move. She kept her head straight. He moved again, this time to kneel in front of her. "I think this may be the best that can be done with you. It's shorter than mine, now."

She slid her blanket off her shoulders and reached up to touch her hair. "Goodness," she said as she felt just how short her hair was. Foye scooped up a handful of the hair he'd trimmed and took it to the window. He opened one of louvers and threw it out. "There's almost nothing left."

When he returned, she'd brushed most of the hair off her blanket and was scrubbing the back of her neck, trying to dislodge the stray hairs. Foye sat in front of her again. Sabine pretended to be busy brushing more hair from her blanket. The truth was, the loss of her hair bothered her more than she wanted to let on.

He put his hand under her chin and lifted her head, holding her chin and turning her head from side to side. "You make a tolerable boy," he said.

She raised her eyes and found him studying her. Her stomach filled with butterflies. "Do I?"

"Yes."

She studied his face, too, trying to bring back the way she'd first seen him, with such awkward features and a hooked nose, all parts uneven and awkward, but all she saw was the light in his eyes and the gentleness of his mouth.

His was a face of character and intelligence. To her, he was beautiful. A man who tried to see the world as it was rather than what it was said to be, and still retained his hope.

"Let this be a lesson to you," he said.

"What?"

He grinned. "Never let an ugly man cut your hair."

She pushed him in the chest, and he pretended to be injured. "Stop, Foye. You're not ugly. You're not at all." He let go of her chin and fell to the floor, clutching his chest.

"I'm injured. Injured I tell you. Brought low by some snip of a boy."

"Oh, stop that, too." She planted her hands on the floor on either side of his face and bent over him. He was laughing, and she was trying to hold back her own mirth. She couldn't get a deep enough breath to laugh anyway. "I'm going to sketch you. I will. And you'll see I'm right. You are not ugly." Briefly, she lifted a hand and brushed a fingertip along his cheek. "Repeat after me. I, the Marquess of Foye, am not an ugly man."

"I, the monster of Foye—" The words didn't make it past his laughter.

"Come now." She bent closer. What was left of her once waist-length hair fell over her forehead and no farther. There were no waist-length curls to fall over her shoulders. She touched her forehead and found only a few lank curls to sweep back. She looked down again and said, "Say it, my lord, or I shall be forced to deal harshly with you."

But Foye had stopped laughing, and he was looking at her with such heat her breath caught in her throat. He reached out and cupped his hand over the back of her neck. She didn't move. If she moved, this moment, whatever it was, wherever it might lead, would end, and she didn't want that to happen. "You are so very young, Sabine."

"Twenty-three isn't so young."

His fingers tightened on her nape but not enough to bring them closer. She wanted him to. She wanted to be closer to him. She wanted this to happen between them, whatever he intended, she wanted that and more.

"It is compared to thirty-eight."

"If only you were thirty-seven or I twenty-four," she said, rolling her eyes. "Then everything would be all right."

"Are you mocking me?" he asked. One corner of his mouth twitched, and Sabine's heart gave a clench at the sight.

"Never."

Foye slid his hand off her neck, and Sabine realized that he wasn't going to do anything. Despite the heat between them, the feeling that only the two of them existed, nothing was going to happen between them. "Good," he said. "Because it wouldn't do at all if you were to mock me."

"Foye," she said. But she didn't know how to tell him what she wanted, because he had been so adamant that nothing would happen between them. They shouldn't. He was right in that. But she wanted him to kiss her, and she could see that he wouldn't. She lifted a hand to her hair, as short as a boy's, and yet shorter than Foye's. It barely reached the top of her neck.

He rolled away until he was sitting up. "We should both be asleep," he said. He shrugged out of his coat, and laid it over his saddlebags. He reached for his cravat.

Sabine said, "Allow me, effendi."

"I can undress myself," he said. His voice was gruff.

"Don't be difficult, Foye. We're both tired and tense, and there's really no need to take my head off, is there?"

"No." He sighed as she pushed herself up to a sitting position and deftly untied his cravat. "I didn't mean to snap, Sabine."

When she leaned forward to pull the strip of linen off his neck, he breathed in. She folded his cravat and placed it very neatly and precisely on his coat. "It's all right. It's very strange, us being here like this."

His waistcoat was next. She unfastened his watch, that was easy enough, and tucked it into a pocket. There were eight cloth-covered buttons. He kept very still while she pushed it off his shoulders, and then, well, the contact was too much. Too intimate. Though she had imagined doing this more than once, the reality was nothing like what she

had imagined. Her body reacted in ways she hadn't anticipated: nervous, aroused, uncertain, even guilty. She didn't
feel confident the way she had in her imagination, not of
herself, or of Foye, for that matter. There were matters
between men and women of which she was ignorant and
he was not, and yet she thought she'd never live if he didn't
want her, too.

She drew away her hands, leaving him with his waistcoat halfway down his arms, and she had never in her life
seen any man but Godard in his shirt, and it wasn't the
same at all to see Foye in this state of undress.

"Thank you, Pathros," he said, shrugging off his waistcoat on his own. He was trying to make light of a moment
that wasn't. "You are an able valet. Now, it's time we went
to sleep." He stood up—my God, in only his breeches and
shirt!—and dimmed the lamps until the room was almost
completely dark. Then he lay down, pulled his blanket over
him, and closed his eyes. "Sleep, Sabine."

"Yes, my lord."

But she lay in the dark, listening to Foye breathing and
fighting the tears dammed up in the back of her throat.

Twenty

❧

About one o'clock in the morning. A caravansary in the oldest section of Aleppo, Syria. A room shared by Lord Foye and Sabine. The room was unnaturally quiet. Foye lay on a mattress too short for the length of his body; Sabine lay on another, curled into a ball.

SABINE AWOKE TO DARKNESS, MOMENTARILY DISORIENTED. Everything around her was unfamiliar, the room, the scent of dust, the pallet on which she lay, the air and the weight of everything that had happened to her. She wasn't certain of the time, except that it was still dark out. She'd been dreaming, nothing pleasant, unfortunately. Though the specifics faded before she opened her eyes, a residue of fear and grief clung to her so resolutely she could hardly hold back a sob.

Her life wasn't going to come right. How could it? She was thousands of miles from home. The world she'd known no longer existed. Godard was dead, and her safety was no longer a given. She would never mend things with her uncle and never have the chance to tell him she loved him. And this thing with Foye. My God, she was one moment relieved that he'd turned his back to her and the next near tears with the conviction that he no longer wanted her. As for her feelings? When Foye looked at her, she wanted him, her body ached for him, longed for him to touch her or kiss her.

She held her breath and willed herself not to move, but she couldn't stop her tears. They continued to slide down her cheeks. Eventually, she had to sniff. She did so slowly, trying to make it sound as if she were merely taking a long, deep breath in her sleep.

"Sabine?" Foye said in a voice just above a whisper.

Oh hell. He was awake.

She used her sleeve to wipe her eyes. "Forgive me," she said when she could speak without risk of betraying her emotion. "I'm sorry if I woke you. I didn't mean to."

"Are you all right?" He spoke slowly, as if he might be about to fall asleep again.

She doubted he wanted to know the answer. Why would he? His mattress rustled as he moved, resettling himself under his blanket. She didn't dare move. The slightest motion might break her apart. She wasn't a weak-willed woman, or so she liked to think. All she needed was a moment to gather herself. Just a moment, and she would have herself in hand.

"All is well, Foye. Go back to sleep. I did not mean to disturb you."

"Are you certain?"

"I could not sleep. That's all." She had to speak in one breath lest her voice tremble and betray her. By the final word every last atom in her lungs had been expelled, and she couldn't get a decent breath of air afterward. Foye moved closer to her. She shifted too late to avoid him. But all he did was press a handkerchief, or some bit of silk anyway, to her cheek.

"Thank you," she whispered.

"It's nothing, Sabine."

"Have I told you thank you for coming after me?"

"I should have come sooner. I wish I'd come before your uncle died."

"Thank you, Foye."

"I am very sorry for your loss," he said.

"I'm sorry, too." The backs of his fingers brushed over her cheek, an incidental contact that, nevertheless, sent a shiver through her, and, inexplicably, made her feel even more alone than ever. "I miss him," she said. "I miss him terribly."

"I know you do, my love."

"You're probably wiping off my color," she said. Her stomach fluttered, and that so disconcerting heat settled between her thighs.

"I'll inspect you in the morning," he said with a low laugh.

She did so love the sound of his voice. "That would be wise, I think."

As her eyes adjusted to the dark, she could make out the shape that was Lord Foye, but not much more. The features of his face were lost in shadow. She took his handkerchief from him. She expected him to move away from her, but he didn't. His hand remained on her cheek, his fingers moving over her, along her temples, beneath her eyes. He meant only to comfort her, of course, but the slow motion of his touch set off shivers that pulled deep in her belly.

"I was shocked when my elder brother died," Foye said. "I hadn't even heard he was ill. I expected he would continue on living and before long produce an heir or two and the Marrack line would go on as it always had."

"I'm sorry he died," Sabine said.

He let out a short breath. "One day I came home—I had a modest home then, in Hampstead Heath, which I still have—to find the family solicitor waiting for me in the parlor. He stood up when I came in, I remember that particularly, and before I could say good day, he addressed me as "my lord." That was enough for me to know what had happened. Two terrible words and I knew. Even so, I didn't believe it at first. My brother ought to have lived many, many more years. I'd assumed he would. His son had died the year before, and his wife conceived right away. The week before he died, she delivered a girl. Without warning, there was but one Marrack left to carry on the family name and traditions."

"Didn't you want the title?" she asked.

"God, no." His voice fell like velvet on her ears. "When it meant my brother had died? No. But what choice had I? It made no difference that I was happy with my life as it was or that I would have preferred to have my brother alive."

"I often wished I'd had a brother or sister."

"It's not as though we didn't have our differences. We did. But I miss him still," he said. He removed his hand from her cheek. She was disappointed.

"You shall miss him for the rest of your life," she said. "As I will miss Godard."

"Yes, I think so. And now I am the last Marrack. There are no more of us."

Silence fell between them. At least this time the quiet was not an uncomfortable one. "If I'd known you then," she said, "I would have told you how sorry I was."

"Thank you." His voice was a gravelly, sleepy rumble. "The words do help."

She caught his hand in hers and held tight. "Why did you come after me, Foye?"

"For you," he whispered. She kissed his fingers, and he drew in a breath. "Why else? To convince Godard . . . of whatever he needed convincing of."

"What's to become of us?" She tightened her fingers around his. "What will happen now, Foye? The truth. No lies between us. Tell me the truth now. I'd rather know now. Before it's too late for me."

Foye levered himself up and leaned over her. "Do you doubt me?"

"No," she cried out softly, just managing to choke back a sob. "No, Foye. I love you. But I doubt my future. Mr. Lucey said you don't want to be married. He said he thought you still loved Rosaline." In the dark she pressed her fingers to her eyes. "I don't know what I think, Foye. Sometimes I think you can't possibly want to marry me, or that you only say so because you feel you must. Sometimes

I think I'll die if you don't love me, and other times I'm
sure you still love Rosaline."

"I don't love Rosaline." He leaned over and kissed
her forehead. "It's true you are completely unsuitable."
He laughed softly. "You read my fate in my tea leaves,
Sabine. Don't you remember? So, let me tell you what's
to become of us so that you are sure of your future with
me. We'll return to England and be married in St. Paul's
Church. You'll carry orange blossoms and scarlet roses in
your bridal bouquet, and everyone will marvel at my good
fortune."

"I've always liked peonies," she said. Her heart clenched
hard. Such happiness didn't seem possible for her. "Can't I
have peonies in my bouquet?"

"Whatever you like, dear heart. We'll honeymoon in
Cornwall, and if you like, I'll help you finish Sir Henry's
book."

"Yes, that sounds lovely, Foye."

"And now, my love, close your eyes and sleep."

"Yes, Foye." Quiet descended again, and that was as
unfamiliar as everything else. Somewhere in the khan,
men were laughing in the rhythm of a language other than
English. Sabine was once again overwhelmed by how
alone she was. What if Foye had not come? The thought
shook her deeply. Scenes replayed in her head, unpleasant ones that she could never make come out right. The
pasha's advances to her. Godard's final illness. The weeks
after Crosshaven's lies when she'd hardly spoken to anyone, even her uncle.

Quietly she sat up and hugged her arms around her
upraised knees. She missed the familiar weight of her hair.
Her clothes were unfamiliar; she was not used to having
a garment covering the whole of her lower body and legs.
The very fact of her being dressed in men's clothes was
wicked and improper and sinful. Foye was here, but she
still felt alone.

"Sabine," Foye said in the dark. He reached over and
found her hand.

"Go back to sleep, Foye."

He sat up. His voice came from low in his chest, gravelly still. "I can't. Not when you're awake."

She turned her head toward him, her chin resting on her knees. He'd gone to bed in shirt and breeches. No waistcoat. No coat. No cravat. The breadth of his chest beneath that white linen was impossible to miss. "Usually when I can't sleep I read," she said because she didn't want the quiet again. Horrible things filled her head in the silence. Her chest tightened with repressed tears. "Something dull if the case is desperate." She shrugged. "I've no books, dull or otherwise."

"Nor I." His shoulders were terribly broad. "What about drawing? Do you ever sketch when you cannot sleep?"

She rested her chin atop her knees again, her arms still wrapped around her shins. "Yes," she said. "I do. But I've no pencil and no sketchbook."

"If you had supplies, would you sketch?"

Sabine faced him in the darkened room, grateful for his willingness to distract her. "Tonight? Yes. I'd sketch you if I could. I'm determined to do you justice one day. Don't laugh," she said. "I am determined."

"I am not laughing."

She saw the edge of his mouth twitch. "Liar."

"Damn it all—" His eyes widened. "I beg your pardon."

"If I could," she said, "I would draw you from the nude."

Foye blinked rapidly.

Sabine closed her eyes. Had she really just said that? Apparently, her capacity for humiliating herself was boundless. Well. It was true, wasn't it? If she could, she would draw Foye like that.

"What a thought," he said.

"Male artists draw women from life." There wasn't much chance of recovering her dignity now, so she just blundered on. "It's considered a requirement for an artist's proper training."

"That," he said, "is because the female form lends itself to artistic expression."

"The Greeks did not omit the male nude," she replied. Talking to Foye distracted her from the residue of her nightmares. "And lest you attempt to distinguish between sculpture and a two-dimensional representation of the human form, let me say first that art is art no matter the medium and second that I have seen the relevant amphorae."

"Your uncle did not shelter you nearly enough."

"Probably not," she replied.

He reached for one of his saddlebags, left on the floor by his bed. "Have you drawn from the nude before?" he asked while he opened one and rummaged inside.

"If I tell you I haven't, that does not mean I shouldn't."

"Do you think I implied that?" Foye turned back to her with a pencil and a small notebook, soft bound and covered with oil paper. He held them out, but she didn't take them. He put them on the mattress beside her.

"It is too dark for me to draw."

He rose and relit the lamp he'd put out and brought up the level of light in the other. Not much but enough that if she wanted to, she could, in fact, sketch.

"Fiat lux," he said. He held out both hands, palms up. Let there be light. Back on his mattress, he lay on his side, facing her with a hand propping up his head.

"You should go back to sleep," she said.

"I'm not the least tired." He reached for the sketchbook at her feet and opened it. "I'm not much of an artist."

She glanced down and put a finger on one of the pages. The drawing there was of a ruined building. "What castle is this?" she asked.

He leaned closer to look. "Maraat Al-Numan. And all I did while I was there was think of you."

"Godard and I went to Serjillo with Nazim Pasha. On our way to Kilis. I kept imagining some Roman elder was going to return home and demand to know what we were doing in his house." She traced the outline of a door in a crumbling castle wall. He'd captured the desolation in the landscape quite well. Architectural details he'd rendered particularly well. She turned a page. "These are very good, Foye."

"I haven't your talent, but I like to draw a scene when I can." He sat up, knees drawn up under his blankets and his arms wrapped loosely around the outside. His hair curled willy-nilly over one side of his forehead, and the tilt of his head made the awkward angle of his cheek all the more apparent. "Draw something," he said.

She turned another page or two. He'd captured a view of the bazaar in Constantinople. On another page was the Great Mosque. Very competently done. She picked up his pencil. "You?"

His eyes stayed on her. "If you like. Or fix one of those things I tried to put down."

She chose a blank page and started to sketch as she spoke. She knew the lines of his face so much better now. "I began to hate him," she said softly. "My uncle, not Crosshaven, for taking me away even though I'd done nothing wrong. And yet," she said, "I was glad to be gone from London. From England. Word had reached even Oxford. Some of Godard's friends cut us dead. Even after we left England, we sometimes went days without speaking to each other except for, 'Please pass the sugar,' or 'Yes, that is a magnificent example of an Ionic column.' "

"Are you drawing me?" he asked.

She glanced at him, then returned her attention to her page. "Do you mind?"

"I'm no Adonis, Sabine."

"You have a noble face." His reply to that was a laugh, and she fixed him with a stare. His gaze met hers, one of those accidental exchanges that seemed to happen between them from time to time. Her stomach went shivery again. "Must I be stern with you, Foye? I warn you, you will not find that pleasant."

"No. Please no." His mouth curved into a smile.

"Then stay just as you are." She worked on the line of his cheek and started on his eyes. "You have very pretty eyes," she said.

"You tread upon dangerous ground, Sabine," Foye said. "You might turn my head with such talk."

She laughed. "I doubt that very much."

This time she was succeeding in capturing the strength in his face, but her pencil was losing its edge. "Have you a pen knife? Or a pencil that's less dull?"

He reached into his saddlebag again and pulled out a wooden case that held a supply of pencils. None were as sharp as she liked, but she found one that would do and began on the details of his mouth. His lower lip was fuller than his upper, and there was a tenderness there, lurking in the masculinity of his jaw and chin.

"You are very busy there," he said.

She held out the book and showed him the page. "If I had my own materials I would have done better, but it's a tolerable likeness, I think. Better than what I managed before."

Foye looked at it for quite a while before he said anything. "My God," he whispered. "Me to the very hook in my nose. You are an artist, Sabine." He touched the page. "Did Godard know this about you? I know he discouraged you, but did he understand the extent of your talent?"

She reached over and took the sketchbook back. "He knew a great deal, Foye. But not everything. Now, since you will not let me draw you from life, I think we are done. Surely, now we may sleep."

But Foye stared at her, his eyes intent. "I've lost my soul to you," he said. "My heart."

She stretched out a hand and pressed her fingertips to his chest until she felt the beating of his heart. "Your heart beats here, Foye. In your chest. You carry it with you wherever you go."

"And yet you are its owner."

She thought of Rosaline and how badly Foye had been hurt. She was glad Rosaline had jilted him. Sorry he'd been hurt yet glad that it had happened. "I'll keep it safe for you," she said. "Will you do the same with mine?"

He reached up and over his shoulders to grab the back of his shirt and pull the linen over his head. While she watched, his hands disappeared underneath his blanket.

"What you are doing?" she asked, though it was clear he was removing his breeches. In an instant all the tension from before roared back. She was too aware of him. And aware of him not as Lord Foye but as a male animal to her female. Yes, she far was too aware of herself and her body's reaction to him.

He used his foot to pull away the blanket. "There," he said. He lay back and threw one arm above his head. The other he left at his side, relaxed, his long fingers loose.

The Marquess of Foye was naked.

Twenty-one

🐚

About two thirty in the morning. The caravansary in
Aleppo. Neither Foye nor Sabine were asleep. They
should have been. But they weren't.

JUST WHEN, FOYE WONDERED, HAD HE GONE UTTERLY
mad? What in God's name had possessed him to strip
naked in front of Sabine? Lust, he thought. Pure, roaring,
boiling-his-blood lust. He had no intention of making love
to her. He wanted to. He wanted his body over hers and
inside her, but when they were married. When she was
indisputably his. England was months away by ship, and
the stark reality of that was if he made love to her now and
she conceived, by the time they were home, she'd have
quickened. He could hardly get her to St. Paul's in time,
and even if they managed to disguise her condition, they
would be hard-pressed to explain a child born so early.

At the moment, however, he had an even more pressing
concern. Which was what Sabine would do. He kept his eyes
on her and waited for a maidenly protest or even amused
laughter. But none came. Which was really quite interesting.
She was silent, but hers was not precisely a shocked

silence. She sat cross-legged on her mattress, frozen, so
yes, perhaps she was a bit shocked at what he'd done. So
was he, actually. But he rather thought she was school-
ing her reaction, carefully hiding from him what she was
thinking inside that clever head of hers. Eventually, however, her gaze moved downward from his face.

Now, admittedly, his face was awkwardly put together.
There was not much to admire there. But the rest? Enough
women had expressed their delight with his person that he
thought it likely he pleased Sabine. Though, true enough,
he was imposing in a way some women enjoyed and others
did not. His time among the Turks had stripped him down
to the point where he was leaner than he'd ever been in
London, and he had never been prone to fat. His skin fit
closer to the muscle now.

They were perhaps an arm's length apart. One of his
arms. All his flaws and assets were on display for her. She
still wasn't objecting. Her examination was slow, and yes, she
lingered at his cock—he was erect, no helping that, either—
and if he was not mistaken, her cheeks turned pink before her
attention traveled on. If she'd seen those Greek amphorae,
she knew about a man's before-and-after state, as it were.

The sketchbook he'd given her was open on her lap, his
face captured on the white sheet. She picked up her pencil,
turned to a fresh page, and began to draw. As she worked,
he heard her pencil moving over paper, and he relaxed in
respect of her objections to his nudity. Perhaps she would
decide she didn't want him. She may have decided that
already. Or perhaps she would decide she liked a man built
on his scale.

God help him.

His body reacted predictably to that particular line of
thought. But he didn't move or in any way try to hide the
particular part of him that ached. There were certain reali-
ties of the male body of which, one way or another, she was
not entirely ignorant, and his present physical state happened to be one of them.

He was mad for her, mad to have her, mad to be with

her. That he was entertaining some rather coarse desires where she was concerned did not help matters much. He forced his thoughts to less titillating subjects than unsuitable places for her mouth and brought his physical reaction to a less rampant state. Foye wondered if he could, after all, manage to keep his honor, and hers, intact. Perhaps Sabine would spend all night drawing him and so save them from his base desires.

She turned a page, and he watched her pencil moving again. When she concentrated on a part of her drawing, she had a habit of chewing on her lower lip. It occurred to him as well that she rarely resorted to the bit of gum rubber he used when one of his efforts went awry, which was often.

She was a gifted artist. If she'd been a man she might already be working in oils and be a member of the Royal Academy, painting female nudes and taking commissions for formal portraits. What he'd seen of her work in mere pencil was breathtakingly good. What might she accomplish in oils?

Presently, she put down her pencil and said, "I believe I'm done." She sat with the sketchbook on her lap. Almost immediately, the earlier tension between them returned. In force.

"May I see?"

"If you like." Her cheeks turned pink beneath the coloring on her skin, which made him wonder. Sabine was never coy, but what was this blush of hers? "There is another on the page before."

He was quite comfortable being nude in front of her and didn't bother to cover himself with his blanket or stop to pull on his shirt. He pushed up on one elbow and took the bound sketchbook from her. In remarkably few strokes, she had captured his outsized body and transformed all his physical awkwardness into something heroic. And yet every line was as familiar to him as the face he saw in the mirror. That was his body there, big and muscled beyond the elegance of, say, someone like Crosshaven. And she'd formed him with a series of strokes that rendered him lithe and sensual, a desirable male whose partner was waiting somewhere not far away. Any moment, the man on this sheet of paper would have his lover in his arms.

"They're only studies," she said. "For something more formal later, if I have the opportunity."

He glanced up. "*When* you have the opportunity."

Slowly, she inhaled, and damn, but he wanted to know what she was thinking. "Thank you for letting me draw you. I know how difficult it must have been."

"Not at all. You're talented, Sabine." He turned the page backward and didn't know whether to laugh or shout or be deeply appalled at what he saw there. She'd drawn, in exquisite detail, his erect penis. There was only the barest suggestion of the body to which it was attached.

"I suppose," she said, "you think me wicked."

He pushed himself the rest of the way up. He was going to hell anyway, so he put down the book, looped his arm around the back of her neck to draw her to him, and kissed her. Nothing tender or sensitive, but an open-mouthed, deep kiss that started out electrifyingly arousing and stayed there, getting more intense by the second.

Her mouth was soft against his, accepting. Welcoming. Her palm lightly touched his torso and then flattened on his chest, one finger sweeping over his nipple, and his arousal ramped up to a nearly unbearable pitch.

He pulled away, not far, enough to say, "You understand this is fatal for us, don't you?" he said in a gruff voice. "Nothing will be the same between us if we do this. It means there's no wedding at St. Paul's." No more bloody waiting.

"I don't care what happens." Her lids swept down, briefly hiding her eyes from him. "Not today, nor tomorrow. Or ever. So long as I have lived one day in my life. Just one. With you."

"Sabine." He reached out to brush a finger along her cheek. "A day? Only one out of all the days you have left? Do stop frowning." He pressed his thumb over her mouth. "That's better. Surely you realize that I will have to marry you here, not in England." He pressed his mouth to the side of her throat. "It's for the best," he said. He tightened his arm around her nape, bringing her closer. "I don't think I could have held out much longer anyway."

"Kiss me again, Foye," she said.

He frowned and drew back a bit farther. "You do understand, Sabine, yes? We would have married anyway, but this means sooner, before it's convenient for either of us. We merely anticipate our wedding night."

Her tongue darted out to touch her lower lip, and Foye was swamped with visions of what he'd like for her to do with him. "Are you certain, Foye?"

"Hell, yes, Sabine." He started working at her clothes, an occupation that got him farther away from her, not closer. She took a breath and relaxed. "Jesus," he said in a low voice, "if anyone comes in, he's going to think I'm about to bugger my dragoman."

She gave a soft laugh at that. He found the sound ravishing.

He unraveled the sash around her waist, then slid a hand underneath her outer cloak and pushed it off first one shoulder and then the other. She did the rest, and before long she was free of the garment. Their eyes connected when he pushed apart the two halves of her jacket. His state of arousal was nearly enough to make him forget this was to be her first sexual encounter.

"You'll tell me if I do anything to make you afraid?" he asked. She nodded, and he said, softly, "Do not lie to me, Sabine. There are ways for us to do this without me scaring you to death. If you need time, if you reconsider or want this to be slower, you have but to tell me." He took her head between his two hands and kissed her forehead, her cheeks, her closed eyes. "I promise you that, my love, I will be as gentle as possible."

"I trust you, Foye." She spoke so gravely, he thought his heart would break. She lifted a leg so that the inside of her thigh brushed his leg, and he went back to adoring her body inch by inch. He dropped lower to kiss her while he pushed her jacket off her shoulders, and she shifted her body to make it happen. He decided he loved her mouth.

They worked at her *shirwal* next, and when the garment was loosened, he pulled the thing down her legs, touching skin that was soft and shockingly pale after her artificially brown face and arms. Her skin was warm and smooth beneath his palms. By the time he had her stripped down to that length of silk he'd been thinking about all bloody day and night, he was ready to scream with pure lust.

"You're right," he said. He slid the tip of a finger between her skin and the silk and used that to pull her toward him. He'd tied the knot between her shoulder blades, which meant that she needed to sit up in order for him to get it off her. "This is far too tight. No wonder you couldn't breathe. What benighted oaf did this to you, Sabine?"

"I'm thinking of hiring him as my lady's maid." As she bent toward him, her shorn hair fell across her temples. "I wonder if I should."

He turned her around so he could unfasten the fabric and unwind it from her torso. The knot was stiff and tight and he had to fight to get it loose. "Sack the fellow, I say. There are more interesting things he can do for you." When he had it off, she stayed with her back to him, leaning down with one hand pressed to the mattress and the other on her upper torso while she took a deep, deep breath.

Foye stared, transfixed, aroused beyond belief. The flickering light made her skin gleam like closely woven silk. Despite her being so small a woman, her curves were luscious. He drew a finger slowly down the line of her spine. Her skin was as soft as it looked, smooth everywhere and pale wherever it was free of the coloring. The slide of her ribs to her waist aroused him as much as the curve of her waist to her hips. He bent to kiss the nape of her neck and cup a hand over one of her breasts. She kept her torso bent.

"Is this all right?" he asked, aware that his position was an aggressive one and that if the difference in their sizes bothered her, this particular arrangement of their bodies would only serve to emphasize that disparity. On the other hand, it was possible she liked it.

"Yes," she said on a breath.

He shifted so he was behind her, using his other hand to bring her upright until her back was pressed against his front and she was on her knees while his thighs spread on either side of her. He kept his hand moving upward until his fingers were in her now nut-brown hair, sliding over her skull from back to front. Golden blond sparkled from the uneven brown coloring. Her hair was thick and soft underneath, and he thought about what it would have been like to hold that once glorious mass of golden hair in his hands. He brought her head back to lean against his shoulder.

"Sabine," he whispered. "Oh, Sabine, you're so lovely. Too lovely for a beast like me." He put both his hands around her waist and reverently slid them downward, molding his palms and fingers to the shape of her, pressing her against his erection. He returned to her breasts, looking at her from over her shoulder. Sabine sucked in a breath when he covered her. "Do you like when I do this?"

"Mm."

"That is not an answer." He brushed his palms over her nipples. "Do you like this?"

"Yes, Foye."

She had a narrow rib cage—hell, she was smaller than him by a terrifying amount—but her breasts were magnificent. Not unduly large, but far more than he expected. She was quite pale. Even her nipples were a pale, pinkish brown. He felt a surge of disbelief that he should have gotten them to this point of aching desire and mutual nakedness. And here he was, holding her, cupping her breasts, and feeling the beat of her heart underneath his palm. He wasn't considering anything like sedate intercourse with her. He was, in fact, in serious danger of losing his self-control.

That could not happen. Not for her first time with him. Her first time ever. He would be gentle. Tender. Restrained.

His hands, the backs browned by the sun, looked

entirely, wonderfully masculine on her, large and border-
ing on coarse. He caressed her and dropped a line of kisses
along her shoulder. "Such a lovely body, Sabine. Divine."

He laid her down on the mattress and knelt between her
legs, looking at her. Another shiver of arousal shot through
him. He drew a hand along one of her thighs, bringing his
fingers around to the inside. He knew he could all too easily
overwhelm her. The last thing he wanted was to see her looking at him with fear. He was trying his best, really he was.

He cupped her sex, tangling his fingers in her pale, crisp
nether hair. She might change her mind. She could. She
might take a long, hard look at him and decide she would
never accept him. This was not, after all, a true wedding
night, where there was, in essential fact, no possibility
of his wife denying him. He pressed his hand over her,
between her legs, sliding a finger along the folds of her
body, and Sabine, quite gratifyingly, bowed toward him.
Her eyes fluttered open, and she raised her knees to give
him access. He came up against her maidenhead. They
locked gazes. "I'll try not to hurt you, Sabine."

"It's all right, Foye."

There wasn't any possibility of going back now. Foye
smiled and lowered himself in order to taste her, sliding
down to kiss the inside of her thigh and then her quim. So
much for restrain and reserve. Her skin was salty, and he
didn't give a damn about much but seeing to her thorough
pleasure. He slid farther down and nudged her thighs apart.
"Lovely, Sabine." He breathed the words against her skin.

Her sex was warm and damp for him, and when he
kissed her there, she tensed, but not with fear, with desire.
"Foye," she said on a long, low inhale. "My God, keep
doing that. Please."

He was happy to oblige. He adored bringing a woman
to climax this way. The taste and texture against his mouth
and tongue never failed to arouse him, the pleasure that
ended with them both sated.

He listened for the changes in her breathing, waited

for the tension in her body to tell him she was close, and adjusted touch and kiss to bring her to the point where her body would belong to him, when she would allow herself to surrender to her body, to pleasure, and to him.

After he'd brought her to climax, he pulled himself over her, careful to keep himself well above her. Sabine gazed at him with sleepy, pleasure-sated eyes. His cock brushed her belly; he could not help that contact while he lowered his head to her breast and still kept his weight off her.

She groaned when his teeth found her nipple, a light scrape, a touch, a sweep of his tongue around and across the taut nub that meant she was responding to him. She arched against him, and before he could think, he pressed his cock against her belly, imitating the motion he would make when he was inside her.

Her legs came up, the soft, sweet inside of her thighs brushing against the outside of his. He fell deeper yet into his own arousal. He pulled away long enough to reach out and drag his mattresses next to hers. When he'd done that he rolled onto his back and brought Sabine over him to straddle his lower torso.

"Foye," she breathed.

Just the sound of her voice aroused him. He had the loveliest view of her body this way. He slid his hands from her belly to her breasts, palming them. Her short hair swung forward past her temples until she arched her upper back, filling his hands. His fingers tightened on her, plucking at her nipples. She clasped his wrists with her brown-dyed hands, then brushed her hands along his forearms.

"Foye," she whispered as she looked down and into his face. She wasn't afraid of him. Not at all. Not afraid and not repulsed. "When you touch me . . ." She drew a breath. "It's so lovely. You make me feel . . . unsettled." She bit her lower lip. "I need you, now, I think."

He managed a smile at her. "Now? Are you certain?"

"Please, Foye." She tightened her hands around his wrists. "I don't want to wait any longer."

Hell, he could barely speak he was so out of his mind with desire for her. He pushed himself up, holding his weight on one arm while he put her on her back. With her supine, he bent his head to kiss her mouth, then trail his lips down her throat to her breast. Her nipple budded hard when he tongued her. He reached between them and put a hand around his cock, and oh, hell, he was close.

"Sabine," he whispered. So close. So close to sliding his cock inside her. "Sabine, tell me this is what you want."

She looked into his face. "Fiend," she said. "You torture me on purpose. I'll never forgive you for this. Never."

"Tell me," he said, settling his belly against hers. "I want the words from you."

"Yes, Foye! I want this with you."

He put his mouth by her ear, one hand planted on the mattress near her shoulder, holding his weight. "I'm going to put my cock inside you," he said. "I'll be inside you, warm and snug, and it will be the moment I've lived for since I met you."

Her hands rested on his shoulders, moving lower, sliding over his chests, touching him, burning him. "Stop torturing me." She bowed against him. "Beast. You are a beast."

Foye pulled back his head. "Listen to me." He waited until she opened her eyes. "I've not made love to a virgin in a very long time. If I hurt you, it's because of your maidenhead, not because that's how it is for women. It's just this once. Only this time, my love."

She nodded, and then he let go of himself and got the head of his cock at her entrance, very aware that he was bigger than she was. He pushed his hips forward, and, he pushed through her maidenhead with very little trouble and just hell, his foreskin slid back with the friction of entering her, and he flew to an even higher level of arousal. She was hot and tight around him, and it was all he could do not to drive himself as far into her as he could.

With one arm around her body just above the slope of her hips, he rocked forward. He went slowly because she was very tight, and she arched her throat and he watched her mouth open on a moan of pleasure. She put her hands on his shoulders, fingers angled toward his back. "Now," he whispered. "Now, Sabine. I love you." He held her, and with a single thrust, he penetrated fully, and God help him, he adored the sound of her breath catching in the back of her throat, and the give of her body to his. She enveloped him, hot and slick around his cock. Heaven. Bliss. He was inside her where he had dreamed of being for far too long. Jesus, he was at the edge of his control.

His. She was his at last.

"Are you all right?" he said. Her body was tense against his, and he didn't want to have hurt her, though of course he must have. Her fingers gripped him hard, digging into the skin of his shoulders. His balls were tight, and he had to fight the urge to thrust. Sabine drew in a long, trembling breath.

"Foye," she whispered. She twined her arms around his neck. Her fingers tangled in his hair and brought his head down to kiss him. He fit his mouth over hers and kissed her back.

Yes.

He drew partially out with a backward tilt of his hips and upward pressure from his free hand on her hip. She slid her hands to the top of his shoulders, not pushing him away at all. She bent her knees again, and her inner thigh brushed his hip. Foye pushed into her again, muscles tensing as their bodies merged.

"Like that," he said. "Hell, yes."

Heaven. Considering that he was a large man, and she was so small and elegant, they fit together very well. When he was all the way in again, he stayed there, wanting to be sure she was all right. But she was slick around him, and he wasn't mistaken in his interpretation of her groan. She opened her eyes and they looked at each other.

"Foye," she said, settling a hand on his cheek. "Oh, Foye." He pressed forward, and his world narrowed to just the two of them. "Foye," she whispered. "Why are you torturing me like this? Am I as awful as that?"

"No, Sabine," he said when he had the wits to speak. He slid deeper inside her. "I am torturing you because I intend to see you break apart while I watch. I am a selfish man when it comes to your pleasure. I intend to see it all."

"Beast," she said with a smile.

Words filled him, a dozen, a thousand, a hundred thousand, but he couldn't speak a one. He put his palms on the mattress at the top of her shoulders and drew back, then forward, slowing watching her face the entire time. His breath hitched as his foreskin slid back, exposing the sensitive head of his cock to her body. "Sabine."

Her answer to that was a tilt of her pelvis that sent his cock sliding inside her, into the warmth of her body. The sensation was so exquisite he forgot everything but that. But her. Their bodies matched very well. This was all he could manage. Just the two of them, just his body inside hers. Her eyes took on a drugged look, and he thought he'd expire just from looking at the way her expression changed. She'd caught on to the essential motion, and damn her, she'd learned already how to move so as to drive him mad.

He slipped a hand between them and found the exact spot that would bring her to climax. "I adore your body," he whispered. "Your breasts, your mouth, your eyes." As he, too, hurtled toward orgasm, she leaned in and kissed the side of his throat. His hips were moving harder now, faster, and when she did break apart, he threw back his head so he could watch, and then he let go of himself, and it didn't matter that he came inside her because in the morning he was going to marry her anyway.

Twenty-two

❧

WHEN SABINE OPENED HER EYES, FOYE LAY FAST ASLEEP less than a foot from her. She was, for a moment, disoriented and wondering how the marquess had gotten into the pasha's palace, let alone into her room. But then she remembered, and the familiar fell away. He'd gotten her out of the palace and away from Kilis. They were in Aleppo, in a khan, and last night they had become lovers.

She had no idea what time it was, except that it was no longer night since there was enough light for her to see the room and, very clearly, Foye's face. She could study him without rudeness or worrying that he would misunderstand the reason for her stare. He knew too well the ways in which others found his features inelegant. She thought he didn't know well enough the ways in which he compelled. He'd pulled his quilt up to his chin and slipped one hand underneath his cheek. The butt of a pistol protruded from the edge of his pillow.

In repose, his features still had that ill-fitting jumble but the sight made her heart feel light—and anxious. Looking at him now made her belly shiver with the recognition that she wanted him again. She wanted his arms around her, his mouth on hers. How interesting, though, that she did not find him unattractive now, when he was not awake to imbue his face with sheer force of personality. His beard was growing, dark along his cheeks and the line of his chin. Thick, dark lashes lay on his cheeks, and his hair was disheveled. He was a very large man, but only in the way that one man is taller than another.

He lay between her and the door. Quite ready, she was certain, to die for her should they be discovered by the pasha's men. What other reason was there to make a barrier of his body? Godard would be—she caught herself. Her uncle was dead, and a part of her wondered if the pasha hadn't played some role in his illness.

If Foye had come for her even a day later, she was convinced she would already have been beyond rescue. But Foye had come for her. On his own. Despite all her letter writing and sending Asif to Aleppo with a letter for the British Consulate. Foye had come. Not some official from the Levant Company nor anyone else in an official capacity.

She reached out and touched his cheek with her fingertip, to a spot above the whiskers growing. His skin was warm. She was a fallen woman, this time in truth. Lord Foye was her lover. Sabine brought back her hand and saw his eyelids lift.

"Good morning," she said. "Though perhaps it's afternoon."

"Sabine." He caught her hand and brought her fingers to his lips for a kiss.

The angles of his face came together in interesting ways. She could no longer look at him and see him as unattractive, though she knew others might think so. There was too much intelligence in his face. Too much honor. Too many memories of his face as he came to pleasure with her. He threw aside his covers and reached for his clothes. After some searching, he extracted his watch from his waistcoat and consulted it. He stood barefoot on the rugs covering the floor, unconcerned by his nudity, while he wound his watch by the light coming in through the windows.

Foye, Sabine thought, was a magnificent man.

"Midmorning," he said, still with his back to her. He peered out the window. Camel bells tinkled in the interior courtyard; a few of the beasts protested. Men's voices, the cadence of the local languages, Arabic and, though she did not speak the dialects, Druze and Kurdish, too.

"The time?"

"Thirteen past ten." He consulted the watch again. "And fifty-three seconds." He snapped the face of the watch closed. "I suggest we dress and find some breakfast. I want to send one or two men out to see if there is any sign of Barton and the others. Or the pasha."

How strange it was to be lying in bed, conversing with a man who happened to be standing before her naked, as gloriously lovely as Michelangelo's *David*. She knew his body, the texture of his skin, his taste, his scent, the sound of his voice as he whispered in her ear.

She knew his temperament, too, that he was calm and possessed a sharp intellect. That he would do what he promised. He was the Marquess of Foye. A nobleman. And he claimed to love her.

He fixed her with a penetrating gaze. "When we've found something to eat, you and I have business to attend to at the consulate."

"I wrote to them about Godard."

"Did you?" She could see him assessing that. "Before or after Godard died?"

"After."

"Are you certain your letter was delivered?"

"I gave it to Asif."

He nodded. "Then they'll know of his death. We'll need the official documentation in England." With a frown, he said, "They ought to have sent someone to investigate. I wonder why no one came?"

Sabine shrugged. "Perhaps they did, and Nazim Pasha sent them away."

"Then what good are they?" He stood there with his hands on his hips. "Useless. Worse than useless if that's what happened."

"Who knows what lies the pasha might have told them?" She sat up, keeping her blanket around her. She felt unaccountably happy. "Do you intend to tell them Nazim Pasha demanded a ransom for me?"

"That and more. Detaining a British citizen against her will won't be looked upon kindly," Foye said. "No matter what they think of the man." He clasped his hands over his head and arched his back in a long, luxurious stretch. Every muscle was on display. There was not an ounce of excess flesh on him. When he was done, they ended up looking at one another. He smiled. "What are you thinking, Sabine? That I am shameless?"

"No." She put her chin atop her knee. "I am thinking that you are beautiful."

His smile turned serious. "Thank you, Sabine."

"Come here, Foye."

He did, and holding and touching him in the brightness of morning made her heart overflow. Afterward, Sabine held him close and tried to memorize the way he felt in her body and in her arms. The scent of him, the texture of his skin and the taste. The way she felt safe and adored and physically sated. He pulled away with a charming reluctance.

"I wish we could stay here all day." He traced the line of her collarbone with the tip of his finger. "We could forget the world outside and spend all our time making love."

"That would be lovely." She pressed her hand to his cheek, and again her heart hurt at the happiness. "Very lovely."

Foye dropped his head and kissed the underside of her throat. "Mm. Sabine. What is it you do to me?" He lowered his body to hers, his weight on his hands by her shoulders. "I think you make me very stiff," he said with a wicked grin.

"Is that proper, my lord? I think that sounds very improper."

"Mm. I think it's proper, my dear." He dipped his head again. "Lovely, lovely Sabine. You make me properly stiff."

"What an unhappy occurrence. If you were to ask me. Is there something I can do to help you with your condition?"

"I wonder." He nuzzled her throat again. "Can you? Would you be willing to try to give me some relief?"

"I'll endeavor, effendi."

"What an excellent servant you are. Remind me to raise your wages next quarter. Now, my lovely dragoman, will you let me have my wicked way with you again?"

"Oh, yes, please," she said. She meant it, too. With all her heart.

"My pleasure," Foye replied. He used his thigh to nudge her legs apart, and since she now knew what he intended, she shifted, and he pushed inside her. And yes, he was very much bigger than she was, and she loved the difference between their bodies. He felt good inside her, so very good, that before long she wasn't thinking about much except for Foye and the place where their bodies joined. His eyes flashed, but she knew he was being careful. Too careful. There was more he wanted from her.

"Foye," she whispered. "I know you won't hurt me. I know."

He paused and dropped his head to her. "I never would. Never." She arched against him, but he didn't let go of his restraint with her. "Sabine. My love."

She held him when he came and knew with an ache in her heart that she wouldn't ever be the same without him.

"It's time we got you dressed," Foye said later when they had their breath back. "It's two days to Iskenderun. The sooner we're on our way the better."

"Trussed, you mean."

"Yes, trussed. What a sin that is." He dropped a kiss to her breast, one then the other. "I won't be able to ogle your bosom."

Sabine sat up and between them they transformed her back to Pathros, and then she helped him become the very proper and alarming Marquess of Foye. He kissed her after he was dressed, too, and her heart melted at the tender way he held her.

"I don't know how I'm going to keep anyone from thinking I've unnatural affections for you," he said.

"Don't joke about that," she said.

His expression turned serious. "Before we leave Aleppo, Sabine, we will be proof against the pasha. There'll be no need for subterfuge." He smiled broadly. "I'll be forced to give Pathros the sack."

"Are you sure that's wise, Foye?"

"I don't think my wife would tolerate my involvement with the boy." He put his hands on his hips. "Do you?"

She widened her eyes. "You mean us to be married? Here? So soon?"

"The consul here can perform the ceremony, Sabine." He frowned. "We did nothing to prevent conception either last night or this morning. And that is not a circumstance I would have allowed if I had not intended to marry you, and quickly, too."

"But—"

"We are not in England yet, Sabine. The law is different here. A young woman without a husband and without a male relative to take charge of her is in a precarious situation. Nazim Pasha made it clear he did not agree that I had standing to take you with me." He drew his eyebrows together. "Why do you think I had to resort to kidnapping you? Believe me, I had exhausted all other means at my disposal before choosing this."

"I await your point, Foye."

"My point, Sabine, is that should Nazim Pasha overtake us, he might succeed in regaining you. Based on past experience, I doubt anyone at the consulate would mount a formal protest with the pasha or the Sublime Porte before you have been sold or made a gift. If we are not married, there will be no relative of yours to protest on your behalf." His eyes went hard. "If my wife were to be abducted, I assure you, the authorities would act. Without delay."

She lifted an eyebrow. "Foye—"

"Need I remind you that I am a peer, and my title, all that Foye is now and in the future, is subject to primo-geniture. We *must* be married now. It's months by sea to home. You'll be well advanced if I've got you with child." He raised a hand. "Do you think for a moment I will per-mit anything to happen to you? All I ask is that you do not make my efforts on your behalf more difficult. You may well believe, Sabine, that the consulate would move heaven and earth for me and my wife."

Sabine looked at him. "You're certain of this, then?"

"Yes." He wasn't worried that she doubted him; he was worried she doubted her feelings for him. Matters had moved too quickly between them from the very first. He had no doubts. To her, their future seemed perilous indeed.

Twenty-three

❧

SABINE FOLLOWED FOYE OUT OF THEIR ROOM, FEELING as if she were a prisoner headed for her last meal. Her interlude with Foye had for a while taken away her troubles. She had lived, for a time, in a world in which she was safe. Now she was walking back into uncertainty. She adjusted the saddlebags she carried, all but the heaviest, which Foye had slung over his shoulder.

Footsteps echoed on the stairs, coming up. Foye slowed and removed the pistol he'd tucked underneath his coat. He checked the weapon and held it behind his back. There was a great deal of noise from downstairs. Sabine drew her pistol as well.

"Remain calm," Foye said as they continued walking. He sounded horribly nonchalant. "You are my employee. Nothing more. Nothing less."

When they reached the top of the stairs, Foye put his saddlebag on the floor and stood at the top, blocking any access past him. Sabine stopped, her pulse thundering. She could not see around him. But his shoulders relaxed, and he took a step or two down. He did not, she noticed, replace his pistol. The weapon remained in his hand. "Barton," he said.

Sabine went to the head of the stairs and peered past Foye to see Barton about halfway down the stairs. He panted as he stood there, bent over, one hand on the wall, the other clutching his hat. "My lord. Thank God I've found you."

She replaced the pistol in her sash.

"What is it?" Foye asked in a low voice.

"Nazim Pasha himself is in Aleppo," Barton said as softly as he could over his hard breathing. He must have run quite a ways before he found the khan. "The news is everywhere. He stopped us an hour or two out of the city. Furious. He beat Sir Henry's servant within an inch of his life, my lord. I don't know how he managed to stay with us. And now the rumor is the pasha's called on Mr. Barker himself . . ." He put a hand to his chest and took a deep breath. His face was flushed. "On a matter of grave importance it's said."

"Has he?" Foye sounded bored by the subject. He signaled to Sabine to pick up the saddlebag he'd dropped and continued down the stairs, Barton and Sabine following, saddlebag in hand. She slung it over her shoulder with the others she already had. Barton hardly spared her a glance. "What on earth for?"

"Sir Henry's niece has vanished from Kilis. I heard that from one of the men in service at the consulate. The pasha blames that fellow he nearly killed, Asif."

Sabine's heart thudded against her ribs, but Barton wasn't paying any attention to her whatever. Her dark skin and boy's attire made her invisible to him.

Foye slowed down. "Miss Godard?" he said. "Vanished?" He was a perfect picture of astonishment. "I don't see how that could be. I very much doubt she's actually vanished. It's a ruse to extort more money from me. Or

else he never intended to turn her over and he's looking
to solidify his excuse when I raise hell over his refusal to
return her."

Her knees felt a little wobbly. Foye was right. She was
not in Britain where she understood the law and what was
expected of her and what rights she had and did not have.
The Sublime Porte might be the voice of the sultan, but as
with governments everywhere, the law tended to operate
according to the whims and appetites of the local officials.
Nazim Pasha had made a point of being useful to the French
and the English alike, and his power was felt far from Kilis.

"His men are all over the city, my lord. They are armed,"
Barton said. "I've seen them myself. There is no question
of it. They are asking after you and Miss Godard."

"Hmm." Foye shrugged and continued down the stairs.
"Were you recognized on your way here?"

"I don't believe I was, no," Barton said.

"But you can't be sure." As he walked, Foye rechecked
his pistols. Both of them. "Pathros," he said casually.
"I advise you to check your weapons as well."

Sabine nodded and again pulled out the larger of her
two pistols.

"It was my impression, my lord, that the pasha believed
you may have made off with Miss Godard."

"Ridiculous," Foye said. "As you well know."

Sabine didn't know how Foye could remain so calm.
Her pulse was pounding in her ears as it was, and her hands
were shaking.

"Where are the others?" Foye asked.

"In the courtyard, my lord."

"Excellent." He put one pistol in his pocket and returned
the other behind his back. "Pathros, come along."

"Sir." Sabine's chest constricted until she could hardly
breathe. Barton didn't look twice at her.

"Are the horses ready?" Foye asked Barton as they continued out of the khan.

"Yes, my lord"

"Good man." Foye clapped his servant on the back. "I'll

need you on your way to Büyükdere before long. Make sure you take Asif with you. Bring him to England if he wants to come."

"And you, my lord?"

"I've a ransom to gather. A business that may take me to Iskenderun if I cannot scrape up enough here."

"But she's gone!" Barton said. "What good is a ransom now?"

Foye headed for the door but paused to address Barton. "I want Miss Godard returned, and I intend to see it happen. I won't give him the excuse of a failed ransom to withhold her from me." His voice hardened. "Nazim Pasha is lying about Miss Godard, Barton. He means to make a gift of her to the sultan. And these lies of his are the perfect way to have her vanish into the Seraglio."

They exited the interior of the khan into the enclosed courtyard. The caravan they'd heard from their upstairs room was gone. Asif was there with Godard's trunks and the men Foye had sent to Kilis with her and Godard. He leaned against the courtyard wall, one arm held across his waist. His lower lip was split and still bleeding, one eye swollen shut, and there were several livid red stripes across his face.

Sabine's first task was to make sure Foye's Janissaries were ready for departure. Instructions were duly conveyed to their captain. That done, she hurried to catch up with Foye as he crossed the courtyard to Asif. The servant stayed in the shade cast by the wall, holding the reins of his horse with one hand. He nodded when she and Foye approached. Nabil stood beside him.

"Asif," Foye said, "you've done well, my friend." Sabine translated, and that earned her a scowl from Nabil. "If you've a mind when this is done, come to England. Barton will see your passage there. You've a job for life with me. I hope you'll come."

The Turk nodded, barely moving his body as he acknowledged Foye's gratitude. "Effendi," he said through stiff lips.

Foye put a hand on Nabil's shoulder. "And you, my

dear young fellow, can you continue a little longer for me?" Nabil nodded. "Good. You'll stay with Barton, then. Barton, when you've gotten Godard's things to Büyükdere, see their house is packed up. My things as well. Ship the Godards' belongings with mine directly to Maralee. And if Asif elects to come, get him decent passage."

The horses were ready now, and Foye gave final instructions to Barton before they each rejoined their original parties: Foye and Sabine with the Janissaries captained by the Druze, Barton and Asif ready for the probably monthlong trek to Büyükdere. Her stomach rumbled as she walked to her mare. She was famished, but she didn't think she could swallow a single crumb even if she had one to eat. And though her mouth was dry as dust, she didn't think she could drink anything, either. Nazim Pasha was in Aleppo. He might find them yet.

Barton kicked his mount until he was at her side. She flashed him a grin and pretended to be engaged in resettling her saddlebags. She did not want to talk with him. But Barton stayed even with her, eyeing her far too closely for her comfort. What if she did something to betray herself? Or had already? Would all be lost? Surely, he was wise enough to keep silent if he'd guessed who she was? Asif certainly had. She mounted without any difficulty.

"Peter, is it?" Barton asked. His gaze raked her, deeply suspicious, she thought. Her heart thudded against her ribs, and she had to force herself not to grip the reins too tightly. He knew, she thought. Barton knew who she was.

"Pathros." She gave the native pronunciation, which was not so very far from "Peter," and buried herself deeper in her guise of a young dragoman. She cocked her head at him and did her best to appear calm. "Yes, Mr. Barton?"

"His lordship seems to depend on you."

She shrugged. "I am helpful to him, I hope. It is why he employed me."

"You speak English well enough," he said. He took out a stained and dusty handkerchief, removed his hat, and wiped his face and temples with the square of cotton. "And that's

a mercy. I can hardly understand that other fellow, Nabil."
He put away the handkerchief. "Damn. I don't know how
you natives bear the heat. It's not natural, this weather."

"Perhaps tomorrow it will be cooler."

Barton shot her another glance. "Don't be cheeky, my
boy. It bloody well is too hot." After a moment, Barton
continued. "You bunked with him last night." Sabine said
nothing. He couldn't know. He just couldn't know what
they'd done. "Probably for the best. A boy your size doesn't
take up much room, and him such a giant." Barton chuckled
and waited until Sabine thought to smile in return. "Did he
sleep at all?"

"Very little, sir." She relaxed when the expected accusa-
tion didn't come. "He was restless."

Barton nodded and wiped his forehead again. "He is
concerned for Miss Godard and her safety."

"The woman he will pay ransom for." She bowed her
head, keeping her face down.

"If she hasn't bloody vanished. You know how these
things are in this godforsaken country," he said. "Tell me,
what do you think? Is there any hope for her? Or is his lordship haring off to gather a king's ransom for no reason?"

She bobbed her head. "Nazim Pasha has released others
before. When Lord Foye has paid her ransom, he will
release Miss Godard."

Barton's expression darkened. "She's an exceptionally
pretty girl from everything I've heard. He won't let her go,
you mark my words. Straight to the Seraglio, if you ask me.
If she's not in his, that is."

"Do you think that is so?"

"No hope for her now, that's what I say." He gave a
mournful shake of his head. "Mark my words, boy, that
pasha has sold her into slavery. She's already lost, and his
lordship's going to take it hard when he discovers that."

"I pray God you are wrong," Sabine said. She crossed
herself.

"Back in Büyükdere, he was . . . fond of the young
lady," he said. "He's taking this hard. Very hard. You keep

a sharp eye on him, lad. He'll run himself into the ground
if he's not looked after. Especially if it's true she's lost to
us all." Barton fixed her with a stare, and Sabine returned
his gaze unblinkingly. As far as he was concerned, she was
Pathros, a young native boy. Barton didn't even know what
Sabine Godard looked like. How could he recognize her?
He would see what he expected to see. "He is a very great
man back in England. When he returns, there's much he
might do to help your nation."

"I am sure that is so, sir."

They remained in silence for a while. "His lordship says
you're one of those Christian heathens."

"Heathen?" she said. She put some heat into the
inquiry.

Barton flushed redder. "Perhaps not a heathen if you
believe in God and Jesus Christ." He shook his head. "Keep
your head about you, lad, and he might take you back to
England with him. Would you like that? To live in a Christian nation?"

"It is very far from home," she said.

"That it is. That it is. Keep it in mind, my boy. Look after
him. He treats his staff well. You couldn't have a better
employer in the whole of the British Empire than the Marquess of Foye. I've been with him for nearly fifteen years
now. There's no better man. None better." He glanced at
Foye, who was inspecting his horse before they left. "Look
out for him for me. See he gets some sleep when you stop
and that he eats, too. Will you promise me that?"

Sabine nodded. "I will."

Foye mounted and rode to Barton and Sabine. "Is there
a problem, Barton?"

"No, milord." He wiped his handkerchief across his
face. "Just having a word with the young lad here."

Sabine stood straighter. "Do you require my services,
Lord Foye?"

"If you please," Foye said. Nothing in his tone or
expression that suggested he thought of her as anything but
Pathros. There was a great deal of noise in the courtyard,

and Foye had his back to the high, arched exit to the khan, which was why he did not see the newcomers. Sabine, who was facing him, did.

"My lord." Sabine reached over and grabbed his arm, squeezing hard. Her heart shriveled in her chest. "Effendi!" she said in a low voice.

"What is it?"

She nodded behind him with her spine solid ice. Her knees went weak. "Nazim Pasha," she said.

Twenty-four

&

NAZIM PASHA WAS HERE.

He would discover her, if he hadn't already guessed, and abduct her in front of Foye and everyone else. Foye would try to stop him, and the pasha would kill him. Without remorse. She swallowed hard and tried to relax on her mount. So far no one but Asif and possibly Barton knew who she was. Why would the pasha suspect her when he was looking for an Englishwoman?

There was a ringing silence in the courtyard. Asif confronted one of the pasha's Janissaries, and the two now stood across from each other, glaring at one another. The soldier had his musket leveled at Asif's heart. In the hush, thirty or more men filled the courtyard, all of them armed Janissaries. About half stayed mounted, blocking the exit. The rest rode forward, behind the pasha. One of them carried the two spears with their tails signifying the pasha's rank.

Nazim Pasha continued his leisurely ride into the courtyard, heading toward Foye. Was this what it had been like
for the Mameluks in Cairo? Had they, too, faced this infinite silence before the attack that took their lives?

Foye's personal guard came to attention. The Druze
captain of his Janissaries pulled his rifle from his back
and kicked his stallion until he was just ahead of Foye.
The other Janissaries did the same. All around her, she
heard the sound of weapons being released and readied. It
occurred to her that, as Pathros, she ought to do the same,
but Foye reached over and stopped her.

"Stay calm," he murmured. "You are Pathros, my dragoman, not a soldier. Keep the pistol at hand, though."

Nazim Pasha emerged from among his Janissaries. The
handle of the bejeweled pistol protruding from his sash
glittered with refracted light. Upon reaching Foye, he made
an elaborate bow, a mockery of the European custom.

"Marquis," he said in French. "Good morning."

"Pasha." He held his pistol down, across his lap. "I confess," he replied in the same language, "I am astonished to
see you here."

"Perhaps we might call for coffee and refreshments,"
the pasha said with a nod of his head in the direction of the
khan.

"Forgive me," Foye said. "But I have a long journey
ahead of me and don't wish to be delayed."

"You cannot conduct your business here? Cannot
Mr. Barker assist you in gathering the funds you need?"

Foye shrugged one shoulder. "In the amount required,
no. I'm afraid the bulk of my monies are held in Iskenderun. That's two days' hard riding at best. Three if we're
delayed."

The pasha's gaze swept the men surrounding Foye, dark
eyes moving constantly, searching. Sabine concentrated on
breathing evenly. He would look past her. She was Pathros,
a young Christian boy, an infidel of no interest to Nazim
Pasha. Her palms were sweating, her back cold with fear.

Nazim Pasha gestured and one of his Janissaries

immediately rode to his side. In Arabic he told the mercenary to take some men and search the interior of the building for the Englishwoman. Her. With a sense of the world being out of its natural order, Sabine understood the Pasha meant her. He was sending soldiers inside to search for an Englishwoman. And that meant he did not suspect her.

The Janissary nodded and wheeled around in the now crowded space. While Foye watched him gather companions, Sabine leaned over to translate.

"We have had a hard journey from Kilis, Marquis," the pasha said. "You and I have a great deal to discuss."

Foye leaned forward, one hand propped up on his hard-muscled thigh. He glanced in the direction of the khan. "I assume Miss Godard is well?"

The pasha stroked his mustache. On each of his fingers was a ring of some precious stone. Not that his choice in jewelry would prevent him from firing his pistol, or ordering someone else to do so, for that matter. "I am unable to say," he said.

"Is she not in Kilis?" Foye said. "I was under the impression that she was to enjoy your hospitality until I returned with her ransom. Surely, Pasha, you haven't lost her, have you?"

"I would have been delighted to entertain her for as long as she was pleased to be my guest." He urged his horse forward, closer to Foye. Close enough that a gun shot would not miss. "But she disappeared, Marquis. The very morning you departed."

"Really?" Foye said. He looked and sounded bored. "That is unfortunate. However, it seems to me you had misplaced her before my arrival. If you'll recall, she was not available at any time during my visit. I never saw so much as a glimpse of her. I am indeed distressed to learn you could not keep one insignificant woman under your control. This is a quite serious matter, as I am sure you know. I hope you notified the authorities the moment you discovered her missing."

"I assure you I did. And, who, may I ask, is that behind you?" the pasha asked.

Foye turned, as if wondering the same. "Do you mean him? My dragoman." Sabine saw Foye slip the trigger lock on his pistol, and her pulse beat so fast and so hard she could barely hear.

Nazim Pasha addressed Sabine directly, in French. "Do you speak French, boy? What is your name?"

Heart in her throat, she looked at Foye for direction, by pure luck stumbling onto the very reaction Pathros was most likely to have. Foye, she recalled, had told her what to do. She was not to speak French, but she may already have ruined everything merely by paying attention too closely. Had the pasha guessed she understood?

"He doesn't," Foye replied, still in French.

"This is not the dragoman you brought with you to Kilis," the pasha said.

Sabine tried to stay relaxed, but my God, her heart was going to burst. Someone inside the khan shouted. *You do not speak French*, she told herself. She must appear as if not a word of this made sense to her.

"No," Foye said. "I bid that one to stay with my valet during the removal from Kilis. He's just there." His hand was steady as he gestured in the direction of Nabil. "My valet does not speak a word of the local language. He needed someone to tell him what was going on. I hired this one"—he nodded at Sabine—"when we came through Aleppo yesterday."

"You, boy, what is your name?" the pasha demanded of her in rapid French.

Just in time, Sabine remembered to look at Foye, who smiled at her—his blood must be ice, she thought. Her pulse pounded in her ears, and she prayed the pasha interpreted her fear as only natural to the tension of the encounter.

In English, Foye said with utter calm, "Nazim Pasha would like to know your name. Please oblige him with an answer."

She cleared her throat, and it was a wonder she could speak at all. "Pathros," she said. The word came out roughly, and she had to clear her throat afterward. Her mouth was bone dry. She bowed to him. "Pasha."

Nazim Pasha brought his horse around to her. He moved in close enough to jostle Foye's stallion, who objected and would have bitten the pasha's mount had Foye not pulled hard on the reins. The pasha turned his mount sideways and stared at her with his dark, dark eyes full of suspicion. He wondered, Sabine thought as terror slid down her spine. His eyes slid up and down her body, taking in the clothes, her complexion, searching, she was convinced, for womanly curves. She knew her face was probably still dirty. The clothes weren't hers; her hair was gone. She was Pathros. Pathros. She didn't dare breath. Thank God, thank God, Foye had bound her tightly this morning.

In Turkish, the pasha said, "How long have you worked for the Englishman, infidel?"

"Do please translate your conversation, Pathros," Foye said with a lazy gesture in her direction.

Sabine didn't have to pretend to be nervous. It wasn't hard at all to appear to be a nervous young Christian boy who was all too aware that a pasha could have him beaten for no reason other than that it amused him to do so. She made the translation into English before answering the pasha in Turkish. "Since late yesterday, Pasha." She repeated her answer in English for Foye.

"Did he, at any time," the pasha continued in Turkish, "have a woman with him? An Englishwoman?"

Sabine translated the question for Foye and then gave her answer in English before she replied to the pasha in Turkish. Her dry mouth made her voice scratchy, and she did her best to keep the tone lower than her natural speaking voice. "No, Pasha." She bobbed her head, touching her forehead. "I never saw an Englishwoman with Lord Foye. Perhaps one of the others saw something I did not?"

The pasha laughed, and Foye tightened his grip on his pistol. The pasha's Janissaries came out of the khan.

Without an Englishwoman and with no reports of anyone inside having seen Foye in the company of any woman.

"Then you have lost her." Foye shook his head. "That is unfortunate."

"I think when you return from Iskenderun you will find she's been enjoying my hospitality all this time." Nazim Pasha addressed Foye again in his exquisite French. "She has been in Kilis all this time, Marquis. Awaiting the day when she may return home to the bosom of her family."

"You do not want England to be your enemy. And that," he said, "is what you will have if Miss Godard is not returned to me safely."

"I wonder at your interest in the woman," the pasha said.

"You might have succeeded in convincing the authorities to look the other way when you were arranging to kidnap an innocent young woman." Foye stared him straight in the eye. "All you need to know, Nazim Pasha, is that Sabine Godard was never without a man's protection. I am not an invalid with no influence here. No matter how often you dine with the consuls here in Aleppo or Constantinople, the fact remains that I am not an Englishman you can trifle with. If I return to Kilis, Pasha, and find that Miss Godard is not with you, safe and sound, and ready to leave with me, I will bring the might of England down on you, so help me God, I shall."

The pasha stood unmoving for quite a while. At last, though, he bowed to Foye. "God's will be done," he said. He gestured to several of his Janissaries. "You will be pleased to know that I have many more men assisting me in looking after her. And since she is so well cared for in Kilis, please allow me to be certain that you return safely from Iskenderun," the pasha said. "With all the money required."

"Oh, I shall return," Foye said.

Nazim Pasha smiled. "My men and I will accompany you to Iskenderun and back." He lifted a hand. "I insist. It is the least I can do to assure your safety."

"And what of the safety of Miss Godard?" Foye asked.

"My men will continue to protect her. My servants will spend every hour of their day seeing to her entertainment. Never fear in that regard, Marquis. When she is at last returned to you, she will regale you with all the tales of her pleasures."

Foye stowed his pistol. "Come along if you wish. But don't slow me down, Pasha. I won't wait for you."

Nazim Pasha merely smiled in return.

Foye swore under his breath. He leaned to Sabine and said in a low voice, "Stay close to me at all times. And keep your weapon at hand." His mouth gave a wry twist. "If you can toss out a few obscenities or curses in some other language from time to time, do so."

She bowed her head to him as she had to the pasha. "My lord."

For Sabine, the next quarter of an hour passed in a blur. She relayed Foye's instructions to his men about when they might expect to leave and did her best to stay far away from the pasha while he informed his Janissaries of his change in plan. Five of them were to stay behind and continue searching for the Englishwoman. Another five were dispatched to procure supplies sufficient for the trek to Iskenderun and back; they were to catch up to the main group as soon as possible. The remaining men, thirty at least, stayed with the pasha.

Before noon, they were heading out. They made a considerable party as they rode to the city limits. Dogs chased after them until they reached the outskirts of Aleppo. A few of the dogs pursued them onto the rocky plain, but eventually even the most persistent cur gave up.

They continued west on the Iskenderun road into the Nur Mountains, faced with the seventy or eighty miles that stretched between here and the Syrian Gates, the narrow mountain gap that was the only passage to the port city of Iskenderun and the Mediterranean.

About noon, she and Foye ate a breakfast of nuts, cheese, and dry bread washed down with a mouthful of water, on horseback. By midafternoon, they'd left the plains that surrounded Aleppo and the northern province for the eastern side of the foothills. The arduous climb through the mountains had begun. For the most part, the pasha stayed back with his men. But it was clear to her and Foye both that the pasha suspected Foye had arranged for Sabine to meet him on the Iskenderun road, and that he had deployed his men accordingly, so as to intercept any secondary party.

Long before there was any hope of seeing a sunset, Sabine had a pounding headache from the heat and the constant reflection off the white stones everywhere one looked. If they ate, it was bread and cheese consumed while mounted, with a mouthful of stale water to wash it down. During their few stops, Sabine snuck off to relieve herself in private, often using her horse as a barrier. Once or twice she saw the pasha watching her, but his gaze was dismissive rather than curious. She'd learned to stand with her legs apart, arms over her chest, and if she walked, by God, she had bollocks.

The Janissaries of both men, Foye's and the pasha's, made coffee during their stops, brewed hot and thick and sweet. The Druze captain made Foye's coffee. He seemed to take it as a point of honor. Another of the Druze soldiers made hers. It was possible, she had heard, for a native traveling with coffee-making paraphernalia to journey for hours on very little sleep. If she was right about Foye's determination to reach Iskenderun as quickly as possibly, they were about to put that tale to the test.

The invigorating effects of the coffee they'd consumed during their last stop had worn off and still they rode on, winding higher into the mountains. Hours in the saddle became a painful reminder of each and every muscle in her body. She was sore and tired and very put out that Foye, who hadn't slept any more than she had, wasn't showing signs of dropping off to sleep in his saddle. He might at least have the decency to look ragged around the edges. And he didn't, even though he hadn't slept any more than she had the night before. Like many of the others, she kept a cloth wrapped around her face so that only her eyes showed.

About an hour before dusk, Nazim Pasha joined Foye, engaging him in conversation, again in French. Nothing very interesting. To be sure she did not give away her comprehension, she dropped back and let the two men ride ahead. Once or twice as they talked, Foye laughed.

The pasha's presence plunged Sabine into a world where everything was topsy-turvy. She was not Miss Sabine Godard. She was Pathros, a Christian ethnic Nazrin, employed as dragoman to an English lord. She did not speak French and therefore, understood nothing of what Foye and the pasha were saying. Aside from her facility with Turkish and Arabic, she was unimportant. Her function was to translate for her employer whenever required. Nothing more.

They rode on. Her lower body was numb, her knees in permanent agony from the short stirrups of her high-backed native saddle. Her spine and shoulders were a mass of permanently contracted muscles. Someone was hammering nails into her head. As often as she could she rode with her eyes closed. But, though her mare was sure-footed, the terrain was treacherous, and there were times Sabine had no choice but to watch the way, if only to prevent herself from being pitched over the mare's head.

They kept riding. Without cease and without conversation or remark on the sights. They passed two Bedouin men, tall and wrapped in dark red cloth, so at home on their horses that they seemed one and the same creature. The Bedouin were known for their ferocity and for having no qualms over attacking Europeans or anyone else. Despite government claims to the contrary, the Bedouin were not well controlled. They did as they pleased when they pleased to whom they pleased. All the Janissaries paid more attention to their surroundings for several hours after the encounter.

When, at last, the sun was disappearing behind the mountains, they rounded a corner of the path, and there, as if presented to them as a gift, just a few yards off the road stood a small khan. Camels lay in the sandy dirt in front and to the side. An Arab boy kept watch over tethered asses and mules. Inside, there would be cool water and respite from the heat. There would be food other than crumbling bread and stale tea; there would be lovely hot tea and a place to lay down her head.

The closer they came, the more fervently she imagined herself sliding into a bath and washing away the dirt and grime of all their days traveling. Heaven! Foye and the pasha were the first to come even with the turn to the khan, but they passed by the entrance without slowing.

Foye signaled to her to ride beside him. When she pulled even with him, he said, "I need a favor."

Twenty-five

❧

Approximately eight o'clock in the evening. A moonlit night on the road between Aleppo and Iskenderun.

SABINE COULD NOT LOOK AWAY FROM FOYE EVEN THOUGH she knew she ought to. He didn't look away, either. Butterflies took off in her stomach. Where Foye was concerned, she had too many conflicting emotions to know for certain what she was feeling. Anxiety over Nazim Pasha and whether he would discover who she was. Uncertainty about their sexual relationship. Foye had been so tender with her last night. So careful of her. He'd held back some part of himself, though, and it worried her.

"Your favor?" she said. "What is it?"

"Ask our Druze commander to join us, please."

Sabine nodded in reply and dropped back to summon the captain. When they were back with Foye, he said, "Please ask him how much longer we can expect to safely ride. I'm given to understand there is a small inn about four hours ahead." Foye shot a glance at the pasha. "Ask the captain if he agrees we can safely ride until then."

As she translated, she was horribly aware of the pasha listening. Her accent was good; mimicry was a talent of hers, and she'd been listening all day to cadences of the Arabic spoken among the Janissaries who were not native Turkish speakers. God help them all if she did not have the accent down. She felt her attempt to keep her voice in a lower register only increased the chances that she would stumble linguistically. But she managed to convey the questions without anyone accusing her of being anything but Foye's dragoman.

The Janissary listened quietly, stroking his mustache as he did so. "The horses," he replied in his accented Arabic, "will be fine until midnight." He held out a hand and wiggled it back and forth. He didn't seem to suspect she wasn't a boy. Why, she thought, after all this time so near to the pasha, would anyone else? So long as she continued with caution. As long as she didn't make a mistake. She might get them all killed if she did. "After that, we would be better off to rest if the Englishman hopes to arrive in Iskenderun on schedule."

Sabine thanked him and translated for Foye, who looked happy with the opinion. "We'll continue until we reach the inn, then."

Shortly after this exchange, the pasha left Foye to confer with his men. Foye leaned close as she rode beside him, speaking in a soft voice. "I believe he's convinced I intended to rendezvous with you at the first inn. He'll be expecting me to dash off without him now, heading back there."

"But we won't."

"No," he said. "I hope he goes mad wondering why I haven't. After tomorrow, we'll have to be even more careful." He let out a breath. "Damn but I wish this trip were shorter." He glanced at her. "You've done well so far, Pathros."

She swallowed hard. "Thank you, my lord."

Twice as they rode, they heard horses behind them. Both times several of the pasha's Janissaries moved off the road until they were out of sight. On both occasions, innocent travelers passed by. The Janissaries who'd split off rejoined them. Oh yes, Sabine thought. The pasha did indeed believe Foye had arranged to have Sabine join him somewhere on the Iskenderun road. So long as he believed that, she was safe from overt suspicion. But how long before he began to wonder?

Dusk turned to twilight and twilight to a moonlit night so bright the stars faded overhead. Before long, even the mercenaries drooped in their saddles, dozing as their mounts picked their way through the sandy, rock-strewn terrain. The horses, too, showed signs of fatigue. They had by now been on the road for so long she'd lost count of the hours, pushing through the mountains without cease.

They reached the inn shortly before midnight. This particular establishment was a plain mud building with narrow windows and a sagging roof, with no enclosed inner courtyard to protect the animals of a caravan. Most of the men would have to sleep outside. While the others dismounted and led their horses to the side of the structure to feed and water their animals, Sabine and Foye stayed in the front.

Foye surveyed the building. "It looks . . . unsavory at best." The building was ramshackle, just one story with walls in poor repair. But there was food to be had inside. Hot food. Foye dismounted. "Negotiate our terms with the innkeeper," he told her as he reached for her mare's bridle. Sabine nodded and dismounted without help. She was quite good at it now. "I'll wait for you here," he said.

"And the pasha?"

"He can fend for himself. Keep your pistol at hand."

She bowed to him. "Yes, my lord."

Sabine secured their accommodations without incident. There was a rather exhilarating freedom to conduct such business entirely on her own. Foye had given her a purse for that purpose, which she kept tucked into her sash and brought out to count out the coins for their meal and room. Their Janissaries would be sleeping outside, however.

"There is a warm spring a quarter mile beyond the building," she told Foye. "A small one, but we are welcome to use it to bathe. The path, I have been assured, is well marked. They are happy to provide us with coffee and a narghile, my lord."

A servant showed them to their room. He carried in one hand a lamp that he hung on a hook on the wall by the door. When she saw the condition of the room, a far cry from the khan in Aleppo, for a stomach-curdling moment Sabine thought Foye would insist they remount and ride to the next available inn—God knew how long that ride would be.

Three or four men would fit inside this crude room, no more. That was not so unsatisfactory an arrangement since the inn, with its single story, had rooms that were open at the back but for a low wall so that travelers could sleep with their horses or pack animals near at hand and within sight. Their men would not be far. Neither, of course, would the pasha's men. Or the pasha himself.

From over the low back wall, she could see that the pasha's men had just finished setting up a tent. The spears of his rank were already planted outside, and there were men standing guard. Since Nazim Pasha was nowhere in sight, she assumed he was already inside the tent.

Foye's Janissaries had already set out their bedding and blankets on the other side of the low wall that separated Foye's room from the outside. Another of the soldiers stayed with the horses, holding onto the picket line. The pasha's men were farther away. Some had already lit fires; others were quite plainly on guard. The rest went inside to eat.

The interior of the inn was not large enough for Foye to eat separately from the others as ought to have been the case for a man of his rank. Instead, he sat at the head of a table with the rest of his Janissaries and servants crowded around the sides and opposite end. She had negotiated a meal for all his men. The elbow of the soldier sitting next to her dug into her ribs.

The pasha entered with two servants and a broad-shouldered Janissary who took up position behind the pasha's seat.

At Foye's instruction, she ordered meals to be sent to the two guarding the horses, leaving the table by herself to do so. No one thought it odd or unusual. Quite the opposite in fact. This was what it was like to be a man, she thought. To be free to conduct one's business and expected to be competent enough to do so without need of supervision. When she returned from making her request, she retook her place at the end of the table and dug into her food.

The pasha and Foye had fallen into conversation. The subject was poetry, of all things. A speciality of hers. She and Godard had made a thorough study of French poetry. She bent her head over her bowl, concentrating on blocking out Foye's conversation.

The meal was rice with lentils and a small amount of meat. She didn't care whether the meat was chicken or goat or mutton; it was marvelously good to put hot food in her stomach after so many hours gnawing on dry bread and hard cheese. The others, Janissaries and servants, felt the same, for they all sat in silence for some time as they ate. Only the pasha and Foye spoke.

"Pathros," Foye said when she pushed away her empty bowl, "please tell the others they may go to the spring to bathe when I've returned from the same. Have the captain and one other come along to guard the path." He blinked twice and rubbed a hand over his eyes. Was it possible he was as tired and out of sorts as she was? Up to now, he'd seemed impervious to any of the hardships of the day. "Tell them as well that they're to take turns standing sentinel. Our captain may choose his guards as he sees fit for the task." He stared at her a moment. "Tell me if that's clear, or have I only babbled at you?"

"Perfectly clear, my lord." She bobbed her head and quickly relayed Foye's instructions to the Druze captain. He nodded. Foye made his good-nights to the pasha, and Sabine hurried to follow him.

Foye continued walking. "We'll need a change of clothes. You'll have to valet me, Pathros."

"My lord."

One of the Janissaries sat with his back against the half wall, holding the rope that bound the horses together. She ignored him while she gathered clean clothes for herself and Foye and what bathing items of Foye's she could find.

There were windows in the wall opposite, tall and latticed as was the fashion here. Another Janissary was just visible in the darkness, sitting on the other side of the wall, not far from the horses. Another had a small fire going and was grinding the coffee beans for the drink that would keep them awake while they stood sentinel. Most had already said their evening prayers and laid out their own bedding.

The Druze captain and a second man appeared, and Sabine adjusted her own weapons in her sash. The four of them headed for the springs under the full moon and the watchful eye of Nazim Pasha, standing arms crossed in front of his tent.

Twenty-six

☙

Approximately one thirty in the morning. The Nur Mountains. The warm springs about a quarter mile from a small, rather crude inn on the road between Aleppo and Iskenderun. Foye and Sabine were bathing, with two Druze mercenaries standing guard.

BOTH THE JANISSARIES WERE ON GUARD TWENTY YARDS down the path from the spring, having been instructed they were to watch for any of the pasha's men and give a quick whistle if it appeared they would be interrupted by anyone at all. Foye had stripped down quickly and with his help she did the same.

They were alone, naked, and Foye was helping scrub her clean as quickly as he could. Every noise made her jump, every second she expected they would be interrupted by the pasha or one of his men. When they were done, Foye waded out of the shallow pool, and they went to work drying her off and getting her breasts rebound and her dressed in clean clothes. He brought out his ointment and worked more through her hair, concentrating underneath where the blond showed through and along her center part where there were just faint signs of new blond. They left her mostly unclothed, with just the *shirwal* and shirt over her re-bound breasts.

"There," Foye said with a relieved sigh. "If anyone comes now, you're Pathros once more."

She gave a nervous glance over her shoulder. But there wasn't anyone on the path, only the captain and the other soldier, both with their backs to the springs.

"We will get through this." Foye set a hand to her cheek. "Come now, Sabine. If he's not guessed yet, he's unlikely to now."

"Pathros," she said in a near whisper. "I am Pathros." She was the marquess's dragoman, a boy who knew how to curse in Arabic and Turkish and walk like he had bollocks and who could make arrangements for their accommodations without anyone thinking he should not. She was competent and self-sufficient.

But when she looked at Foye, standing naked at the edge of the spring, she was Sabine Godard, and she and Foye had been as physically intimate as a man and woman could be. She wanted to throw her arms around him and whisper to him how dear he'd become to her. Most of all she wanted this to be over, this constant tension and fear of being found out.

Foye stood as silent as she was, still touching her cheek, fingers moving gently along the line of her jaw. Shadows and moonlight played over his face, so familiar to her now, and for some reason the very fact that he looked as he did made her heart feel too big for her chest.

Tears welled up, but she refused to cry in front of him. She couldn't. She wouldn't disappoint herself and him with such weakness or put them in that kind of danger. Tears gathered anyway, filling her heart and her very soul. How was she to reach across the gulf between them when she was no longer sure of the man who stood on the other side?

The Foye before her was not the amiable gentleman of their early acquaintance. Nor was he the man who'd held her so tenderly last night, while he'd made her feel things that had changed her forever. When she accepted his body into hers, he had changed her forever. That made her want to cry, too. She wasn't the same person who'd fallen in love.

He'd turned into a stranger men followed without question. She knew the difference between a man who was followed because of what he was to others—pasha, earl, sultan, king—and a man whom others followed because of who he was to himself—decisive, honorable, decent, quick thinking. Foye was both, and she had woefully, horribly misjudged him because she had known nothing of men and perhaps remained ignorant still. She would love him until the day came that she drew her last breath, and yet she feared she did not know him nearly well enough.

A sharp whistle cut the air.

"Blast," Foye said. He stepped away from her, back into the spring. He dunked his head in the water and was bathing by the time several men approached the spring. Nazim Pasha, with two servants and several of his Janissaries, all of them armed. The two Druze separated from the pasha's men.

Sabine tried to make herself inconspicuous, but that seemed impossible, given she was bareheaded and only partially dressed. Lord, please let her loose shirt and *shirwal* be enough to hide her shape. She sat down and put on her slippers and boots, ignoring the conversation.

"Marquis," the pasha said, in French of course. "This is a pleasant place to bathe." His servant came forward and helped the pasha remove his outer cloak.

"It is," Foye said. He washed his chest as if he hadn't a care in the world.

Sabine looked away as the pasha continued to disrobe. He was nothing like Foye, not as tall, not as lean. He waved away his servant and faced her, stroking his beard. How well could he see her in the dark? Foye waded out of the spring. That was a distraction. He towered over the pasha.

Sabine scrambled for the satchel containing a towel and Foye's clothes. As she passed the pasha on her way to join Foye, the pasha stopped her with a question. She turned just her head.

"Have you ever worked in the public *hamam* in Aleppo?" he asked her in Turkish.

She was about to answer him when Foye said, "You seem quite interested in my dragoman, Pasha." Sabine put down the satchel and used the towel to dry Foye's damp skin. He stood as if it were nothing to have someone else looking after him this way. "May I ask why?" Foye said in French.

The Pasha reverted to French. "I asked if he'd been a *hamam* boy." He shrugged. "Such a boy as your dragoman could become quite rich, if he were skilled. If he caught the attention of certain men."

"I've no idea," Foye replied. In English he said, "Pathros?"

"No, Pasha," she answered in Turkish. She bowed deeply. "My father would never permit that."

The pasha chuckled as he walked past them to the spring. "There was once a very rich man of Aleppo who fell in love with a bath boy. He came to the *hamam* whenever he knew the boy was to be there. But another man also admired the bath boy, and they soon became aware they were rivals." His servant followed him to the water, carrying a jeweled metal box that contained the pasha's bathing utensils.

"What happened?" Foye asked. He was dressing now, with Sabine's assistance, in a clean set of road-worthy clothes. Smallclothes, breeches, shirt. She worked as quickly as she could, and when it wouldn't be too obvious, Foye helped. At least the pasha wasn't looking at her anymore. He seemed intent on Foye.

"Ah," the pasha said at Foye's question. "One of the men became jealous and killed the boy."

"A tale with a very sorry ending." Foye shrugged on his coat and let Sabine adjust the garment around his shoulders. He picked up his boots and slid his feet into the slippers. "Good night, Pasha," Foye said. "Come along, Pathros."

Sabine knelt to pack away Foye's dirty clothes and finish putting on the rest of hers.

"Good night, Marquis," the pasha said.

Sabine, delayed by dealing with Foye's clothes and her own, heard the pasha tell his Janissaries to follow them.

Slinging the satchel over her shoulder, she hurried after
Foye, followed by two silent Janissaries.

At the inn, the proprietor brought them coffee and a
narghile as well as a selection of tobacco, which he presented to Sabine. She relayed the choices to Foye, who
merely lifted a disinterested hand. She handed over a coin
in exchange for some of the honey-infused tobacco Godard
had preferred. The Druze captain settled himself in a corner of the room, standing, arms over his chest and staring
over the low wall at the Janissaries gathered there.

On the floor by the fire, Sabine laid out Foye's rug and
blanket, then did the same with her own gear. In this tiny
room, there was no way to put much distance between them.
"Tell the captain he may go, Pathros," Foye said. "And that
I would be grateful if he kept an eye on our friends out
there." She did so, and the Druze bowed and went outside,
leaving her and Foye quite alone.

Foye sat on his blanket. He paid no attention to the
narghile, but he did take the coffee. Sabine was too tired
and anxious to have any coffee herself, though she badly
wanted something to do with her hands. He poured coffee into one of the cups and, one eyebrow raised, said,
"Pathros?"

She, too, squatted. She leaned forward and took it from
him despite not wanting it. "Thank you, effendi."

Foye shrugged off his outercoat and draped it atop his
gear quite as if his doing so was proper between them.
Was it? Was he thinking of her as Sabine Godard or as his
dragoman Pathros? She leaned her head against the wall
behind her back and wished last night had never happened.
They were so ill at ease. Well, she was uncomfortable, at
any rate. She could not tell if Foye was bothered at all. He
reached for his pistols and set them on the ground between
his legs.

She had seen him naked, she thought to herself as she
watched the tension in his body. More than once. Her
palms had felt the shift of muscle and sinew underneath his

skin, the slide of his cock into her. "Do you think the pasha suspects?"

Foye thought about that as he reached for the narghile. "He certainly suspects that I made away with you somehow. But if he suspected you were not Pathros, he would have acted by now. No. He continues to look for a woman, the fool." He reached between them and tapped the side of her head. "I thought I'd have apoplexy when the pasha came down that path with you hardly dressed at all."

She took the narghile from him and deftly, from her long practice doing so for Godard, inserted the tobacco and lit it. She handed it back. "Yes, I as well."

"I think your poor-shorn head convinced him. It's lucky we trimmed it last night. Or was that this morning?" He, too, had his back to the wall. With one leg extended straight out and the other bent up at the knee, he took back the narghile.

"What did he mean by that awful story of the bath boy?" Sabine watched smoke drift toward the ceiling. Her stomach ached from tension.

Foye laughed softly. "Come now, Sabine—"

"Pathros."

"Very well then, Pathros. You've read the Greeks. You can't be ignorant of their notions of love in its various forms." He took another draw at the narghile and blew a smoke ring. "He saw me alone and naked with a very pretty boy and drew his own conclusions."

She sat up and looked him in the face, astonished. His eyelids were lowered partway, but she could see some of his blue irises. "He didn't think that," she said.

"He did." He laughed. "And if he thought I wanted you, well, Pathros, he was right."

She sat back and picked up her coffee. She didn't drink any.

"It's just as well," Foye said. He reached for his coffee, too, and emptied the glass. "Better he finds you a convincing boy and think I want my own *hamam* boy than to have him realize who you are and the real reason I want you flat on your back or on your knees."

"Foye . . ."

"Go to sleep, Pathros."

"You should as well." She put her coffee down only to have Foye pick it up and empty it, too. She frowned. "You'll never sleep now."

"I don't intend to."

"No wonder Barton is worried about you."

"He's always fussing over me." He took another draw on the narghile. "Like a mother hen. Don't you do the same. I assure you, I can handle myself."

She reached across her mattress to adjust his bedding. "He thinks you'll overextend yourself. Having watched you today, I must agree."

"What choice is there?" he said. "The sooner we reach Iskenderun the sooner you'll be safe. You can disappear into the consulate, and the pasha will not be able to touch you. Until then?" He set aside the narghile so violently he had to steady it lest it topple over. Sabine jumped. "You should have sent for me the moment your uncle became ill. I would have come, and perhaps this might have been avoided."

"It happened so fast, Foye. There was so much going on. Godard fell ill, and I don't even know how many hours I sat with him, praying he would recover. But within days he was dead."

He reached out and hooked his palm around the nape of her neck. "Hush, Sabine. I am out of line with you."

"I did write you. Every day."

Still with his hand on her neck, he said, "I imagine he intercepted your mail."

She shook her head. "I thought the same. It's why I sent Asif to Aleppo after Godard died."

Foye slid his hand from her nape to her cheek, curving his long fingers over her cheek and jaw. "That was brave of you. You kept your head about you. Now, sleep, love."

What she wouldn't give to have all this upset behind

them. Her doubts and trepidations rose up in her, choking her, cutting off her words while she fought to suppress the urge for weak, feminine tears. This would be easier if he wasn't being so infernally reasonable and gentle with her. "Was this a mistake, Foye, what happened between us?"

"No." He cupped the other side of her face, too. "I can't stop thinking about you. You were driving me mad with desire before, and it's no better since last night. That wasn't enough. One night with you will never be enough. I want you right now, Sabine, and I will want you tomorrow, too, and for the rest of my life. Do you doubt that?"

"I don't know what I think anymore."

"Then think this, Sabine . . ." Foye bent to her and gently, tenderly, brushed his lips across hers, then again not so gently. "You are a first for me as well." He pressed his forehead to hers. "This is a damnable time to fall in love."

"I'm afraid you'll not want me anymore. After all this. And I'm too young for you." She was shaking inside. Trembling like a leaf. "You said so yourself. I am not suitable for you at all."

"Next year you will be older." He shrugged. "I find that is more than sufficient for me. I've not changed my mind. I won't."

She turned her face and quickly kissed his palm, then moved away. "This is madness, Foye. Madness."

"Then let us go straight to Bedlam." A sharp noise outside made them both freeze.

"You see?" she said in a low voice. "Madness."

Foye straightened and got to his feet. Sabine did the same, and they ended up standing less than an arm's length from each other. But the sound was nothing after all. She was quite close enough to see that his beard was heavier than before, still stubble, but growing longer. His face was tanned darker, too. The deeper color made his eyes an even brighter blue. Her heart hurt just to look at him. His expression, while not exactly soft, was at least no longer devoid of emotion, as it had been for most of the day. "Then let me be mad, Sabine," he whispered.

"That could have been anyone coming back. We might have been seen."

"What will the pasha think?" The corner of his mouth quirked.

"My God," she said. "You're impossible."

"And you are lovely. Even dressed as a boy, you're lovely beyond words. And brave and quite probably more intelligent than I am."

"You were on Godard's list, so it's doubtful."

She stayed where she was, too close to him, but unable to move farther away, either. Where else could she stand in such a tiny, crowded space as this? The room was not large enough to get anywhere near far enough away from him, and if she sat on her mattress, then Foye would not be able to sit without them being too close again. The way he watched her made her stomach shiver with the recognition that here stood a man with whom she had been intimate. He had touched her places she generally pretended didn't exist. He'd made her feel things she didn't know were possible.

"It's a pity we couldn't reach the consulate in Aleppo," he said. "We'll have to be married in Iskenderun instead, and that cuts it rather close. Fortunately," he said evenly, "the vice-consul there is a friend of mine." He let out a breath. "This will come right," he said. "We have only to reach Iskenderun and all will come right." He took her hand in his and gently pressed. "You'll see. Who but I will appreciate all the arcane knowledge packed into that head of yours? Is there any other man who will be proud to hear you list the plays of Aeschylus?" She made a face at him, but he just laughed and leaned over her, so close. Perilously close. "Come now, Sabine, list them for me. You know them all, and I long to hear the words fall like dewdrops from your lips."

"*The Persians*," she said. She licked her lips.

"Go on."

"*Seven Against Thebes, The Suppliants, Agamemnon, The Libation Bearers*, these last three being a trilogy, then *The Eumenides* and likely, *Prometheus Bound*."

"I adore your mind, Sabine." He leaned closer yet, then threw a look over his shoulder. "I adore you utterly." He put a hand on her hip. "Hearing you speak like this arouses me." He chuckled. "You will keep me amused for the rest of my life."

"You're mocking me."

"Never." He grew serious. "Never, Sabine."

Sabine studied the way his cheeks were not perfectly even, the way they slashed down so haphazardly, high and sharp and forcefully there. She remembered, too, the way his skin had felt beneath her fingers, how soft and warm, slick with sweat, the taut muscle beneath. Her stomach had quivered at the sight of his strong features when he looked at her with tenderness—and desire. He touched her cheek, just resting the tips of his fingers on her. The pressure of his fingers brought her head around so that she must either close her eyes or look at him. Their eyes met, and Sabine thought her heart would break just from the simple act of looking at him. "I do love you, Foye" she whispered.

"And I, you. You're exhausted. Lie down and close your eyes. I'll wake you in the morning." Foye reached out and tugged on her hand until she relented and let him hold her hand. They were too close. Too close, considering how terribly she wanted him to hold her. "I'll wake you when it's time to go."

Twenty-seven

❧

FOYE STRETCHED OUT ON HIS PALLET, ONE LEG CROSSED over the other, waiting for the inevitable lull in the night when sentries lost their edge. Perhaps he should have taken Sabine outside somewhere, past the springs, to some copse of wood to lie in the moonlight and whisper to her of his desires while he proved just how deep they ran.

Outside, on the other side of the inn, another caravan was passing on its way to Aleppo, traveling through the night to take advantage of the cool air. They were nearly halfway to Iskenderun. It was possible that with a quick start and hard riding he could get them safely to Iskenderun sometime in the next twenty-four hours.

He sat up. The pasha's Janissaries did not have a change in guard duty; he'd have heard them if they had. When he looked over the rear wall, he saw them sleeping. Several of his mercenaries were asleep as well. His Druze commander was stretched out by the wall. Awake. The captain sat holding onto the rope that secured the horses, in a line of sight to the pasha's tent.

Soft noises came from the horses on the other side of the wall. With the moon so bright, he had a good view of the pasha's tent and the two men asleep outside the door. The last of the camels had finished passing by. He rose and went to the window overlooking the front of the inn, where, in the bright moonlight, he had a good view of the road. A man came behind driving several asses before him, then more armed men, following the caravan on its way to Iskenderun. Soon, they too passed out of his sight.

Foye packed his bedding under the captain's watchful eye. He found Sabine's saddlebags and gear. The soldier nodded and silently rose. He separated Foye's stallion and Sabine's mare from the others, then pegged down the rest so they wouldn't wander. The Druze pointed, silently conveying that he would meet Foye in the front.

He bent down next to Sabine and woke her. Her eyes popped open, but he put a hand across her lips, and she nodded, understanding the need for silence. While she rolled up her bedding, Foye stuffed his coat into one of his saddlebags and took out a set of native clothes of his own. He stripped quickly. Sabine turned and helped him dress, then tucked his tightly rolled-up clothes into his saddlebag. By the time they were done, Foye was a blue-eyed Arab.

Together, they packed up the rest of their gear and crept out.

The Druze waited for them by the road. Foye handed over a heavy purse, which disappeared into the depths of the soldier's sash. Then he and Sabine mounted and they were off, riding hard for Iskenderun.

They continued the climb into the Nur Mountains, letting their mounts pick their way around boulders and through sandy terrain, and occasionally making way for other travelers heading in either direction. No one paid them much attention. Two natives heading into Iskenderun was nothing to remark. Once daylight came, however, anyone who came close enough to see Foye's eyes would penetrate the disguise.

As night worked its way toward dawn, she and Foye dozed in their saddles. They were both dead tired. Still, they stopped only to feed and water the horses and take care of the inevitable pressing needs. Whenever they heard someone behind them, they moved off the road until they were certain it was safe. About ten o'clock the following morning, they reached Balen, the city that spanned the infamous Syrian Gates where Alexander the Great had engaged and ultimately defeated Darius and the Persian army. Their mounts, slow but sure, carried them downward into the western foothills of the Nur Mountains.

Exhaustion pulled at Foye, dragged at his eyes, and clouded his thinking. He could, and had, literally, slept on his horse. Sabine had done the same. The thought of stopping was a siren call to sleep. But Iskenderun meant the end of their journey. They would be safe there. The nightmare of these last few days would be over.

With the heat beating down on them, they rounded a bend, and Foye's breath caught in his chest. Before them the blue Mediterranean stretched out to the horizon. Ships bobbed in the Iskenderun harbor, from which the city spread outward.

They worked their way through the foothills, but before they reached the flatlands of the city itself, Foye turned his horse off the main road. They followed a narrow packed-dirt road, passing several native houses of dark carved stone. He knew from experience that an unprepossessing exterior spoke nothing of what they would find inside.

At one of the homes, Foye unwrapped the cloth around his face and dismounted. Sabine did the same. "This is *Bayt Salem*," he told her. "The home of my friend Hugh Eglender. The vice-consul I told you about." He rubbed his eyes. "I did tell you. Didn't I? He'll marry us."

"Yes, Foye."

His legs felt like water. He wanted so badly to sleep. "You must remain Pathros awhile longer," he said.

"Effendi."

The entrance to the house was a corridor that made two turns before it opened onto the main interior courtyard, a device that ensured it was not possible for passersby to see inside. An English servant met them at the edge of the courtyard. He knew Foye immediately, despite his native costume.

"My lord," he said. He smiled at Foye. "How pleasant to see you."

"Is Eglender at home?" Foye asked.

"No, but he will be very pleased to know you've come to see him, my lord. Come in, come in."

Another servant came to take their horses. Sabine kept her head down and her arms folded around the saddlebags she'd taken from her horse. Two more servants hurried toward them to take their things. Another appeared with a pistol thrust through his waistband. They followed Eglender's butler upstairs to a room with a ceiling painted in deep blue and gold and elaborately carved cabinets lining the walls.

"After such a long journey," Foye said to Eglender's butler, "I should very much like to bathe, please." He made a careless motion in Sabine's direction. "The boy will look after me, no need to disturb anyone else."

The man nodded. "Very good, milord," he said.

"I know the way," Foye said.

"My lord." He bowed and left them alone in the room.

Truly alone.

They locked gazes. He'd done it. They'd reached Iskenderun ahead of the pasha, and he was so tired he could hardly think straight. "Come along, then," he said. "I presume you want a bath at least half as much as I do."

"More than you, Foye." She opened their saddlebags until she found both the metal containers that held the items necessary for bathing.

Since the arrangement of Eglender's house was the traditional one, the baths were located downstairs. Foye led the way past an open storage room to stairs that descended to ground level and an orange- and lemon-tree-lined path through a garden. Another set of stairs took them down to the household's private baths.

Foye already knew the baths here were nothing short of spectacular. An intertwining pattern in the marble floor repeated on the walls and ceiling. Pale white marble columns held up a domed ceiling in which there were insets of thick glass to filter daylight to a soft glow without the danger to modesty that would have been posed by the usual latticed windows. The side nearest the entrance had tiled niches where they could remove their clothes in privacy. In the center of this space was a marble platform where, under normal circumstances, they would lie down while a servant massaged them. There was an awkward pause during which Sabine's cheeks flushed under her darkened skin.

"What are you thinking, Pathros?" he said. Jesus, he felt stupid with exhaustion.

She smiled at him. "That I'm to be your bath boy after all," she said.

The only thing left for them was to undress. Foye stood there for too long, thinking of Sabine and her body and how foolishly, wonderfully giddy he felt when she touched him. And how incredibly lucky he was that she wanted to.

Twenty-eight

👋

Approximately four in the afternoon. The private baths at *Bayt Salem*, Mr. Hugh Eglender's home in Iskenderun, then a province of Syria under the control of the Sultan Mahmud II. Eglender's decision to live in the foothills, rather than the pestilential marshes of the city proper, explained his longevity in his position.

SABINE WAS ALREADY IN ONE OF THE NICHES, REMOVING her clothes. Foye tried not to think about her stripping down to her bare skin, but he didn't have much success. Visions of her refused to leave his head, visions that were accompanied by indelible recollections of him holding her tight while he came. Inside her. With no attempt to spare them both from the consequences of conception.

He was acutely aware that Rosaline had once found herself at a similar crisis—not as to any possible conception but on the cusp of marriage. He knew too well the outcome of that. He and Rosaline had never done more than kiss—but as to feeling pressured into a marriage she didn't want and perhaps wasn't ready for. The result of that had not been happy for him. Engaged to marry a man she did not love, no doubt pressured by her father, Rosaline must have felt a great deal like Sabine did now. Trapped. Resentful. Full of doubt.

He stepped into a niche and removed his travel-stained clothes. He bundled up his fresh clothes but instead of walking out, he sat on the marble bench and wondered what the hell was going to happen to him this time. They were not out of danger, he and Sabine. She'd been through too much, lately, to be sure of anything. Devastated by the death of her uncle, harried by Nazim Pasha, dressed as a boy, and now his lover.

He let his head fall back against the marble wall behind him. He was too damn tired to think straight. He knew if Sabine left him, he would be shattered beyond repair.

"Foye?" Sabine called softly.

He rose and tied a silk *pestamel* around his hips and slipped on a pair of pattens that would keep him from falling and breaking open his head. He stepped out of his niche. "Yes?"

Sabine stood in the middle of the room with her shockingly short hair and brown face and hands, and he didn't understand how the pasha or anyone else had ever failed to see her for the woman she was. Like him, he wore pattens on her feet. He was reminded of the pasha's story about the *hamam* boy, and, Jesus, his mind was so unclear, so fuzzy with exhaustion, he didn't know what to think.

"I cannot untie this." Her cheeks were bright pink. She meant the cloth that bound her breasts. She'd wrapped a *pestamel* around her hips, too; other than that, and the cloth around her bosom, she was nude, and he couldn't help himself. He looked a very long time at her legs and bare midriff.

Eventually, he recovered himself and helped her unfasten the knot he'd tied between her shoulder blades. He had to work at it because the material was damp and had tightened during the course of their traveling. When he had the two ends separated, she put her hands over her bosom to keep the cloth in place. He trailed a finger along her spine.

She slowly turned around. "Thank you, Foye."

She wasn't Rosaline. Sabine would never leave him the

way Rosaline had. She would be honest with him if she changed her mind. "If you decide to leave me," he said, "you will tell me, won't you?"

Her eyebrows drew together, but she seemed to understand he wasn't asking her a question. She nodded. "Yes, Foye."

He stayed where he was. They were both dirty, and they both smelled like they'd been traveling long and hard. Her head did not reach his chin, nowhere near, actually. He put his hands on her shoulders, his thumbs parallel with the nape of her neck. He was glad, fiercely and deeply glad that he'd met Sabine.

"And if you leave me?" she asked.

"I won't," he said.

"You don't know that."

God, what they needed was two consecutive weeks without disaster. Time to know each other, to learn and love without the threat of death or betrayal hanging over them.

"I do," he said.

She gazed at him. He knew she was analyzing his every word, every nuance of his expression, looking for meaning within meaning within meaning. Except, it was so very simple. He watched her arrive at the same conclusion. She nodded again. "Of course," she said. She took his hand and pressed his fingers. He reached out and tugged at that damned cloth. After a bit, Sabine let go and he pulled it away, letting it drop to the floor. She'd already bundled her clothes, the cleanest she had left, as he had, and he reached down to pick up her things and tuck them under one arm.

"Come, Sabine." He walked into the warm room via a short, right-angle passage constructed so as to prevent a direct line of sight from the first to the second. He heard her following him, and it took all his self-discipline not to look over his shoulder at her. He'd damn near run her into the ground over the last few days, and not a word of complaint had come from her. Not one.

Marble benches lined the walls in this room. Every few yards was a fountain where one could turn a tap for cool,

clear water to rinse off the soap and dirt. In the middle of
the room were two shallow pools, one larger than the other,
both with patterned marble bottoms and wide steps into
the water. He put their clothes and bathing kits onto the
marble bench by the nearest pool and immersed himself
in the water. Bliss, he thought, as the water surrounded
him. Unadulterated bliss. He opened his eyes and, God,
he thought he'd never in his life seen anything as erotic
as Sabine walking toward him. Other than the *pestamel*
around her waist, she wore nothing. He clearly saw the
uneven demarcation of her dyed skin and the pale white-
ness of her elsewhere.

At the edge of the pool, he held out his hand. She hesitated. "My love," he said softly.

She slipped off the pattens and got into the water. He
didn't regret his promise of restraint. He would not disgrace
them both by allowing the possibility of one of Eglender's
servants interrupting them engaged in something that must
be private between them.

"When we are back in England," he said while he
scrubbed his arms without looking at her—anything to
take his mind off all the things he wanted to do to her, "I
am going to build a Turkish bath at Maralee House." That
remark required a glance in her direction. She was scrubbing her leg, her head tilted toward him. "Perhaps I'll even
hire Turkish servants to staff the addition. What do you
think? Shall we have a Turkish bath?"

"That sounds very nice." She stared into the water,
keeping her back turned away.

Foye put a hand on her bare shoulder. He was far, far gone
from trying to pretend he didn't want her or that he wasn't
going to touch her again. He was. As soon as they were private. Just not now, when they were both tired and hungry
and nervous with each other with so many things between
them unsettled. "You're so lovely, Sabine. I haven't told you
that near often enough. Nor how much I admire you."

She looked over her shoulder at him. There were dark
circles under her eyes. "Thank you, Foye."

"What you need," he said, smiling at her, "is your very own *hamam* boy."

She laughed at him.

"At your service," he said.

He stretched for his bowl and used that to scoop water to get their hair thoroughly wet. When he'd done that, he grabbed her hand and walked with her to the bench where he'd set his bathing supplies. She had none of her own, of course. He put his between them and set himself to washing his hair. Sabine did the same. He adored the way her short hair exposed the line of her throat and shoulders.

When he poured the last basin of water over her hair, she let her head drop back and closed her eyes. She let out a sigh. "Heaven. This is heaven. I've been dreaming of a bath forever."

Foye stared at her bare breasts because he was too damn tired not to. She was lovely beyond words. While he stared he knew deep in his soul that she was the woman with whom he wanted to share his life; there was no question in his mind whatever. He wanted them to be married now. Yesterday. This minute.

She opened her eyes and caught him staring. Foye didn't bother to pretend he hadn't been. He no longer cared about trying to keep his reactions subdued. Her cheeks turned pink, but she didn't look away from him. He ran his fingertips along the underside of one of her breasts. "When we are alone, Sabine, I will adore you properly, I promise. If you'll let me. If you want me to."

"Oh, Foye," she whispered. "What am I to do with you?"

She was so very young in some ways, with so little experience of men in the usual social sense. She had never been given a season, never been presented to men as a marriageable young lady. She'd had no interactions with men to whom he might be compared so that she could be certain she preferred him to anyone else. She had lived her entire life believing she would always be taking care of her uncle.

"Whatever you like," he said. He was careful to smile so

she wouldn't read more into his reply than she was ready to hear. He picked up his soap and worked up a lather. Between them, they washed the dirt and stink from their bodies. He didn't see any reason for modesty between them, so he moved aside his *pestamel* and soaped himself everywhere. He didn't dare do the same for her; he knew where that would lead, and this was neither the time nor place for that.

While she stayed in the pool, he waded out and propped the kit's mirror on one of the ledges above the tap that fed water into the basin. Barton would have been astounded that not even a nick marred his cheeks or throat when he was done. He put his razor under the water to clear away the soap and ended with a thorough rinse of his face.

"There," he said, rubbing his newly smooth chin and checking to see that he'd not missed any spots. "I am as handsome as ever now."

Sabine didn't say anything to that, and when he looked over, he saw why. She was fast asleep. Her head rested against the tall marble decorations carved above the next basin and tap, and her rinsing bowl bobbed in the basin beside her. Her hair was partially dry. One curl, part gold, part brown, was damp enough to cling to the side of her cheek. She'd refastened her *pestamel* around her waist. Drops of water glistened on her skin.

Even though he had touched her body everywhere a man could desire to touch a woman, even though he'd had his mouth on her there, he felt he was seeing Sabine for the first time in his life and falling in love with her like some damn fairy tale in which the monster was redeemed by the maiden. Well. He was a beast, and he was in love with her.

His conviction about the state of his heart left him shaky and uncertain. Had he felt this way about Rosaline? He knew he'd believed he loved her. If anyone had tried to tell him he hadn't he'd have called him a fool. He had loved Rosaline, that was so. He'd been pleased—no, happy, intensely happy—when she accepted his offer of marriage and had only fallen more deeply in love with her afterward. After they were formally engaged, he'd been faithful to her. A changed man compared to his previous ways. There had been no more mistresses, no more affairs with widows or married women.

But had he ever felt that if something were to happen to Rosaline his life would end? He wasn't sure. He remembered the giddy happiness of loving Rosaline. And how little of himself he had shared with her. Because, he knew, to his shame, that she had not been his equal. Sabine was. And he was quite sure that without Sabine he'd be destroyed. Indeed, he had loved Rosaline, but he loved Sabine in an entirely different way. More deeply. More dangerously.

Foye returned to his belongings, bundled them up, and went to Sabine. He knelt at her side. "Sabine?" he said. She didn't respond, so he touched her shoulder—God, her skin was soft—and gave her a gentle shake. "Sabine?"

Her eyes twitched under her closed lids.

"Sabine," he said softly. She opened her eyes, but he could see she wasn't fully awake. "Sabine, wake up."

She lifted her head and blinked slowly. "Foye?"

She needed him, he thought. Whatever reservations she had about him, she did need him. She was alone, with no family to worry about what happened to her, no one to keep her safe. Her eyes focused and something in him twisted painfully when he saw how she fought to wake herself up. "My goodness. I fell asleep."

"Come, Sabine," he said. He was proud of her and all she had endured without complaint. "It's time we went upstairs."

She more or less succeeded in staying awake from sheer force of will. He tucked away his sexual response to her as he picked her up and carried her into the cool room. There, he wrapped a towel around her hair and two more around her shoulders and waist and settled her on a divan while he went back to fetch their clothes and bath items.

When he returned, she was awake and sitting cross-

legged on the divan combing out what was left of her hair.
She had put on her *shirwal* but left the towels covering the
rest of her. Pity, that. She worked a comb through her hair,
then switched to the other side, beginning on the tangles
there. When she was done, she set her comb very precisely
on the table beside her.

"I need help getting dressed," she said.

"Of course." This was accomplished quickly enough.
Once they'd bound her bosom again, his primary contribu-
tion was to hand her the various parts of her costume. She
was all too soon Pathros.

"I'll arrange to get you more suitable clothes in the
morning," he said while she adjusted her headdress. "Perhaps Eglender knows someone whose wife or daughter is
your size." He threw aside his towel and began dressing.
He looked at her sideways while he wrestled to get his shirt
right-side out. "I'll see about finding a ship to get us home.
Tomorrow. Or later today. I've lost track of the days. After
we've slept." He glared at his shirt; one of the sleeves was
now wrong-side out. How had he not noticed that? "I can't
think straight anymore."

She left the divan. "Do you need help, effendi?"

Foye let out a short, hard sigh. "Hell, yes."

She took his shirt from him, and he ducked his head for
her so they could get the thing on him. They succeeded,
eventually, in getting him dressed, while he did his best
to ignore the intimacy of her hands on him, touching him,
shaking out his clothes, smoothing them out, buttoning,
fastening, even tying a very decent knot in his cravat. Hell,
he even put a hand on her shoulder for balance when she
bent to get his stockings on his feet.

He couldn't wait to get her upstairs and both of them
undressed.

Twenty-nine

❧

About half past seven in the morning. *Bayt Salem*, in the foothills above Iskenderun. An upstairs room with carved cedar cabinets and a painted ceiling. A finch sat in one of the high windows trying to convince a lady finch to visit his most excellent perch.

FOYE RESTED HIS WEIGHT ON ONE FOREARM AND LOOKED down at Sabine. It was sometime in the morning since there was enough light for him to see despite the room lamps being out. She was naked and felt remarkably good tucked against his body. Tenderness welled up in him because she was Sabine and the woman who made his heart whole. He would take care of her. No matter what happened or how she did or didn't feel about him.

She lay on her side, facing him, her hands up close to her face, head bowed toward his chest. His uppermost leg was draped over her lower body. The color on her face, although lighter than it had been, remained darker than the rest of her skin, which was immensely and beautifully pale. So very English of her. Her hair was, of course, still a mutilated walnut streaked with gold.

Sabine, still asleep, moved closer to him, burrowing her face against his chest, and he was touched that she sought him out. He caressed her shoulder with the tip of his finger, tracing a circle on her very pale skin. She made a soft sound in the back of her throat, and Foye leaned down and kissed her shoulder. She smelled of attar of roses from the scent bottles left on hand in the cool room, and he was viscerally reminded of how he'd felt when he was inside her, when he was looking into her face, sweat between their joined bodies, and her looking at him as if he were the handsomest man she'd ever seen. There weren't many women who looked at him like that.

All in all, he was very much at peace with what they must do. He ought to be more bothered by his predicament than he was; marrying a too-young woman when he'd been so certain he did not want to marry at all. He would be doing well by them both if he could make Sabine content in their marriage. And himself. He kissed her earlobe. He looked forward to returning to England to settle into a country life where the most excitement they were likely to face was whether they would walk to church on Sunday or drive.

"Mm," she said without opening her eyes. "Foye." She stretched slowly, luxuriously, and his belly tightened with desire for her as her body slid against his. "Is it morning already?"

How sublime it was to hold Sabine in his arms, to feel her against him and know the woman he loved returned the emotion and more. He wouldn't trade a single day with Sabine for anything. None of the heart-pounding fear, none of the days fighting his feelings for her. Not a minute of any day since he'd walked into Anthony Lucey's parlor and seen her sitting there.

He shifted himself over her, only partially so that he did not crush her, and slid down to kiss one of her breasts. The minute he did, his cock went full-on hard for her. When his mouth closed over her nipple, she moaned softly and arched into him. She wasn't, after all, despite her small size, the sort of woman who did not like a large and rather beastly looking man. As he recalled, she liked him very well indeed.

Her arms wrapped around his shoulders, and Foye felt himself slip away, far from anything that was right or proper or gentlemanly, and into a world where all that mattered was Sabine, who loved him.

She adjusted herself, and he watched her eyes open and focus on him. He was poised to enter her, but didn't yet. He wanted to be sure she was ready for him and that he had a firm grip on his need for her.

"Foye," she whispered in a low, desirous whisper. She pushed at his chest, and he submitted himself to whatever fancy she had in mind. He ended up on his back with Sabine over him. Her hair fell forward as she leaned down to his chest, tiny curls almost as unmanageable as his own. Her tongue came out and swept over his nipple, and he felt the pull of that all the way to his balls.

She slid one hand along his rib cage and down to his hip and then across to his aching cock, and all the while she was kissing his body, his chest, his nipples, then his belly, and the, oh hell yes, the inside of his thighs.

"Jesus God, Sabine," he whispered when her tongue dipped into his navel while her hand was being very bold beneath. She cupped his bollocks in her palm, and by then he wasn't thinking of much besides whether she was going to take him in her mouth and whether he would go out of his mind before she did. When she put the matter to rest, Foye thrust his pelvis toward her and buried his fingers in her hair. "I am your slave," he said while he still had something of his wits about him. "Your abject slave." Her tongue touched the rim of his cock. "God, help me, yes. Like that."

He was a damned lucky bastard no matter what because, as it turned out, she was able to take a good deal of him into her mouth, and he couldn't see any sign that she minded this in the least. She proceeded to send him mad with pleasure. Her fingers, too, stayed quite busy, touching, stroking.

He was quickly at the point of climax and trying to delay the inevitable.

"Sabine," he said. "Sabine, I want to finish inside you. God, please."

She stopped but not before he had to exercise every ounce of his willpower not to let himself fall, and even then, he held her tightly because for some time he was in danger of a single touch from her dropping him off the edge. "Did you like that?" she asked.

"Hell, yes." At some point, he thought, he would have to relearn how to control his language around her. At some point.

"Mm," she said. She still had her head by his parts, one hand on his thigh, the other on his belly. She had a calculating look on her face, as if she'd been taking mental notes of his reaction, and the thought that she was analyzing what they'd just done, what he'd just let her do, wound him tighter yet. Where might a mind like hers end up on the subject of his pleasure? "Perhaps I'll do that again," she said, and hell if she didn't run her tongue along her lower lip. "I want to see you lose control. I want to know what you look like when that happens."

"No," he said, very serious now. He pulled her onto his chest. It was crucial to him that she understand he would never lose control with her. Ever. They would have a very controlled and proper marriage. None of this overlarge emotion that had plagued them. "You would not like that at all." He buried his hands in her hair and summoned a smile. "A great beast like me, Sabine? I'd terrify you."

"You wouldn't, Foye." She gave a tight shake of her head. "I don't want you to hold back." She reached up and pressed a hand to his cheek. "I won't break. I can promise you that."

He rolled her underneath him but kept her on her stomach. He kissed his way down her spine before he slid a hand underneath her hips and brought her up so that, with him on his knees and holding her hips with both hands, he

entered her from behind. "Is this all right?" he whispered.
"Am I too wicked for you?"

"Foye." She gave a soft moan and pressed back
against him.

That was certainly an encouraging development, wasn't
it? He watched his cock disappear inside her, felt the slick
tightness of her pressing around him when he was in as
far as he could get. He held her hard against him, working
himself in her, dying.

Someone, some godforsaken, addlepated fool, knocked
lightly on the door. Once and then a second time. Someone
said something in Arabic.

Sabine went still. He bent over her, one arm holding his
weight, and careful not to let his torso touch her back. He
got his breath under control.

"Don't even think of stopping this," he whispered. "Not
until we are both quite done." He pushed back and wrapped
the fingers of one hand around her hips. He held her tight
against his groin while he circled his pelvis. "Pathros," he
said in a voice made rough with passion, "tell whoever it is
that I am not fit company yet, but that you will soon make
me so."

She called out something in Arabic, but only a word or
two, which was not enough for her to have said anything
that would prevent someone from opening the door and
discovering that Foye was breaking the tenets of his faith
and the Mohammedans', too. At least with her naked, there
would be no doubt that his conduct was with a woman
rather than his young dragoman.

There was a response from the other side of the door.

"Tell him the rest, Sabine." He kept his fingers on her
soft, soft skin while he continued moving in her. He had to
put his other hand on the floor to keep his balance and hold
his weight off her while he put his mouth by her ear. "I am
not to be disturbed just now. You, personally, will see to
my every need and have me downstairs shortly."

She said something again, several sentences of which he

understood not one word. Whoever was on the other side of the door said another word or two, and he and Sabine stayed quiet enough to hear him walking away. He got an arm around her, fingers stroking her hard until he felt the beginning of her climax. Foye pulled out of her and put himself on his back.

"Foye," she whispered when he was inside her again with her on top. "Foye."

"You are delicious," he said. He had the presence of mind to keep his voice low.

"I love you," she said. She put her palms on his chest and worked her hips on him while he put a hand over her nether hair and stroked her. He wanted this to last, this time when they were both at more leisure than they'd ever been. "Foye," she said. He heard the strain her voice.

"Make love with me like this, Sabine." He slid a hand around the back of her neck. He was very close to a climax. It wouldn't take much more. "I'm going to make our son now," he said, because he was there, about to come without taking any precautions. "Right now."

It was remarkable, really, that just over an hour later they rode to the British Consulate to call on his friend Hugh Eglender. He'd spent a preposterously long time getting dressed, but when he was done, he was sartorial perfection, down to the polish of his boots and buttons. He was now conspicuously armed with a pistol and a sword, and Sabine, in her guise as Pathros, wore her pistol tucked into her sash as well as a dagger.

They were in Iskenderun proper now, with the scent of the sea on the air and the cry of seabirds over the harbor, and they were very nearly safe from Nazim Pasha.

Had he ever thought that his wedding day would be like this?

She brought her mare even with his mount and bowed her head before she addressed him. She sat her native saddle easily now, quite used to it. "Foye, are you absolutely certain of this?"

He kept them moving, though his heart had gone still.

She was quite clever enough to argue her way out of this, if she'd changed her mind. There was always the possibility that she would refuse to go along. It was difficult to marry a woman who would not say "I will."

Foye was not without mental resources of his own. He'd been on Sir Henry's list, for pity's sake. "Am I to be jilted again?" he asked. He meant to sound harsh and so he did. "That is badly done of you, Sabine, if you intended this all along."

"No, Foye," she said. "No."

"Then it's tedious to repeat myself," he said. He leaned toward her, keeping his voice pitched low. "I made no effort to prevent conception, Sabine. None whatsoever. I will not sail to England knowing we might well discover halfway there that you are in an inconvenient situation and unmarried. And you cannot stay here, you know that. I won't have you in that sort of danger when we do not know yet where Nazim Pasha is or what he plans to do."

"Perhaps nothing," she said.

"Nazim Pasha has leveled entire villages from a perceived slight to his honor. He will seek revenge against me if he realizes what's happened before we are safely married and on our way home. That's a given. Even if that were not so, we have very little choice in the matter now, Sabine. It's what's done in situations such as this." He speared her with a glance. "It's what's done. What's proper and honorable."

She pressed her lips together.

"Sabine." He allowed himself to relax. "I want to marry you. I want you to be my wife." They were now mere yards from the consulate. He drew up and sat his horse calmly. "If you are having doubts, consider, Sabine, that you are alone in the world. I will take care of you. As my wife, you'll want for nothing."

"That is unfair—"

"Though it was not my intention to return to England anytime soon, I am happy to do so now, with my bride on my arm. But I will tell you now quite bluntly that it was never my intention to marry a woman who is too young and too intellectually blind to see the facts before her."

"Intellectually blind?"

"Fear not, my love." He kept a straight face, but the urge to laugh at her outrage was nearly irresistible. "I am in charity with all your shortcomings. Be assured, Sabine, that if this madness of ours has given us a child, then you and my child will have the protection of my name. Do not suppose for even a moment I would let you bear me a bastard. There is no counterargument to that."

She opened her mouth to object and didn't. Because, after all, he was right. "This cannot end well."

"A disguised attack ad hominem, Sabine? That does not become you. I submit this will end quite well. I shall have a legal wife, very young and very pretty, to bear the Marrack scion, and you shall have a husband who tolerates your many eccentricities."

"You will regret this."

He shook his head. "In fact, my love, I doubt it. You read my fortune in my tea leaves and, if you will but recall, my fortune was to be lucky in love."

"So you resort to absurdities." But she was smiling, and that was something. "Really, Foye. That does not become you."

"Consider our marriage a condition of my plucking you from the pasha's harem or preventing you from becoming a gift to be installed in the Seraglio to await the sultan's whim. Or, if you prefer, consider this my just reward for everything I have done since I went haring after you."

"Why did you?"

He shrugged. "Because I realized that I had not laid my case before the one person whose approval you required. I went to Kilis intending to convince Sir Henry that you must be my wife. I intended, if you must know, to tell him that he would not lose you if you were to become mine." He let out a long breath. "Or, if you must, Sabine, consider our marriage your burden to bear for your sins with me.

So long as we put an end to this ridiculous discussion and attend to our wedding day."

"Very well, Foye." She lifted her chin. "I merely wished to point out there might be alternatives."

"Duly noted. I reject them, of course."

"Entirely out of hand," she said.

"Yes. Shall we, then?"

"Mr. Eglender might refuse to marry us, you know."

"He won't. You may rely on that, my dear."

Thirty

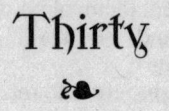

THEY COVERED THE REMAINING DISTANCE TO THE consulate without another word between them. Good, he thought. At least she accepted that this would happen. Outside, they dismounted, and while Sabine held the reins of both horses since she remained, ostensibly, his servant, Foye gave a coin to a young boy waiting in the street.

"Tell him," he said to Sabine in a measured voice, "that I will give him another coin if he and our horses are here and happy when we return."

She did, and Foye opened the consulate door and in they went. They were greeted by a young Englishman who sat at a desk copying out documents. Foye walked to him.

"The Marquess of Foye, here to see Mr. Hugh Eglender," he said when he had the young man's attention.

The clerk's chair scraped the floor when he jumped to his feet. "My lord." He bowed a bit too deeply, but Foye was by now used to such reactions when he identified himself. "I'll tell Mr. Eglender you are here."

"Thank you."

Five minutes later, the clerk returned to usher them into Eglender's office. The vice-consul was standing behind a desk when Foye walked in with Sabine. Hugh Eglender was a moderately tall man with thinning brown hair and dark brown eyes. Behind the affable exterior, Foye knew, was a sharp mind. They had been at King's College together. He wondered if Eglender had made it onto Sir Henry's list. He ought to have. A question for Sabine later.

"Foye," Eglender said, smiling broadly. "Good to see you." He thrust out a hand and they shook briefly. "I am sorry I didn't see you before I left this morning. I was hoping we'd sit down to coffee first and have a few moments to catch up on what you've been doing since you left Iskenderun. I've never known you to sleep so late. You must have been tired indeed."

"I was," Foye said. "Very tired." He reached back to pull Sabine forward and establish her in the chair. Eglender's eyes rose. "We'd been traveling for days without adequate sleep. I'm afraid we would neither of us have been fit company for you this morning."

Eglender narrowed his eyes at Foye's use of the plural. But other than another puzzled glance at Sabine, he paid no attention to her. "Is there something I can do for you, my lord?"

"In fact there is. I am about to tax you grievously, Eglender. I need passage for two on a ship bound for England, the sooner the better."

"There are two in the harbor now waiting to sail." He tapped his desk. "Captain York in command of the *Thunderous* is leaving in a fortnight, I believe."

"Not a military ship unless it cannot be avoided. And a fortnight is too long. We cannot wait." Like hell he was putting Sabine on a ship sailing for His Majesty's Royal Navy. "It's essential we be on our way as soon as possible."

"The other is a merchant marine. The *Eos*. Bound for Portsmouth if I'm not mistaken. She's waiting for the evening tide. That will be tight, if you're to sail with them."

"That will do. Can you arrange it for me?" There were advantages to his title, and he intended to use every single one that he could. "I fear I am here without any of my staff."

Eglender bowed. "Of course, my lord. Consider it done."

"The passage is for two, Eglender. Specifically, me and my wife."

His eyes opened wide. "Your wife?"

"If you will but oblige me, yes." He gripped Sabine's hand. Jesus. He was actually nervous. "Allow me to present you to Miss Sabine Godard."

Quite plainly, Eglender recognized the name. His eyes opened wide. "Miss Godard? Sir Henry Godard's niece?"

"Take off the headdress, Sabine. If you please."

"Good Lord," Eglender said when Sabine complied.

"It was necessary to disguise her as my dragoman in order to get her safely out of Kilis. Nazim Pasha, I fear, had designs on her."

Eglender leaned forward, pressing his hands to the desktop. He looked from Foye to Sabine and back. "I have a letter from Mr. Barker in from Aleppo, dated nearly three weeks ago now, that confirms Miss Sabine Godard perished from the illness that took her uncle."

"A lie, as you can see." Foye brought Eglender current with all, or nearly all, that had happened since he'd left Büyükdere and ended with the request that Eglender, with his authority as vice-consul, marry them before they returned to England.

Eglender sat down hard. "I don't think I've heard a more remarkable tale in my life, Foye, and I have been in the Levant long enough to think myself immune to surprise. Are you quite sure?"

It was a measure of his frustration with Sabine and her similar hesitation about an immediate marriage that Foye's voice hardened more than was necessary. "Yes, Eglender," he said brusquely. "I am quite, quite certain." He drew himself up. "I trust I need only assure you that I am certain this must be done since no one will listen to what I wish to be done."

Eglender blanched. "My apologies, Foye."

"So long as you marry us, all is forgiven." He forced himself to smile. He would have what he wanted. And very soon, too.

"Very well, my lord."

Foye produced a ring from his pocket. He had last night sent Eglender's butler instructions to purchase what he needed. Though he'd described a plain gold band, this morning the servant had put into his hand a ring set with sapphires and citrine. He didn't care what it looked like. This one, or any other, would suffice until he was back in England and could see to having the union consecrated by the Church of England.

A quarter of an hour later, he was a married man, and Sabine Godard legally no longer existed.

His. She was his at last.

Sabine was silent on their ride back to *Bayt Salem*, and Foye decided it would be best to leave her to her thoughts for now. They'd been through enough, for pity's sake. Hell, he needed some time to adjust himself. Besides, it was done. She was his wife. Lady Foye. The fact was, he liked the sound of that. She was his. They had a lifetime to learn how to live with their love, but only a few hours until the *Eos* sailed. Between now and then, he had a great deal to see to, not the least of which was obtaining suitable clothing for her. He could hardly bring his wife home with nothing but the clothes on her back. When they were home, he'd bring her to London and see she had a wardrobe befitting a marchioness.

"Foye." Sabine grabbed his arm, squeezing hard. "Foye!" she said in a low voice.

He stopped. Without his noticing they'd reached the interior courtyard of *Bayt Salem*.

They were not alone. The courtyard teemed with men

and horses. He recognized his Janissaries, his Druze captain, and the pasha's men as well. Most of the Janissaries had their weapons drawn. The captain had confronted one of the Janissaries, and the two stood across from each other, glaring at one another.

As Foye took in the scene, a solitary man emerged from among the Janissaries. He held a pistol himself. His splendidly embroidered kaftan rustled as he walked. Nazim Pasha caught the soldier's arm and said something in a sharp voice. The soldier kept his musket trained on the Druze.

"Sabine," Foye said. She dismounted and stayed behind him, a hand pressed into the small of his back.

Nazim Pasha pushed forward until he stood before Foye. In French, he said, "Marquis. How delightful that I have caught up to you at last."

"I'm afraid I can't say the same," Foye replied.

"Perhaps you might call for coffee and refreshments," the pasha said.

"Alas." Foye crossed his arms over his chest. "This is not my house, Excellency. Such hospitality is not mine to extend. I do not think the owner would appreciate learning that your Janissaries have been here, terrorizing his household."

"Where is Miss Godard?" the pasha asked. "I know you have arranged to meet her here." The rings on his fingers sparkled in the light.

"Beyond your reach at last." Foye grabbed the reins to Sabine's horse and walked out of the corridor, leading both animals. He kept Sabine behind him.

The pasha said something in his own language.

"Was that as vile as it sounded?" he asked Sabine.

"Yes, Foye."

He heard the ominous sound of a pistol being cocked. "Now that I look closely," the pasha said, "she does not make a convincing boy at all." He took a step toward Sabine. "She is too lovely a woman to be dressed in such clothes and treated in so low a fashion."

Sabine lifted her pistol and aimed it at the pasha's heart. "One more step, Excellency, and you are a dead man," she said in perfect French.

"My love," Foye said, "please tell Nazim Pasha's men that you or I will shoot him dead if they do anything but turn about and go back to Kilis." When she had complied, Foye looked the pasha straight in the eye and said, "Pasha, you would do well to forget Sabine Godard entirely. She no longer exists."

The pasha had his hands up by his ears. He was still smiling. Behind the pasha, Foye's Janissaries had moved into a better position to react should this come out badly. His odds of getting Sabine out alive improved a great deal. "Marquis, you overreact."

Foye kept his own pistol trained on the pasha. "You might have succeeded in convincing the authorities to look the other way when you were arranging to kidnap an innocent young woman." The pasha's grin grated on him. "I promise you, they won't look the other way when the woman involved is my wife."

"Wife?" He took a step back and clapped his hands in mock delight. He stopped when Sabine took a step forward, aiming her pistol at the pasha's heart. Foye had no idea if she was any kind of a decent shot, but the focused look on her face was probably enough to convince the pasha that this was not the time to find out. "And this is something you can prove?"

He gazed steadily at the pasha. He saw the rage in his dark eyes, and it was no comfort to see. "Does it matter, Excellency?"

"Perhaps not at this moment, no."

"I promise you, it's so. Sabine Godard is my wife." He leaned forward. "She is no longer without a man's protection, Pasha, and you should be quite certain that I will protect her with my last breath. Or yours, if necessary." He smiled. "I do so hope it is, Pasha."

Nazim Pasha stood unmoving for quite a while. At last, though, he brought his hands together and bowed. "What a shame that I cannot stay to drink a toast of felicitations to your happiness."

Foye didn't relax until every last one of the pasha's men had gone. Only when he heard the distant sound of the outer doors being locked did he put away his pistol. After which there was an explosion of sound, with everyone speaking at once in too many languages to keep straight. There were a great many explanations and directions to convey to too damn many people, in too damn many languages, all of which were somehow duly made. Foye made sure his Janissaries were paid and their services extended until such time as he and Sabine were sailing for home.

Later, when emotions had settled down and the household was once again quiet, Foye and Sabine went downstairs to one of the storerooms where Foye had left a trunk of his. Eglender's butler had produced, from God knows where, two valises sufficient to stow such things for their voyage as they would be able to procure from among Foye's belongings or from the bazaar in Iskenderun. Servants were busy packing what belongings Foye had on hand.

An hour later a letter came from Eglender that changed everything. "What is it?" Sabine asked after Foye read it and said nothing.

He reread the letter, but the result was the same. "The *Eos* has no room for more passengers. No berth can be procured for love or money." He resisted the urge to crumple the paper. A duke's mistress was on board, with an extensive retinue.

"We'll take the next, then," Sabine said. "The military ship."

"I won't put you on a fighting ship, Sabine, and that is at present all that sits in the harbor."

"What of Constantinople?" Yes, he saw she understood very well the danger of them remaining within Nazim Pasha's reach. "Can we not sail from there?"

"It's nearly a month from here to Constantinople." He walked to her and held her face between his hands. "I want you safely out of Turkey. I want you home. At Maralee."

"There are no ships, Foye."

"You'll go alone. On the *Eos* as planned."

Her eyebrows drew together. "Even if I wanted to, how could I, Foye, if there is no room?"

"Eglender moved heaven and earth and found two women who agreed to share their cabin with you."

She shook her head.

"You must go, Sabine. You know you must."

"Don't send me away without you," she whispered.

"I'll take the very next ship possible. I promise you. The *Thunderous*, if I must." He kissed her forehead and then her mouth, and her lips were so soft beneath his. Foye pulled back with a long sigh. "We haven't much time. The *Eos* sails in less than two hours."

After some discussion about her final destination once she arrived in England—Foye wanted her to go directly to Maralee—they agreed Sabine would proceed to Oxford and see to her uncle's estate. He'd come afterward as soon as passage could be obtained for him. And they would, at last, begin their married life together.

In the storeroom, Foye hung a lamp on a hook in the wall. He pulled out his kit and saddlebags and went through them for anything that might be useful to her. His scissors. His brush and comb were upstairs. Flint. Half a candle. He opened the trunk he'd left behind when he first arrived in the country weeks ago.

As he lifted out items, he set things aside for her to look at. Books mostly. A sheaf of paper. A spare writing case. "You'll have something to read," he said. "And to write and draw with." He put a hand on the books. "Take them all if you like."

"Thank you, I will." She too intently examined the book.

"Sabine."

"Yes?" She wouldn't look at him.

"I wish you could stay with me. I wish it were possible, but it's not. Do you doubt for a moment that the pasha has not given up thoughts of revenge? If we stay in Turkey, I assure you he'll find us."

She lifted her head at last. "That is precisely the point, Foye. What is to keep the pasha from extracting his revenge on you while you wait for another ship?"

"I need you safe. I need to know you are safe and on your way to England." He took her in his arms. They had very little time now. He swallowed the lump in his throat. The fact was, he did not want her to go. He wanted to keep her with him, and damn the risk. "I wish you did not have to go so far on your own."

"It's all right, Foye." She bowed her neck until her forehead rested against his chest. After a bit, she said, "Promise me you'll be careful?"

He kissed the top of her head. "I promise."

She looked into his face. "I'll wait for you in Oxford, then."

"I would prefer you go to Maralee to wait for me, but Oxford suits." She would need time to see to her uncle's effects and to make whatever personal amends were needed. He nodded and opened the portable writing case. He opened the bottle of ink and took out paper. "A letter for my solicitor. If anything should happen, if you should find yourself in need of funds or assistance of any sort, he'll see to it. I'll give you the papers from Eglender as well. Best you have those with you." He wrote quickly, signed his name, and when the ink was dried folded and sealed the letter. He took out two more sheets of paper. "My banker. And another for the butler at Maralee House." He looked at her while he wrote. "For my peace of mind, Lady Foye. Maralee is your home now. Always. No matter what."

She took the sealed papers from him. "I can't shake the conviction that something will go wrong."

"All will come right, Sabine. You'll see."

But it didn't.

Thirty-one

&

10 Walter Close, Oxford, England,
NOVEMBER 22, 1811

The home of the late Sir Henry Godard and the former Miss Sabine Godard. The weather was exceptionally wet that day. It was impossible to escape the sound of water, dripping from eaves, falling from the sky, spattering onto windows and streets.

EXHAUSTION SANK DEEP INTO SABINE'S BONES AS SHE stood in the center of her uncle's study. Rain pelted the windows behind her. The cold that had once seemed so dearly familiar and often missed now chilled her to the bone. She wished she had a warmer cloak. She hadn't and was fortunate to have the thin cloak she did wear. A warmer cloak was nowhere to be found anywhere in Walter Close. A fire in the fireplace would be a more practical wish, since there wasn't one of those, either. That, at least, could be remedied.

No one would have faulted her if she had not recognized the room upon following the butler inside. But for the furniture, there was nothing left of Sir Henry Godard. She recognized the desk, but the surface was stripped clean of his papers, books, and personal belongings. His ebony inkstand was gone. So was the brass spyglass he'd kept on the corner of the desk. All his books and papers were gone. The very smell of the room was different.

"Miss Godard," said the butler, Dawes. He dry-washed his hands. "This is quite extraordinary. We never dreamed . . ." He paused to clear his throat. "We were told you'd died, miss!"

"Oh, Dawes." She took one of his hands between hers. "As you can see, I haven't."

Dawes had been the butler at 10 Walter Close for as long as she could remember. She had grown up with him and thought of him as eternally middle-aged. Now, for the first time in her life, she saw age in that beloved face; the wrinkles creasing his cheeks, the jowls and gray hair. But that poignant sight wasn't what broke her heart. Walter Close had been stripped bare. Nothing was left but the furniture.

It seemed Nazim Pasha had succeeded in reaching across an ocean to extract his revenge. He hadn't lied about his letter to the British authorities in Aleppo. His information had not been ignored. Someone from the consulate in Aleppo had troubled himself to send her uncle's death notice, and hers, to the *Times*. Dawes, in fact, had brought it out for her, and it now lay on the bare desk, edges curling with age. A line toward the conclusion of the notice informed any reader who read that far that the philosopher's niece, Miss Sabine Godard, had perished not long after Sir Henry.

She had been dead for months, as far as anyone in England knew.

She looked around for a chair and at last saw one tucked up against the far wall. Sabine walked there and sat, pulling her cloak tight around her. Her skin prickled with cold. She hugged herself and rubbed her hands together for warmth. While she had been fleeing Kilis, her home had been sold out from under her.

"Is there anything left, Dawes?"

He extended his hands in a gesture of futility. "Only what you see with your eyes, miss."

She'd been traveling for days since the *Eos* landed at Portsmouth, and she wanted nothing more than to go upstairs to her room and sleep. From Sicily onward, the weather had been rough. Several of the passengers, herself and her two cabinmates included, had suffered from a nearly constant mal de mer. And now, with her stomach convinced she was still on board the *Eos*, she must accept the stark reality that the home she'd held in her heart for so many weeks no longer existed.

She forced herself to concentrate on what Dawes was saying. "Was everything sold?"

"We'd given you up for lost, miss." She gave him a look, taking in the black armband he wore, and relented. She did not doubt his sincerity. His astonishment when he'd answered the door to see her standing there in her Turkish garb, not a boy's costume, but a Turkish woman's traditional gown, two battered valises in hand, had been genuine. The man had flung his arms around her and hugged her hard. "Sold, miss. Or sent to the rubbish heap."

"Given me up for lost." She shook her head. Whatever had been done was not Dawes's fault, she reminded herself. None of this was anyone's fault. She had been reported dead, and Godard's solicitor had acted accordingly.

"As you see, Dawes, I did not succumb to any illness." She sagged against her chair. The sea voyage had utterly depleted her. Her entire body ached, and with the slow, bone-jarring journey to Oxford across muddy roads, she was now beyond exhausted.

Dawes looked and sounded miserable. "The house is to be let, miss."

"Not sold?"

"There is a distant relative. A cousin of a cousin or some such thing." Dawes shrugged. "They've asked that the house be let."

It occurred to Sabine that she had almost no money left. She'd spent a goodly portion of what Foye had given her on her cloak and in hiring a driver and equipage to get her to Oxford, and then inns along the way. She still had the emeralds Foye had given her, but she was reluctant to convert them to cash as yet, and in any event, was not entirely certain how one went about doing so.

Based upon what she'd found here, she did not expect there would be any ready cash on hand. London and Foye's banker were much too far away to solve her pressing need for funds. She stood and immediately, her stomach revolted. She was perilously close to being ill. She reached back to clutch the top rail of her chair and willed her belly to settle.

"Miss?" Dawes took a step toward her. "Are you unwell?"

"Tired. Nothing more." She took a deep breath through her nose. "I have been traveling for days since I arrived in England. Months, if you count the time since I left Iskenderun."

"Shall I call a doctor?" He touched her arm and helped her to sit down again, and she was grateful for his assistance.

"No," she said. She leaned against the back of her chair and patted his arm. "Thank you, Dawes, but that will not be necessary."

What, after all, would a doctor tell her that she did not already suspect? When Foye arrived, at last, he would be so pleased to know.

"You're white as chalk, miss."

"I'll be well enough in a moment. I stood too fast, nothing more. There's no need to call a doctor." She held out the clipping and smiled as he took it from her and folded it carefully into a pocket of his coat. "I must rest before I go out again." She considered Godard's study and sighed. "I suppose my room has been stripped bare as well?"

"Yes, miss, but I can start a fire and see to fresh linens, and you can rest there good as ever you did. When you wake up, I'll have tea and a hot meal for you."

"Thank you. That would be splendid, Dawes." She walked upstairs with Dawes carrying her valises. Nothing had been spared. Even the paintings were gone. His library had been sold, too. Dawes hurried ahead of her to open the door to her room. As with the rest of the house, her room had been stripped of every sign of her having lived here. All her possessions, gone. Her own books, her artwork, her private notes and papers. Everything gone. She couldn't help herself; she let out a sob, a sound between grief and outrage.

She was supposed to have come home. Home. Not to an empty shell, but to her home, with her familiar possessions. Her own clothes. Her shoes and hats, and books. And instead, all that made the house home was gone.

"There, there, miss." Dawes patted her on the shoulder. "It'll all come right. You'll see."

Hearing Foye's own words only made her sob the harder. Foye wouldn't want to see her give in to weakness, but she didn't seem able to stop herself. She sat on the bed and cried uncontrollably. Her misery mounted, deepening the hole inside her that she couldn't reason away.

She'd been trying to deny it for weeks, and now, she simply gave up trying. She missed Foye. She missed her husband with a power that shook her to her core. If he were here, she'd hold him in her arms and never let him go. She searched through her pockets for a handkerchief.

The butler was bending over the hearth, starting the promised fire, but he stood and dug a large handkerchief from his pocket. He shook it out. "There, there, miss. There, there." He handed her his handkerchief, and she took it gratefully. "You have a good rest, and when you wake up, why, you call for me, and I'll bring you some nice hot tea and something from the kitchen. That will make everything better. You'll see."

She sniffled. "Thank you, Dawes. That's so very kind of you."

"You rest now, miss."

Sabine slept until three and awoke with an empty stomach that propelled her out of bed and to the pull that would let Dawes know she was up. She dug through her valise until she found the comb she'd brought with her from Iskenderun. Between that last rushed visit to the Iskenderun bazaar and Foye's emptying out his kit for her, she'd had nearly everything she needed for the voyage. She ran the comb through her hair and repinned it. The walnut color had faded completely so that when she looked in her dresser mirror she saw her familiar golden blond hair. Since leaving Turkey, her hair had grown out enough that she could pin it back and expect it would stay out of her face.

She straightened her gown, if that was the correct word for her Turkish garb, and headed for the stairs. Somehow, she would have to find something more suitable to wear. English fashions were quite different from the Turkish, after all.

When she came downstairs with her hair combed and her face freshly washed, Dawes was in the parlor, setting out the food. The simple fare made her wonder if he had raided his own larder. He must have. A house this empty would not have provisions for anyone but the staff left behind.

There was bread and butter, some cold ham, an apple, cored and neatly sliced, and the promised hot tea. Her stomach rumbled. Her appetite these days was inconsistent at best. For example, the thought of eating the ham made her ill. She buttered a thick slice of bread. Oh, divine, divine bread and butter. She poured the tea before it was properly brewed. Strong tea also tended to make her stomach roil.

"I'll need to call at the bank, Dawes." Godard's banker would be able to tell her whether there was any money that could be disbursed to her, and his solicitor would tell her how to regain Godard's estate. "Would it be possible to hire me a cab?"

"Yes, miss, of course."

She finished her tea and stared at the leaves in the bottom of her cup. "There is something you should know, Dawes," she said. She swirled the leaves and upended the cup on her saucer. Not because she believed she would read her future there but because it reminded her of Foye.

She righted her cup and looked at the leaves. What future was there for her? Would the tea leaves tell her how soon Foye would be here? She saw no horseshoes. Nor portents of love or good fortune.

"Yes, miss?"

She looked at Dawes, How strange that she had thought all this time that she would tell no one about Foye until he was here with her. Quite the contrary. She was eager to share her news. She sat, arrested by this sudden and unexpected result of her feelings for Foye.

"Yes, miss?" Dawes said.

She curled her hand around her teacup, threading a finger through the handle. "I was married before I left Iskenderun."

"Married?"

"To the Marquess of Foye." Dawes gaped at her, and she grinned at him. "It's perfectly true. Foye should be here before much longer. There was business he needed to attend to before he could leave Turkey. I came on ahead. He'll be here any day I'm sure." If he'd gone aboard the *Thunderous*, he was two weeks behind her. "We agreed I'd wait for him here in Oxford."

He bowed to her, smiling at her. "Felicitations, miss— my lady."

"In the meantime, I must see Godard's banker."

The cab was summoned and money paid sufficient for transportation there and back. What she learned was not comforting. The process of reversing the legal disbursement of her uncle's estate was not a simple one. Walter Close was let, the tenants to take possession within days. The banker took pity on her situation, though, which was a mercy since all the money she had in the world consisted of a handful of Turkish coins and two pounds sterling.

Her next step, it seemed, was for her to go to London and settle things with Foye's solicitor. And then she would go to Cornwall and wait for her husband's return.

Thirty-two

🐌

The Temple Bar, London, England,
DECEMBER 12, 1811

The law offices of Mr. George Brook, solicitor to the
Marquess of Foye. The rain from Oxford had followed
Sabine to London. She did not have an umbrella and
so hurried to the door through the rain with her cloak
inadequate to the task of protecting her from the cold
or the wet.

THE FIRST THING SABINE SAW WHEN SHE HAD CLIMBED
the stairs to Mr. Brook's office was a statue of Minerva in
a niche above the transom. That seemed auspicious. The
sight made her smile. When she opened the door, a slender
clerk came to his feet. The fingers of his right hand were
ink stained. He brushed at his coat, clearing his throat and
setting a hand to his cravat. Three other clerks looked up
from their copying as well.

"Ma'am," said the first clerk. He smiled at her, looking her up and down. Sabine decided she did not like him
much. His face was round, for someone as thin as he was.
His shoes were scuffed, something Foye would never have
tolerated in his dress. "May I be of assistance?"

"I should like to see Mr. George Brook, if you please."
She had Foye's letters with her, all of them. She felt, rather
superstitiously, that actually using them was an admission that something had gone wrong. Nevertheless, she

had them with her and now slipped them from her reticule to find the one addressed to Mr. George Brook. She did not hand it over immediately. Her heart lurched. This was Foye's writing. She remembered so vividly watching him write this very letter. "Is he in?"

The clerk came from behind his high desk. "He's with a client, ma'am. Is he expecting you?"

She resisted the urge to smooth back her hair. Now that it was growing out, it curled around her face as Foye's was wont to do. She had not, of course, removed her hat, merely pushed back her hood. "No." The clerk knew very well she was not expected. "But the matter is urgent."

"Have you a card, perhaps?" the clerk said.

She swallowed. "I haven't a card." Her stomach was not at present inclined to charity, and the climb up the stairs had exhausted her. She looked around for a chair and sank down on it. Before she left Oxford, she'd found a length of inexpensive cloth in a trunk tucked away in the attic. She'd dyed it black and made herself a gown. Not worthy of a marchioness, she thought, but it would do better than her Turkish costume. Now, she wasn't so certain.

She wore the black-dyed gown now and thought she looked quite hideous. With black-dyed slippers and a black ribbon threaded through her black cap, there was no mistaking her mourning state. Godard deserved no less from her. She had no jewelry but for the ring Foye had put on her finger in Iskenderun, and that was at present hidden by black gloves bought secondhand and dyed along with her frock.

"May I tell Mr. Brook your name?"

She looked up. Her name. She very nearly said, Miss Sabine Godard. "Lady Foye," she said. She handed the clerk Foye's letter to Mr. Brook. "I am Lady Foye, and I have urgent business with Mr. Brook."

No more than five minutes passed before the clerk returned. An older gentleman in tan breeches, a green waistcoat, and a coat with a ridiculously high collar stood behind the clerk. He held Foye's letter in one hand. Sabine decided not to stand. Her stomach was not settled, and she was nervous on top of that.

Brook walked to her and extended his hand. "Lady Foye."

"Mr. Brook, I presume."

"Yes, my lady." He nodded at her, taking in her black gown. "My condolences for your loss, Lady Foye."

"Thank you."

"May I bring you anything to drink? Tea, perhaps?"

"Yes, thank you." Not so much because she wanted tea but because when it came she would have something to do with her hands.

Brook gestured, and one of the clerks left his chair and disappeared through an interior door of the offices. "Shall we speak in private?"

"Please." She put her black-gloved hand on his and stood. Brook said nothing until they were inside his office. It wasn't large, but he had a window that scattered light across his desk. There was a long table covered with papers along one side of the room. Rain dripped down the window.

She sat down, brought her hands to her lap, and waited while Brook seated himself at his desk with Foye's letter before him. "I'm sure this is a surprise to you, Mr. Brook. But Foye has not returned from Turkey yet, and things have come to a pass here. We had agreed, sir, that I would wait for him to arrive—that is not relevant, I suppose. The fact is that I was reported dead, erroneously as you can see, and at present I no longer have the home at which Foye and I expected to meet upon his return to England."

"Well." He cocked his head and returned her smile, but so briefly she wondered at it. "I can see that you are most certainly not dead, Lady Foye."

"No, sir."

The clerk came carrying a salver with the promised tea and a plate of powdered cakes. Water speckled his breeches, from which evidence Sabine presumed that he had gone outside to purchase the food. She ignored her tea but did accept one of the cakes. She sat with the plate on her lap.

"Is there anything that can be done to recover my possessions? And my uncle's." She explained her situation with Godard and the house in Oxford while Brook stirred milk and sugar into his tea. "I've been told the house is let and there is nothing to be done about that."

His eyebrows drew together. "It is certainly a matter I can look into on your behalf, Lady Foye."

She smiled. "Thank you, Mr. Brook. I am would be very grateful for anything you can do."

Brook picked up Foye's letter and studied it in silence for a very long time. He schooled himself too well. Sabine had no idea what he was thinking. "Have you proof of your marriage, Lady Foye?"

"Yes." She opened her reticule again and handed over the documents from Hugh Eglender. "We were married in Iskenderun. At the consulate there. Mr. Eglender is a friend of my husband's."

He took the papers and examined them carefully. Sabine reached for her tea and held it, letting the cup warm her hand. "There is a great deal that must be done," the attorney said. "And quickly." He lifted his head from his study of the documents she'd given him. "There seems little doubt that you are indeed Lady Foye."

"I should certainly think so," she said. But her heart beat hard in panic now. Could there be any doubt? Did Brook intend to deny her?

"Forgive me if I am indelicate. Is there any chance that you are with child, my lady?"

She sat very still. "Why do you ask that question now, sir?"

"My dear Lady Foye." He put the pages on his desk. "You are in mourning."

"For my uncle, Mr. Brook."

Brook turned white. "Is it possible? You do not know?"

"What?" She stood up, forgetting the plate on her lap. It clattered to the floor. Her legs shook so hard she had to reach behind her to steady herself with a hand to the back of her chair.

"How am I to tell you this?" he said in a low voice.

"Tell me what?"

"Lord Foye did leave Iskenderun, I presume not long after you did. He took passage on the *Hecla*."

"The *Hecla*. I expected he would sail on the *Thunderous*. Why the *Hecla*?" She watched him. "How is it you know what ship he took while I do not?"

"It was in all the papers, Lady Foye. They were caught in a storm off the coast of Gibraltar. A ship of the line, the *Thunderous*, was nearby. They, too, were caught in the gale. The *Thunderous*'s captain was no doubt the better sailor. His account of the wreck appeared in the *Times*. The *Thunderous* saw the *Hecla* founder and go down. When they were able to approach, which you must image they did with all possible haste, it was too late to save anyone."

Sabine's world stopped.

The lawyer stood up and started around the desk. "I am very sorry to tell you this, but all the passengers on board the *Hecla* perished."

"No."

"The Marquess of Foye is dead."

Thirty-three

🐋

The legal office of Mr. George Brook, solicitor. Mr. Brook was presently disconcerted for the first time in his life. Understandably so. Unfortunately, matters were about to get worse. Far worse. His very livelihood passed before his eyes.

IT WAS, FOYE DISCOVERED, A MASSIVELY INCONVENIENT thing to return home a dead man. But once he'd presented himself to his solicitor, the process of resurrection began. Matters had not gone far enough to be dire, thank God. By all accounts, he'd been dead only a few weeks, and Mr. Brook, in whose offices Foye now sat, bless the man's soul, had been actively working on the assumption that Foye would make a miraculous return to the living, preserving his fortune for future generations. To that end, they were both pleased with the outcome. But there was a deuced lot to take care of now.

The *Hecla* had indeed gone down. But he had not been a passenger, though he was supposed to have been, and had, in fact, been listed on the manifest. But for Hugh Eglender catching him just as he was heading for the quay, he would have been. Inclement seas had delayed his obtaining alternate passage for another fortnight.

Foye leaned back, one leg crossed over the other, holding the cup of tea the clerk had brought him. He swirled
the nearly empty cup and watched the tea leaves settle at
the bottom. He had a strong urge to upend his cup and read
his fortune there. For that, however, he needed Sabine's
expertise.

Brook clasped his hands on his blotter and gave Foye a
grim look. "May I say, my lord, welcome back among the
living."

"Thank you." He didn't smile. "It's good to be alive." He
leaned forward. "Did my wife contact you?"

"Yes, my lord, she did."

"Thank God. We were to have met in Oxford, but her
house has been let to complete strangers and the attorney
had no notion where she'd gone." He did, however, and
Brook confirmed it for him.

"She is at present at Maralee House." His lawyer
cleared his throat. "Perhaps you are aware that she, too,
was reported dead."

"Yes," Foye said wryly. "I knew before I left Turkey that
a notice had been sent."

"I am handling the matter of seeing her possessions
and inheritance returned to her." Brook clasped his hands
on his desk. "Given her condition, your title and entail-
ments are in abeyance for the time being. Now, of course,
the abeyance is a moot point, given that you are not de-
ceased."

"Her condition?" Foye straightened on his chair. "She's
with child?"

"Indeed, my lord."

"My God." He leaned back. "I'd no idea." He looked at
his lawyer. "I suspected she could be, but . . . My will must
be changed. Immediately."

"Understood."

"What do you need to know? She is to have her own funds
and a substantial jointure should I actually predecease her.
Payment guaranteed. Invest it, Brook. If something should
happen to me, she must not suffer financially."

"It will be as you wish, my lord." Brook took up a pen and a clean sheet of paper. "If you will return later this afternoon, my lord, I will have documents for you to execute."

"How soon?"

"Four o'clock?"

"Three." Foye started for the door. "She thinks I'm dead, Brook."

Brook nodded. "Three is agreeable, my lord."

Foye returned at precisely three o'clock, signed his new will, and twenty minutes later was on his way to Cornwall. He faced easily seven days from London to St. Ives, the nearest town to Maralee House. Seven days before he could hope to see Sabine. He traveled hard, ten hours a day driving, changing teams when he could, through poor winter-condition roads, sleeping in the coach rather than stopping at an inn. More than once he drove the coach while his driver slept inside.

He was six days on the road before he came upon the drive to Maralee. The two posts that marked the road meant he was just under a mile from the house. He rode the rest of the way, hell-bent and as fast as his mount would carry him. Outside the house, with its view of the bay, Foye dismounted, practically jumping off the animal. A groom came from behind the house to take his horse.

The man's eyes got big when he saw Foye. His face split in a grin. "It's the master!" he shouted. "The master's here!"

Foye didn't wait. He climbed the stairs to the door, and only when he threw it open did he think to wonder how he ought to present himself to a woman who thought he had died. He went inside. "Sabine?" he shouted.

His butler came out from a side room, hurrying to see who could be shouting, and stopped in shock when he saw Foye. "My lord, is it you?"

"Yes, by God, it is me."

"You haven't drowned, then?"

Foye heard a door open upstairs, and he called out again, shouting, "Sabine?"

More servants were appearing, having heard from the groom or heard him shouting. Foye pushed past the butler and took the stairs two at a time. When he reached the top, he came full stop, because it wasn't Sabine waiting for him. If he'd been hit with hammer he couldn't have been more stunned. Not Sabine, but the Earl of Crosshaven stood there.

"What the hell are you doing at Maralee?" Foye said.

At the same time, Crosshaven said, "Good God, Foye." He took a half step from the door he'd exited. "We thought you were dead."

We?

A smile of pure joy turned Crosshaven's face from handsome to radiant. He walked forward and enveloped Foye in a bear hug that actually lifted him off his feet. Cross released him and pushed his shoulders. "What the devil, old man?"

Foye grabbed Cross's wrist and leaned in. "What are you doing here, Cross?"

Nightmarish anger flooded through him. Every self-defeating thought he'd ever had rushed back, filled him with self-loathing. Sabine had left him. Fallen out of love with him. My God. The woman he loved beyond anything had left him.

"Where the hell is my wife?"

"Foye," Cross said. He took a step back, both hands lifted. "It's not what you think. Foye, it's not. And Lady Foye isn't here."

"Get out."

"I didn't mean—"

Foye grabbed Crosshaven by the lapels and brought him up off his feet. White-hot anger lanced through him. "You never meant. Damn you, you never meant." He wanted to throttle the bastard. Jesus, he was more than a little tempted to toss him headfirst down the stairs. "What happened because of your lie that night turns my stomach, and for that, I'll never forgive you though St. Peter himself denies me entrance to heaven."

"I'll not forgive myself, either," Cross said.

"Then why are you here?" He released and pushed Crosshaven's wrist so hard Cross's arm jerked in the air. "Why the devil are you here?"

"Rosaline," he said, and he had the effrontery to sound and look angry. "Her parents live near St. Ives. You know that, Foye. Better than anyone." Crosshaven took a step back, pulling on the end of his coat to set it back to rights. "We were visiting her parents when we heard the news about you, and then about Lady Foye. About there even being a Lady Foye."

"You brought Rosaline here?"

"No. They don't get on, actually, your wife and Rosaline."

"But you two do."

Cross flushed. The bastard. "If you must know, Foye, she's cold to me as well. I don't blame her. But Rosaline's father insisted on calling. Today of all days." Crosshaven inclined his head toward the open parlor door. "He's not well, Foye, but he insisted on paying his respects, and since I am home and able-bodied and he is not, I brought him here. He admires you still, Foye, Rosaline's father. He took the news of your death hard. We're here, waiting for her, your wife, Foye, so that a man who hasn't done you any wrong can tell her how sorry he is that you're gone."

Foye stared at him. He could hardly believe this was Crosshaven.

"She doesn't know we're even here, for God's sake, your wife." He grabbed Foye's arm. "Listen to me. She's out, Foye. Not even at home yet. She doesn't talk to me unless it can't be avoided, and she doesn't even know I'm here."

Foye didn't know where to look, what to do, what to feel. His heart was still pounding in his ears.

"Cross?" called a thin voice from the parlor.

"Come tell the old man you're alive, Foye," Crosshaven said. "Please? Not for me. For him."

Foye took a deep breath and went into the parlor to say hello to Rosaline's father.

He was frailer than Foye recalled. Too thin, his hair mostly gone. But he gripped the old man's hand and told him the tale of his survival, and all the time he could hardly concentrate but for thinking about Sabine.

Cross had the decency to stay out of the conversation. He kept to himself on the far side of the room and didn't say anything unless it was to remind his father-in-law of some name or event he'd forgotten or gently correct him when it became plain the old man's mind had wandered and had suddenly mistaken Foye for his late father.

He could hardly concentrate, but all the same, he knew the moment Sabine came into the room.

Thirty-four

❧

SABINE STOOD IN THE OPEN DOORWAY, BLINKING HARD. She couldn't understand why Lord Crosshaven was in her house. He must know he was not welcome. But then another man came forward, and her heart stopped beating.

"Foye?" she said.

It must be someone else, she thought. Someone else as tall as Foye. The stranger came out of the shadows where he'd been. And her entire body flashed hot and then cold as ice. She trembled from head to toe. It couldn't be. He was dead.

"Foye?" she whispered.

"Sabine."

It was his voice. His voice. She'd never in all her life fainted, and she would not now. She put out a hand to catch something. The edge of the door. A table. A chair, anything sturdy enough to help her keep her balance when her head was swimming and her legs threatening to crumble.

There was a table by the door; her searching hand hit the edge and that served. She clutched it, hanging on as hard as she could.

"It's me," he said. He came toward her, and all she could think was that she must be imagining this. The sun was coming through the window behind him, this man who looked like Foye, and she wasn't sure at all of anything. She could not see him well enough. "My love, I wasn't on the *Hecla*."

Sabine held out a hand. "Is it you?" she said. "Is it really you?"

"Yes." He crossed the room, walking out of the sunlight, and he took her in his arms. And though a part of her still believed Foye was dead, she wrapped her arms around his neck and pulled him tight to her, and their bodies fit exactly as she remembered. Perfectly.

She was dimly aware of Lord Crosshaven helping a frail old man to his feet. She recognized Crosshaven's father-in-law from church. Since coming to St. Ives she had met everyone who attended their church. She had withstood all the introductions, even the exceedingly difficult one to Lord Crosshaven and his wife, whom she disliked a great deal. At first on mere principle and then because she would not have liked the woman in any event.

Sabine stepped forward, still with one hand on Foye's coat, stopping Crosshaven by placing a hand on the old man's arm.

Crosshaven took a breath and said, "He wanted to pay his respects, Lady Foye."

She nodded. "Thank you for coming, Mr. Prescott."

He bowed, slowly, and, leaning heavily on his son-in-law's arm, spoke in a voice that trembled with age. "He's a good man, Foye." He lifted his head. "A good man, my lord."

"We'll call, Mr. Prescott," Sabine said. "If we may. Lord Foye and I."

He chuckled and patted her hand. Mr. Prescott smiled at her, and she was reminded very strongly of Godard.

Not because there was any great resemblance between the
men but because of his age and the way Lord Crosshaven
supported his arm. Mr. Prescott was older than Godard
by several years, and she knew precisely what it had cost
the older man to travel so far, how deeply he must have
felt his obligation to Foye's memory. "That would be
delightful."

"We look forward to it, sir," Sabine said. She pressed
his hand and leaned in to plant a kiss on his cheek. "You've
brought me luck, sir," she said. "You came to call and
brought me back my husband. I'll never forget that."

"Come along," Crosshaven said to his father-in-law.
"We'll get you home, and you can tell Rosaline all about
how you brought Foye back from the dead." He looked at
Sabine and said, very softly, "Thank you." Cross glanced
at Foye and nodded. "Good day, my lord."

"I won't wish you the same."

"Foye," Sabine murmured. "Don't be unkind."

He looked down at her. "I won't, my love."

When Crosshaven and Mr. Prescott were gone, Sabine
turned back to Foye and slipped her arms around him, resting her cheek against his chest and stroking his back until
she stopped shaking.

"Tell me again it's you, Foye," she whispered. "Tell me
I'm not dreaming." He held her close, stroking her head.
Tears burned behind her eyes, and there was nothing she
could do to stop them.

"You're not." He pulled her hard against him. "I drove
from London to here as quickly as I could. I couldn't get
here any sooner."

She went up on tiptoe so she could put her palms on
both sides of his face. She traced every line of his face with
trembling fingers while Foye produced a handkerchief to
dab at her tears. She looked to the door and saw the butler
there with the housekeeper and several of the maids and
footmen. Through her tears she said, "It's him. It's really
him. We'll have a feast tonight, won't we?"

Foye set her back and said, "Lady Foye and I will dine

in our room tonight. If you wish to celebrate tonight, do so, with full permission." He slipped an arm around her waist and held her tight against him. "But we'll feast the entire house tomorrow."

"My lord." The butler had the sense to retire, shooing away the rest of the staff.

Foye took Sabine to his room, and he looked around slowly. Sabine realized it was patently obvious to anyone that she had moved in here, into his room and not the lady's chamber, and there they had an awkward moment. "I felt closer to you here, Foye," she said. The silence between them horrified her. Had he changed? Had he fallen out of love with her?

"It's quite all right."

She stayed near him and kept her hand on his arm, and he let her. He faced her and removed her hat. Some plain thing she'd bought at the milliners at St. Ives and had dyed black, not caring at all what she looked like. Her gown was a horrible, hideous black as well. Her shoes, too. He stood there in the center of his room that she had turned into hers, and ran his fingers through her hair.

"It's grown quite a lot since Aleppo," he said. "And all of it gold again."

"It has." She touched the curls around her forehead. "These remind me of you. I didn't know I had them until recently. Before, my hair was too long to curl this much."

"Brooks told me you're with child, Sabine. Is it so?"

She nodded. "I've seen the doctor."

"You're wearing mourning," he said. "Widow's weeds."

"For you, Foye."

"I dislike you in black." He stroked her hair, her cheek, and she turned her face into the curve of his palm. "I hate particularly to see you in clothes that are out of fashion and too plain." He was holding onto his emotions as tightly as she was, and she wasn't sure how to get them past this awkwardness. Turkey was thousands of miles away, and now, after all that had happened, could they really make a life together?

What a pair they were.

"Knowing you," he said, "you haven't anything else to wear."

"I haven't."

"I'll buy you a new wardrobe. In colors. Any color you want, Sabine. A rainbow of them if you like. I'll take you to London and visit all the shops in the world."

"I don't care about that." She reached up to put her hands on either side of his face. His skin was cool underneath her fingers. She trembled when she touched him, and he covered her hands with his. "Thank God you came back to me, Foye."

He took a deep breath, and she tried to work out what would happen now. If she didn't know, or couldn't guess, did that mean they'd grown too far apart? "I confess," he said eventually, "to some relief on that score myself."

His smile took her breath.

"You do make me laugh, Foye," she said. She slid her hands to his shoulders and then to his chest, where she left them so she could feel the beating of his heart. He let his hands slide off her until they ended up at her hips. She tilted up her chin to look at him. "I am still in love with you," she said.

"Are you?"

"Yes." She nodded, a very determined bob of her head. "I've been giving the subject a great deal of thought over the weeks since I left Iskenderun."

"There is not much to do on board a ship but think a great deal," he said.

"Quite true."

He reached up to bracelet her wrists with his fingers. She'd taken off her gloves when she came home, and her gown had short sleeves that left her arms bare from just above her elbows to her hands. Foye swept the last two fingers of each hand down her arms from the bottom of her sleeves to her wrists. "I've been dreaming of this moment for months," he said. "Of holding you in my arms again and hearing you tell me that you love me."

"I love you, Foye. How many times shall I tell you? A dozen, a hundred? A thousand?"

"We'll be married again in the Church of England, Sabine." He slowly breathed in. "Wherever you like. Here or in London. Or in Oxford, if that's what you'd prefer."

"Here," she said without hesitation. "The church in St. Ives is pretty, and I like your reverend. Besides, this is home."

"St. Ives it is."

She unfastened the first button of his coat. He kept his fingers around her wrists. "I told you I could not leave Godard," she said. "But I never got the chance to tell that by the time we reached Kilis I'd changed my mind about not telling him. I was so very unhappy, and all I wanted was to be with you."

He touched her cheek, cupping the side of her face in his warm hand. "Please don't regret staying with Godard. You mustn't do that."

Her breath caught, and Foye briefly tightened his fingers on her. But only briefly. "I wanted to, Foye." Her voice dropped so low he had to strain to hear her. "I wanted to leave him."

"I understood you could not."

"So much happened when we went to Kilis." She unfastened another button of his coat. "I thought I'd given you up forever." She swallowed hard. "I imagined you'd return to England and marry some other woman. And then . . ."

"Sabine," he said, "I do understand."

"All that happened and I didn't think it was possible to love you more, but I did. By the time we were in Iskenderun, I loved you more. And more. And more, Foye, and there didn't seem to be the words to tell you in a proper way." She looked at him with a frown. "When I arrived in Oxford, there was a hole in my heart. From missing you. All I could think every minute was how much I missed you and wanted you to come back to me. And how happy I would be when you were with me at last."

She unbuttoned the rest of his coat. When she reached up to push it off his shoulders, he released her to let the garment slide down and off his arms. She lay her head against his chest. "I missed you, Foye. And I wanted to tell you that I love you. More than anything, I wanted to tell you that." He cupped the back of her head, and she turned her face to his. "I did not say things to Godard that I ought to have. Words that ought to have been said between us. And then one day he was dead, and I shall never be able to tell him that I loved and admired him."

"He knew, Sabine."

"Therefore," she said resolutely, "I decided that I must tell you how I felt before it was too late. That you are the finest man I have never known. Lovely and generous, and, oh, Foye, I wanted to tell you how lucky I would be to spend the rest of my life with you, and I should have. I should have. Only—" She swallowed hard again. "You were dead. And when I thought you were dead a part of me died with you. "

Oh hell, she was crying, she realized. Those were tears blurring her vision. She swiped at her face, and her fingers came away wet.

Foye touched a finger to her cheek. "Don't cry, my love. Please don't cry."

"I thought you were dead, and it killed me. It killed me, Foye. And now you are here. Standing before me, alive, and I won't go another moment without telling you that I love you and that I already know that I cannot bear the thought of living without you. Because, you see, I thought I would have to. I have been living without you all these weeks." She clutched the front of his shirt. "And I was destroyed."

Foye brushed his thumbs along her lower lip. "If you love me, Sabine, I can honestly tell you that I am the happiest man in the world."

"Make love to me, Foye." She curled her fingers against his chest and looked into his eyes. She blinked once and his face came into focus. "Please, make love to me."

He smiled down at her. "I would be delighted."

It wasn't long before Sabine was naked and Foye was in a similar state of undress. He ran a hand down her side, looking her up and down as he touched her. "I've never seen you all the same color, Sabine," he said.

She shifted, arching her body and stretching herself. "What do you think of me, Foye, when I am only Sabine?" She smiled as wickedly as she knew how. "Instead of Pathros?"

"Delicious, madam." He touched her hair, too, which was still short, but longer than when she'd left Iskenderun, and even curlier now. He gathered a handful and kissed the locks. "You smell of violets instead of roses."

"Foye," she whispered, putting her arms around him and pulling his head down to hers. "Now. I want you now."

"Your every wish is my command," he whispered. He rolled onto his back and brought her with him, and his hands slid down to the curve of her belly and he rolled them again, on his big, wide bed and kissed her there, where their child lay.

The sight of him made her body melt for him; it brought out every female instinct that said he needed to be inside of her, claiming her this very minute. And she claiming him. She took a deep breath and tried to ramp down the lust roaring through her body.

"Why are you not inside me, Foye, where I long to have you?" She tangled her fingers in his hair and brought his head up to hers. "You are mine, my lord. Mine and mine and mine forever."

He entered her, and she pressed her head into the mattress, sucking in a deep breath. Her thighs came up around his hips. Her body surrounded him, his warm, hard flesh, and she was wet for him, ready for him.

"Foye," she whispered, "tell me you love me. Tell me again."

"I love you, Sabine." He put his mouth by her ear and stroked forward until he was deep in her. "I love you," he said slowly.

She could feel herself losing the battle for her control, but she wanted this to last. She wanted to see his face, but everything felt too big and vast and she could barely keep back a shout of frustration. He filled her. She dragged her eyes open and saw that he looked quite fierce. Determined about whatever was going on inside his head. She drew her hands down his back, along either side of his spine. "No, Foye. Not tender. Fierce like you are right now. Fierce, the way I love you. Fiercely, love me fiercely. Like this." And she brought him forward into her.

She looked directly into his eyes as she rocked her hips toward his, her legs pulled up. He squeezed his eyes closed, and for a while, so did Sabine. She concentrated on anything but the man who was driving her mad with lust, with love. He drew nearly out of her and then pushed back inside. God. She closed her eyes and mastered herself again.

"Foye," she said, and her voice broke on a sob.

She forced her eyes open, and to her, he was the most beautiful man in the world, naked atop her, in her, touching her, and God help her, she knew a man in passion when she saw one. Without reservation. She pulled his head down to hers and her mouth opened underneath his. They kissed, she kissed him, and he gave back every ounce of the passion there.

He let himself go then, stretching himself over her, driving hard and harder until she couldn't think. She matched him every bit of the way, and when she heard the hitch in his breath that told her he was about to come, she held nothing back, and it was the most magnificent experience of her life to have Foye there with her, whispering that he loved her.

Her entire body clenched as her orgasm shook her, made her tremble with pleasure that was almost pain until she fell and fell and fell, hard and fast and with her husband. And for this moment, her life was perfect. Exactly as she had dreamed.

Sometime afterward, he drew a hand down her bare

shoulder as she lay beneath him, wondering where her wits had gone and if she would ever get them back. "Foye."

"Yes, love?"

"You are heavy," she said. "A beast of a man, if you must know."

He pushed up, and he leaned in and kissed her nose before he pulled out of her and rolled onto his back. "I love you, Sabine," he said.

"And I you, Foye." She turned onto her side, one hand holding up her head while the other brushed down the mid-line of his torso. "I'll need to draw you again. All my pictures of you are gone."

"You may," he said. "Whenever you like." He tightened his arm around her. "You were right the day we met, you know."

"I often am," she said. "What was I right about?"

"The tea leaves."

"I said they were nonsense as I recall."

"But they weren't."

She looked at him from beneath her lashes. "Have you gone mad, my lord?"

He was smiling at her, softly, with a gentleness that brought a lump to her throat. "You foretold that I would be lucky in love."

"You cannot know your future from looking at the dregs in your teacup. I should think you're sensible enough to know that."

"My love," Foye said, "I beg to differ. My fortune was uncannily correct. And you were uncannily accurate in your reading." He kissed her. "I have been lucky in love. Luckier than I deserve to be."

"It's I who am fortunate." She touched him again, drag-ging the tip of her finger across his chest. "Are you happy, Foye?"

"I am, Sabine." His hand drifted to her waist. "Never happier in all my life." His voice fell. "You? Are you happy?"

"I think it was my fortune I read in your tea leaves, Foye."

"Is that so?"

"Oh yes. As you know, my readings are never wrong. I am very happy in love."

Enter the rich world of historical romance with Berkley Books.

Lynn Kurland

Patricia Potter

Betina Krahn

Jodi Thomas

Anne Gracie

Love is timeless.
penguin.com

M9G0907